PRAISE FOR **THE HOLY ROAD**

"*The Holy Road* confirms that Blake's laurels for storytelling
and scholarship [for *Dances With Wolves*] were
deserved. The man writes like a poet."
—Baltimore *Sun*

"Epic, tragic . . . Inhuman agony, brilliantly portrayed."
—*Kirkus Reviews* (starred review)

"A more powerful historical novel [than *Dances With Wolves*] with a
much wider scope. Blake's ability to evoke sadness and joy, action
and emotion is as strong as ever, and the ending hits hard."
—*Publishers Weekly*

"A book that not only lives up to the first one, but actually enhances
it and enriches our understanding of the characters and the world . . .
A lyrical, well-researched, moving look at the death of the
Indian nation . . . This is an epic, sprawling and messy and alive. . . .
The action in this book is thrilling."
—*Ain't It Cool News*

"Evocative."
—*People*

"Poignant . . . With a minimum
of sentimentality, *The Holy Road* tells a sad tale."
—*The Dallas Morning News*

ABOUT THE AUTHOR

MICHAEL BLAKE lives on a

ranch in southern Arizona with

his wife and three children.

THE HOLY ROAD

THE HOLY ROAD

MICHAEL BLAKE

The HOLY ROAD

A NOVEL

 RANDOM HOUSE TRADE PAPERBACKS | NEW YORK

Copyright © 2001 by Michael Blake

Reader's guide and interview with the author copyright © 2002 by Random House, Inc.

All rights reserved under International and Pan-American Copyright Conventions. Published in the United States by Random House Trade Paperbacks, a division of Random House, Inc., New York, and simultaneously in Canada by Random House of Canada Limited, Toronto.

Random House Trade Paperbacks and colophon are trademarks of Random House, Inc.

This work was originally published in hardcover by Villard Books, a division of Random House, Inc., in 2001.

LIBRARY OF CONGRESS CATALOGING-IN-PUBLICATION DATA

Blake, Michael

The holy road: a novel / Michael Blake.

p.   cm.

Sequel to: Dances with wolves.

ISBN 0-375-76040-7

1. Comanche Indians—Wars—Fiction.   2. Railroads—Design and construction—Fiction.   3. Ethnic relations—Fiction.   I. Title.

PS3552.L3487 H6 2001   813'.54—dc21   2001025842

Random House website address: www.atrandom.com

Printed in the United States of America on acid-free paper

First Trade Paperback Edition

Book design by Barbara M. Bachman

THE HOLY ROAD

THE HOLY ROAD

*T*HE SCALP WAS RED AND THICK BUT WHAT MADE IT ESPECIALLY extraordinary was its great length. It was the longest shock of hair anyone had ever seen, so long that its owner had to sit on the shoulders of another warrior to tie it to the rafters of his lodge. Had it not been tied so high the hair would have dragged the ground and people living in the lodge would have been forever brushing it aside, reducing it from a vaunted trophy of war to an unwanted, everyday annoyance.

Still, it fell to a point about chest high and Wind In His Hair's wives grumbled about its presence from the moment it assumed a prominent place among the many other scalps hanging in their large home. The grumbling was something the wives did under their breath and out of earshot of their husband for they knew that to complain openly about such a thing would cause unnecessary trouble. And it would be unfair to a husband who had sired so many healthy children, had unfailingly provided an abundance for his family, and was widely revered as the highest-ranking member of the elite warrior society known to all as the Hard Shields, the combat unit that viewed protection of the village and its people as their most sacred responsibility.

They might challenge their husband on the proximity of the family lodge to water, or the sleeping habits of the children, or the preparation of a feast, but they kept their misgivings about the white woman's scalp to themselves. How their husband displayed his souvenir, taken in honorable combat at the cost of his own disfigurement, was simply none of their business.

Nor was it the business of anyone else in the village, and, like the wives of Wind In His Hair, every member of the community kept his feelings about the scalp hidden from public view. But the unvoiced opinions only added to a sense of dread that had been growing steadily among them for years. The presence of the white woman's scalp in the village served as a constant reminder of the strange, unfathomable threat that had come to dominate their lives. It was the worst kind of threat a people can endure, an invisible horror that disturbs good sleep, confuses clear thinking, and makes the steadiest heart skip with odd, little ripples of fear at what tomorrow might bring.

Even Wind In His Hair was not immune. In the deepest reaches of his instinctive, reactive soul, a soul as purely Comanche as any that had ever been born, he could feel occasional and upsetting echoes. He had always slept well, but in the last year he often woke inexplicably in the night. And sometimes as he lay blinking in the dim light of his fire's embers, his eyes would pick up the outline of the long, red-haired scalp and he would wonder how many white people he might have to kill to safeguard the only life he knew.

Having no answer grated against his mind, and it was only when he had reassured himself that an answer was not important, that his only responsibility in this life was to be a father, a husband, and a warrior without fear, could he turn on his side and let sleep descend once again.

CHAPTER II

*T*EN BEARS, TOO, HAD TROUBLE SLEEPING, A CONDITION THAT had been unknown to him for most of his long life. The anxiety that dogged all of his band was a heavy burden for an old man already weighted down with increasing infirmity.

He could no longer ride, and when camp was moved he was forced to travel like a piece of baggage sprawled on a travois. Having outlived half a dozen wives, the last of whom had died the spring before, he depended on his daughters to boil his meat and tend his fire. The eyes that had served him through so many snows were as hazy as twilight and he knew that they would never grow brighter, only darker. He tired easily and would doze between daily interviews in which he arbitrated disputes, listened to complaints, offered advice, or fielded questions about news from the wider world. He talked less and less, preferring to meditate carefully on the words of others before uttering brief, concise opinions packed with wisdom.

As his sight diminished, his hearing seemed to grow sharper, so sharp in fact that he began to hear the words of others just as he heard the wind waving through the grass, or the percussive rhythms of rainfall against the walls of his lodge. He had begun to listen to an eternal communication beyond mere language that enabled him to hear into a person, to hear the heart and lungs and blood.

He had stumbled onto this wondrous gift of concentration in an effort to stay awake during conversations. For a time he had fallen into a pattern of losing consciousness in mid-discussion, a development that chagrined him so greatly that he wished for death to spare him further embarrassment. But despite his longing for release from the rigors of life, the old man was unable to throw himself away.

If a generation ago he had wanted to make such an exit, he could have done so by simply refusing to move on the breaking of camp. His lodge would have been struck around him and he would have been left to sit like a shelled pea on the ground, a cup of water and a bowl of food beside him. The sun would glare down upon him, the wind would rush over his wrinkled flesh, and eventually he would recline on his back, never to rise again, content with the thought that soon he would melt back into the body of his mother the earth.

Such a death seemed a luxury now. He imagined it in the same way a boy dreams of winning honors in battle or a girl looks forward to making a family of her own. But no matter how much he wished it to be, Ten Bears could not take the hand death had extended. The present generation was the most challenging he had ever known in his life as a Comanche. In any other era his time would come and go and his own earthly presence would be replaced by another, just as it had happened with the Comanches since they first appeared on the earth. But now the great wheel of life seemed to be slowing and whether it would continue to revolve or stop completely was impossible to know. The whole of Comanche life was hanging in the balance, and so long as it did Ten Bears willed his tired lungs to draw breath. If he were to begin his long journey across the stars today, he would leave his people to be scattered like chaff in the coming whirlwind. So he stayed, listening carefully to the blood of all those who came before him.

When the sun was starting down, one of his granddaughters, Hunting For Something, usually came by with a small bowl of buffalo and berries which she herself had pounded into a mush. If the day was fair, Ten Bears would wrap the food in a piece of cloth, grab up his walking stick, and stand listening at the entrance of his lodge, waiting for a lull in the rhythm of human traffic outside. At the appropriate moment Ten

THE HOLY ROAD · 7

Bears would bend his creaky frame and start into the sunlight, charting a course for the open prairie and whatever scant stand of trees lay by a spring or pond or stream close to camp.

No one interrupted these sojourns. The entire community knew that Ten Bears had somehow acquired the ability to "hear blood" and that for him to maintain the gift it was necessary that he be free of distraction. When people saw him stride stiffly out of camp they let him go, in the knowledge that surely he was sifting weighty and mysterious thoughts.

No one could have guessed that Ten Bears' primary objective was to find a secluded spot where he could nap uninterrupted. But by the time he reached his place of peace the idea of napping usually gave way to a sense of wonder that his old legs had been able to carry him this far from camp yet again.

If he was lucky he would find a small grove of cottonwoods situated next to running water. He would finger the medicine in the pouch hanging from his neck or perhaps he would light his pipe as he sat listening to the breeze make music in the cottonwood's leaves, and to the eternal trickle of the stream. At times he would lie flat like a corpse and gaze as best he could at the clouds overhead, opening his mind to anything that wished to enter.

That scalp at Wind In His Hair's . . . no one likes it. I don't like it. But who is to blame? Not Wind In His Hair. Not the Comanches. The Comanches didn't fire first. The white woman had a gun that shoots twice. She shot out Wind In His Hair's eye. He took her scalp and brought it back and hung it in his lodge. That's his right. He's a warrior.

Kicking Bird doesn't like it. He doesn't go to Wind In His Hair's home anymore. He wants peace. How can there be peace? If I got up now . . . I won't get up now, I'm happy on the ground. If I were on my feet at this moment, if I looked in the four directions, perhaps I would see them. No, I wouldn't see them, not here. But they are out there somewhere. They are in the east and the west, in the north and south. They are all around us. They are closer every day.

This country is good. It gives us everything we need. It will last all summer. But where will we go when the leaves die? Where will we go that doesn't carry us closer to them? How could you forget, old man! The great hole in the earth. You were born there. The Comanches will go down into the earth this winter as they always have. The Kiowa will be there, and the Cheyenne too. And the buffalo. Food and water and space for everyone in a place where no white person has ever walked. We will sleep as the snow banks up against the lodges. Hunting For Something will bring me treats and tend my fire . . .

Those hawks circling in the sky . . . perhaps they are vultures. Maybe they are two vultures trying to decide to come down. If they fly down here I'll close my eyes and lie still. I'll wait while they land, wait until I hear the rustle of their wings coming closer. Then I'll sit up and give them a shock . . . ha!

I can't see them anymore. Must have been hawks. No white person has walked this country either. Oh, I hope they never will. But Wind In His Hair's scalp says they will. What is to be done? A whirlwind might come and carry that scalp beyond the stars. Maybe there is a whirlwind big enough to carry all the white people there too. I have never seen one that big. Maybe there is a song that could be sung, a dance that could be danced. There must be something. The Kiowa always want us to join their sun dance; maybe we should dance with them this summer. They are good people, good friends. But they are too superstitious. How can their ceremonies be trusted?

The earth feels warm on my back. I love the earth. Nothing is better. It is soft on my back. My arms and legs are like feathers on the skin of the earth. Am I floating? Am I rising? Am I dreaming now? Am I dying? Does it matter? . . . What am I doing?

It was always the same. Ten Bears' mind would wrestle the unending line of questions clamoring for answers and invariably the mental exercise would wear him out. Then the old man would succumb to sleep, sometimes dozing until the chill of twilight woke him. He would roll onto his stomach, pull his wrinkled hands close by his shoulders, and, using all his strength, raise himself onto hands and knees. He would lift one knee up, plant a foot, and, trembling with effort, get to his feet.

He would stand still for a few moments, reacquainting himself with the elements while he regained his bearings. Then he would start back for the village, his step firmer than when he had left, confident that he would have the strength to deal with any development that had taken place in his absence. On the way back he would think, *I am Ten Bears, still walking the earth, the oldest of us all*, wondering at the same time if he might find something good to eat when he got home.

CHAPTER III

O F ALL THE PEOPLE DWELLING IN TEN BEARS' VILLAGE NONE was more perplexed by the red-haired scalp than Kicking Bird. The scalp nagged him with possibilities for the future that he did not want to think about. It depressed him in ways that his brethren could not conceive, making him still more a stranger to his people than he already was. It was no coincidence that Kicking Bird's long face seemed to grow even longer and stay that way about the time of the scalp's arrival. For him the scalp told an old story of revenge and retribution that never led to anything new, and newness was the one thing that Kicking Bird truly craved. In the years since Dances With Wolves had come, the craving led him away from his traditional calling as a medicine man and into an ever-expanding, self-made role as a Comanche statesman.

Kicking Bird spent as much time away from camp as he spent at home. He traveled with his large family to the boundaries of the immense Comanche territory and beyond, attending ceremonies, councils, seasonal feasts, and trading get-togethers.

Twice he had ranged very far to the east for treaty talks called at the behest of exotically clothed, hair-mouthed representatives from the faraway place called Washington. He was the only member of the great

Comanche nation at the inconclusive meetings, and since he had no authority to speak for any of his people, he stayed on the fringes of the sessions, content to listen and observe and learn whatever he could of the wider world.

To his surprise he was pursued by the white men, and though he told them curtly he had nothing to say, they singled him out at the end of the talks, presenting him with a heavy silver medal bearing a likeness of the one they called the Great White Father.

On their return, Kicking Bird and his family were confronted by an excited group of warriors from his own village ready to do battle. From a distance they had spied a persistent flashing, which they took to be the reflection of some ornament, or, more ominously, the glint of a weapon being borne toward the village. They quickly gathered their ponies and, fully armed, galloped onto the prairie to meet the intruder. One young man loosed an arrow which whistled a few feet above Kicking Bird's head before his identity was discovered.

From the day of his return, the white man's peace medal was regarded as a prize of the highest order by the people of Ten Bears' village. It was a constant feature of Kicking Bird's costume, and no eye could resist the dazzle of the metal disk with the white people's chief emblazoned upon it. When Kicking Bird was at home the medal could often be found hanging on the shield stand just outside his lodge, a magnet for the attention of anyone passing by.

But the effect it had on people went deeper than curiosity. Like the woman's scalp that dangled from Wind In His Hair's lodge poles, it, too, served to remind the Comanches of the threat that prowled the borders of their country. It made people nervous, not only about the whites but about Kicking Bird himself. He was one of them yet he was always looking beyond camp. The presence of the medal, so prominent in Kicking Bird's appearance, made him seem stranger.

None of this diminished his status among them, however. The wearer of the medal remained one of Ten Bears' closest advisers, standing shoulder to shoulder with the old man in every council and ceremony. The former medicine man's far-reaching journeys had endowed him with insights and information no one else possessed. On matters that extended beyond the village itself, people naturally looked to Kicking Bird for advice.

Still, there was talk about him, and though these doubts never reached him directly, the impeccable man whom the former John Dunbar had once described as "a magnificent-looking fellow" knew that his thirst for the future set him further apart from the life and people he loved.

Kicking Bird himself did not know what was to come. He knew only that a collision with the white people was inevitable, and that when it came he wanted to be ready to lead, to help his people navigate in any way he could. Perhaps it would cost him his life, but he didn't worry. He was bound to the path he had taken.

Wisely, he chose not to speak of the future or what it might bring. He went about the business of being a Comanche: providing meat, visiting with his wife, investing himself in the life of his six children, keeping his lodge flap open to all who needed his counsel, and acknowledging the Great Mystery with daily prayer.

He had come to realize that the object that hung about his neck spoke for him without words. Kicking Bird knew, better than anyone, the meaning of the silver medal and the red-haired scalp that dwelt in Ten Bears' village. Together they made a perfect picture of the Comanche predicament: the people called the Lords of the Plains were divided and doubtful.

CHAPTER IV

*T*HEIR LODGE COULD USUALLY BE FOUND AT A MODEST DIS-
tance from the main village, apart but not separate. The people inside
conducted their lives as full Comanches and were accepted as such. They
wept at funerals, swallowed at weddings, shared the same danger, the
same laughter, and the same timeless pattern of everyday life as if they
were descended of generations of wild, free people.

An unknowing eye could not have seen the difference between the
family in the set-apart lodge from any others. But the difference ran
deep. The family of Dances With Wolves and Stands With A Fist and
their young children, Snake In Hands, Always Walking, and Stays Quiet,
were Comanche in every aspect but their blood. Their blood was as distinct from that which flowed through Comanche veins as the color of
earth is from sky. They were seeds blown from another world which had
worked into Indian soil and germinated, drawing sustenance season after
season until they had achieved a strength and harmony that made them
as natural to the landscape as the blades of grass that covered the plains.
Yet they were eternally different, and perhaps they lived a little apart in
subtle acknowledgment of the gap that could never be bridged.

It could also be said that the extra steps it took to reach the lodge of

Dances With Wolves were the only traces of that gap. The two white people, and then their children, were fully accepted, and after so many years no one thought of them as white.

If anything, the uniqueness of the family was a point of pride, a pride that had not diminished over ten winters. Dances With Wolves had long ago taken the warrior's road, dedicating himself to the principles and skills demanded of Comanche manhood. There had been about him none of the self-centeredness that curses youth, and the idea of service beyond self was one he embraced smoothly and steadfastly. He was a great killer of buffalo and the meat he made always found the fires of the poor and aged and infirm before it reached his own.

People raised eyebrows at the breadth of freedom he gave his wife, but none could deny that the match was made to last and that the couple's good citizenship was unassailable. If Dances With Wolves occasionally carried water, or helped in the striking of the lodge, or stayed with his children while his wife visited her friends, that was their business, not anyone else's.

If the little girl, Always Walking, wanted to follow her father around camp instead of staying home with her mother, that was all right. And if the oldest one, the boy Snake In Hands, wanted to help his mother tan a hide, that was all right too. Even if Dances With Wolves carried the infant girl, Stays Quiet, around in a sling, no one condemned it. Of course they might tease him, as they often did with little jibes like "You're a good mother to that child," but there was no malice in it. People expected the Dances With Wolves family to be different and found no fault with their eccentricities. They would always be a little odd in their customs and there was nothing wrong with that.

In truth, people would have overlooked far greater eccentricities in Dances With Wolves and his family for a reason that overrode every other. As a warrior Dances With Wolves was unexcelled, having demonstrated on many occasions a strength and dependability that put him on a level with Wind In His Hair.

It was seen as fitting by all that three summers ago, under sponsorship of the great Wind In His Hair himself, Dances With Wolves had been inducted into the elite circle of Hard Shields.

The new inductee's mettle was proven that season in a dawn attack by a large party of Utes who hit the village hoping for plunder and scalps. While the village took flight, Dances With Wolves, Wind In His Hair, and five other Hard Shields stood their ground, outnumbered two or three to one. To be a Hard Shield meant to fight to the last breath, and that morning the seven Comanches fought the enemy with extraordinary tenacity, repelling wave after wave of Ute charges, even after each of the defenders had been wounded. Not one of them withdrew, and once the main body of the village had safely removed itself from the fighting, many warriors came back to turn the tide, driving the Utes off.

When the battle was over, six Ute warriors lay dead on the ground. One Comanche, a genial, heavy-set Hard Shield named Woman's Heart, lay among the dead, his brains half out of his head. The rest of the village and its people were unscathed.

From that day on, people regarded Dances With Wolves as one of their most powerful protectors, and he lived up to the perception. He was always among the first to get a weapon in his hands and among the last to put it down. His loyalty to the band was unquestioned, and when the red-haired scalp arrived in camp, no one questioned his feelings because Dances With Wolves had been part of the raid in which it was taken. In fact, he was with Wind In His Hair when the woman had picked up the two-shooting rifle and fired it. He had seen Wind In His Hair leap through the smoke of the blast and club the woman to the floor. He had seen him bend over her body and slice the hair away from her head with a knife. Dances With Wolves returned as a warrior who was already part of the scalp's history.

He had suffered the same privations as his friends on the deep drive into Mexico, where they had been chased relentlessly by huge numbers of Mexican soldiers. He had crossed the great muddy river at full flood and nearly been swept away. He had stumbled toward home with nothing in his belly, and he had seen his strong-hearted pony lie down on the trail and die. He had crept with his brothers to the isolated white man's house on the edge of Comanche country in hope of finding something, anything, to eat. He had been fired on and he had returned the fire. He had helped storm the house and he had helped kill all those inside. He had ridden off on a stolen horse and he had seen by morning that they were being pursued. He had, like the others, made a desperate run for his life, scrambling up the great caprock cliffs and onto the staked plains.

And then, like his fellow warriors, he had walked those parched plains for almost a week before finally trudging into the village, deep in the night of a waning moon.

For Dances With Wolves, the scalp in Wind In His Hair's lodge was but one memory counted among many from the long, disastrous raid into Mexico. He sat under it often, as he visited Wind In His Hair frequently. Everyone knew that the two were as brothers.

Like all Comanches, Dances With Wolves was uneasy about the shrinking space between Indian and white, more so perhaps because he had more to lose. But, in itself, the scalp meant nothing to him.

The person it terrified was his wife.

CHAPTER V

*T*HE LOVE SHE HAD FOR DANCES WITH WOLVES WAS ABIDING. They suffered through divisions as any man and woman would, but most days she counted herself lucky to have found such a considerate and faithful husband. That in itself would have been plenty, but Stands With A Fist also enjoyed a special status accorded her by his achievements.

And he was a perfect rudder for her emotions, for Stands With A Fist was not a woman who walked the middle of the trail. She had always found herself to one side, blowing hot or cold, and she often wondered what might have become of her were it not for her husband's ability to love her through unpredictable swings of temperament.

But even with all they held between them, Stands With A Fist knew that the one thing in this world she could not be without was her children. It was the children who had smoothed the rawness of her edges. Motherhood had entwined the disparate strings of her personality and forged her into a whole person, moving her through life with a freedom from doubt and fear she had not known before.

It was difficult to believe that Snake In Hands was in his ninth winter. Was it possible he could have come out of her so long ago? And was it possible that a being who came into the world so helpless could now be a boy racing toward manhood? He was taller and stronger than any boy his age and was blessed with an ability to retain everything he learned. Information, of whatever sort, seemed to stick in the inquisitive boy's head forever.

Their firstborn had been slow to show himself, and for a long time they had been unable to name him. His skeptical expressions hardly changed in the first year of his life, as if he knew his own vulnerability. As an infant people had marveled at his fine, fair hair and his white skin, and more than one made the practical suggestion that they call him White Boy. It was an amusing thought and for a time it circulated as a joke in the village. The parents took the ribbing good-naturedly, and when prodded to find a name they offered the same reply again and again, a reply the boy's godfather, Kicking Bird, was the first to make: "Let's see what happens."

The child's physical development was astounding and when the moon of his birth was marked for the first time, he was already standing on a pair of thick, beautiful legs, legs that would soon be propelling him around camp and onto the fringes of the grassland. One summer morning he trundled back into the lodge holding a young garter snake in both tiny hands. His mother was not fond of snakes but her son was so happy that she could not bring herself to discourage him and soon he was gently cradling every harmless, legless serpent he could find.

The only real falling-out he had ever experienced with his father took place when Dances With Wolves killed an obstinate rattlesnake outside the lodge entrance. His son had upbraided his father for days after, and from then on Dances With Wolves was forced to gingerly remove all dangerous snakes to a place of safety.

The boy's affection for these special animals never lagged, and even now he would jump down from his pony whenever he saw something slithering through the grass. Intent as any hunter, he would creep after the wriggling object of desire and, at just the right moment, clamp a pair of fingers on its tail and lift it off the ground. If the snake was agreeable, he would take it with him, and it was not unusual to see the head or tail of his find poking out of a shirttail or trouser leg as he rode along.

The second child, a girl, was born less than two years later, and the Comanches, who had gotten over the surprising whiteness of Snake In Hands' skin, were jolted again when they found that not a single hair could be seen on the little girl's head. An infant without hair was as inconceivable as a sky without stars, and the strange being that dwelt among them was constantly discussed.

Again the parents looked to Kicking Bird and again he gave the same reassuring advice.

"Let's see what happens."

The naming of the second child, as with the first, was put off, and in the meantime a growth of light, extremely fine hair began to appear on her head. That and the passage of time put an end to many wild speculations.

Though smaller and less sturdy than her brother, the new arrival grew just as rapidly, and in her own way just as strongly. She, too, was walking early. Whatever she might have lacked in boyish strength she more than made up for with a singular sense of purpose that dominated every aspect of the little girl's personality.

From the time they could carry her, the girl's legs were moving her fearlessly around the village and she was forever popping up in the homes of people she didn't know. These solo flights were taken without warning at odd hours, and it became routine to see Stands With A Fist going from lodge to lodge, her boy in tow, searching for her little girl.

Although the wayward child was repeatedly lectured about the importance of obtaining permission for her daily jaunts, the admonitions did little to deter her, and on one mild winter day the worst fears of her parents were realized when it was discovered that she was missing. After the village had been searched twice, from end to end, all available men and boys went to their horses and fanned out across the prairie in all directions. She was found more than a mile from camp, striding resolutely across the open grassland.

When the horsemen came alongside she refused to break stride, acknowledging them with an irritated glance before turning her light blue eyes forward again. And when one of the men laughingly inquired, "Where are you going?" the toddler replied curtly, "I'm walking."

She complained loudly when one of the warriors plucked her off the grass, and kept up her squawking all the way back to camp. After that she was known as Always Walking.

Always Going would have suited her just as well, because being on the move was how she wanted to be. She loved helping her mother, and she was good at entertaining herself. She could spend all morning with a doll and a toy lodge. But if her father went outside to relieve himself she wanted to go along, and Dances With Wolves' generosity toward his children was such that he found it hard to deny them.

Instead of diminishing, Always Walking's penchant for action swelled as she grew, along with a flinty obstinacy for getting her way. When her mother reminded her that a girl should be a girl and that she should pay more attention to her place, Always Walking would reply, "I am a Comanche, Mother. Comanches can be anyplace they want to be."

If the logic of her arguments was overruled, Always Walking stubbornly sulked, refusing to be herself until the next opportunity to exercise her will was realized. So deep was her determination that by her eighth summer there was almost nowhere that her father and Snake In Hands went that she didn't go, too.

Stands With A Fist's third child, a girl, was now nearing two summers and had yet to demonstrate anything beyond the reticence that marked her older brother's early years. She was neither meek nor bold, neither leader nor follower, seemingly content to take in the life swirling all about her. Perhaps she was awed by the individuality of her older brother and sister. Or perhaps she was slow in developing. Or it might have been that cautious observation was simply her nature. They called her Stays Quiet.

Like her husband, Stands With A Fist had no interest in pushing her children. She provided safety and sustenance and a mother's love. What the destiny of each child might be was not to be imposed. Destiny was something to be provided by the Great Mystery and it was up to each child to discover his or her own.

The greatest satisfaction Stands With A Fist took as a mother was to see her children healthy, happy, and growing. She still slept with them, and feeling those three warm bodies that carried her blood breathing next to her was the ultimate pleasure, her hope and salvation rolled into one.

Motherhood also represented her greatest fear, the same blinding fear she had experienced when Lieutenant Dunbar made his appearance so long ago. Her first life had been torn away from her when the Comanches seized her as a little girl. The thought that her life as a Comanche, too, might be taken away was a bad dream that dogged her day and night.

After the disastrous raid into Mexico it was impossible to keep it in the back of her mind. Dances With Wolves had already fought the whites. Wind In His Hair had taken the white woman's scalp. She could not escape the conclusion that more contact was inevitable. What would happen if the whites discovered her? What would happen to her children?

The possibilities made her mind buzz so chaotically that sometimes the rattle of it made her faint. Since the men had walked in from Texas in the middle of the night, each day had become a trial. When her children asked questions about the whites the best answer she could make was, "The whites are none of our business, that's why we stay away from them. They have nothing to do with us."

In sleep she sometimes lost her children. Once she had a horrifying dream of soldiers riding through camp, killing everyone in sight. She ran onto the prairie, dragging the children behind, but still they were pursued. When she stopped and looked back all of the soldiers' eyes were red and they were breathing fire. With her own hand she cut the throats of her children, each of them hysterical with fear. Then she drove the same knife deep into her own heart and fell back. Faceup on the ground, she realized she was not dead. Unable to open her eyes, she lay vibrating to the power of horses' hooves pounding the earth, listening to the screams of the soldiers and the explosions of their guns as they bore down upon her. She cried so hard that tears ran in streams down the length of her body.

She was sobbing when she woke and frantically checked her sleeping children to make sure they were still alive. Drawing them close calmed her enough to stop her tears.

But still she could not sleep.

CHAPTER VI

*H*IS REPUTATION AS A DREAMER HAD ENDURED SINCE HIS long, hazy days with the pony herd, and while it suited him perfectly, it had divided people as to his worth. Many regarded him as lackadaisical and shiftless. Just as many tolerated his slow development and defended his unique skills with horses as indispensable in tribal life.

But as he entered his twenty-first summer, Smiles A Lot was finding it more and more difficult to follow the poorly defined path he had taken. He daydreamed about taking his place as a warrior and sometimes imagined himself sitting in the Hard Shield circle. But the chance of his ever winning membership in that elite society was a remote possibility.

Smiles A Lot would be the first to admit that he was far behind. Boys four and five years younger had already been on many dangerous raids, and a number of them had even won honors. He had been on only one major raid, the doomed incursion into Mexico, and the only honor he had won for that was his own survival. There was as much to be ashamed of as there was to take pride in, and every action he had taken seemed to have mixed results.

It was true that he had single-handedly stolen twelve excellent horses from under the noses of heavily armed ranch guards. But it was also true that he had been confused about the precise rendezvous point because he had not listened carefully to Wind In His Hair's instructions. As a result he had waited in the wrong place with the horses while the main body of warriors, most of them on foot, had to fight their way out of a Mexican trap. The whole skirmish could have been avoided had he been in the right place at the right time, and Smiles A Lot shuddered at the thought of what might have happened to his standing if the warriors had not escaped the Mexican net.

Wind In His Hair had said it all when he gave the young man a public scolding.

"What good would a hundred horses be if there were no warriors to ride them? You think more about horses than you do about people! You are useless to me!"

To feel the wrath of Wind In His Hair beat down on him was humiliation enough, but to have his friend Dances With Wolves, the man who had sponsored him, witness the upbraiding was devastating. The man he had once called Loo-ten-tant, the man who had been so kind to him, was forced to stand by passively as he was tongue-lashed by the most respected warrior in the band. There was nothing Dances With Wolves could say or do for his young friend because Wind In His Hair was right. He had endangered everyone.

Smiles A Lot thought about his failings constantly in the weeks it took them to get back to the village. How could he restore his standing? What could he do? Where could he begin? His eyes had welled and overflowed as he stood a half mile away, holding the worn-out reserve horses, as his brothers in arms risked their lives in the attack on the white man's house where Wind In His Hair took the woman's scalp.

Now, two moons later, Smiles A Lot hardly thought about the red-haired scalp or the looming threat of white people coming into the country. There were too many personal problems pressing him, problems that a part of him felt were unfair.

Hadn't he been encouraged in his gift for managing horses? Hadn't he given his youth in service to the people and their animals? He was the one everyone else turned to when a mare was foaling, when a favored buffalo runner went lame, when there was trading to be done. Hadn't they depended on him to locate good pasture and the right breeding stock? Hadn't he enriched all of his people?

It was as if none of that mattered. He had alienated himself from Wind In His Hair. His own parents wondered aloud how long he planned to live in their lodge. His mother kept asking if he had his eye on anyone, and his father kept pronouncing that he would never be able to take a wife if he didn't elevate his status to that of his peers.

Though the warriors were kind enough not to make him a pariah, in the many stories they told and retold about the awful raid into Mexico, they did not include the exploits of Smiles A Lot. He had been omitted. It was as if he had not gone.

Even the bitterness inside him was not enough to effect any wholesale change. He was still the genial Smiles A Lot who provided reliable, good-humored company in any setting, the boy who was not going forward and not going back. To all who dwelled in Ten Bears' village, Smiles A Lot was just Smiles A Lot.

Among legendary horsemen he stood out, but what good was it really? The wonderful things he could do on the back of a horse were regarded as mere novelty. He had no family to hunt for, and while others his own age were out risking their lives for the good of all, Smiles A Lot was back in camp, applying poultices or delivering foals.

That he was such an easy young man did not help him, either. Apart from his devotion to horses, he had never demonstrated the passion expected of youth. That, of course, did not mean he was devoid of feeling. If anything, youth's hopes and desires ran deeper in Smiles A Lot than in most, but it was not in his nature to express them openly.

The tall, good-looking young man had kept his feelings hidden from view all his life. But as the village twisted in mute turmoil over the issue of the whites, Smiles A Lot writhed in a personal agony, a dilemma he shared with no one. It took a big effort to keep his torment secret, for it was like a sickness. He had suddenly and inexplicably fallen in love.

This lovesickness was easily the most monumental thing that had ever happened to him. In sunlight he often had to shake his head to clear out the thought of her while he was trying to concentrate on something else. At night it was much worse. He rolled back and forth under his covers, trying to fend off a constant bombardment of images that denied him sleep.

There were times when these visions would force him from bed. Wrapped in a blanket, he would stumble out of his parents' lodge and make his way through the pitch to the horses. In the grass he could writhe without anyone seeing, talk to himself, moan when he felt like it, stare dreary-eyed at a canopy of stars until he was so exhausted by her that he was able to lose consciousness for a few hours.

How he had tumbled into this inescapable captivity was a mystery to Smiles A Lot. He had known her all his life but had felt nothing special until a fateful afternoon when he stopped by Ten Bears' lodge to discuss a few trivial matters about the condition of the old man's horses. From the time of his boyhood, Ten Bears had kept the shy young man who knew so much about horses under his wing, and on quiet days the two passed a few minutes together. It was on such a day that Hunting For Something had come in with a bowl of pemmican for her grandfather.

Greeting Ten Bears, she dropped to her knees on the opposite side of the fire and with a single look that lasted no more than a second or two, turned Smiles A Lot's world upside down. It was nothing more than a shy glance, delivered under lidded eyes. But it was directed squarely at Smiles A Lot and carried the power of a mortal blow. In that instant she changed from a skinny girl of barely fifteen summers to a woman of profound mystery whose spell was paralyzing.

From then on she was never far from his thoughts, and Smiles A Lot, without any experience as a suitor, pursued her. Whenever possible he watched Ten Bears' lodge, hoping to see her go inside so he could make an entrance of his own. He made it a point to look in on the old man each day, and every time he came to the lodge flap it was with a heart that threatened to jump out of his chest.

Her family lived on the other side of the village from his own, and he conjured any excuse he could to travel that way, hoping to catch a glimpse of her. He loitered along the path to water, joining other young men with crushes on various girls. And suddenly he was in attendance at any communal gathering that might include her.

But he had no success. Every time he went to Ten Bears' lodge it was as if all the forces of earth and sky were conspiring against him. She was never there. He had seen her only once as she disappeared into the traffic of camp. The fleeting view of the glistening black hair trailing below her waist, the long dress, and the moccasined feet had held him transfixed as he wondered about her feet and arms and legs, the smell of her skin, the touch of her finger, the sound of her voice.

His surveillance of the trail to water yielded only two sightings. Each time she was with her mother, and when he saw them he immediately turned away, too nervous to look in their direction. As he stared at the ground, or into the branch of a tree, he thought of himself as foolish beyond words. She was passing so near. It was the opportunity he had sought to the exclusion of all else, yet he could not act. He could only subject himself to torture. And if he found the courage to cast his eyes about in time to see the fading form of mother and daughter, that was worse. All he could see then was the impossibility of his vain dream.

It was just as bad at a dance or ceremony which brought everyone together. A public setting made any contact out of the question and all he could do was peer through the fire and into the faceless crowd of girls steeped in shadow on the other side.

At times Smiles A Lot wished fervently that she had never looked at him because all the difficulties of his life were nothing compared to the fix he was in now.

And what if she looked at him again? What if they talked? What if they touched? The obstacles that lay beyond were insurmountable. Her father, Horned Antelope, was the son of Ten Bears and a Hard Shield. Smiles A Lot's father was a craftsman, a master of bow-making, but nothing else. Matches like that were not made.

It was terrible to be stuck. It seemed to take all the power he possessed to get up each day, to walk and talk and sleep. He was a fluttering piece of chaff whose every motion was under the absolute control of a momentary meeting with the eyes of a girl.

Yet there was a strength coming out of it, a hardening in Smiles A Lot he had never felt before. He possessed the heart of a dreamer and the sanctity of dreaming was something to be protected. At his darkest moments, the lonely, desperate heart that beat inside him grew suddenly large and powerful at the thought of defending his dream. In a strange way it didn't matter if they never spoke or touched. She was already in him. A dream of blinding, beautiful purity was buried in his heart. No one could take it away. He didn't care about Wind In His Hair's scalp or the coming of the whites. He didn't care if the earth yawned one morning and swallowed the whole village, for he knew that as he drifted down, spiraling head over heels into the void, he would be encased in the cocoon of her being . . . of the girl called Hunting For Something.

CHAPTER VII

*A*LL COMMUNITIES ARE SUSCEPTIBLE TO EXOTIC INFLU-
ENCES, and this was true of Ten Bears' village. Kicking Bird's deviation
into the wider stream of political life had created a vacancy in the spiritual life of the band which was now occupied by the secretive, mysterious
man known as Owl Prophet.

In many ways he was as traditional as any Comanche. He was
happily married, the father of two likeable daughters. He practiced the
medicine of healing and curing with better than average results, steadily
building a lucrative practice that largely freed him from the time-
consuming labor of the hunt and the inherent dangers of raiding.

But Owl Prophet's true specialty was not medicine. Medicine was
but a sidelight to his true calling of prophecy and Owl Prophet conjured
the future with a magic so dazzling that he was able at times to hold the
entire village in sway.

He operated out of a lodge adjacent to his family's. No one
knew what went on inside, because no one had ever entered. In fact,
the power that resided within was so daunting that it stifled the natural curiosity of children. Not one among them was brave enough
or foolhardy enough to lift the flap of Owl Prophet's lodge and peek

inside. What prayers he softly chanted, what charms he maintained, what spells he concocted were known only to him. Since childhood he had been the most inscrutable member of Ten Bears' band and the mystery about him only deepened as more and more of his predictions came true.

Everyone knew about the owl. It was the one object inside the special lodge that people had seen, and its rare appearances were not to be missed because his most spectacular forecasts had come after publically consulting with his animal assistant.

Owl Prophet routinely predicted dry summers, difficult births, and spectacular weather. Of course he was not right every time, but his many successes made his failures, especially ones without import, easy to forget.

He was particularly adept at sorting out omens, and none was more spectacular than the mystery of the rat. Shortly after Wind In His Hair announced that he and several Hard Shields were going into Mexico and that any able-bodied men could join them, a dead rat, its entrails bulging through an opening in its stomach, appeared one morning in the center of the village as if it had dropped from the sky.

Wind In His Hair thought the rat had been dropped somehow by a hawk or owl passing overhead, an explanation readily accepted by Dances With Wolves and the rest of the Hard Shield membership. Ten Bears peered down at the rat and wondered if it hadn't disemboweled itself in a freak accident. Kicking Bird dismissed the rat as a trivial matter, not worthy of thought. But talk persisted and theories of one sort or another fluttered around the village like scattering birds.

The rat's corpse was snatched up by one of the camp dogs before Owl Prophet could examine it but that evening he hired a crier to circulate through the village, inviting all who desired information to assemble in front of his medicine lodge at the falling of night's first star.

Many eyes watched the sky that night and when the first star flared and died, a crowd gathered at the appointed place. Oddly, there was no fire inside the lodge and people began to grow restless, wondering if Owl Prophet was even inside. Suddenly the tent flap flew up and he stepped out. The crowd was silent. They could make out the outline of the famous owl perched upon his head. A few people gasped as the owl's head swiveled.

"I know the meaning of the rat," Owl Prophet proclaimed. "Come again in two sleeps and I will tell if it is good or bad."

Owl Prophet slipped back into the lodge, dropping the flap behind him, and the crowd broke up in confusion. Two nights later the throng that gathered outside Owl Prophet's medicine lodge was large and expectant. The glow of a fire could be seen inside the place of mystery and the crowd waited silently as if holding its collective breath. For several minutes a flurry of shadowy movement held the onlookers' full attention. Then the flap was thrown open by unseen hands and the viewers pressed closer together, craning frantically for a better view of the amazing tableau that had sprung up before their eyes.

Filling the entrance was a large square of canvas, a screen illuminated by the light of the fire behind it. Out of nowhere the silhouette of a man appeared which everyone assumed was the form of Owl Prophet. But before anyone could be sure, another silhouette appeared behind the screen. There was no mistaking the distinct outline of an owl. Its head swiveled on its neck and its body expanded and contracted with what appeared to be living breath. The bird's movements were stiff and mechanical, but instead of inviting skepticism they had the opposite effect. The queerness of the action behind the screen held the audience rapt. Not a soul had ever seen anything like it before.

While the owl performed, incantations were uttered, incantations that seemed to be coming from the silhouette of the man, though the voice sounded different from Owl Prophet's.

"Great Mystery," the voice intoned, "speak to your servant. Tell me of the rat with the hole. The people want to know its meaning. They are afraid. Let them understand it, Great Mystery. They seek only to serve you."

The request was repeated three times, and all the while the owl gyrated. A long silence followed during which both silhouettes ceased to move. And then, in a measured way, the owl astonished the Comanches by slowly and dramatically spreading its wings. This action was also repeated three times and was so deliberate as to leave the impression that something was about to happen.

When it did, the effect was overwhelming. Gasps of horror broke out in the ranks of the audience. Several youngsters ran away and two people slumped unconscious to the ground as the owl's silhouette began to talk.

It was nothing anyone could understand, an otherworldly blend of high-pitched screeches, low grunts, and prolonged sighs all delivered with dizzying rapidity. The creature spoke for no more than a minute before it spread its wings once more, issued a final piercing screech, and fell away from the screen.

The figure of the man fell away too, and for a few moments the crowd stood still, staring at the black canvas in complete bewilderment. Before anyone could move, heavy, scraping sounds were heard, and moments later, to the astonishment of all, Owl Prophet himself crawled through the entrance. He flopped down in front of the lodge and, with much effort, raised himself to his knees.

"The Mystery has spoken," he gasped. "The rat with the hole . . . a bad sign . . . many rifles in Mexico . . . death in big water . . . a scalp coming back . . . a red scalp!"

With that Owl Prophet pitched forward and lay heaving on the ground, unable to move.

The people closest to the medicine man were wary at first of going to his aid, thinking he might be dying. But Owl Prophet continued to breathe, and when he lifted his head slightly, those with the courage to do so lifted him up and carried him through the dispersing crowd, depositing him in the family lodge across the way. For several hours, Owl Prophet lay in fevered delirium before slipping into a sleep from which he would not wake until twilight of the next day.

People wandered back to their homes drained by the experience, their minds packed with unforgettable images that kept the camp awake long after bedtime.

One who stayed up late was Wind In His Hair. He did not dismiss Owl Prophet's performance. In fact, he was as deeply impressed as anyone. But he was also angered by the turn of events. He snapped at his wives and children before retreating to the special Hard Shield lodge, where he sat for an hour in solitary contemplation, angry that the delicate chemistry of an important raid, so long in planning, had been upset. Owl Prophet had power, to be sure. But what about his own? Was his own power to be thrown away because an owl talked? Was the might of all Comanches to be subverted by a spectacular show of prophecy?

The call went out to the Hard Shields that same night and when they assembled in Wind In His Hair's meeting place, he spoke out of his heart, saying that while he could not doubt the truth of Owl Prophet's words, he was not ready to surrender to them either. Owl Prophet might have the ability to speak with the Mystery, but he could not guide an arrow to its mark. He had never faced an enemy in battle, and while Wind In His Hair admitted he knew little of magic, he knew how to lead men in war. That was his specialty. He then asked each man at his fire how he felt and if each still wanted to go.

All of them did, and two days later the large party with Wind In His Hair at its head rode into a stiff breeze from the south, leaving behind them the anxious hopes of friends and relatives.

When the bedraggled war party returned it was learned that each part of the prophecy had proven out. There were many guns in Mexico, far too many. Three good warriors had been drowned in floodwaters. The scalp hung in Wind In His Hair's lodge. All had been predicted with awesome perfection. Overnight, Owl Prophet's influence increased tenfold, and when the crier went around two moons after the party's return from Mexico, everyone put aside their business and came to the medicine lodge. This time Wind In His Hair stood at the front of the crowd, fingering the sewn lids of his missing eye, waiting as anxiously as anyone for Owl Prophet to appear.

The medicine man did not consult the owl behind the screen that evening. There was nothing flamboyant about his condition or the words he spoke. He was perfectly matter-of-fact, but the absence of a show did not matter to his audience. They were intent on his every word.

"In less than five sleeps, friends from the north will come to our village," he announced. "They will bring with them a strange story."

CHAPTER VIII

*T*HEY APPEARED LATE IN THE AFTERNOON FOUR DAYS AFTER OWL Prophet's pronouncement, a long line of travelers occupying a narrow band of light on the horizon, heralded by the hollow boom of thunder from ominous skies.

Wind In His Hair and his family were visiting one of his wives' relations in the south, and Dances With Wolves, accompanied by his two eldest children, had taken a small hunting party off to the east. Everyone else was in camp and they all turned out to greet their friends, the southern Cheyenne.

Because Ten Bears' strongholds were found only in the most far-flung sectors of the measureless space that comprised the Comanche homeland, such visits, especially with the Cheyenne, were extraordinary. From the moment the visitors were sighted an atmosphere of celebration swamped the village.

People rushed to their lodges to make themselves presentable. A welcoming committee was hastily assembled to provide the honored guests with everything they needed: a practical campsite, fresh water, pasture for their animals.

Once the new lodges were erected visiting began in earnest, led as always by young people. Initially shy, children of both tribes were soon tearing around camp, cavorting together as if they had known one another all their lives. The adults followed suit. The Cheyenne were an exotic disruption in the routine of village life, and the isolated Comanches relished the change.

The visitors were generally taller and leaner than their hosts. Their clothing and accessories were different, as were their prayers and taboos and humor. The only thing truly abhorrent about them was their reputation for eating dogs. But since no Comanche had actually witnessed such a barbaric practice, the unsettling quirk was quickly pushed to the back of people's minds so that the best of times could be enjoyed.

The Cheyenne leader, a stately, elegant man of middle age whose name was Wolf Robe, immediately paid a visit to Ten Bears. The men had met twice over the years, and their acquaintance, though slight, made this occasion a reunion. Wolf Robe and his band were on an expedition to Mexican traders in the west and sought permission to camp with the Comanche for a few days before proceeding on, that is if water and game were plentiful. Ten Bears insisted that was the case. The old man also insisted that Wolf Robe and his leading warriors come to dinner that night, suggesting Kicking Bird's lodge as a good site for the feast.

The dinner at Kicking Bird's was the last of many on a night when everyone stayed up late. The children were too excited to sleep, and so were the adults. There were many new people to meet and, like all Indian get-togethers, the trading began at once, not stopping until the Cheyenne left. People began to eat and that didn't stop, either. On the first night the camp crier announced half a dozen calls to eat at various Comanche homes.

Men with high standing from both tribes filtered in and out of the public dinners. They enjoyed themselves but they ate little and expended little energy. The feasts of real importance, feasts they could not miss, were coming later. The Hard Shields were sponsoring a party for their Cheyenne counterparts, a handful of Dog Soldiers who were riding with Wolf Robe. That was to be followed by the gathering at Kicking Bird's, where information of real weight was to be exchanged. It had been announced as a dinner, but everyone knew it was to be a high-level council.

As might have been expected, the meeting of the two warrior societies was a full-throated, free-wheeling orgy of anecdotes concerning combat and hunting laced with hilarious stories, many of them off-color. At its conclusion an intermission of almost an hour was observed, giving people time to make ready for the rendezvous at Kicking Bird's lodge.

Comanche men arrived first. The most influential placed themselves around the fire next to Kicking Bird and Ten Bears. Then a constant stream of Comanche men, their thick hair combed and oiled, their shirts and leggings and moccasins resplendent with beadwork, their scalplocks and ears and fingers festooned with sparkling metal, flowed into the lodge until it was bulging. They sat or stood quietly, uttering nothing above a murmur as they waited for their guests to come.

The Cheyenne arrived shortly after the last Comanches had wedged themselves into the tent.

Led by Wolf Robe, they came as one, and, though the Comanche men looked formidable, the Cheyenne warriors ducking into Kicking Bird's lodge eclipsed them. It was as if a delegation of gods had alighted from a cloud to file mutely into a common lodge, their glistening copper faces masks of dignity, their every movement a testament to the impeccable grace of power. The twelve men were part of a very few who lived at the pinnacle of Cheyenne manhood. They had endured every privation their wild country could produce. They had survived the illnesses and accidents of youth to reach maturity. They had triumphed over the hazards of the hunt and each of them had survived combat many times. The sullen, confident men filing inside that night represented the finest blood, the richest essence of all Cheyenne life. To call them gods might have seemed far-fetched in another society, but in their world no greater men existed.

When Wolf Robe appeared Ten Bears was helped to his feet, and though he stood unsteadily, the old man's face was bright with animation as he welcomed his guests to the fire and cordially invited them to be seated. Ten Bears drew his pipe from its case and there was silence as the smoking began.

It was silent outside as well, which was unusual because a meeting of this gravity normally attracted eavesdroppers who pressed close to the walls in hope of hearing what passed inside. On this night, however, the vicinity around Kicking Bird's lodge was deserted. People were worn out from eating and visiting, and from overtired children who had stayed up

too late. Nonetheless, they would have come had there been anything
to hear. But anyone trying to listen would have been disappointed because this council was not being conducted by voice. The tribes knew a
few words of each other's tongues, and both counted Spanish-speakers
among their ranks, but neither was adept enough to make meaningful
talk so they naturally resorted to a language whose fluency was shared by
all: the language conducted as music by fingers, hands, and arms, the art-
ful language of signs.

There was only one soul lurking outside the meeting place that night,
and he had not come out of curiosity. Loitering close by, he had happened
to see the Cheyenne delegation arrive at the lodge and drifted closer with
the idea that spying on the gathering might provide a respite from his
misery. He had already attended several feasts but had been unable to appear at the one hosted by the father of Hunting For Something. He
would have walked through fire to see her face and it would have been
simple to stop by and pay his respects to the Horned Antelope family. But
courage had failed him. If he had showed his face, no mask, however
thick, could have hidden the hopeless ardor in his bleeding heart.

As Smiles A Lot moped about, hoping to pick up any sound from inside that might distract his despair, he noticed a sliver of light. There was
a tiny rent in one of the lodge's seams, and as he placed one eye against
it, the lovesick young man found that it afforded a complete view of the
principal men seated around the fire.

He was in time to see Ten Bears offer his visitors still more food.

"If there is room in your bellies," the old man signed, "you are welcome to more."

"No," Wolf Robe countered amiably, "your generosity has made
every Cheyenne belly heavy. Some of our people can barely walk."

Smiles flashed through the lodge and the two headmen chatted
easily for a few moments about the prospects for a successful round of
trading with the Mexicans. The assembled warriors listened passively to
the preliminaries, knowing full well that the meat of the discussion was
yet to come, and when Ten Bears made a casual inquiry about the quality
of hunting in Cheyenne country it opened the gates to a flood of alarming news.

Wolf Robe had remained cross-legged throughout the small talk but
now he rose to give everyone a full view of all he had to say.

"Our brother the buffalo has given us all we need. The grass is good and the buffalo are plenty, but they are acting strangely. They gather less and less in great herds. They are acting like ants scattered from their nest. They act lost."

"Why is this?" Ten Bears asked.

Wolf Robe paused as if pained. Then he signed curtly.

"The whites are overrunning our country."

Silence pervaded the lodge and Wolf Robe listened to it for a few moments before continuing.

"They are popping out of the ground like grass after rain. There is nothing but trouble everywhere we look. That's why we are here now. We are hoping some of these troubles will have passed by the time we get back."

The Comanche looked at one another for enlightenment but each face showed only puzzlement.

"Tell us about these troubles," Ten Bears asked.

"White hunters are camping everywhere. They come in small groups but they have far-shooting guns that can kill as many buffalo in an hour as we can take in a week."

"Are you killing these men?" Ten Bears asked.

"We kill as many as we can. It is not easy to ride against the far-shooting guns. A party from my wife's brother's band killed six in one raid but it turned out bad. The white men were infected with the spotted sickness and the warriors carried it back to the village. It killed many. My brother-in-law is dead from it. Our band has killed a few of these hair-mouthed hunters but every time we do they send soldiers out to chase us . . . in our own country! There are two soldier forts, in the east, on the edge of our country. We learned before we left that they are making another one."

Ten Bears' brows pinched together. "Why are they doing this?"

"They want our land," Wolf Robe replied. "They're on it now, all along the Vermillion River off to the east. They make square houses of mud to live in."

"I have heard of these square houses," Ten Bears interjected. "It is said that these houses cannot be moved and that inside there is no air."

"I have only seen them from afar. I have never touched one. These white people put blades in the ground and skin the earth. They drill holes and plant seeds and eat the green things that grow out of the holes. . . ."

One of the Cheyenne warriors said something to Wolf Robe.

"Trees are being felled everywhere they can be found," he went on. "They cut the trees into pieces and push the pieces into the ground and stretch wire between them . . ."

"Singing wire?" Ten Bears asked.

"The wire doesn't sing. It sits there."

Another Cheyenne mumbled something to Wolf Robe and the headman made more pictures in the air.

"If we kill the earth skinners . . . soldiers chase us around for that, too."

Still another warrior spoke up. Wolf Robe listened, nodding at what the warrior was saying. Then he turned to his Comanche listeners.

"Some of our people are trading robes for colored water that white men make. Everyone has a name for it. I call it crazy water."

"I know about that," Ten Bears put in. "It's the water that burns the throat and makes people wild."

"Yes. Don't let it into your camp. People can't stop drinking it. They get tired and fall down, or they get so crazy they can't see who they are . . . they fight . . ."

"Indian against Indian?"

"Indian against Indian. People get killed sometimes. One man I heard of gave his woman to a white man for pleasure just to get more of this water. People get sick when they drink it, yet they still want more when they get better. Don't let any of your people get hold of this water. It always brings trouble."

As the Comanches sat in stunned disbelief, several of Wolf Robe's warriors beseeched him to tell something more. Wolf Robe's head twisted back and forth, trying to catch everyone at once. Then his hand went up for silence and he signed again to Ten Bears.

"Have you heard of the holy road?"

Ten Bears glanced over his shoulder at the warriors who sat and stood transfixed behind him.

"No," Ten Bears finally replied. "What is this holy road?"

Wolf Robe considered the question a moment. Then he turned and nodded to a warrior sitting close by. Wolf Robe sat as the new man rose to speak.

The Comanches paid close attention to this warrior. He was tall, even for a Cheyenne, and particularly resplendent in heavily beaded moccasins and leggings. His bone-pipe breastplate extended to his waist and a heavy disc of hammered copper hung about his neck. Tied in his scalplock was a huge claw taken from a humpbacked bear. His eyes were lidded, his lips thin and delicate, his nose long and straight. The most spectacular thing about him, however, was the tight-fitting white soldier jacket with its brass buttons lining one side of its open front and golden bars of fabric sewn on its shoulders.

"I am Fast," he signed. "I have smoked the pipe tonight. My words are true."

Outside, Smiles A Lot was not aware of the stiffness in his legs, nor was he bothered by the light rain that was falling. He was not even aware of Hunting For Something. As a boy he had sometimes spied on high-level councils but that was only because he had nothing better to do. But what had been a lark in his early youth was suddenly something more. He was spellbound by the exchange taking place between the two tribes' best warriors.

The new speaker's quiet presence stood in sharp contrast to the sublime action of his arms and hands. Perhaps it was because the boy outside had never paid attention, or perhaps he was witnessing a true master, but whatever the reason, Smiles A Lot remained entranced by the exquisite perfection of Fast's every gesture as he spun out his story.

"White men with long looking-glasses came into the country last year at the first melting of the snow. The whites had said they were going to build a road on which a fire wagon of steel would pull boxes on wheels behind it. We didn't want to see a road like this coming through our country. My brother and I and a few other warriors overwhelmed one of these parties while they were in camp. We killed all of them and took the long looking-glass and tried to see what the white men were looking at, but it was worthless. We never saw anything.

"From then on, white soldiers were with the looking-glass people and we had a hard time driving them off. When the grass started out of the earth this year, some Kaws told us that the road for the fire wagon was being built. They said there were many white men doing this and that the road was aimed at our hunting grounds.

"Council fires burned for many sleeps until it was decided that we should make war against this road. A great party of a hundred warriors set out to the east when the ponies were fat. We wanted to stop the road. Our hearts were strong. We were willing to fight the fire wagon.

"After five sleeps we found the fire-wagon road. There were many white men making it . . ."

"How does this road look?" Ten Bears interrupted.

"Two ropes laid side by side. Metal ropes. The white men we saw were pounding these ropes into the earth. We decided to drive these whites off and circled behind them so we could come out of the sun when we attacked them in the morning. We did this and they scattered over the prairie. We took two scalps but some had the far-shooting guns and we fell back.

"We were going to attack once more when two scouts galloped in from the east. These scouts had seen something coming toward us on the metal rope road. It was not a fire wagon but some kind of wagon bed without sides. It had wheels and a stick with handles which two white men were pumping up and down like drinking birds. A third white man was riding on this thing.

"We saw it come over a little hill and rush down to where we were sitting our horses. The two pumping white men rolled onto the ground and ran off. Our horses were so frightened that they began to jump into the air. It was hard to hold them.

"The third man did not run away. He came down the hill, standing straight up on the funny wagon. He wore a black robe. Around his neck were two pieces of crossed silver. He pulled the silver over his head and waved it as he drew closer. He pulled a black thing from his robe, the thing white men call a 'book.' He held these things over his head, screaming words we did not know. The man was not pumping and the little wagon lost power. It stopped in front of us and the man stepped off.

"Many stout warriors did not want to look at the man. He had no meat. His skin was the color of wax. His nose was as thin as a needle and his eyes popped like a frog's. He waved his arms and yelled and paced back and forth. He pointed the cross at people. People were getting scared.

"Then he fell down in the grass. He began to roll on the earth. He talked in many strange voices and his eyes turned up into his head showing only the whites. Saliva poured from his mouth. All could see that some spirit was inside him and that he was deranged. The strongest warrior has no power against such things. We rode away, hardly stopping until we were home."

Kicking Bird, who had followed Fast's strange story with rapt attention, got quickly to his feet as the rain outside began to fall faster.

"Did anyone find out who this being was?"

"We have counseled with all who know anything of whites," Fast replied. "It might be a white man priest. It might be that the road for the fire wagon is some kind of holy road. People are calling it the white man's holy road."

"And the fire wagon, the thing the white man calls a 'train.' Have you seen this thing?"

"Two times," Fast replied. "It makes a horrible noise and is covered in armor. Nothing can penetrate. We have tried to pull the road up from the earth but it takes many men to get one piece out. And the whites always put it right back. We are still trying to find a way to fight the fire wagon. It is a hard thing to fight."

Fast let his arms drop to his sides and stood, surveying the crowd of Comanches across the fire. Then he sat down. A hush filled Kicking Bird's lodge and for a few moments only the rain, beating steadily on the conical hide that surrounded them, could be heard.

Ten Bears' chin had dropped toward his chest but now he raised it and started shakily to his feet, rising with the aid of the strong arms around him.

"We have heard your talk," he signed. "We pity the Cheyenne for their troubles. What will you do?"

Wolf Robe rose to answer.

"What can be done to fight an enemy that is everywhere," he replied, "an enemy with weapons no one understands, an enemy that becomes larger every day no matter how many we might kill? No one can answer these questions but we are all warriors and a warrior knows but one thing and that is to defend his people and his country. It may be that the next time the snow flies our bones will be scattered over the earth but none of us are afraid to die."

Ten Bears nodded as Wolf Robe sat. "It is the same with the Comanche. Who knows what fate the Mystery has planned for us. But if Cheyenne runners reach this village and ask us to come and help, we will do it anytime. We have fought side by side in the past and we will help the Cheyenne if they want us to. Comanche fear no enemy."

Ten Bears blinked as he looked out at his guests, wondering briefly if it was possible to fall asleep on his feet. "Our hearts are glad to have old friends in camp. It makes everyone happy. The rain is coming down now and I long to be under the good robe in my lodge. Good night."

Everyone who had been sitting got to their feet. Those standing stirred perceptibly for the first time since the meeting had been convened. Outside, Smiles A Lot pulled back from the lodge wall and receded into the darkness.

But he was still watching as the conferees ducked out of the lodge and moved off through the driving rain with as little care as if they were strolling in the sun. Smiles A Lot, too, was unfazed by the rain that had soaked him through and was now running down his face.

He had read the words of the warriors disappearing into the night as if for the first time. He had seen them as if for the first time. The dreamer he had been all his life was no more, shed as if by magic. It had joined the water pooling around his feet. Confusion had suddenly lifted and he knew he would no longer worry about what he might do.

His dilemma over Hunting For Something was gone, too. His feelings for her were the same, but he no longer felt sick.

Something strong had invaded him, a force with the power to erase the past and set the future. There was only one thing he wanted now. He wanted to be a part of the talk he had just witnessed. When there was a call to arms, he wanted to catch up his strongest pony and ride to battle. He wanted to sire children and provide for them, and from that night on, Smiles A Lot possessed a single, all-consuming ambition.

He wanted to die a warrior.

CHAPTER IX

*T*HERE WAS STILL DEW ON THE GRASS WHEN THE CHEYENNE headed west like a flotilla of small ships sailing slowly away on a flat, endless ocean. Impromptu councils sprung up as soon as they were gone. They had enjoyed the company of their visitors, but the people of Ten Bears' camp were itching for the moment when they could get down to the business of speculating on developments in the country of the Cheyenne.

Though it was far to the north, it wasn't as if no one had ever been there. A few people knew that country well and most had at least touched it in their far-ranging travels. Now that soldiers and buffalo-hunters and settlers had invaded it, everyone wondered if the Comanche might not be next. The Kiowa nation was just to the north, a buffer between the Cheyenne and Comanche, but that was little consolation in light of the monstrous power of what the Cheyenne had called the holy road.

The road and what it carried and what it might mean for all of them was too incomprehensible for consensus to emerge in the endless round of meetings that day. A significant number of warriors refused to believe that the whites would ever consider invading their country, and at many fires there was talk about how quickly the whites would be destroyed if they were so foolish as to try to encroach on Comanche lands. Soldiers especially. Soldiers couldn't ride. They couldn't shoot well, and their big American horses gave out quickly. If soldiers came, they would probably die of thirst before Comanche warriors had a chance to kill them!

The older men shared a more measured approach to the Cheyenne revelations. Kicking Bird and his contemporaries had been trained from birth as warriors, and fighting was second nature to them, but the weight of age and experience gave them a more practical view. Still, there was no consensus here, either. Should they move farther west? Should they go to war with the Cheyenne? Should they think about attending the next time whites sent runners with invitations to a council? These and many other issues were raised, but no one could agree. How could there be agreement on what could not be understood?

Kicking Bird smoked the pipe in many lodges that day, so many that by the time he returned home he wondered if all the smoking had not made him ill. Everyone inside was asleep, but lying down did not soothe his queasy stomach. It rolled in persistent waves and he soon went back outside, hoping the fresh air would take his sickness away.

The back of his lodge faced the open prairie, and as he stood staring at the night, Kicking Bird suddenly felt as if he were the only person in the world. How could this be? The earth was under his feet. The stars were filling his eyes. His wives and his children were asleep with full bellies. There was no sickness in camp. The season had been prosperous and there was no reason to think it would not continue. Comanche enemies were far away, and if they were foolish enough to come near they would surely be defeated. Even the whites, with all their guns and all their people, would be defeated if they came out here. How could they think of coming? What could they possibly want with the country of the Comanches except perhaps to walk across it? The more he thought about it, the more Kicking Bird realized that whatever the whites might bring was not as troubling at this moment as his own people's lack of readiness to meet the challenge.

Smoking so much had not made him sick at all. It was a sickness of the heart that had settled in him. Outside of himself no one in the village knew any white-man words and he had never practiced the words pried whenever possible from Dances With Wolves and Stands With A Fist.

They could speak the words, but it was well known that the couple who had been born white would be the last to want anything to do with their birth race.

From all he had heard, the white man's talk was confusing. They had made many promises to the Cheyenne and Kiowa, not one of which had been kept. Even the presents they had promised rarely found their way into Indian hands.

Anyone who treated with the whites would have to be prepared. Kicking Bird was the best prepared of them all, yet he knew almost nothing of white ways. And what if he did? Would it really matter if he were smarter than all the whites put together?

Kicking Bird concluded, wistfully, that it would not matter. The Comanche could not agree on the significance of a single dead rat lying with a hole in its stomach in the middle of camp. How could they agree on a course of action for dealing with a nation of strange people whose numbers were staggering, whose clothes and customs and armaments and food and machines might have come from a world beyond the sun and the moon? Kicking Bird saw no way for the Comanche to remain as they were. He could not imagine the Comanche, or any other tribe, meeting the white threat as one people, and without unity all would surely be lost.

He resolved that night, standing alone behind his lodge, that he would never allow himself to feel this queasiness again. He could no more change the condition of the Comanches than he could reach into heaven and shuffle the stars. But he could still do all in his power to serve his people, his wives, his children, and himself. He could not allow himself to be crippled with doubt. Then he would serve no one.

He did not sleep in the family lodge that night, retiring instead to the tent next door, the place reserved especially for him, the place where the peace medal from the whites hung. His stomach trouble had disappeared completely and he quickly fell into a deep sleep, dreaming a terrible dream that the buffalo had vanished, returning to the earth from whence they had sprung, brothers no more to the Comanches or anyone else. The Indian people were left to wander in starvation, crying ceaselessly for their relatives the buffalo who had deserted them.

Late the next morning, his children, unable to wait any longer, flooded into the lodge of their father and, as they rolled over him in a happy pile, Kicking Bird knew more than ever that no power on earth could sway him from his course. He would do his best to handle what was coming. He would offer all of his experience and wisdom to the cause of leadership. He knew that whatever happened he would not disappoint the tangle of arms and legs in which he was now entwined, and that was good enough for Kicking Bird.

CHAPTER X

SMILES A LOT HAD NO BAD DREAMS. IN FACT, HE SLEPT soundly and deeply for the first time in weeks.

He was up long before Kicking Bird began wrestling with his children and spent most of the early morning with his horses, trying to figure out how best to exploit his wealth. *So beautiful*, he thought as he meandered back and forth among them. They all knew and trusted him, and as he passed by, dragging a gentle hand over their slick coats, the ponies would nicker to him or lazily blow the dust from their nostrils in a sign of contentment. He, in turn, felt unbounded affection for them. But he was not thinking how much he loved them this morning, he was trying to decide which ones he could do without.

In the past he'd sought peace in the company of his horses, a living shield against the doubts he had about himself. But now there was no vestige of doubt. Smiles A Lot looked upon his many horses as weapons, and before the sun was at midpoint he was back in camp fully armed.

Smiles A Lot had no capacity for guile, and as a trader he had never displayed the adroitness at bartering that came easily to others. He had never sought anything more than a fair return on the value he offered and that spirit had guided his selection of the half-dozen sturdy ponies he brought into camp that morning.

Three of the ponies he left picketed in front of his father's home. With the other three in tow, he crossed the village to the lodge of Horned Antelope's sister, the newly widowed Magpie Woman. She had lost her husband in the raid into Mexico and her sudden dependence on the charity of others made her a good candidate to provide what Smiles A Lot needed.

She was at home with her two children and seemed happy to see Smiles A Lot. Her chopped hair and the unhealed cuts on her arms made it plain that she was still in mourning, and when Magpie Woman warmed to the offer he made, Smiles A Lot knew he was doing the right thing.

It was common knowledge that his horses were the finest. Any one of them was a prize and he was offering three to the impoverished widow, two for materials and one for labor. Magpie Woman seemed delighted and assured him that the lodge he wanted her to make could be completed before the next full moon. She had enough hides already on hand, and though she might be short a few poles, she assured him she could find more without any trouble.

Returning home, he found his father and mother outside, curiously inspecting the three horses he had left staked to the ground.

"Are these your ponies?" his father asked as Smiles A Lot came up.

"No, Father, they are yours."

"Mine? What do you mean?"

"I want to trade them for a bow and set of arrows."

"A bow . . . and arrows . . . for you?" his father asked.

"I want a long-shooting bow of ash, and maybe twenty arrows."

Smiles A Lot's father scratched the side of his head. "Twenty arrows . . . that's a lot, son. There is no ash here. I would have to travel one or two sleeps to find it."

"That is why I'm offering three good ponies instead of one."

The older man cocked his head quizzically at his boy.

"Why do you want a bow and arrows?"

"Any man has to have such things in his lodge."

"What lodge?" his mother suddenly spoke up.

"Magpie Woman is making me a lodge of my own."

Smiles A Lot's mother stepped in front of her husband. "How can you have a lodge of your own? Who will keep it? Who will make your food . . . your clothes?"

"Maybe *I* will," Smiles A Lot replied stoutly.

"This is backwards," his father started, "what will you do—"

"How can you have a lodge without a woman?" his mother interrupted.

"I will have a woman."

"Who?"

"I don't know . . . someone good."

"People will laugh," his mother cautioned, "a grown man with a lodge and no family."

"Let them laugh," said Smiles A Lot. "I am a Comanche man. I can do what I want. I want a lodge and I'm going to have one. Father, will you take the ponies I'm offering or should I walk them over to Powder Face?"

"Powder Face!" his father exclaimed. "His arrows can't hit anything."

"Is it a bargain?" Smiles A Lot asked.

"You will have to be patient . . . an ash bow takes time."

"I'll be patient."

Leaving his stunned parents, Smiles A Lot set off once more and a few minutes later was standing at Owl Prophet's lodge flap. He announced himself and waited.

After what seemed a long time the flap opened and the slit-eyed prophet stooped through the opening. He said nothing but stood staring down at Smiles A Lot, waiting for the boy who was good with horses to state his business.

"I am taking the warrior's path," the young man said evenly. "I want you to guide me."

Owl Prophet continued to stare at his caller. He looked at the sun. "Come back when there is shade on the other side of my lodge," he said. Then he ducked back through the flap.

When Smiles A Lot returned early in the afternoon he was leading another of his ponies. Again he announced himself and again Owl Prophet emerged. He glanced expressionless at the young roan stallion Smiles A Lot had brought and told the boy to come inside his family's lodge.

No one was at home and Smiles A Lot sat in the spot Owl Prophet indicated, on the other side of the small fire burning in the center of the floor. The prophet did not offer his visitor a pipe. He sat still, his long unbraided hair spilling down his shoulders, his eyes so narrow that it looked as if he might drift off to sleep at any moment.

After a long silence, his lips moved almost imperceptibly. "Tell me how this has come to pass."

Smiles A Lot told of the night he had spent in the rain outside Kicking Bird's lodge. He told of the arrangement he had made with Magpie Woman and the bargain he had struck with his father. He was tempted to reveal his feelings for Hunting For Something but decided that such an admission would only distract Owl Prophet.

It was hard to tell what Owl Prophet was doing. His eyes had shut as soon as Smiles A Lot started to explain, and they remained closed even after Smiles A Lot had stopped talking.

But all the while Owl Prophet held his head up, as if the eyes were somehow seeing through the lowered lids. Smiles A Lot started when the lids suddenly flew open and the prophet's eyes, round as eggs, stared straight through him. The words Owl Prophet spoke were flat and trancelike, delivered with an authority that discouraged questioning.

"Journey to the country of the Kiowa. Seek out the place of mystery, the great bluff with sides that slope back to the earth, the bluff whose rock face looks like a bear has clawed it. A creek runs along its base and winds around behind. Secret your horses and possessions there and climb the back side of the place of mystery. Sit near the edge where the rock face falls to the creek. Do not eat. Do not drink. Only pray. Pray hard. Ask the Mystery to reveal your destiny. When you see something, come and tell me what it is."

Owl Prophet trembled. His eyelids closed then opened into slits once again. "You have heard me," he said lowly. "Make ready and go. Leave that pony where he is."

Smiles A Lot wasted no time. He asked his befuddled mother to prepare enough food for a week of sleeps, then picked up his old bow and a few arrows and cut three favorite ponies from his herd. His preparations were so single-minded and hasty that to say good-bye had not occurred to him. His only thought was to follow Owl Prophet's instructions, and when his father asked when he would return, Smiles A Lot answered simply, "I don't know."

Then he vaulted onto a dapple-gray pony and, with horsehair lines to the other two in hand, started off through the village. People noticed him leaving but no one spoke to the boy, whose eyes were fixed straight ahead to the northeast.

One, however, followed him to the edge of the village, there to stand watching on the lip of the prairie as the young man and his horses shrank to specks. For a long time she had wished he would look her way or speak to her. For a long time she had been unable to think of much else and her heartstrings had been jumping all morning with the news that Magpie Woman was building a lodge for him, that his father was going to make him a bow, and that he had been sequestered with Owl Prophet.

What mission he was undertaking she did not know. She only knew that whenever a man left camp there was no guarantee he would return, and she stood squinting until the black dots moving in the distance vanished below the horizon. All along she had hoped that the rider and his horses would by some miracle grow larger again and that he would be riding toward her instead of away. But now he was gone and inwardly she chided herself for being shy. Life was uncertain these days. It seemed like something new was happening every day and there was no knowing what tomorrow promised. And now there was nothing she could do but wait and hope for his return. Then she would do something, she told herself.

For now her heart was on the ground. She stared down at her moccasins with wet eyes and with the wild thought of jumping on one of her father's ponies and racing out to catch up with him. But when she lifted her eyes once more and saw that he was truly gone, she put herself back in the hands of fate and walked gloomily into the village. It would do no good to mourn a missed opportunity, she told herself. Might as well go home and make up grandfather's bowl of pemmican.

CHAPTER XI

WIND IN HIS HAIR DID NOT MUCH CARE FOR DOMESTIC life. Left to his own, he would have little to do with anyone, even those connected to his blood. But his sense of dedication defeated him. He recognized that a part of his responsibility as a warrior was to make himself available to family beyond his wives and children, to occasionally make long journeys away from the home village. He avoided such forays to the scattered villages of the plains whenever possible, but his wives were shrewd. Several times a year they laid careful traps for their celebrated husband, traps which once sprung were rarely evaded.

Such was the case with his most recent trip, a trip to the south one of his wives had asked for as they slept together on a snowbound night many moons before. In the time that followed she had taken care to remind him of his promise only at moments when his spirits were especially good, and he finally declared that they would go soon after his return from Mexico.

Any attempt to wriggle out of the domestic mission was made especially hard by One Braid Trailing's status as his youngest, prettiest, and favorite wife. She was devoted to him and didn't lose her temper often.

And they never had to go all over the country because her only family resided with the Honey-Eater band in the south.

Her father was a Comanche, her mother a lifelong Mexican captive, and Wind In His Hair liked them both, especially the father, who was esteemed as a member of the Honey-Eaters' equivalent of the Hard Shields.

What he didn't like, aside from the unexciting social nature of the visit, was the country. The country had too many small hills and trees. Hills and trees made him nervous because he was used to gazing as far as he could see.

The worst thing about going to the Honey-Eaters, however, was their closeness to the whites. The slow-spreading infection of whites eating into the body of the Comanche empire was most pronounced in the southern extremities, and though the band he was visiting was the largest and strongest among the remaining Honey-Eaters, it was still tiny in comparison with the powerful communities farther north.

Attrition from constant conflict with the whites had tattered the community's once cohesive quilt. The village was top-heavy with the old and infirm. Mature warriors seemed to grow scarcer each year, and few were the young men ready to take their places. So many of them had been killed by what the whites called "rangers," deadly bands of heavily armed whites who roamed the borders of Comanche country looking for Indians to exterminate. They killed Comanches in any way they could and were more likely to poison a spring or knock a man off his horse with a far-shooting gun than they were to engage him in face-to-face combat.

They were good at hiding in the eastern country of hills and trees and that made them hard to kill, aside from the rare occasions when they were found in the open. If found there, they would invariably retreat, hats flying in the dust of speeding horses.

Ambush was their forte and a Comanche party wandering into one ran the risk of losing every man. The whites always had guns, several for each man, and they never seemed to run out of bullets. The end result was sad news coming back to camp, news that made for widows and orphans, and gave cause for new war parties going out, part of a never-ending cycle of remorse and retribution that fractured the pleasures of living as surely as a splintered mirror cuts an image to pieces.

This was the woeful scenario that greeted Wind In His Hair's arrival at the Honey-Eaters' village. The hollow air carried the wails of grieving women to his ears even before he entered the village proper. They were mourning a hunting party that had been forced by lack of game to travel farther east than they wanted and had been surprised as they watered horses on the banks of a stream. The hair-mouthed Comanche-hunters had driven them back against a cut bank where the warriors had to fight with nothing in the way of cover. Four of the party of eight were killed during the day, and all of them would have died had it not been for the intervention of thick clouds which covered the moon long enough for the survivors to escape.

The loss of four warriors was sad enough, but there was another aspect to the debacle that made it particularly bitter. The bodies of the dead had not been retrieved—and it was essential that they be brought back, lest their spirits be left to wander in lonely, earthbound confusion.

Especially revolting was the reported presence of Tonkawas, one of the Comanches' bitterest enemies. Long subjugated by the whites, the Tonkawas had fallen into the habit of taking the white man's money in exchange for guiding them against the Comanche. Not only did they kill Comanches and take their scalps, it was known to all that Tonkawas coveted the flesh of their enemies. Comanches taken alive were sometimes thrown whole onto large fires, their meat roasted black before being taken into the mouths of the Tonkawas.

A member of Wind In The Hair's extended family, a brother-in-law, was one of the dead, and now, instead of relaxing at the end of their journey, the great warrior from the north found himself attending a round of councils. There was no question but that a party had to go out and fetch the bodies back, and that speed was important, but putting together the party was, as always, a complicated undertaking. The size of the party, the warriors it would comprise, and the time it would consume were all weighty issues, and all were aggravated by the weakened condition of the Honey-Eater band.

People were eager to have Wind In His Hair at their councils. It reassured them to have such a great warrior in their midst, but the standing he enjoyed in his own village was not transferable. If it had been, Wind In His Hair would have organized a party and put it into the field as quickly as possible. Instead, he was forced to stand back as the depleted and demoralized Honey-Eaters debated how to commit their meager resources.

After three sleeps of constant wrangling, a rescue party consisting of only twelve warriors, two of them barely tested boys, finally departed. Wind In His Hair rode with them as a full-fledged member.

Heavy Runner, a middle-aged warrior with a lifetime of honors, headed the small group. He kept Wind In His Hair by his side, but even the presence of these two outstanding warriors did little to bolster the group's spirits. This was not a Comanche war party of old, a juggernaut of heavily armed warriors sweeping all from their path. It was a small band of men with only six rifles, driving deep into contested country, whose focus was not on victory but survival.

None of the men who had escaped the white rangers had been able to agree on the exact spot of the skirmish, and since all of them had been shot and were recovering, no one was along to pinpoint where the dead had fallen. They were traveling blind, and as the party pushed east the country became even more hilly and dense, and Wind In His Hair, unused to such terrain, began to feel more nervous. To maintain silence, all in the party were forbidden to use rifles unless there was an emergency. Animals were to be taken by bow, and Heavy Runner prudently insisted that the camps they made be dry and fireless.

There were no incidents and on the morning of their fourth day out, the small band of warriors reached the vicinity of the fight with the rangers.

Two men were dispatched to scout both sides of the stream while the balance of the party remained sequestered. At mid-morning the scouts returned to camp with the news that they had located the site. White men were there—two hair-mouths in long white coats with six blue-coated soldiers to guard them. They had two wagons and had pitched a few tents along the slow-running river. The blue-coated soldiers had not established a perimeter but were lounging around their tents while their horses grazed untended.

What the hair-mouths in the long white coats were doing the scouts could not ascertain. Two fires had been built on the banks of the stream. Over the flames sat two large kettles filled with boiling water. The white-coated men seemed to be in charge of the cooking because when the scouts saw them they were going back and forth between the kettles stirring the bubbling water with wooden paddles.

A hundred yards upstream from the strange camp the scouts had discovered a wagon and had crept close enough to confirm that this was where the Comanche warriors had lost their lives. The wagon was covered with a canvas tarp, but they could see two sets of moccasined feet resting on the downed tailgate.

The Honey-Eaters and their famous friend from the north immediately convened a council to sift through the information brought back by the scouts. For a time they discussed what purpose whites might have in camping at the ghoulish site, particularly the white-coated hair-mouths whom the soldiers were protecting. Could it be that they were feasting, that they were imitating the hated Tonkawas? Perhaps they were trying to draw power from the slain warriors? Was some dark, unknown magic being performed by the whites? Wind In His Hair knew that white medicine men sometimes wore white coats and theorized that they might, for some inexplicable reason, be trying to raise the dead.

But it was all conjecture, and since no one could understand it, this line of inquiry was soon dropped in favor of what could be done to retrieve the remains of their friends and relatives. The younger men wanted to attack, taking as many scalps as possible, but Heavy Runner and Wind In His Hair both spoke against this notion, reminding everyone of the purpose of their mission, and pointing out the foolhardiness of putting themselves in needless jeopardy. They were already surrounded by danger and little could be gained by exposing themselves to more.

The plan they decided on was designed to frighten the whites, driving them off long enough to let the party gather up what remained of their comrades and escape back to the west.

The two youngest members of the team, both of whom had strong, fast ponies, would cross the river far upstream, then backtrack under cover, stopping at a point opposite the main party. There they would wait for a signal to be given by one of the warriors who was particularly adept at mimicking the feeding sounds of quail. At that moment the boys would burst from their hiding place on the other side of the river, waving blankets at the whites' loose horses. They were to chase these horses downstream. At the same time the ten remaining warriors would loose their arrows at the white camp. They would do this with as much whooping as they could muster, hoping that the whites would envision a much larger force of attackers. Then they would emerge on the banks of the stream and pretend to pursue them. If the whites continued to flee, the warriors would gradually peel off and backtrack upriver to perform the real work of their mission. The few warriors who continued the chase could then fire their rifles if they felt it was necessary but until that time no one would fire unless it was absolutely necessary.

The plan worked to perfection. When the sun dipped close to the horizon the signal was given and the boys burst from the undergrowth on the other side of the river. Most of the American horses were still loose and stampeded downriver. A split second later the main body opened up with a tremendous cacophony of yelling. The two white-coated men scrambled onto a canvas-covered wagon. They were ungainly, and as they clambered into the wagon, one of them took an arrow high in his leg. Screaming, he tumbled into the back of the wagon while the other man desperately urged the horses forward. The soldiers were too surprised to do much more than fire a few wild shots in the direction of the attack as they flailed about for their horses. Some of them rode double as they pursued the wagon, which was plunging frantically downstream.

Three warriors kept after the small party of white men, and the two boys who had started the American horses disappeared downriver. That left seven warriors, including Wind In His Hair and Heavy Runner, to investigate the odd camp on the riverbank.

The fires were still going and the big black pots were still bubbling. The men peered into the huge kettles. They could see bits and pieces of things rolling about in the frothy water but could identify nothing. Rifling through the still-pitched tents, they found a stout wooden pole, which they used as a lever to tip over the pots.

The warriors danced back on tiptoe as the scalding water and its contents hit the sand at the edge of the river. Riflefire cracked in the distance but the Comanches did not lift their eyes. Their eyes were fixed on what lay before them. Two human skulls, cooked nearly to the bone, had rolled out of the mammoth vats and lay steaming on the dark, flat sand. For a few moments they were too stunned to move, but when the initial shock at the grisly discovery had been absorbed, several men fell to their knees and sang death songs. Others turned away to vent their fury on the white man's camp. The boys who had spooked the horses were coming upstream with three captured animals but no one gave them more than a glance.

Heavy Runner and Wind In His Hair jumped onto their horses and ploughed upstream to the unhitched wagon. Throwing back the tarp, they confirmed what they already suspected. The putrefying, headless bodies of two Comanche warriors lay side by side in the wagon's bed.

Within twenty minutes the Comanches had wrapped and tied the bodies and their parts in blankets, slung the macabre parcels over the backs of the American horses, and were riding grimly upriver.

Rounding the first bend in the stream, they spotted the remnants of a large fire on the other side and swung across to investigate. Sprawled across the remnants of the blaze was the charred half-eaten body of a third Comanche warrior. Tonkawa sign was everywhere.

They packed up the corpse in the same way they had the first two, and, wary of possible pursuit, rode long into the night, not stopping until an hour or two before first light.

The party had succeeded. Three of the four dead had been recovered, horses had been captured, a full crate of bullets had been found in one of the soldier tents, and no one had been lost. But there was little talk on the long, sad march home. No stories were swapped about the encounter with the enemy. No laughing or joking or bragging. None of them expressed what was in his heart, because every heart was empty. There was never sweetness in bringing home the dead. And there was little honor in running off a few white men who, unbeknownst to Wind In His Hair and his compatriots, had ventured into the field to retrieve a few aboriginal skulls for scientific study. The heads of the dead that had spilled from the kettles only served to further drain the warriors' spirits. It was debauchery on an inconceivable plane, so vile as to defy explanation.

On the long, silent ride back to the Honey-Eater camp, Wind In His Hair tried to comfort himself with brave thoughts. A Comanche warrior was afraid of nothing. Comanches honored their dead. Comanche people would endure because nothing could kill a spirit fed by the hand of the Mystery . . . the Comanche spirit.

He told himself these things many times but in the end there was little solace in such thoughts. The arrival of the bodies in the Honey-Eater village set off a new wave of mourning and a sad overcast settled on the place.

Though they had never been close, Wind In His Hair felt a special sorrow for the family of his brother-in-law, for his was the body that had not been recovered. But what provoked his greatest agony was the nagging, disheartening conclusion that the Honey-Eaters had grown weak, and to feel that he was part of such weakness made his stomach turn.

Having to be a part of an aftermath that saw so many people rendered helpless through the twin blows of grief and horror made him wish only for home, and the day after the rescue party's return, Wind In His Hair gathered up his family and led them north.

He brooded all the way, and when they reached the village—a few hours after Smiles A Lot rode out of camp—the dark cloud that had settled over Wind In His Hair's spirit was evident to all who saw him. When he was told about the Cheyenne visit and the troubles they were having with the whites he sent a crier to every Hard Shield lodge with the news that an urgent council was being convened.

Wind In His Hair had decided that war must be made on the whites before it was too late. He would make a strong talk for the idea of raising a large party that would travel to the country of the Cheyenne and help them drive the whites out. No one could make an impassioned proposal for war like Wind In His Hair, and it is likely that the Hard Shields would have jumped to their feet at his behest.

But nobody ever did ride up to the country of the Cheyenne, because on that same night Dances With Wolves came in with news that changed everything.

CHAPTER XII

THE VILLAGE CAME INTO VIEW AT TWILIGHT, ABOUT THE SAME time Wind In His Hair's council was getting under way. In addition to his children, seven hunters were with Dances With Wolves. It was the same with his party as it had been with Wind In His Hair's. Joy and laughter had not traveled with them. Even the reliable buoyancy at seeing home again was absent.

They had been on the trail for two weeks but the search for game had yielded practically nothing. They had ranged far to the north, penetrating the Kiowa hunting grounds, but they had found no large herds, only pockets of animals who were so skittish that even the best buffalo-running ponies were hard-pressed to draw alongside. Eight seasoned hunters had managed to fell only two buffalo, most of which had been used to keep Dances With Wolves and his party fed while they looked futilely for more. They were coming back with two robes. Their pack animals carried three deer, shot on the way home because no one could bear to come in with nothing to show for their efforts.

Taking one of the deer, Dances With Wolves, Snake In Hands, and Always Walking broke away as their friends entered the village, taking the long way around to the set-apart lodge sitting on the far side of camp. It would have been easier to cut straight through the village and the few minutes they might have saved would have been welcome, for all three were disheartened and exhausted. But Dances With Wolves rode wide of his home village because he didn't want to see or exchange words with anyone. He wanted Stands With A Fist to be the first person he spoke to. He wanted her ears to be the first to hear because he felt too much for her to be anywhere but face-to-face when she learned the devastating news he carried.

Stands With A Fist and Stays Quiet were waiting outside the lodge when they rode up. It had been her practice to wait through the twilight the past few days in hope that she might see them coming before it got dark. She always got nervous when they were gone more than a week.

She and her daughter began to dance and shout and squeal when they saw them. The incoming riders answered with cries of their own as they urged their tired horses into a last lope.

Seconds later Snake In Hands and Always Walking were in her arms. Both children were played out with fatigue and when Snake In Hands blurted, "There wasn't any game, Mother," she looked past him and saw at once that Dances With Wolves was wearing an uncharacteristic expression. It was more a wince than a smile, manufactured with effort.

"No buffalo," he said with a quick shake of his head. He could not bear to look at her and turned back to pull a single deer from the packhorse. At any other time he might have left the meat where it lay for a few minutes but he was afraid to show her any more of his face and was relieved when he heard her moving the children into their lodge.

As he gazed out at the last light of day he wished for the first time since he could remember that he could be somewhere, anywhere else. It sickened him to feel like this and he wondered, as he had wondered so many times since he happened on the camp of his Kiowa friend Touch The Clouds, if there was some way he could keep what he knew to himself. He laid his forehead against the withers of the pack pony and sighed a long, sad sigh. His time had run out. He would have to tell her.

Like most women, Stands With A Fist had an uncanny nose for change in her husband. She knew right away that something was wrong. He was avoiding her face, and as the children recounted the adventures of what they called their "empty hunt," Dances With Wolves said little. Once in a while she would catch him in a glance and see the same sad smile. It seemed now as if it were painted on and it kept her on edge.

When the children were finally asleep she went outside to shake some bedding. She had already shaken it out that afternoon but she wanted a few moments alone. Something was coming but what it might be she could not guess. Perhaps he wanted another wife. Perhaps there was a sickness inside him. She could imagine nothing worse and, steeling herself for whatever might come, she ducked back into the lodge.

He was sitting in front of the fire but only looked at her from the corner of his eye.

Unable to wait any longer, she stood and faced him with folded arms.

"What has happened?" she demanded quietly.

"Sit down," he said, indicating a spot across the fire.

She sat and waited. Dances With Wolves' eyes shifted restlessly.

"What?" she asked again.

"Touch The Clouds was out there. I saw him."

"Is he well?"

"His mind is stirred up. It is the same with all the Kiowas."

"Why?"

Once more Dances With Wolves dropped his eyes to the fire. Then he looked up, trying to speak calmly.

"There are white soldiers coming into the country of the Kiowa— many white soldiers."

Stands With A Fist's eyes widened but she didn't move. It was if she had stopped breathing.

"They are making a soldier fort near the great Medicine Bluff."

Stands With A Fist only blinked. She still could not move nor could she speak. She sat enveloped in a cocoon of blinding shock. The world seemed to have collapsed onto her meager shoulders and she was so powerless under its weight that the generation of something as small as a tear was impossible.

"The whites want the Kiowa to come in and live in small places. They are promising to feed people and take care of them if they will come into these places called reservations and stop making war. The whites are saying that if this is not done they will war against the Kiowa."

He looked to her for a response but saw the same dead stare in a pair of eyes fixed so completely on the moment that they were mindful of a look he had seen many times: the upturned face of a corpse gazing into eternity.

Dances With Wolves was reeling too, but his role as messenger drove him on. The words flowed out of him, and though he flattened them as best he could, they could not be changed.

"Other whites, called 'agents,' are there. They want to talk. They say they want to be friends, protectors to all the tribes. They are saying all will be well if people come in. Touch The Clouds smoked the pipe with me. His words are true."

Struggling, Stands With A Fist made a few words. Her mouth was trembling.

"What will Touch The Clouds do?"

"He doesn't know."

At last she moved, lowering her face for a moment, her lips quivering. She mechanically lifted her face to his and spoke again.

"What will we do?"

Dances With Wolves shook his head slowly.

"I don't know."

He started to get up and she jerked to life.

"Don't leave. Don't go now."

Dances With Wolves stepped over the fire, placed his hands under her arms, and lifted her.

"We will always be one," he whispered, guiding her gently toward the bed, where the children slept. He raised the robe and tucked her inside. Instinctively, she groped with closed eyes, pulling the bodies of her young close as Dances With Wolves knelt next to the bed.

"Sleep with our children," he said softly. "I will be with you, but I have to tell the Hard Shields this news."

"They are all at Wind In His Hair's," she mumbled, eyes still shut.

She turned her face and buried it in the familiar odors of her bed and children. She did not hear her husband's soft footfalls. Nor did she hear the flap slap against her home as he stepped into the night. She was already far away, cut off from fear and trouble, deep in the tiny world of her bed and the little beings she had brought to life. In seconds she had succumbed to the self-administered drug of the only place she felt safe, and as she slipped into unconsciousness, Stands With A Fist imagined a sleep that would carry her and the little world she now occupied far beyond the stars on the long drift into eternity.

Dances With Wolves had intended to alert Kicking Bird first, but on the way to his lodge he encountered several warriors who, seeing his agitation, inquired what errand he might be on. When he told them of the need for a council they naturally persisted in asking why and he had no choice but to report that there were white soldiers in the country of the Kiowas.

At that moment a fast-running, inextinguishable firestorm of alarm burned through every lodge in camp. By the time Dances With Wolves had roused Ten Bears, his simple pronouncement that white soldiers were in the country of the Kiowas had mushroomed into the popular belief that blue-coated soldiers were about to ring the village.

Warriors from every corner of camp were streaming into Kicking Bird's special lodge. Women and children were milling about in anxious confusion. The Hard Shields had suspended their own meeting to investigate the confusion, and when Dances With Wolves and Ten Bears pushed into the mass of men already assembled at Kicking Bird's they were greeted with the kind of chaos that would lead a casual observer to conclude that the sky was about to fall.

It was fortunate that Ten Bears still lived, for the respect his presence demanded calmed the inflamed crowd of warriors long enough to bring them under control. As room was made for Ten Bears' place of prominence at the fire, warriors who could find a patch of ground to sit on followed suit, their excitement diminishing in the process. Ten Bears drew out his pipe and smoked, wisely waiting for silence before allowing the council to begin.

At last he passed the pipe around the first circle and by the time it came back to the old man all was quiet. Ten Bears looked across the fire at Dances With Wolves.

"Tell us what you have heard."

He told of his meeting with Touch The Clouds and the mention of such a warrior sharpened the attention of all present. But by the time Dances With Wolves had finished his report, the excitement mounting in the lodge threatened to explode. Young warriors shouted out that they would take the trail against the whites that night. Their passion was infectious and every soul who heard them was stirred by their zeal.

But as Wind In His Hair rose to speak everyone quieted. Regardless of their courage, young warriors had no real standing. This warrior did, and everyone wanted to hear what he had to say.

Wind In His Hair had learned that when one had true power it was not necessary to use it loudly. Though there were still inflections of his hallmark impulsiveness, Wind In His Hair spoke only a little above a whisper, the sweeping grace of his gestures a marked contrast to the gruesome disfigurement of his face. The single eye still burned, however, reminding all who saw him that Wind In His Hair was indomitable.

"We always knew the whites would come this way. The Cheyenne, now the Kiowa . . . the Comanche next. Comanche always throw back the enemy. That is all I have to say."

This declaration was supported by ringing cheers, but they soon died down. Other strong men had to be heard. Kicking Bird, as was his custom, stayed seated, directing what he had to say toward the leading men in the first circle.

"What Wind In His Hair says is true," he began. "Comanches throw back their enemies and make them cry. But these are not the Utes or the Pawnee. This enemy is different. When the Utes and the Pawnee get whipped they go home and do not come back for a long time. For every white soldier we have killed, two more come in his place. Every Comanche knows that it is foolish to fight if you cannot win."

Kicking Bird stopped speaking, and a somber air settled over the meeting.

"Kicking Bird's talk is good," Horned Antelope said. "But look at what the whites are doing to the buffalo. Do they see Comanches differently? I say no."

A Hard Shield named Red Jacket jumped to his feet.

"The whites say one thing then they do another," he shouted.

The crowd parted as Milky Way pushed his way to the fire. The sad-faced warrior, though nearing fifty, was still regarded as a vital man.

"All this talk is right," he said, chopping the air with a fist. "Every Comanche might die if we make a big war on these people. Milky Way is not afraid to die. I worry for my children. I do not want them to wander hungry. I do not want them to die of want. Milky Way does not mind killing white soldiers, but I wonder how many."

For more than an hour men stepped forward to speak what was in their hearts, and each eloquent confession, no matter the course of action it favored, was brimming with anguish.

When it seemed that every man in the lodge had spoken, Dances With Wolves rose.

"I have not much to say for Dances With Wolves. His brothers have spoken for him tonight. Dances With Wolves is not afraid of Comanche enemies. He loves the Comanche and wants them safe."

He turned his face toward Ten Bears, then hesitated. The old man's head was drooping. His eyes were closed. It looked like he was asleep. Dances With Wolves feared that if he asked a question Ten Bears might not answer, and for a moment longer he hesitated. But all eyes were on him.

"What is in the mind of Ten Bears?"

Ten Bears did not move and the lodge held its breath in the stillness. Slowly, he lifted his head. He placed one weathered hand on the earthen floor and started to push. The arms of those around him came to his aid, steadying his ascent and settling him on his feet before they fell away.

Ten Bears coughed into his hand.

"I have thought a long time. It would be good to wake tomorrow and find that all the whites have gone back into the earth . . . or that the sun has burned them up."

Laughter rolled through the lodge and an ease that had been absent from the start spread over the meeting.

"I do not think they will go away. I do not think Comanches will stop behaving like Comanches, either. Every man here has told what is in his heart. We are not of one mind, and that is neither bad nor good. In the way it has always been, each man will decide what is best for him."

He stretched a thin arm and wagged his fingers. "What is best for you, Wind In His Hair?"

"Wind In His Hair will lead a party of strong-hearted warriors to the country of the Kiowas. We will see what can be done to help them. If they want me to fight, I will."

Ten Bears nodded toward Kicking Bird.

"I, too, will visit the Kiowas. If the whites want to fight I will fight. If they want to parley, my ears will be eager to hear their words."

The support for Wind In His Hair was loud and clear, yet there were many murmurs of assent for Kicking Bird's position, too.

Ten Bears focused his glassy eyes on Dances With Wolves.

"I go to hunt," he said firmly. "There is little food here. A warrior must make meat."

Ten Bears bobbed his head as if he approved. Then he glanced slowly about until his eyes found Owl Prophet. The medicine man had been silent all night but now he got up. Whatever might be read in a man's face was hidden behind his lidded eyes.

"Only the Mystery knows our fate. The Mystery is not ready to speak. I will stay in camp and listen. If the Mystery says anything, I will tell it."

Owl Prophet's words, though not conclusive, were an apt end to a council that had produced no answers, only declarations. The men who had been present filed out into the night with little trace of the bounding exuberance or staunch comradeship that signals unity.

Few warriors returned to their homes and families that night with their minds made up. Each was leaning toward one path or another, but it would have been a mistake to interpret their uncertainty as weakness.

The knowledge that their common fate had finally commenced gave them strength. They were no longer frozen in the clutches of what might come to pass. The time had come for each man to decide. By coming in force to the country of their neighbors the whites had issued a clear challenge, and to meet a clear challenge was what every Comanche warrior had been trained to do. What the final outcome might be was, for the moment, not so important as standing up and every warrior in camp was primed for action.

At that moment the Comanches remained confident of their power.

CHAPTER XIII

*T*HOUGH HE HAD NEVER SEEN THE MEDICINE BLUFF HE HAD been in the vicinity on several occasions and knew it resided somewhere in a string of queer, misshapen hills that rose out of the grassland on the eastern edge of the Kiowa territory. It was said to be the largest of the hills, no more than a mile in length, each end gently sloping upward to resolve in a distinctive hump that marked its center.

He did not doubt that he would find it. As he left camp with his ponies trailing behind, a mantle of confidence unlike any he had experienced before settled over him. Perhaps it was the freedom he felt in taking action. His ears and nose and eyes all seemed keener, and in the many miles he logged, every ripple in the landscape stood out and every faint odor on the breeze seemed to speak to his nose. Even the footfalls of each pony, sounds he had always taken for granted, seemed separate and distinct.

When Smiles A Lot reached the region of the strange hills, on the afternoon of his fourth day out, he crossed and recrossed a shallow, winding creek as if guided by forces beyond his understanding, until suddenly he found himself facing a long, wide incline dotted with a few scrub oaks. The land pushed up before him and at its apex a smoothly formed hump stood out against the sky.

The winding creek flowed languidly at the base of the odd hill and he hobbled his ponies in its cover. He drank long and deep from the cool waters of the stream before setting off with a clump of sage, two pieces of flint, and the clothes on his back.

The day was fair and the climb so easy that his breathing was hardly labored by the time he reached the top. No trees of any kind grew at the summit and the ground was as smooth as it had appeared at a distance. Then the earth suddenly gave way as if it had been sheared and when Smiles A Lot peered down the drop-off was straight and steep as any true cliff, falling a hundred and fifty feet to the meandering creek that encircled the bluff. Looking from side to side, he could see that the clawlike marks Owl Prophet had described etched the whole of the formation's rock face.

Heights had never appealed much to Smiles A Lot. In the few times he had sat in the high limbs of a cottonwood, he felt a certain turning in his stomach and an instantaneous weakening of his arms and legs. He felt the same things now. Standing at the edge of the precipice, he felt his stomach climbing into his throat and his knees quivering. But the sensations were fleeting in comparison to the whole of his spirit, which seemed to have been grasped and flung into the ecstatic space ahead.

The horizon stretched before him in limitless glory, so dazzling that for a time he was uncertain if he was still standing on the earth. The breeze rushed against his body in busy, little eddys, leaving in its wake a silence so profound that for a moment he imagined himself arrived at the top of the world. Without meditation he spontaneously raised his arms skyward in supplication.

At the same time he closed his eyes and immediately his head began to spin. Fearful that he might reel and fall, he tottered back, settling effortlessly on the ground. There he lay for several minutes, staring straight up. With the earth pressing against him and the sky looming over him, Smiles A Lot, for the first time in his short life, imagined that all he needed to know about existence was to know the place he now occupied, between the earth and sky.

When his rapture subsided, Smiles A Lot roused himself and set to work. He cleared a small patch of ground near the edge of the bluff and plucked a few handfuls of dry grass. Then he struck his flints until one of the sparks ignited the fuel. When tiny flames appeared he lit the tightly bound sage and passed the bundle over himself from head to toe and, satisfied that he was chaste in the eyes of the Mystery, sat cross-legged on the ground. Owl Prophet had given him the barest of instructions. To sit and wait was all he had been told. But Smiles A Lot did not feel the slightest sense of bewilderment or apprehension or trepidation. He knew he was in the right place.

Halfway through his first full day at the top of the world his thirst became unbearable and he waited out the hours, fighting back the desire for water. The compulsion for relief became so great that he thought he might die. Then, by some miracle of will, it began to recede, until at last his thirst became a part of him, as common as breathing or feeling. The same thing happened with his hunger. At the end of his second day it, too, became so much a part of him that he no longer knew it was there.

His body, which rebelled at the stillness imposed upon it, caused him constant, excruciating pain. What began as mild discomfort grew like a fever, until his body was consumed with an array of cramps and cricks and throbs and kinks and aches and chafes. Fiery needles tortured his shoulders and spine and knees and hips. Even his head seemed to catch fire, and for a time he was certain that the pain would carry him away.

Then all at once it, too, disappeared, and, as his third night on the bluff began, the stars seemed close enough to be plucked and the moon that rose could have been picked out of the night sky as easily as taking an apple off a branch. He imagined rolling it back and forth on the ground from one hand to another. All was bliss and so great was his contentment that instead of fighting against sleep he could do no more than sweetly wish it away, thinking dreamily that he might somehow remain as he was for all time.

Whether or not he slept that night Smiles A Lot did not know. It seemed as if he had, for there were stretches of time he could not account for. But when he heard the call of a bird and saw that the sun was up, he realized that the peace he had reached the day before was still with him. He had no thirst and no hunger. There was no complaint from a body that, aside from subtle, nearly imperceptible shifts, had stayed in the same position for hours, maybe days.

But something was different. He opened his eyes a little and discovered that the skin of the earth had come alive. It was moving.

He turned then, swiveling his head and twisting his spine, first one way, then another. The skin of the entire hill was moving and in an instant he became cognizant of what was causing the phenomenon. Crows, multitudes of them, were milling back and forth over the ground. Every oak on the slope behind him was heavy with the big black birds. Their voices came to him, a raucous din of screeches and mutterings.

He knew he must be dreaming. They inhabited every inch of ground. Through the masses of strutting birds he could glimpse little sparks of earth in the same way one might see an occasional flash of light reflecting off a field of stones.

As he watched the fantastic assembly of birds, Smiles A Lot began to wonder at their purpose. Had they come to feast on him? Were they trying to contact him, trying to show him something? Was he now in the Crow nation? Would he have to remain?

As he teetered on the verge of panic a sudden fluttering made him swivel his head once more. A commotion was going on in the oak closest to him. A crow took wing, flapping heavily into the air. The first was followed by a second and a third. The whole tree came to life as the crows pushed into space.

The birds on the ground began to hop into the air and the sky turned black as they climbed toward heaven, thousands upon thousands of them calling to one another.

Smiles A Lot watched, stupefied. How much time had passed since the flight began he did not know. Nor did he know what compelled him to tilt his head back and raise his eyes. When he did he saw that they had formed a gigantic funnel directly over him. The great mass of birds was circling lazily, their huge, hollow column reaching for infinity.

It came to him then that crows were thought to have a direct connection with the dead, and Smiles A Lot wondered if he himself might have passed over. He raised his arms to see if he was still alive, and to his astonishment felt himself lifting off the ground. He ascended, still sitting cross-legged, and when he reached the cloud of crows he, too, began to circle in the same lethargic way, revolving slowly upward. As he went higher the speed of his revolutions grew. He turned faster and faster until at last he was spinning crazily through space.

All at once he felt a jolt. He was sitting on the ground again but was so disoriented that he could not help but fall back. On his way to earth his spine struck something solid, something alive. He felt it burrow under the small of his back and suddenly he was rising again. As he was lifted into the air he felt himself sliding down something he knew well. He could smell a familiar smell too and in the time it takes to blink he had completed his slide to find himself straddling the back of a horse whose flesh was hard as metal.

He let a hand drop to the animal's withers. Its coat shimmered black as onyx, and when Smiles A Lot glanced up he saw that the horse had craned its neck for a look at who might be sitting astride its back. A dark eye, its pupil black as its coat, stared back at him with inscrutable intent.

The next thing Smiles A Lot knew, a stallion's scream rent the air and the animal below him was diving and leaping, corkscrewing frantically to unseat him. It plunged and reared as if it were some monster of the deep, alternately sounding and surfacing the length of the bluff and back again. All the while, its rider sat as easily as a man might sit against the willow backrest in his lodge, enjoying a tranquil smoke.

At the zenith of the bluff the magnificent horse abruptly halted his gyrations and gazed once more at its rider. With a long-winded sigh it raised and lowered its handsome head as if in agreement with some unposed question. It spread its front legs, dropped its head between them, and exploded backward.

At the same instant Smiles A Lot's perspective shifted. He was watching himself at a distance, watching himself ride this great engine of a horse as it powered backward down the long approach to the top of the bluff.

In a flash he was atop the horse again, looking up the slope. Debris from their descent, chunks of earth floating in silt, were raining down on the ground, and as it slowly settled, he could feel the animal beneath him gather itself. It bounced up and down on its front legs and shook its neck and head as a stallion does before it charges. It took deep breaths, each one more rapid than the last.

Whether the force came from behind or below or in front Smiles A Lot could not tell but in a single stroke they were blasted up the hill, though the horse under him did not appear to move. An unseen power had flung them forward and the energy it generated seemed to grow as the cliff ahead rushed up to meet them. They were already in the air when they soared over the abyss, climbing as smoothly into the sky as an eagle sails on an updraft.

But the sky was not the sky. It was filled with enemies. Pawnee horsemen charged them, each with a war club poised to strike a fatal blow. Smiles A Lot and his mount swept through them with the precision of a blade. He could see them rolling off through space like particles in the wind. Utes were rushing toward them on foot, knives raised in one hand, bloody scalps in the other. They, too, went down. A regiment of Mexican lancers was vanquished as effortlessly as a hand passes through smoke.

A cluster of wagons came next. Kneeling behind the wagons were blue-coated soldiers, the smoke of their rifles hanging like tiny clouds in a windless sky. As horse and rider reached the wagons they rocketed straight up, leaving the white soldiers far below. It was amazing to see the bullets they fired race up from the ground, then waste themselves, then begin a long descent, the spent slugs finally bouncing off the heads of soldiers darting for cover.

When Smiles A Lot looked down he saw the horrifying sight of a white people's thunder gun and its dark mouth. He and his mount sped into its black maw. As they raced down the enormous barrel, Smiles A Lot could see the silvery contours of its rifling.

Far in the distance there was an explosion and an enormous round ball hurtled toward them. It was pushed by a flowering orange flame which crashed like water against the sides of the barrel. At the moment of impact Smiles A Lot closed his eyes and to his great surprise felt nothing. He did not reopen his eyes but somehow he could see. They were flying down the barrel in a shower of metal fragments from the exploded black ball. Some of it had been reduced to orange and black dust. He could taste it. It tasted like earth.

The earth was in his mouth. He could feel gritty particles of it grating against his teeth. Smiles A Lot tried to open his eyes but only one lid raised. The other eye was pressed against the familiar skin of the bluff. The drop-off was only a few feet in front of him.

He could hear voices, happy, human voices shouting words he did not understand. He could hear the faint sound of splashing, too. Dazedly, he pulled himself over the ground and gazed down the cliff face. Wagons were parked at the side of the stream below. Blue-coated soldiers were standing next to the wagons. There were men, their bare skin glinting snow-white in the sun, cavorting in the water.

Smiles A Lot hung over the cliff, trying to decide if he was dreaming, when a fly landed under his eye. When he brought a hand up to brush it away, every joint in his arm throbbed. Then he realized that his entire body was aching, that his tongue was swollen and dry as cloth, that he was faint with hunger.

He wriggled a few feet back from the cliff face and tried to stand but was barely up before his legs collapsed. Again and again he tried before he finally gained his feet. He wobbled a few steps and collapsed again, pitching forward on his face. Too weak to walk, he straightened his legs, tucked his arms against his sides, and rolled slowly down the slope, finally bouncing to a stop against the willows that flanked the creek at the base of the bluff. He crawled into the cool water and immersed himself there for almost an hour, rolling onto his face, then onto his back, repeating the action over and over. He wet his swollen lips and dabbed drops of water on his parched tongue. Before he got up he allowed himself a few sips from the stream.

Barely able to stand, he staggered through the undergrowth and finally found his hobbled horses, standing together on the open grassland. Fumbling weakly at the flap of his traveling pouch, he at last succeeded in retrieving a stick of jerked meat, which he ate in tiny bites, sucking all the juice out before he swallowed.

Repeatedly he tried to pull himself onto one of the ponies but when he finally gained its back he fell off the other side and had to rest another hour before trying again.

When he was finally able to climb up and sit, the sun was dipping toward the horizon and he rode south, clinging feebly to his horse's mane. Several hours after sunset he came across a spring at the mouth of a ravine. He tumbled down, turned on his back, and slept as if he would never wake.

When he opened his eyes again it was at the behest of one of the horses, which had been nudging him in the ribs with its soft muzzle.

Smiles A Lot drank as much as he could hold, chewed up half a dozen strips of jerked meat, and continued south. He was feeling much better now and was anxious to get home. He wanted to tell Owl Prophet about what he had experienced on Medicine Bluff. Surely the prophet would have something to say when he told him about the crows and the horse and the enemies falling before him and the white men in the stream.

It was possible of course that the prophet would recoil, thinking that Smiles A Lot had lost his mind. *It could be,* he thought to himself as the country flattened out ahead of him. *My mind is in pieces. Maybe in the ride ahead they will come back together.*

It was true that the young man who wanted to die a warrior had undergone a fragmentation of the mind. Yet as he rode home with the breeze in his face one thought stood out in the jumble that was floating freely in his head. Whenever danger found him, he had better make sure he was on the back of an all-black horse. If he couldn't find one, he would do well to steal one from an enemy. No prophet needed to tell him that from here on out, a black horse was essential to a long and happy life.

CHAPTER XIV

KICKING BIRD WAS THE FIRST TO BREAK CAMP. HIS WIVES packed up the household and struck their lodges as Kicking Bird counciled with a number of middle-aged warriors, all men of solid standing. Gap In The Woods and Big Bow, Gray Leggings and Island, Bird Chief and Powder Face all came to the special meeting lodge because, like Kicking Bird, none was sure that war was the answer. Each of them had fought the white man, as had their fathers and grandfathers. None was afraid of war, but in the back of each man's mind lurked the same seed of doubt that had taken root in Kicking Bird's. Perhaps the persistent white tide could not be turned, and if that was so, it might serve the survival of all to at least make contact. Neither Kicking Bird nor anyone else could say to themselves what contact might yield. But how could the depth of a stream or the strength of its current or the shape of stones beneath the surface be known without walking across? It was this understanding that brought Kicking Bird and other middle-aged warriors together.

Each man that came that morning backed the statesman's position. They, too, packed up possessions and families and, not long after the sun had burned off the morning haze, Kicking Bird led his column of men, women, children, dogs, and ponies out of the village for what was expected to be a protracted stay in the country of the Kiowa.

In the Hard Shield lodge across the village Wind In His Hair was also having a busy morning. His loyal core of Hard Shields had been augmented by the arrival of many others, promising young men like Iron Jacket and Left Hand and Hears The Sunrise, all of them vowing to lend the limit of their skill and bravery to his enterprise. It warmed Wind In His Hair's heart to see so many clamoring for action. The power that beat beneath the breast of every Comanche warrior was coming, as it always had, to the fore. Each warrior retreated to his home that afternoon to settle family affairs, inventory horses and weapons, and perform the rituals essential to safety and victory.

The following morning, a line of Comanche men forty strong filed east with Wind In His Hair at its head. It was the largest party in years and its sullen nature, bereft of the customary excitement that marked such departures, reflected the seriousness with which they regarded the enemy. It was hoped that an encounter with white soldiers would take place, giving them an opportunity to "chop at the enemy's head," as Wind In His Hair put it.

Accompanied by renowned buffalo-killers Lone Young Man, Red Moon, and Feathered Lance, Dances With Wolves also left camp that morning, eager to strike a herd of substance in the west.

He should have been feeling just right. The sun was at his back, his two eldest children were at his side again, and his skillful counterparts and their families were in high spirits.

But he and Stands With A Fist had argued the previous day, creating a tension between them that carried to the moment he had swung onto his pony and ridden off, the sour feeling of estrangement sticking in his craw.

The argument had begun over the children. Snake In His Hands and Always Walking wanted to go out again with their father. He and his wife had both been reluctant to grant permission, but the brother and sister were adamant, finally challenging their parents to cite a good reason for them to stay home.

Dances With Wolves had responded to the challenge with silence. In his heart there was no good reason, but he hadn't wanted to undercut his wife and remained quiet.

Stands With A Fist had understood his silence as a betrayal. If he had wanted to support her he would have spoken up. At the least he could have asserted his authority as a father and told them both that the decision to keep them in camp was final. Instead, he had shifted the weight of deciding to her, a weight that, when added to all the recent talk of white soldiers and war and reservations, she was incapable of shouldering.

She barked rather icily at the children, "Go with your father if that's what you want to do!" and busied herself stoking the fire. Snake In Hands and Always Walking ran happily out of the lodge, leaving Dances With Wolves to confront his unhappy wife.

"Come with us," he said.

She flicked a cold glance in his direction but said nothing.

"Come with us," he repeated. "I'm tired of being away from my wife." He thought this last remark might make amends, but it didn't.

"I can't do that," she said, as if a gauntlet had struck her face. "Every man in camp is gone. There's more work when men are gone. Children need to be watched, people need to be helped. Women have to double their work. It's not easy."

"No . . . women's work is not easy. Come with us," he asked again.

"I can't. I won't. Stays Quiet and I will stay at home. Go out as long as you want."

They took little bites at each other all that evening, and the division between them was still there the following morning. The tug-of-war left no space for affection or understanding and each performed the preparations for his leaving in the edgy atmosphere that drives men and women away from one another. They avoided touching and shared only a few curt words when speech could not be avoided.

When the horses were loaded with provisions and the children were on the backs of their ponies, Stands With A Fist hugged each of them and wished her husband good hunting with the briefest of looks. Then she took Stays Quiet by the hand and disappeared into the lodge.

Dances With Wolves rode onto the plain with a heart so unsettled that even the comical sight of Owl Prophet did little to relieve it. The prophet's family was marching into the prairie on foot, the women and children carrying containers which they probably hoped to fill with sweet plums or berries. The great man himself was trailing along behind, a utility bag on his shoulder and a look of mortification on his face. At any other time the image of Owl Prophet's wives prevailing on him to join the ignominious trek might have made Dances With Wolves laugh out loud, but today it did no more than remind him of his own unhappy circumstances, and he rode on without giving the plight of the prophet a second thought.

Alone in her lodge, Stands With A Fist brooded, wondering if she might have been too hard on her husband. No conclusion could be reached. Her every thought was riddled with emotion and it took all her mental strength to keep from giving in to the temptation of tears. Tears seemed to be the best way to wash everything clean. But she couldn't let herself go.

When she noticed the pony her husband had left tied outside, she briefly thought how easy it would be to jump on with Stays Quiet and catch up with the rest of her family. But she couldn't do that, either.

Everything was pulling her in different directions, and for the moment something so small as putting one foot in front of the other seemed to take more energy than she could command. Stands With A Fist could look forward to the afternoon of that particular day only because she knew that night and the careless release of sleep would follow.

Ten Bears knew nothing of the squabbling between the unhappy couple who lived in the set-apart lodge, yet he felt something of the same torpor that Stands With A Fist was experiencing. He had seen Dances With Wolves ride out with the hunters late that morning, and when they were clear of camp a strange, inexplicable silence had fallen over the village. It was as if the whole community had been emptied. Only a handful of men remained behind, and most of them were, like himself, old and infirm. There were many women and children, of course, but their presence seemed suddenly invisible.

No one was carrying water or gathering wood. No one seemed to be working outside. Day had turned to night. Everyone had melted into their homes.

Ten Bears went back into his lodge and lit his pipe and thought about what could be wrong. It wasn't that all the men were gone, he decided. It was the way they went, drawn out in different directions, for different reasons. The splintering of his people was becoming visible, and the more he thought about it the more Ten Bears felt his dread confirmed. The threat of the whites, still so far away, was dividing the people already. And there was nothing he could do about it.

These thoughts were so disturbing to Ten Bears that he had to get up and out. He loved his routine, especially the daily arrival of Hunting For Something, but he decided to deviate. He needed distance and fresh air and sunlight and solitude. Without these things he could imagine himself starting a slow turn to dust.

Shaking with desperation, the old man struggled to his feet, grabbed hold of his stick, and started out of camp, his eyes stuck on the horizon, determined to walk out as far as his withered legs would carry him.

When Hunting For Something came around in early afternoon with her bowl of pemmican and found her grandfather not a home, she, too, decided to make a change. All morning she had felt uneasy. The village didn't seem like home to her. No one wanted to talk. No one wanted to do anything, not even work. Everyone was going through the motions of living. It made her feel sticky, like she needed to bathe.

She had counted on seeing her grandfather. Standing alone in the deadness of his uninhabited lodge, the girl was seized with a rash impulse. She couldn't say why but she had to do something she had never done before. She had to look for him. She had to find him.

She located him at mid-afternoon. He was reclining against the exposed roots of an ancient sycamore, his legs spread out on the flat, sandy bank of a slow-running stream.

His eyes fluttered when he heard her whisper, "Grandfather!" and before he could make a move she was curled against his side, pressing urgently against his bony chest.

"What is it?"

"I had to find you, Grandfather. I thought I might die if I didn't."

"Why, girl, what's wrong?"

"I got frightened. I don't know why. I wanted to be with you."

Ten Bears pulled her close and stroked her soothingly.

"You're not going to die."

"Not if I'm with you. Can I stay with you?"

Ten Bears smiled at the thought of her needing him. It made him feel good all over.

"You stay with Ten Bears," he said. "Stay as long as you want. No one will bother us."

The old man and the girl, so widely separated by age and experience, achieved the peace that had seemed so out of reach in the simple act of clutching one another on the banks of the unspoiled stream. Ten Bears released his own restlessness, and Hunting For Something felt her sudden bout of anxiety take flight.

CHAPTER XV

*T*HE LINE OF RIDERS, THIRTY-SIX WELL-ARMED MEN, HAD BEEN on the trail for several days. Not one of them, not even their leader, knew exactly where they were. No one had ever hunted this deep in Comanche country before, and having come this far, they found their thirst for retribution growing stronger with every mile that fell behind them. All were united in a single, common desire—to make the earth run red with the blood of those that had retarded the taming of the frontier for decades. They had answered the call of their kinsmen, the confederation of merchants and ranchers and farmers who lived in a long string of settlements along the eastern edge of the Comanche barrier.

Each man in the band of rangers had lived wildly imperfect lives, and even a cursory review of their backgrounds would have led one to the conclusion that they were an unsavory group. Some had operated outside the law when it was convenient, some were shackled with impoverished intellects, some were ruled by homicidal instinct, and some, like their leader, a gaunt, black-bearded man who occasionally preached damnation in stark, airless structures when the Sabbath came around, were guided by visions of mass adulation.

But who they were, where they came from, and how they lived did not describe them as clearly as what had brought them together. Each had stepped forward when the civilization that spawned them offered a free and clear license to kill.

In idleness the thirty-six men might easily have been at the throats of each other. The seemingly limitless stock of liquor most of them had swilled from the outset of their journey would have spurred offhand insults or tangled misunderstandings, setting the murderous natures of some free to rampage. But the simple purpose of their mission kept them focused on the potential prey awaiting them farther out on the prairie. Though the majority passed each day in an alcoholic haze, there was no quarreling and no violence in their ranks.

On the trail they stayed attuned to every variation in the country they passed over, ever-watchful for a glimpse of their quarry and the chance to chase and kill it.

When they made camp for the night they were careful to throw out a perimeter, keep their cookfires small, and speak in low tones, no matter how often they tugged at the ever-present bottles. Even their conversations, bound to be rancorous and abrasive in the more civilized setting of an established drinking place, were free of conflict. The tales they shared as they ate their dinners and smoked their pipes and kept their weapons clean followed, with few exceptions, the wealth of each man's experience on the subject of gore.

Stories of men staggering about with entrails in their hands, shattered bone jutting from sheaths of skin, cleaved heads that afforded close-up views of the fissured brains inside, blood spurting in jets from severed arteries, limbs dangling by the slender thread of tendons, exploding faces, holes as big as melons, whimpering pleas for mercy—any anecdote remotely related to the carnage they loved to inflict was discussed with boundless relish and good humor.

The singular pursuit of slaughter in every imaginable form was at the forefront of every ranger's mind, and its careful cultivation, over many days of searching, culminated in the discovery of a good-sized village.

One of the flankers had glimpsed the tops of the lodges as he passed through a thick stand of elm situated not more than half a mile from the village. He watched for a few seconds, long enough to see that the target was located on flat terrain at the confluence of two streams. Then he galloped back to the main group, certain that he had not been detected.

The gaunt leader, addressed always as "Captain," though he had never served in a formal military body, quickly brought his men to the elm grove and, sighting through a field glass, ascertained that the village was totally unaware of their presence. Ponies were scattered in front of the Indian town but there was no massed herd. In the minutes the captain scanned his objective he saw no more than half a dozen human forms outside the tents, and it was obvious that none of them suspected the wrath about to befall them.

Twelve men were selected to circle wide of the village and position themselves behind it, there to kill as many of the escaping enemy as possible. They were given thirty minutes to get in place, before the main force of rangers would assault the village head-on.

"You rangers who wish to fortify yourselves do so now," the captain intoned solemnly, and a score of men hastily brought their bottles to their lips.

"Don't waste rounds on them animals out yonder," the captain cautioned. "We'll take 'em home afterward. Let's get the people first. Now," he grunted, digging through one of his saddlebags, "I've got a shiny new Colt I'm offering." He held the pistol up with both hands, waving it back and forth in front of the eyes of his followers as though it were solid gold. "This goes to the first man who kills and scalps one of them heathen scum." Then he added with a wink, "Babies without hair don't count."

The roar of laughter such high wit would normally have elicited was stifled by the rangers' hands, many of which flew coquettishly to their mouths lest the guffaws carry in the pleasant breeze blowing toward the treasured target.

"You men go ahead now," the captain ordered and the twelve selected to cut off escape filed out of the grove. When the squeak of saddle leather and the footfalls of the horses had faded to nothing the gaunt leader straightened in the saddle and cleared his throat.

"Boys, I'm a man for prayer. I could quote scripture to you right now for I'm tempted. What we're about to do's got it bubblin' up in me. But I think all I got to say is let's check our weapons over one more time. One more time won't hurt us now and I'd hate to see anybody miss out on the fun 'cause his weapon wadn't right."

The rangers jumped down from their horses. They tested their cinches, unloaded and reloaded their firearms, and filled the silence of the grove they stood in with the sound of knife blades passing rhythmically to and fro on their whetstones, all the while inwardly damning the slowness of time.

CHAPTER XVI

*T*HE FIRST PERSON TO SEE THEM WAS A TWELVE-YEAR-OLD GIRL named Red Dress, the younger sister of Hunting For Something. She was sitting outside her parents' dwelling, playing house with a miniature lodge and dolls when a random glance at the country in front of camp told her something was wrong. A long line of dust was rolling toward the village.

As she stood up Red Dress realized that the rolling cloud was being made by a band of riders hurtling toward her. She began screaming but her cries were as futile as the squeak of a mouse in the split second before talons lift it into space. The rush of pounding hooves and the hair-raising yells of the riders were already resounding through the helpless village.

Frozen with fear, Red Dress sank to the ground, drove her face into the earth, and covered both ears. Moments later, in an explosion of gunfire, a bullet slammed into the back of her head, ending the girl's life.

At the time Red Dress was shot, the camp was already swarming with terrified residents, fleeing in all directions at once. People fell everywhere as the invaders emptied their pistols and rifles at anything that moved, and the whole village might have died in the first horrendous volley were it not for the voracity of the rangers, many of whom succumbed to temptation, scalping their kills and plundering Indian homes on the spot.

Some jumped off their horses and shot those still huddled in their lodges while others became embroiled in disputes over who had fired a fatal round. At the height of the attack the gaunt leader found himself besieged by several rangers, each clamoring to claim the shiny new Colt by virtue of the blood-drenched hanks of hair they were waving in his face.

Horned Antelope had managed to survive the first wave of firing. As he raced for the rear of the village he spotted two warriors, Shield and Milky Way, cutting the throats of horses in a desperate attempt to make a barrier from which they could drive up the price on their lives, allowing the women and children and old men a few extra seconds to escape.

A bullet tore through Horned Antelope's shoulder as he dove behind the downed horses, and on recovering his senses he discovered that both his friends were dead. The last thing he experienced in earthly existence was a queer thudding all over his body as the fusillade of bullets tore through his flesh.

At the first sound of guns, Stands With A Fist had snatched up Stays Quiet and bolted outside, lunging for the picket line that anchored the pony Dances With Wolves had left for her. She threw Stays Quiet onto the horse's withers, jumped up behind, and kicked for the prairie opening in front of her.

But she hadn't covered a hundred yards when the twelve rangers charged with blunting the escape suddenly loomed into view and opened fire. The pony shifted direction at full speed, leaping away from the white puffs of smoke, and Stands With A Fist, somehow managing to keep herself and her daughter on his back, let him go, trusting the panicked animal to carry them clear.

Unhit, they might yet have reached safety had they not been spotted by a trio of rangers who had reluctantly paused in their labors to perform the necessary but bothersome act of reloading their weapons. Seeing the game afoot, they spontaneously laid whips to their horses' haunches and gave chase.

When Stands With A Fist saw her pursuers, she asked for all the speed her pony could give and flattened herself over Stays Quiet. She didn't want to look back but the fiendish hollering of the men coming behind at last caused her to turn her head.

At the same moment the ground in front of her fell away in the form of a natural ditch, no more than a few feet wide, cutting across the prairie. Startled by its appearance, the pony hesitated a split second before taking flight and, landing slightly off balance on the other side, catapulted his riders awkwardly into space.

She held on to Stays Quiet as they hit the ground, and, clutching her to her breast, Stands With A Fist began to run, expecting at any moment to be shot down. Instead, she found herself suddenly encircled by grinning, hair-mouthed white men jabbering at each other in the language she had long forgotten. This flurry of talk between the rangers, a good-natured joust concerning who most deserved to take her scalp, saved the lives of Stands With A Fist and her daughter.

The gaunt leader, having first given the coup de grâce to another fleeing Indian nearby, suddenly noticed three of his men circling a standing enemy and rode over to investigate. Everyone turned their heads as he came up and the sun swept across Stands With A Fist's head. The cherry hue of her hair flashed in the captain's eyes.

"Hold up, men," he commanded.

The gaunt leader stepped off his horse and stared quizzically at Stands With A Fist. As he stepped warily up, his revolver poised to fire, Stands With A Fist closed her eyes, trying to concentrate on images of her husband and children at the moment of death.

The next thing she felt, however, was the lifting of a lock of her hair, and when she opened her eyes she was staring into the sunken gray orbs of the captain. He was rubbing her hair between his fingers as if testing the quality of fabric.

He holstered his gun, took one of her arms in both hands, and slowly pushed up the sleeve of her dress. Gazing into her eyes as if to hold them quiet, he spat onto his fingers. He rubbed the spittle on her arm and, like a detective following a quick succession of clues, pulled her bodice down and stared at the flesh above her breast.

"This here's a white woman."

Awestruck, he stepped back and looked her up and down, his mind swelling with heroic scenarios featuring himself.

"I think this might be Christine Gunther."

All the men had dismounted now. They stood in dumb silence behind their captain.

Stands With A Fist blinked.

"Are you Christine Gunther?"

She had not heard the name for more than eleven years, not since the time Dances With Wolves had first come among them, not since Kicking Bird had implored her to remember the tongue of her birth, not since she had lain semidelirious in a bed of rushes next to a fast-running stream and remembered her mother call out the name that belonged to her.

It was not in answer to the hair-mouthed man's question that she spoke. In her disoriented state she was merely echoing a long-buried memory when she parted her lips and rolled her tongue and let the word come out of her mouth.

"Christine."

"God Almighty, it *is* her!" the captain gasped.

He lifted his hat and held it lightly against his chest.

"The Maker is with us today, men."

Struck by the piety of the moment, the three rangers who had lately vied to see which of them would rejoice in the taking of her life and the skinning of her cherry-colored head doffed their hats and held them meekly to their chests.

Stands With A Fist stared at them uncomprehendingly, and a ghastly feeling swept over her, the first realization that what was to come might be worse than the death she had thought certain minutes before. Her breath grew faster, her shoulders began to heave, and a torrent of tears, accompanied by piteous sobs, rained onto the ground at her feet.

When they gently tugged at Stays Quiet she screamed and flailed, and it was only after she realized she would be given back to her as soon as she mounted that she relaxed her grip.

As the gentle hands of her would-be killers, stained with the blood of her friends, lifted her onto a white man's saddle she became inconsolable again, abandoning herself so completely to grief that rangers had to ride on either side to steady her.

To a man they regarded her as one of their own, and the profound grief that had overwhelmed her was taken by them as a temporary insanity—an understandable trauma at finally being delivered from the clutches of her Comanche captors. It occurred to no one that leading her back to the slaughterhouse that was once her village would be upsetting.

There she was made to wait, a hand covering the eyes of her daughter, as they piled the bodies and belongings of the women and children and men she had known so well into an unceremonious pile. Red Dress and Magpie Woman, the wives and children of Iron Jacket and Left Hand and Hears The Sunrise, Lone Young Man, Feathered Lance, and scores of others were dragged across the ground before her eyes, unrecognizable except for a dress she knew or a telltale scar or an unusual piece of jewelry.

Women she had danced and sung with or aided in difficult births or comforted in times of loss. Children whom she had loved as her own. Men who had shared equal measures of danger and joy with her husband. All were paraded before her as meat, faces reduced to mush, intestines curling like rope in the dirt, legs and arms and torsos hacked open.

When the piles had been set afire the rangers rode east, taking their legendary prize with them. Stands With A Fist tried valiantly to think one thought over and over to make her heart strong: that Dances With Wolves and Snake In Hands and Always Walking still lived. But invariably that thought would lead to the inescapable conclusion that she would never see them again.

She imagined that she would never stop crying and, as the sun set behind her that evening, she felt the whole of herself going gradually numb. The nightmare she had feared so intensely through all her life as a Comanche was nothing compared to the reality of what had happened.

The woman called Stands With A Fist had been rubbed out as surely as those who had gone up in smoke. But as she cradled Stays Quiet through the long and sleepless first night of what the gaunt leader called her liberation, she envied the fate of those who lay dead in the village.

Before the sun was up the next morning they had taken the trail, making haste for the safety of white settlements in the east. She thought constantly of grabbing one of the ranger's guns and pressing the barrel against her head or of lifting a knife from its scabbard and drawing it swiftly across her throat, but the little girl sitting in front of her made such action impossible.

Every step the big American horse she was riding took seemed to drive her deeper into the bottomless depths of a misery that could only be tolerated through the preservation of hope. But she was unable to construct even the flimsiest hope, and as the country became more and more unfamiliar, she found herself facing a future of unrelieved despair she was powerless to oppose.

CHAPTER XVII

*F*ROM HIS VANTAGE POINT, FAR OUT ON AN OCEAN OF GRASS, THE world was flat as the cloudless sky and the horizon was of a length and straightness only the Mystery could make.

Smiles A Lot had seen the same grand picture every day of his life and the enormity of its simple components never failed to stir his feelings. Unaware of any presence but his own in such vastness made him small and large at the same time, a combination that infused his spirit with an incomprehensible blend of fear and fearlessness.

But on this day, as he sat on his pony, gazing across the infinity that led to home, there was something amiss, something tiny but distinct that disturbed the picture before him. Curling almost imperceptibly at the limit of his sight was a thin, black column of smoke. Pushed by the breeze it angled to one side as it rose like a wisp on the horizon.

The smoke was so out of place that he studied it for several minutes. Smiles A Lot doubted that the grass was on fire. The weather had been too still to start something like that, and even if it had, a wildfire would have spread out across a wide swath of country. This smoke was rising into the sky from a single spot, and for reasons he could not decipher, it gave Smiles A Lot a bad feeling. Though the black funnel was several hours' ride away it lay in the general direction of the village and he pressed on, hoping that his feeling was wrong. His ponies were fresh and he jumped from one to the other as he rode, certain that if he forced the pace he could reach the village before twilight.

The sun was dipping toward the horizon and the column of smoke had long disappeared when he finally neared the village, puzzled at the absence of lodge tips against the darkening sky. A natural berm he knew well lay in front of the village and as he crested it Smiles A Lot saw what had happened.

At first sight none of it seemed real. The village was gone, its place taken by half a dozen still-smoldering piles of refuse. In the heavy twilight haze of dust and smoke, some people were moving without discernible purpose. Others were clustered in small groups at the fringes of camp, huddled as though they were shivering against the cold. Few took notice of him, and those who did regarded him without expression. He could see a handful of ponies near the stream behind the village. Like the people, they were bunched together, still seeking safety long after the danger had passed.

The blackened piles of debris were larger than he first thought, and, coming near, he understood that it was corpses, most of them now burned to ash, that had fueled much of the dark column he had seen hours before. Now there was nothing left but shards of bone, the tips of lodge poles, a cook pot or two, and the lingering heat of the recent conflagration. Only then did Smiles A Lot fully realize that the village and the people in it had been annihilated.

He straightened on his pony to survey the survivors again and was struck this time at the paucity of men. Everywhere he looked he saw the bedraggled forms of women and children. The fired corpses were in the main unrecognizable, but the few he had seen which still resembled people were definitely women or children. Unable to believe that men had not been killed, he scanned the survivors again, more carefully this time.

One of the forlorn groups of women was sitting in a loose circle and now he noticed a prostrate form, lying facedown. He rode closer and discovered the Owl Prophet family. The form at the center of their circle lay with arms and legs spread wide. The nose of its face was pressed squarely into the earth. It was Owl Prophet.

"Is he dead?" Smiles A Lot asked calmly.

Bird Woman turned her gaze to her husband and watched him awhile before looking once again at Smiles A Lot.

"He's meditating."

"What happened?" Smiles A Lot demanded. "Where are the men?"

"They were gone."

"Are any men here?"

Bird Woman glanced around aimlessly.

"Ten Bears is here . . . I don't know where. He's alive."

It was now too dark to see and Smiles A Lot rode about calling out the old man's name. A stirring in one of the shadowy groups drew his attention and a girl's mournful voice sent the word *here* through the stillness.

Ten Bears was still being helped to his feet as Smiles A Lot slid off his pony.

"What has happened?" he gasped.

"White rangers," Ten Bears replied. The old man was lucid as always but he seemed winded, as if he were recovering from a blow to the stomach.

"Where are the men?"

"There were very few here. I was out of camp. And Owl Prophet."

"How many people are dead?"

"Maybe half. I don't know how more did not die."

At this Ten Bears visibly winced and Smiles A Lot leaned toward him. "Do you have a wound?"

"No," answered Ten Bears and he stared suddenly into his questioner's eyes with a look so pitiful that Smiles A Lot felt a startling, unfamiliar impulse to cry.

"Where did they go, the men?" Smiles A Lot asked.

"Kicking Bird took some people north to the Kiowa. There are white soldiers up there."

"Yes, I saw them."

"Wind In His Hair has a large party in the east, looking for scalps. Dances With Wolves is hunting in the west. . . . Do you have any food? Everyone is hungry."

"It isn't much," said Smiles A Lot, turning back to his pony. "I'll give you what I have."

He pulled his little bag of jerked meat off the pony and, lifting the flap, offered its contents to Ten Bears. As the old man's hand disappeared into the bag other hands reached out of the darkness to join it and Smiles A Lot noticed that one of them belonged to Hunting For Something.

It had been a long time since he had turned his thoughts to her but the realization that she had survived threw open the door to his heart. The old feelings that rushed in were as intense as before, yet strangely different.

He still thought she was the most beautiful girl he had ever seen. The shape of her lips, the way she carried herself, the slender frame, the timbre of her voice—all these attributes and many more had retained their full power. But he viewed her differently now. Perhaps it was his experience at Medicine Bluff or perhaps it was the sobering effect of catastrophe. Whatever the reason might have been, the fact that something had changed inside Smiles A Lot was indisputable. He felt straighter, taller, stronger, self-contained, and at peace. The fat of his emotion had been miraculously pared away, and, if anything, he loved and admired her more deeply than before. However, this was no time to be lovesick.

"Are my mother and father here?" he asked Ten Bears.

The old man swallowed what he was chewing. "I think they are dead," he said.

Smiles A Lot didn't gasp or cry. Ten Bears had confirmed what he already sensed, and though his heart sank with the knowledge that they were gone, loss was a part of life that every Comanche understood. As he stood over the crouching survivors, the sole sign of grief Smiles A Lot displayed was silence.

A small voice, made tinier by the stillness, spoke up.

"I'm here, brother."

The voice belonged to Rabbit, the youngest of his brothers and sisters. Smiles A Lot bent at the waist and peered forward.

"Rabbit . . . where are you?"

A little hand reached out of the darkness and Smiles A Lot took it. He dropped to one knee and placed a hand on each of Rabbit's thin shoulders.

"How did you get away?"

"I hid in the grass like a coyote," Rabbit said proudly. "They took Stands With A Fist. I saw them. They took that little girl, Stays Quiet, too."

"But they didn't take you."

"No, they couldn't see me. I disappeared."

Smiles A Lot cupped a hand behind the boy's head and pulled his brother's cheek to his own.

"You did well, little brother."

"Can I stay with you?"

"Yes," Smiles A Lot answered, "you stay with me."

Settling his other knee on the ground, he turned his attention back to Ten Bears.

"We should get away from here, Grandfather."

"Yes," the old man agreed, "everyone will be safe in the west. The canyons will hide us. But you will have to be the leader, Smiles A Lot. We have only you to help us."

The boy who was good with horses spent the rest of a long night walking the killing ground, making a head count of the survivors, and found that remnants of almost every family had survived.

Three women and two children had serious wounds, but Owl Prophet was still prone and likely would have remained there had Smiles A Lot not resorted to dousing him with a pot of cold water. The medicine man did what he could for the wounded but one of the women and one of the children passed into the shadow world before dawn.

When the sun finally came up Smiles A Lot forged what was left of the village into a force for action. Rabbit and the other boys were split into two groups: one to catch the remaining horses, the other to scour the surrounding prairie for small game. Rabbit's group succeeded in gathering seventeen horses and the other boys returned with six guinea fowl and almost a dozen wild hares, enough to give everyone in camp a few mouthfuls of food.

At the same time, Smiles A Lot put Hunting For Something in charge of her surviving peers and the girls scavenged the ruined camp for anything that could be salvaged to use on the trek west. The girls were successful, retrieving much useful material for the trip.

The rangers had not been as thorough as first appeared, and by noon Hunting For Something and her friends had collected almost twenty good lodge poles, a large pile of cooking utensils, enough buffalo hide to stitch together two lodges, and even a few weapons, including two working rifles that had somehow escaped attention.

By mid-afternoon the horses were loaded with what had been gleaned from the camp's ashes, several travois had been constructed for Ten Bears and the wounded, and they were ready to march out. Everyone was relieved to get away from the scene of so much pain.

Ten Bears lay on one side, rocking atop his movable bed, his gray head propped on an elbow. His chance escape from the hands of the rangers had already ceased to prey on his mind, and the ugliness of butchery and burning which resulted in the destruction of his community was beginning to recede. What would be referred to in the future as The Place Where The Rangers Burned Hearts was no longer a part of the present. Distance had diminished its impact enough to be guided toward memory as the long dark line on the horizon which marked the beginning of the canyonlands was sighted.

The simple act of moving had given purpose to people who had lost everything. Curiously, Ten Bears himself felt a welcome surge of renewal as he sat up on the travois to greet the coming twilight.

A beautiful day, this day, he thought to himself. *How could it be so ugly? Nothing can be explained, old, worn-out man.*

Better stop thinking like that, he admonished. *Listen to your lungs. Hear them? What if your eyes are filling with night? What if your ears are getting smaller? Listen to those lungs! No rasping, no wheezing. They are working. Old or not, the Mystery wants you to live. Rejoice in that.*

Deciding to give thanks for the good coming out of the bad, Ten Bears drew out his pipe and packed it before he realized that he had no way to light it on the bumpy travois. He held the pipe anyway, thinking, *What does it matter whether or not my words travel to the Mystery on smoke? This is a special time. My heart is true. The things I'm thinking will get where they need to go.*

He craned his head for a look at the women and children spread around him.

These are all good people, he thought. *They know how to live when life is hard. They don't give up. Hunting For Something is up ahead somewhere, trying to find Dances With Wolves' trail. I'm glad that boy went with her, that Rabbit. He's tough like sinew. A very useful boy.*

For a moment he thought he saw movement up ahead and hoped it was Hunting For Something coming back. But his old eyes were betraying him again. No one nearby showed any sign they had seen anything and Ten Bears reclined to face the sky, resolved that his granddaughter would come back when she would come back. No one could manipulate fate.

The clouds were laid out like bands of smoke against the deepening purple of nightfall and Ten Bears briefly wondered if he might be looking at the residue of the boiling pillars of black he and Hunting For Something had watched the day before from their hiding place in a stand of willows. Weary of heartache, he consciously turned his thoughts to the more pleasant subject of his only surviving grandchild's attributes. He was the only family she had now but it made him glad to think of her determination and bravery in the face of having lost her father, mother, brothers, and sisters.

She doesn't complain, he thought, *she doesn't think of herself. She insisted on scouting the trail ahead. I don't doubt she'll pick up Dances With Wolves' tracks. She can do all of a woman's work and sit tall on her pony, too. The girl looks to be a warrior, she carries herself straight up and down. Now she's doing a warrior's work. She's just what a Comanche woman should be. She can do anything. And she's a good-looking girl, too. Any young man who puts his eye on her had better be a good one.*

Ten Bears looked over his nose at the last light in the east and thought of Smiles A Lot. Here, too, was something to make his heart glad in the midst of dejection.

A young man all by himself, thought Ten Bears, *traveling into hostile country on an urgent mission. That boy has changed overnight. No one thought he could do anything. I didn't think so. But here we are, getting safer every mile because a boy who couldn't do anything stood up and took charge. How could I have been so wrong about him? I didn't give him credit because I couldn't see. I didn't hear his blood because I didn't bother to listen.*

"Nobody knows anything," the old man muttered out loud. He allowed himself a self-deprecating chuckle and gazed back down the trail again.

Why am I so surprised at the strength of these two? he thought, shaking his head. *Comanches are strong. Comanches can get through anything. The proof is in our children. That Smiles A Lot—he's proof. He'll find Wind In His Hair and the other men and bring them back to us. The boy has everything. All he really needs is a wife. Hunting For Something . . . Hunting For Something and Smiles A Lot. Could there be a more perfect match? Oh, what do you know anyway, old man? You don't know if they like each other. Stay out of it. Why are you dreaming like this? Well, anyway, I hope he doesn't get killed. I don't care what anyone thinks or says. I don't care if it's not my business. I can think what I want to think, and I think they would be a couple to make people proud!*

CHAPTER XVIII

*T*HE KIOWA COUNTRY WAS NOT AS MYSTERIOUS AS THAT OF THE Comanches. Nothing equaled the drama of Comanche grasslands flat as the sky. Or plunging canyons that stretched into labyrinths on a scale so great as to be capable of containing entire civilizations. There were waterways of every length and breadth, from rivers that men routinely risked their lives in crossing to tiny hidden springs in terrain where the presence of water seemed inconceivable.

Still, Kiowa country was magnificent, blessed with water of every miraculous form, oceans of rolling grassland, and a sense of self-containment not usually found in other worlds. Like its southern neighbor, the Kiowa country, by virtue of its size and variety, could have qualified as a continent.

Kicking Bird always felt as easy as if he were at home when passing through Kiowa land, especially on this trip at the head of a large delegation.

That the Kiowa seemed to hold him in greater esteem than his own people was a poignant irony. To be sure, there was variety of opinion among the Kiowa, too, but in comparison to the Comanches they were far more worldly. Their contact with the whites in recent years had been much greater than that of their powerful yet isolated allies to the south. And not all of it had been bad.

White scalps hung in the lodges of many Kiowa warriors, and there were many Kiowa women who no longer spoke the names of fathers, husbands, and brothers, men who had been sent on the long journey across the Milky Way by white bullets. But the Kiowa had traded with whites. They had attended big councils where they talked with hair-mouthed men called commissioners. Kiowa warriors had taken the hands of white soldiers whom they had already met in running fights or would meet in the future.

None of them cared much for the plentiful white-skinned people from the east whose behavior was so perplexing, but at least the Kiowa knew something of them—no one more than Touch The Clouds, who had attended almost every plains meeting the whites had asked for and had fought with distinction through every conflict. It was the village of this warrior, made legendary by his extraordinary height, that Kicking Bird sought.

On reaching the camp of Touch The Clouds, Kicking Bird and his delegation settled in as honored guests. The Kiowa insisted they pitch their lodges in an enviable spot adjacent to their own community with easy access to water, fuel, and forage. At once the Comanches were treated to the predictable orgy of visits and feasting. Interspersed with gorging and talking were rounds of horse racing—dominated, as usual, by the Comanches—gambling games that floated from lodge to lodge, and, because a large herd of buffalo had recently appeared just north of camp, daily hunting trips that kept the village supplied with fresh meat.

Yet amid this seemingly constant swirl of activity, Kicking Bird remained focused on the reason for the visit. Room had been made for his lodges in the center of the village, a few steps from Touch The Clouds' home, affording the two warriors the opportunity to conduct their meetings with neighborly ease.

Both men took full advantage, and through the first two days of Kicking Bird's stay, they were rarely seen but in each other's company. At any hour of the night or day they might be found talking over pressing matters of the moment with prominent warriors of both tribes.

The subject of the whites was never tabled for long and Kicking Bird quickly found that the sentiments of the Kiowa closely mirrored those of his own people. Some, like himself and Touch The Clouds, were open to more contact, while others were staunchly opposed.

A significant number of Kiowa, especially a tight-knit clique who followed a crafty, barrel-chested man named White Bear, were of both minds. If the wind shifted toward peace they stood ready to exploit it. If a call for war went out they were eager to participate. White Bear and his devotees, like many of their Comanche counterparts, viewed peace and war as part of a natural cycle, like good weather following bad, or vice versa.

However, the teaming of Touch The Clouds and Kicking Bird gave them great influence. That two eminent men known for their levelheadedness constantly guided the discussion toward the subject of the whites led people to the conclusion that the problem was more timely than ever, and all the better if it could be solved in some amicable way.

But after two days of discussing the question in uncommon detail, the two warriors were losing some of their own resolve. Kicking Bird had received his peace medal as a ceremonial present and had never had what might be considered a true conversation with a white man. Touch The Clouds had met many whites in council but the talks never led beyond vague promises of friendship and, in the ten winters he had attended these parlays, he had never met with the same white man twice. Despite his long experience, Touch The Clouds didn't really know any white men.

By the third morning of Kicking Bird's visit the two friends had come full circle. They sat in Touch The Clouds' lodge making a show of keeping their discussions vital while in truth their talk had become moribund. They had met with every leading warrior and had explored every avenue that might lead to a decision as to what action to take. The most viable approach had come from the vacillating White Bear, who had suggested they ride in force to the vicinity of the great Medicine Bluff, show themselves, and wait for a reaction.

The two friends discussed this idea once more and, in doing so, realized that it had little promise. The chance was too great that the white soldiers would open fire at the sight of armed warriors, thus defeating the goal of talks that might hold out some hope for conciliation.

On the heels of this frustrating review, Touch The Clouds fired his pipe and the men lapsed into an awkward silence as they passed it back and forth. Neither man knew what to say.

At last Kicking Bird put into words what both of them were thinking.

"I have been thinking. . . . This question of what to do cannot be answered by ourselves."

"I have been thinking the same," Touch The Clouds confessed. "Perhaps it is a question only the Mystery can answer."

"Yes," Kicking Bird agreed. His eyes roved helplessly around the spacious lodge. "But nothing has been revealed. I wonder sometimes if the Mystery no longer looks on us as his children."

"I wonder the same."

Again the men lapsed into forlorn silence, but a moment later the stillness in the lodge was pierced by a cry from outside. Many other shouts followed in rapid succession, and by the time the friends had gotten to their feet, it sounded as if a general alarm was being raised.

They ducked through the lodge entrance to an explosion of action outside. Men were leaping onto their ponies. Women were hurrying children into their lodges. A great whooping filled the air.

Swinging onto their ponies, Kicking Bird and Touch The Clouds were able to make out through the dust and shouting words that told them what the pandemonium was about.

"White man on the prairie! White man coming in!"

Following thick clouds of dust, Kicking Bird and Touch The Clouds tore out of the village and had barely cleared the camp before they pulled up in disbelief at what lay before them.

A solitary man dressed in black, his hands thrust into the air, was sitting on a wagon pulled by a mule as dozens of warriors, yapping at the limit of their lungs, swarmed around him.

As they rode closer they saw White Bear's pony jostle the intruder's mule. The warrior bawled out words they couldn't hear, then struck the man hard with his bow and the cause of all the excitement toppled off the wagon and crashed to earth.

The impact of his fall sent the man's dark, broad-brimmed hat flying, and Kicking Bird and Touch The Clouds saw what everyone else saw. The sun reflected almost as in a mirror off his smooth, shiny head. Hair the length of a rabbit's ran in a band above his ears and low down along the back of his skull. Everyone drew back in disbelief. He had no scalp.

"I will kill this ghost!" White Bear shouted, pulling an arrow from his quiver.

Before he could string it, Touch The Clouds' hand was on his arm. White Bear's expression said he resented the intrusion but Touch The Clouds' words flew in his face before he could protest.

"Great warriors do not waste arrows on mice . . . shivering in the grass."

The squabble between White Bear and Touch The Clouds barely registered as Kicking Bird sat, trancelike, on his pony, watching with profound fascination as the white man scrambled after his hat and replaced it on his head. He was quite small for any man and was wearing something on his bearded face that Kicking Bird had never seen before: two tiny discs of what looked like glass suspended before each eye by a delicate framework of wire.

The man walked back to his mule, clasped a hand on one of its reins, and waited, almost childlike, for what might happen next. Who he was or what might be his mission in Kiowa country the Comanche could not guess. He was not a soldier, nor did he have what Kicking Bird imagined to be the stature of an important emissary. That he might be lost was possible, but some indefinable sense told Kicking Bird this was not the case. His eyes seemed to have a special energy that was linked somehow with plaintive hope, and in the few seconds that Kicking Bird watched the apparition, he deduced that this being bore no one ill will.

Inspiration suddenly flashed in Kicking Bird's mind and the excitement it wrought tickled him from head to toe as he realized that he possessed a weapon of great power and that this was the opportunity he had been waiting for to use it.

He had pestered Dances With Wolves and Stands With A Fist to teach him the weapon from the day of their marriage. He had practiced it, in private, for years, checking and rechecking the accuracy of what he knew with the reluctant couple in the set-apart lodge. How much of it he remembered and how well he might pronounce it he could not be sure, but an instant later he found himself dropping off his pony and walking through the grass toward the little man.

The Kiowa and Comanche warriors surrounding the scene were silenced at Kicking Bird's approach, and in an odd way they, too, suddenly realized that this white man represented no real threat. The Comanche they all knew as mild-mannered was of average height but to see him now, standing opposite the white man, he seemed a giant. The little man in black was a thing so puny that the wildest imagination could not have perceived him as an adversary.

Kicking Bird's confidence was reinforced by a close-up view of the stranger's face. He guessed that the diminutive figure must have had at least fifty winters, though his countenance was full of youthful innocence, and as he uttered the first words he had ever spoken to a white, Kicking Bird could not help thinking he was addressing a boy.

"I," he said, lightly tapping his chest, "Kicking Bird."

The white man's face opened as if a cloud had moved away from the sun. His lips pulled apart in a smile so wide that it seemed as if his eyes were smiling too.

"I," he began in a light, high voice, pushing a finger up against his chest in the way Kicking Bird had done, "I . . . Lawrie Tatum. Friend, friend."

"Friend," Kicking Bird nodded for that was a word he knew. "Hmmm . . . where? . . . from?"

"I'm from Iowa," Lawrie Tatum answered, speaking the words in a clipped, precise fashion that seemed to suit the latent energy pent up in his little body. "But I have come from Washington."

Kicking Bird knew the word *Washington* too. "Ahhh," he grunted, nodding again, "Washington." He pointed to the peace medal hanging around his neck.

Lawrie Tatum bobbed his head up and down happily. "That's right . . . well, that's the *man*, I'm from the *place* . . . Washington."

"Hmmm . . . Washington."

"I . . . Lawrie Tatum, want to be your friend. Lawrie Tatum and Kicking Bird . . . friends."

At that he thrust a small hand forward, leveling it at Kicking Bird's waist.

At a conference he had once attended Kicking Bird had seen white men make the same gesture. He glanced into Lawrie Tatum's eyes once more, as if to reassure himself that no treachery lurked there, before lifting one of his bronze-colored hands in the stranger's direction.

The two hands closed on one another. Lawrie Tatum grinned and Kicking Bird, not quite believing what was happening, stared at the pudgy digits enveloped in his own long and elegant fingers.

A few other warriors, including Touch The Clouds, had slipped down from their ponies and drifted closer during the exchange. When Kicking Bird performed the intimate act of taking the white man's hand in his own, shock and curiosity drove them even closer.

There they remained for most of an hour, standing on the open prairie, ringed by warriors on horseback, listening to the talk of Kicking Bird and the tiny visitor who had materialized out of nowhere.

Important information was obtained in that first interview, conducted with a patchwork of signs, Kicking Bird's rudimentary, untested English, and the curt translations for those who had gathered round.

Lawrie Tatum from Washington was seeking peace and friendship between Indian and white. He was offering himself to the Kiowa and the Comanche as what he called an "agent" for Indians who loved peace. He would serve those who sought peace in a variety of ways—as a procurer of food, clothing, and medicine, as a protector and intermediary between military and government authority, and as a guide for those, especially the young, who wanted to take what he called "the white man's road." Lawrie Tatum was some kind of holy man, and there were many others of his cult, called Quakers, who had spread across the country seeking friendship with all tribes. He had one wife, many children, and was one of those who drilled holes in the ground, put in seed, and took what grew to eat.

These revelations, passed on by Kicking Bird, were listened to with care by the other warriors. Many snickered at the idea of Lawrie Tatum protecting them against anything, but for most of the interview the free men of the plains gave their full attention to the exchange.

But more and more questions, some derisive and combative, were being hurled from the onlookers. Taking the white man's road was a baffling and useless proposition to most, and Kicking Bird and Touch The Clouds both sensed that the best way to delve deeper into the mission of Lawrie Tatum was not in a public forum. Nor was the open prairie proper. They had been standing all the while. They had not sat down, not smoked the pipe.

When the crowd's questions began edging toward ugliness Touch The Clouds addressed everyone with his usual firmness and finality.

"I am taking this white man into camp," he began.

Hoots of surprise and some of derision arose from the crowd, but Touch The Clouds was not one to be swayed once his mind was made up, and he had already decided that he wanted to study this Lawrie Tatum man in more depth. Single-handedly he quelled all opposition.

"This white man is my guest," he commanded. "He will sleep in my lodge and no harm will come to him."

Lawrie Tatum then climbed onto his wagon and, escorted by most of the warriors of Touch The Clouds' village, rode back into camp, where the women and children and elderly could not wait to get a look at him.

The Kiowa leader ordered a small lodge to be erected between his own and Kicking Bird's, and Lawrie Tatum was made to understand that this would be the place to store his things and rest his body that night.

The little lodge was up in a matter of minutes and the stranger's gear was unloaded and brought inside. Food and water were given him. Kicking Bird and Touch The Clouds sat across from the little man, watching him eat and drink. Lawrie Tatum commented on the tastiness of his meal and the sweetness of the water, but otherwise the three sat in a fragile silence that was constantly broken by intrusions.

The chatter of villagers continued unabated all afternoon as they milled about the new lodge and its novel resident. Gangs of children clambered on and off the white man's wagon, prompting Touch The Clouds to step out and snap at them to go away and be quiet. He was forced to do this several times, but they did not retreat for long. The moment he sat down again, their presence outside could be heard once more, hushed murmurings that grew inevitably into unbridled shouts and laughter. Touch The Clouds would listen distractedly to the truncated attempts at communication between Kicking Bird and Lawrie Tatum before rising angrily to his feet for another short-lived scattering of the children.

Even the few minutes of peace from the children Touch The Clouds' chiding bought did not free the lodge from invasion. Heads were constantly appearing at the hems of the lodge's covering which had necessarily been rolled up on account of the heat of the day. Curious eyes constantly appeared; prominent warriors dropped by in a steady stream, offering some pretext of other business in order to get some idea of what was going on inside. Shadows of eavesdroppers pressed against the hide-covered walls of the tent, and on several occasions, the whole tent sagged as an unseen interloper lost balance and fell against it.

At last the exasperated hosts and their guest went for a walk but were stymied by a throng of followers who paraded behind them, growing in number until it seemed they had the whole village in tow.

Recognizing the futility of their efforts, the men returned once more to the lodge, and it was only with the coming of twilight, which impelled all but the most inquisitive to return to their homes, that the two Indians and the white man were able to converse with some semblance of peace.

Touch The Clouds lit his pipe again and, though reluctant, Lawrie Tatum was prevailed upon to smoke, his pale complexion turning paler with each pass.

Finally able to concentrate, Kicking Bird's mind kept returning to a single question, one that had nagged at him since he first heard the Cheyenne story of the white man's "holy road." Not knowing enough of the white man's language to frame the question properly, he began with the word he knew, hoping it might lead him to construct what he really wanted to ask.

"Train?" he asked, looking intently at Lawrie Tatum.

"Train?"

"Uhh." Kicking Bird nodded.

"Well, yes," Lawrie Tatum sputtered in his high voice, "what about it . . . train?"

Kicking Bird searched for words that kept flying away. "White man train," he said at last.

"Uh . . ." The white man's hand stroked the hair on his face. "You . . . ," he started, pointing at Kicking Bird, "like train? . . . no like train? You . . . go on train?"

Kicking Bird shook his head. He did not understand the words but their gist told him he was not moving toward the point. He gathered himself again.

"Train road?" he said.

"Yes, I understand . . . train road," came the reply.

"Holee?"

"Holee?"

"Holee?"

Recognition flashed on Lawrie Tatum's face. "Holy? Is that what you mean?" he asked, glancing heavenward.

"Holy. Train road holy?"

Lawrie Tatum winced. "I'm not sure what you're asking," he said pleadingly.

"All white man road . . ." Kicking Bird said and made a circling motion with both arms. "All white man road holy?"

"Is the white man's road holy?"

"Hmmm," nodded Kicking Bird.

Lawrie Tatum thought to himself a few moments, and the more he thought the more he realized how profound Kicking Bird's question was. The Comanche was asking if what the white man had to offer was righteous, and in the Quaker's mind there could only be one answer.

"Yes," he answered firmly, "I believe it is. The white man's road is holy."

"Hmmm," Kicking Bird grunted. The exact outlines of the question and its answer were something he had yet to grasp fully, but he was quite satisfied with the exchange.

Lawrie Tatum had questions, too. He wanted to know where Kicking Bird lived, how many people were in his village, if he was married, if he had children. When Kicking Bird told him he was married to three women, Friend Tatum's eyes grew big and he held up three fingers to make sure he understood. Kicking Bird nodded and a look of concern passed over the Quaker's face.

"Wives bad?" Kicking Bird asked.

"No," Lawrie Tatum replied. "White man have one . . . one wife . . . no more."

Kicking Bird nodded that he understood but was perplexed at the idea. How any race could prosper under such a harsh restriction he could not understand.

The line of questioning ended there as did many others. Given the limits of words and signs there was no way to delve deeper and the remainder of the talk was a battle of simple questions.

Lawrie Tatum was by nature more aggressive and animated, and though Kicking Bird burned to ask about many important things, like the buffalo and the soldier fort and how it might be that Comanche or Kiowas could follow the white man's holy road, his deliberations were often cut short by the little white man's persistent questions.

He wanted to know if Kicking Bird and Touch The Clouds were for peace between Indian and white. Kicking Bird translated this for Touch The Clouds, who laughed and said, "If we were not this man's body would already be turning black out there in the grass." Both men laughed as Lawrie Tatum gazed at them blankly.

The Quaker wanted to know if they were chiefs and Kicking Bird explained that Touch The Clouds was a headman but that he was not. A man named Ten Bears, an old, wise man with bad eyes, was the leader of his band.

But the more Kicking Bird and Lawrie Tatum questioned each other, the more aware they became of their inadequacies, and what had begun as a conversation quickly devolved into the more practical pursuit of vocabulary building. For another hour the names of everyday items found about the lodge and on their persons were translated back and forth in Comanche, Kiowa, and English.

All three were eager to learn and the lessons might have continued all night were it not for the arrival of several Indian wives, whose insistent voices demanded that their husbands break off the meeting and see to the children, who were asking for them.

Kicking Bird and Touch The Clouds made Lawrie Tatum to understand that he was safe. Then they each took the white man's hand and bid him good night.

The Comanche listened as his wives related the events of the day. He played games, visited with each of his children, and generally tried to discharge his duties as husband and father. But his heart wasn't in it that night. His head was too ripe with thoughts that pulled him, from recurring impressions of the white man Lawrie Tatum to the new English words that begged to be remembered to the crowded world of possibility that had flowered in his consciousness. When he slipped under the covers he was still too excited to sleep, and once the other bodies in the lodge were hard asleep he snuck outside to give free rein to his galloping mind.

The moon had risen full and Kicking Bird sat in the inky shadow of his lodge, wondering at the incalculable mystery hidden in the white man's lodge only a few steps from where he sat.

To his surprise there was a sudden movement of the little lodge's flap, and an instant later Lawrie Tatum was stepping into the bright, blue light of the moon. He wore no coat and the sleeves of his tight-fitting shirt were rolled past his elbows. The glass discs no longer fronted his eyes and there were no shoes on his feet. He looked around warily and, satisfied that he was alone, lifted one of his hands which was holding what looked like a small stick several inches long. In the other hand he held what looked like a canteen. He tilted the canteen over the object in the other hand and a little stream of water dribbled over the strange stick.

Having no idea what the ritual might mean, Kicking Bird's curiosity gave way to astonishment as the white man's mouth suddenly admitted the stick and a violent scouring commenced inside.

The best Kicking Bird could deduce was that, though it lacked any hint of elegance or sanctity, Lawrie Tatum must be performing some kind of purification ceremony. Perhaps there was some evil entity residing in his mouth.

After repeating the action several more times, the stick was withdrawn and shaken. Lawrie Tatum lifted the canteen to his lips, sloshed the water around in his mouth, and, bending forward, spat all of it onto the ground. Then he turned as casually as if he had just urinated and disappeared into the lodge.

Any chance Kicking Bird might have had for sleep was doomed by what he had witnessed. Seeing such inexplicable conduct reinforced and sharpened all that was different between Indian and white, and as he continued to sit in the shadow of the moon, contemplating Lawrie Tatum's bizarre behavior, he felt the cloud of euphoria he had been riding all afternoon slowly dissipate.

Exchanges of information and negotiation that might determine how the two peoples could coexist were nothing when compared to the gulf in ways of being that existed between the races, and it was with that mindful realization that Kicking Bird finally went back to his bed.

What little rest he at last achieved was more akin to intermittent catnapping than it was to real sleep. His hopes had sobered but not died, and he floated through a queer twilight of consciousness in which he reminded himself that even if it would be prudent to go slower, the prospect of more interplay with Lawrie Tatum the following day was an exciting one.

It never occurred to him that he would not see Lawrie Tatum the following day. Nor did it occur to him that one of the men who had gone hunting with Dances With Wolves would be standing at his lodge door in the predawn chill.

The weary voice calling for him to come out belonged to Lone Young Man, and when the Comanche statesman looked into his face he knew something terrible had happened.

The lodges of the Kicking Bird delegation had been struck, their horses gathered and loaded, and the entire party had already ridden clear of Touch The Clouds' camp when Lawrie Tatum stepped timidly out of his guest quarters half an hour after sunup.

At first he was disoriented, because he was certain that the man called Kicking Bird had been living in a spot that was now bare. As soon as he saw Touch The Clouds, the Quaker agent tried to clear up the confusion, and after a few minutes of fitful signs and words and playacting, the suspicion was confirmed. The Comanche Lawrie Tatum thought of as intelligent and levelheaded had simply picked up and left, presumably for home, without saying good-bye and without any agreement to meet again.

It wasn't as if Lawrie Tatum hadn't been warned. Anyone who had ever dealt with Indians had told him they could not be trusted—that understanding the Indian mind was about as easy as figuring out the meaning of life, that depending on an Indian to do what he said he would do was like a dry farmer depending on rain in a drought.

Lawrie Tatum remembered these admonitions when he glanced again at the vacant ground lately occupied by Kicking Bird's lodge. He still liked the Comanche and it was not in his constitution to give up— whether it be on a patch of skimpy corn back home or the ambitious peace policy the government was hoping he and scores of other Quakers would find a way to implement.

And yet there was bristling in a remote corner of his mind. As he stared at the ring where Kicking Bird's lodge had lately been, Lawrie Tatum couldn't help feeling that in some way he had been played for a fool.

CHAPTER XIX

*I*T WAS A TYPICAL CAVALRY UNIT: HEAVY WITH MEN WHO HAD not served long, a few savvy veterans with the tenacity to forge a career in the army, and a commander who only needed to shave every third or fourth day.

At the beginning, reports of a Comanche war party had roused the troops with the prospect of relief from the drudgery of work detail and the incessant nitpicking of certain officers who treated the dreary garrison as their personal fiefdom. All but the most chronic goldbricks had jostled for a place in the unit that was formed to take the field, and despite the lack of fanfare that signaled their departure for the wilderness, spirits were high when they rode out.

It was not long, however, before a host of deficiencies began to glare in the bright light of action. Their fuzz-faced commander, little more than an earnest boy from a decent family, was operating under a purposely vague directive: to drive the marauders away from the property of citizens without actively engaging them unless fired upon. The lack of potency in his orders immediately created hesitancy and doubt in the young lieutenant, which soon spread virus-like to each member of his command.

To make matters worse, an individual who was far better suited to the role of confidence man than scout had been delegated by the post commander to guide the lieutenant across country, break trail, and advise him on matters pertaining to modes of Comanche warfare.

The scout looked the part. He wore buckskin pants, a flannel shirt, a plumed campaign hat, moccasins, and a band of silver rings on his wrist. But in truth, most of his getup, like the arsenal of weapons he carried, was plunder from his past career as one of numerous ex-Confederate soldiers who had mined opportunities for mischief and crime up and down the Texas frontier in the years following the War Between the States.

None of this came out when he offered his services to the post commander, speaking in a slow, deliberate drawl. At strategic intervals in his fabricated personal history he directed a stream of tobacco juice into a nearby spittoon with uncanny accuracy, a feat which in the eyes of the post commander lent credibility to all he said. The presence of two scruffy Tonkawas standing silently against the back wall also seemed to underline the scout's veracity, and although he demanded an unusually high fee for his services, the post commander was unwilling to let such a valuable man slip away for want of a few dollars.

The scout had counted on the naïveté of the military and, upon meeting the young lieutenant he was to serve, felt his confidence soar. Neither he nor his Tonkawa assistants had ever been in Comanche country, but the lieutenant had never been anywhere, having only lately arrived in Texas. Duping the post commander had been easy enough and pulling the wool over the shavetail's trusting eyes was about as hard as robbing a church.

Still, the scout's charade might have been exposed. A veteran sergeant had suspected fraud from the outset and he mentioned his misgivings to the lieutenant. But the young officer didn't act on the sergeant's hunch because the scout and his Tonkawas, once they picked up the trail, had been tracking the big Comanche war party with pronounced ease.

The success of the so-called scouts was not due to their expertise, however. It was wholly attributable to Wind In His Hair's clever, timeless strategy of luring the enemy to his doom. The column of horse soldiers had been watched from the moment they took the field, and on several occasions when the hair-mouths hesitated in their trek, warriors were dispatched to show themselves in order to keep the pursuers on course.

The line of march was designed by Wind In His Hair to take the white men through the roughest country possible in hope that they would break down. At the end of the first day, the soldiers found themselves at a stream whose water was so alkaline that horses refused to drink and the troops, even after straining it repeatedly, swallowed the muddy liquid only with great difficulty.

At the conclusion of the second day's march through an arid, treeless country, the troops were on hands and knees in a dry streambed, throwing up great loads of sand to get at a few handfuls of silty, brackish water.

The lieutenant felt compelled to question his guide and was assured that they would hit a clear stream around noon of the following day. This was received as gospel though wholly untrue—the scout had no idea where water might be found.

While the lieutenant was eating supper alone in his tent, the unit's ranking sergeant came to warn him that the men were becoming dispirited and that many of their horses would soon be rendered useless without water and feed. The lieutenant, who was also becoming irascible, reminded the sergeant that he was neither deaf nor blind and did not need to be told how badly things were going.

The sergeant, long used to tongue-lashings from officers, took no offense from the lieutenant's rejoinder, and, asking permission to speak openly, got to the real business of his visit.

"Those Comanches, sir . . . I think they're leading us. Begging pardon, sir, but far as I can tell, all these scouts know how to do is drink whiskey."

"Sergeant," the lieutenant countered, irritably, "these people were engaged by the post commander. Are you trying to tell me that your post commander doesn't know what he's doing?"

"Not at all, no sir," the sergeant said patiently, "but, pardon my language, sir, that fella that calls himself scout is full of shit as a Christmas pie. I don't think he even knows where we are."

The lieutenant glared up from his camp table. "That will be enough, Sergeant."

"Yes sir."

After the sergeant left his tent, the lieutenant considered his misgivings but quickly banished the reservations gnawing in the back of his mind. Preferring to trust the overall wisdom of the army he served, he went to bed early, confident that they would strike water the following day.

The scout and his Tonkawa partners were still up after most of the bivouac had fallen asleep, agreeing, over their last bottle of whiskey, that their options were shrinking and that if conditions grew worse, they had best be ready to cut and run. They had hoped the Comanche war party would melt away, as they usually did, and that a return to the post would be ordered after a day or two of fruitless pursuit. But the trail was too clear and too hot to give up.

As the Tonkawas struggled to stay awake, the scout, undecided as to when would be the best time to make a break, told them to be ready to leave that night. They had already been paid and there was nothing to keep them. He fell asleep with the idea that he would nap for a couple of hours, then slip out of the wretched camp unnoticed.

None of the Comanches slept that night. They counciled not far from the streambed and decided that the enemy was sufficiently exhausted for an attack. Wind In His Hair sent two of his best warriors down to look the camp over, and when they returned with word that all was quiet and that five of the six men guarding the horses had fallen asleep, Wind In His Hair told everyone to prepare for a night assault.

An hour before dawn, nearly twenty warriors with Wind In His Hair at their head swept through the soldier camp, waving blankets, firing rifles, and splitting the still night air with ear-shattering screams that plunged everything before them into chaos.

They had not come to fight the soldiers but made straight for the army horses, which panicked as the commotion bore down on them. They reared and pitched and twisted in the air, ripping out the heavy metal picket pins that had held them anchored to the ground. The frantic animals galloped in all directions, some tearing back through the tents that had been pitched in the streambed. The anchor pins bounced wildly at the end of their lead lines, wreaking havoc on the canvas shelters and severely injuring several soldiers.

Wind In His Hair and his men succeeded in driving a large number of the terrified horses in the direction of a dozen more warriors, who by prearrangement were waiting downstream to receive them.

The whole operation began and ended in less than a minute. No Comanche suffered more than a scratch, and the enemy was instantly deprived of almost half his horses. Chances that all the hair-mouths could be destroyed were suddenly much better and Wind In His Hair nearly succumbed to the temptation to try to overwhelm the camp before it could come to its senses. But in a running council he convinced his exuberant warriors to wait one more sleep, to wait until the hair-mouths were dreaming of death. Then it would be much easier to kill them.

At the first howls of the warriors the scout and his Tonkawa cohorts put their plan into action and, by the time the Comanches had passed through, heading east after the horses, the three dubious guides had grabbed up their own animals and fled west.

During the upheaval, none of the soldiers realized that the guides were abandoning them, and in the confusion of trying to put the camp back together while simultaneously mounting a defense, no one bothered to count heads. It was long after sunup before anyone realized that the three individuals to whom they had entrusted their lives would not be coming back. Only the clique of veterans bothered to imagine what they would do to the cowards if they ever happened on them again.

Though the departure of the scouts had gone undetected by their employers, it did not escape the notice of the three warriors whom Wind In His Hair had posted west of the field camp to observe any man or animal fleeing in that direction.

Anxious to put distance between themselves and the fighting, the three deserters pushed their horses blindly into darkness, thinking that with the coming of light they would make a wide swing back to the east and safety.

But their plan was disrupted shortly after the first rosy hues of dawn appeared in the east, when one of the Tonkawas glanced over his shoulder and saw the silhouettes of three hatless horsemen cresting a rise a quarter-mile behind them. Alarmed, they paused momentarily in their flight and had barely begun to discuss whether to make a stand or run for it when they heard the curious, rushing whir of an arrow in flight. An instant later the shaft buried itself in the midsection of one of the

Tonkawas. With a low groan he slumped forward, then tumbled help-lessly from his horse.

The scout and his remaining assistant spun their horses and saw a young Comanche a few yards in front of them. As his horse danced under him, the Comanche drew a second arrow from his quiver.

Now they heard whoops and, turning once more, saw their three Comanche stalkers coming at a gallop. The remaining Tonkawa put heels to his horse. The scout slid his rifle from its case but as he raised it to take aim at the young Comanche he realized to his horror that he was too late. The boy's bow was drawn. The scout heard the bowstring sing and saw the arrow take flight. His hands flew to his throat as the shaft tore through his windpipe and sent him spilling over the rump of his horse. The scout lived long enough for a single look at the face of his killer, who stood over him with a look of wondrous shock.

Smiles A Lot had never expected to run into a white man and two Tonkawas at dawn on the open prairie. He had stopped following Wind In His Hair when night fell but when he woke in the dark, hearing gun-fire, he had jumped on his pony and sprinted toward the sound. Luckily, he had seen the white man and the Tonkawas before they had seen him and, guided by instinct he did not know he possessed, had strung an arrow and shot. From that moment all he remembered were images: the white man's rifle, the Tonkawa goading his horse, the battle cries of his friends, his pony squirming under him, his second arrow seeking its mark with a slowness that made him think he was dreaming.

Hears The Sunrise glanced at the two bodies in the grass, then stared at Smiles A Lot. That the boy who was good with horses had killed two of the enemy was indisputable, yet Hears The Sunrise still could not believe it.

"Where did you come from?" he asked gruffly, as he could not ques-tion what he had seen with his own eyes.

"I've been following you," Smiles A Lot replied.

A sharp yell drew their attention, and in the distance they saw Iron Jacket and Hawk Flying celebrating the death of their enemy. Their knives flashed in the early morning light as the figures slashed and hacked at the body of the hated Tonkawa.

"Where is Wind In His Hair?" Smiles A Lot said dully.

Hears The Sunrise tossed his head curtly over a shoulder. "Back there."

"I need to see him."

"I'll take you," Hears The Sunrise grunted, stepping over to the dead Tonkawa. He slipped a hand ax from his belt and spat on the body. Then he struck the corpse, slicing deep into its side with the blade of his ax.

Smiles A Lot gazed down at the dead white man. He looked the body up and down, and, guided by the same impulse that had brought death to the scout, he drew his skinning knife from its scabbard.

Deep into the afternoon the lieutenant and his troops waited behind the breastworks they had dug in the dry streambed for an attack that never came. They were sure the Indians would come back, but in the baking heat and dead air nothing moved or made a sound for hours, and at three o'clock the lieutenant assembled a scouting party of a dozen men on the best remaining horses and sent them out. An hour later they returned to report they had seen and heard nothing. The Indians had disappeared.

The lieutenant decided, quite rightly, that he should form up his command and get them back to the post before they died of thirst. With half the bedraggled, demoralized command on foot they started the long, hot march home. Two men were dead, one more would die on the way, and the lieutenant, though he tried mightily, could think of nothing to include in his report that might reflect well on his actions.

What rankled him most, however, was something similar to what had irritated Lawrie Tatum. The lieutenant had ridden out to chastise and scatter a band of ignorant, primitive aborigines led by a wild man with one eye. It should have been no contest, but they had toyed with him. They had killed his men and stolen his horses and then slunk back into the wilderness, leaving him with nothing to report to his superiors but failure.

CHAPTER XX

*D*ANCES WITH WOLVES WAS AS SURPRISED AS ANYONE WHEN the girl Hunting For Something and the boy Rabbit rode into his camp. They had come out of a night storm, drenched and exhausted, like castaways washed miraculously ashore, and the tale of survival they had to tell easily fulfilled the promise of their dramatic entrance.

From the moment he saw them, Dances With Wolves knew there had been a disaster, and as he listened numbly to the details of the devastation and its aftermath, he felt his soul altered in ways that could only be compared with the upheaval that marks the coming of death.

When the girl and boy were finished, he felt as if split in two. A part of him was still alive in the world, comforting his children, making preparations for a night march, and speculating on all that would need to be done to salvage what was left of his community.

The other part of him, separate and distinct from flesh and blood, was floating and rolling as helplessly as a corpse in the currents of an ever-changing river. Past and future had ceased and the present in which he dwelt was curiously inert, devoid of thought or feeling or expression. It was as if he had ceased to walk on the ground, relegated instead to float, rudderless, in the space between earth and sky.

Outwardly, he manifested none of this. In the three days it took for Hunting For Something and Rabbit to guide them back to the spot where Ten Bears and the survivors were sequestered, he clung to the warrior's performance of everyday duties: laying out routes of travel, grasping every opportunity to take game, helping other families with their loads, watching over his children, and maintaining a constant vigil for signs of enemies.

But, inwardly, Dances With Wolves no longer knew where he was. His disorientation was so complete that he himself could not describe it. The only evidence of his spiritual disengagement was a profound stoicism that gripped him and had even spread to his children. There was a dullness in their eyes, as if something vital inside had been extinguished, and while the three family members walked and talked like anyone else, they had become shadow people, people who neither came nor went, who stayed in one place no matter what they said or did.

There was much to do in the name of survival, and on reuniting with Ten Bears and the others who had escaped the attack, Dances With Wolves and his party of hunters threw themselves into the task of resurrecting what remained of their people. Though the hunters' packhorses were loaded with meat and untanned robes, there was not enough game to sustain them and the first order of business was to effect a move.

A day later they climbed onto the plains, secure in the knowledge that the practiced eyes of Kicking Bird and Wind In His Hair would be able to follow the trail. With so few horses most people were traveling on foot, but after two days of marching they reached a well-watered spot they had camped in before. Each heart was lifted by the presence of buffalo, whose sign was heavy and fresh in every direction.

There was no time to mount a long trek to the shining mountains for aspen but they were fortunate to find thick copses of cottonwood and elm within a few miles that yielded enough young trees to provide the framework for new lodges. Women and girls worked day and night, rubbing hides until every muscle ached, to provide the needed coverings, and in a few days' time a new village was rising on the plains.

The buffalo were found in such great numbers that at first glance it might have seemed like the old days, when all a man had to do was ride a few miles from his lodge to make meat. However, the animals to which the people of the plains owed their existence behaved oddly, as if they too had been scattered, but the bounty that flowed into the new village had the effect of a life-giving infusion, and by the time Kicking Bird and Wind In His Hair came in, both arriving on the same day, the village was remarkably well-established.

A week later, any prairie wanderer who happened by would have observed a strong Comanche village, perhaps a little shorter on horses than most, but well supplied with food and water, and a bustling population. But if the same traveler had been able to scratch through the veneer of the picture Ten Bears' restored village presented, he would have found the wreckage of what had once been a tight-knit society. The imaginary passerby would not have failed, upon closer inspection, to be struck by the spiritual fractures that divided the Comanches.

Preoccupied with rebuilding the community and maintaining life, the members of Ten Bears' village did not actively grapple with the weighty issues that had rent their hearts, at least not at first.

When he thought about what the future might bring, Ten Bears now found every avenue he might take barricaded by the obstacle of old age. Through his long reign as a headman he had never sought war. In fact, he had unfailingly counseled against its ravages. But now, with so many winters behind him, his influence in such matters barely existed.

He felt as impotent on the subject of peace. If a roving band of rangers could inflict such carnage on Comanches, what would happen if hair-mouth soldiers flooded the plains with the far-shooting guns that rolled on wheels? The Comanche and all they knew would be reduced to dust so fine that it could only be seen in a shaft of light before it settled on the earth.

In all his life he had learned nothing of the white man. He could count on one hand the times he had seen them. How could he begin to pursue peace with people he had never met? How could he meet such people? How could he talk to them? How could he understand them? He might as well dream of reaching up and pulling the moon from its eternal mooring.

All that Ten Bears could do was what he was doing now: sit in the shade of the arbor that had been erected next to his lodge and observe as best he could through his foggy eyes and pick at the bowl of pemmican Hunting For Something had brought. The afternoon sojourns he enjoyed had been disrupted, and the old man decided that the little value left in his existence could best be served by exercising the gift of listening to people's blood.

He passed several afternoons in this manner and had formed a number of useful conclusions. The people of the village, despite their industry, were still burdened by sorrow. They worked, but without the traditional gaiety that leavened labor. The children played, but joy was absent from their games. Coveys of women hauled water and tanned hides and cooked communal meals without the normal laughter. Impromptu gatherings of warriors were convened, but the manly spirit was missing.

Though he had always tended toward reticence, Kicking Bird had been positively mute since his return from Kiowa country. His way of looking forward had been a goad for activity but when Ten Bears saw him now, he was invariably alone. When he came close enough to offer a salutation, on one occasion squatting directly in front of Ten Bears for a brief inquiry as to his health, the old man had the opportunity to penetrate the mask of pain Kicking Bird wore in common with everyone else. What he saw were sparks and what he heard was a rushing of blood that made his ears ring. In the few seconds Kicking Bird sat before him, Ten Bears became convinced that the former medicine man was engaged deeply, turbulently, in thought. What he might be thinking Ten Bears did not know, but he was convinced that Kicking Bird was soon to leave the village again.

Wind In His Hair had come by a few times to acknowledge Ten Bears in the same fleeting fashion. The rangers had killed two of his wives and five of the seven children he had sired, but the great warrior made no mention of his family's demolition. Nor did he speak of his plans in their brief encounters, but the old man did not have to listen very hard to hear his blood—simply to know him was to know what Wind In His Hair would do. Like a cornered panther, Wind In His Hair would fight. When he might move, and with what force, was all that remained to be seen.

The blood of Dances With Wolves was the hardest to hear, and Ten Bears could only guess at the depth of his suffering. Just once had he stopped at the door of the lodge, and then he had barely spoken as he placed a prime cut of buffalo haunch inside the flap. Ten Bears had been sitting inside smoking and when their eyes met, Dances With Wolves had said, "For you, Grandfather," then ducked out of sight.

In subsequent days, Ten Bears saw him venture out to hunt only twice. The rest of the time he was indoors, and most often his children could be seen just outside their lodge, for they never went anywhere without their father. Snake In Hands no longer ran after snakes and Always Walking now stayed put, except in the company of their father. The boy and girl played with other children only if they came around, and Dances With Wolves had few visitors so far as Ten Bears could tell.

The old man viewed everything with the detachment of age. He had finally accepted what had come to pass, and the fretting he had engaged in so often before the ranger attack all but ceased. It was replaced now with a simple curiosity as to how everything might turn out, and nothing piqued his interest more than the goings-on in the lodge directly across the way from his own.

That particular lodge represented what was left of the joy in life for Ten Bears. It reminded him of the new growth that emerges from the prairie after the grass has been scorched to nothing by fire. He was thankful to be close enough to see the comings and goings there, and watching them was his only pleasure.

In normal times this family configuration could never have happened, but catastrophe had necessitated many odd jugglings of lives. The banding together of the three souls across the way violated more rules of tribal conduct than could be counted. In times past such a thing would not have been tolerated, and if a couple like the one living near Ten Bears had persisted they might face expulsion from the group, a punishment reserved for the most heinous public crimes.

But time and custom had been turned upside down, and not an eyebrow was raised against the union of Smiles A Lot and Hunting For Something and their surrogate son, Rabbit. Circumstance had deprived each of their families. She needed a provider and he needed a supporter. Together they were building something out of nothing and, far from being an embarrassment, they quickly became a prideful symbol of Comanche resilience. That the girl's grandfather, the venerable and unassailable Ten Bears, made no objection to the unsanctified union rendered it palatable to the strictest among them, and the young couple went about the business of life unimpeded.

As before, Hunting For Something came every day, making sure her grandfather had something to eat. Rabbit was in and out of the lodge at all hours, and most evenings Smiles A Lot kept the old man company for an hour or two, listening to stories of adventure and heroism and funny anecdotes.

The presence of this odd trio was a tonic for Ten Bears, invigorating him with a sense of belonging he had not felt since the last of his wives died. The old man sat in the shade of his arbor, his despair tempered by the closeness of his new, made-up family. *Good coming out of bad,* he often thought to himself, *it always happens. What will come next? Who knows? This arbor is a good place—I know that. Kicking Bird and Wind In His Hair and Dances With Wolves . . . does it matter what they are thinking? They are making up their minds. When they are ready they will come and talk with me. In the meantime, I am happy in this shade. There's a little breeze to make it just right. Is that her coming? . . . How I miss my young eyes.*

"Hunting For Something!"

"Hello, Grandfather."

CHAPTER XXI

*T*HE THREE WARRIORS UPON WHOSE ACTIONS THE FATE OF THEIR people might depend did make up their minds, just as Ten Bears knew they would, and they divulged their plans to him in separate visits on the same day.

Ten Bears had actually dreamt such a scenario the night before, and so he was not surprised when Kicking Bird appeared at his door in the early morning, asking to talk.

The two men smoked a pipe in silence, and when the bowl was exhausted, Ten Bears knocked the ash deftly into his flameless fire and said in an offhand way, "You have been thinking a lot."

Kicking Bird smiled. "Yes, Grandfather. I have been thinking since I came back from Touch The Clouds' camp."

He then revealed all that had happened during his visit to the Kiowas, describing in detail his encounter with the white man Lawrie Tatum, placing particular emphasis on the Quaker's offer of protection and support for those who loved peace and would be willing to follow the white man's "holy road."

As he finished his fascinating story, Kicking Bird withdrew his own pipe and tamped a few pinches of tobacco into the bowl.

"Did you smoke the pipe with this man?" Ten Bears asked.

"We smoked the pipe."

"His words were true?"

"There was nothing to show they were not. I have decided to go back up there and find Lawrie Tatum and talk to him some more."

Ten Bears nodded, then lapsed into thought. The men smoked in silence, passing Kicking Bird's pipe back and forth.

"I am wondering," Ten Bears began at last. "This white man's holy road . . . how can Comanches take a road they have never traveled . . . how can they take a road where everything is new and strange and still be Comanches? How can they be happy?"

Kicking Bird listened as he sucked at the pipe and sent a long stream of smoke curling toward the hole in Ten Bears' lodge.

"I don't know, Grandfather. But I want to see this Lawrie Tatum again and talk with him. Your question is good. It says a lot. But it makes a question come into my mind, a question that might be just as good. I think of the buffalo growing more scarce each summer. I think of white soldiers coming into the country. I think of these rangers tearing at our camp like starving wolves—killing our women and children, burning down our lodges. When I think of these things, I wonder what will happen if they continue. You ask how we can walk this holy road, and I wonder . . . how can we not?"

"Ahhh!" Ten Bears exclaimed as he passed back the pipe. "Your question is a good one, too. It vexes me greatly. When will you see this—how do you say it?—Loree Taydum again?"

"We will leave at sunup. Perhaps you should come with us."

"Me? No . . . no . . . I'm good here, but if you come back and tell me the Loree Taydum man is a good one and that all his promises are true and that an old man like me can be happy on his holy road, maybe then I will go."

Kicking Bird smiled and started to his feet.

"Who goes with you?" Ten Bears asked.

"Whoever wants to."

"Well," the old man cautioned, "don't take the whole village. Those rangers might come back again."

"No, Grandfather," Kicking Bird assured him, "I won't do that."

The sun had passed the midway point in its daily journey and Ten

Bears had just settled himself in the arbor with a bowl of Hunting For Something's pemmican when he glanced up to see the confident figure of Wind In His Hair striding toward him.

"Can I speak with you, Grandfather?" the one-eyed warrior asked respectfully.

"I always like to talk with Wind In His Hair."

"I don't have my pipe."

"Nor do I. Mine's in the lodge."

"I can bring it."

"That's not necessary," Ten Bears said, moving over to make room in the arbor. "Wind In His Hair's heart is always true. Come and sit down."

Wind In His Hair settled next to the man he had known all his life and came straight to the point.

"What has happened must be avenged, Grandfather."

"It has always been so," Ten Bears agreed. "But I wonder," he continued, setting his food bowl to one side. "Your father fought the whites, and his father before him. You have fought white people. It seems that after all these winters, almost too many to be counted, that the only thing this fighting has brought us is more white people. After every fight there are fewer Comanches. Maybe we should start looking for ways to walk the peace road."

Wind In His Hair gazed out at the village for such a long time that Ten Bears picked up his bowl and resumed eating. When Wind In His Hair spoke again his eyes were still fixed somewhere in front of him.

"I am different from what I used to be, Grandfather. I'm getting older, and I love peace more. I like to be with One Braid Trailing and our children. But I will always be a warrior, a Hard Shield. I will be that when I die. There will never be peace if an enemy can kill us whenever he likes, can burn our homes and steal our horses without being punished. That is not peace. Peace can't be made when one is strong and the other is weak. Both must be strong. The whites will keep killing us until the Comanches are no more . . . if we let them. How can I let them feast on us and toss our bones to one side? A Comanche cannot do that."

Again a silence descended in the arbor and, as if sent to fill it, a sudden gust of summer's breeze brought the dry leaves hanging on its boughs to life. Then Ten Bears spoke again.

"I am old now and people think I am wise. I am not. I do not know what road to take. All I know is that it makes my old heart glad to hear Wind In His Hair's words."

"Thank you, Grandfather."

"When will you leave?"

"I have sent runners to tell White Bear that the Comanche are making a war on the whites. When he will come, I don't know. We will make a big party of the bravest Comanche and Kiowa. Then we will go."

"Don't take the whole village."

"No, Grandfather, I won't do that."

Ten Bears watched him walk away. Long after his form had blurred and disappeared, the old man was still thinking about Wind In His Hair. He thought about him so hard that Ten Bears' eyes began to run. He bent his head and, as his tears wet the dust next to his feet, he realized that he was mourning. Wind In His Hair would be killed, and his passing would take the strongest, most beautiful bloom of Comanche warriorhood. After Wind In His Hair, there would be no more.

A few hours later, Ten Bears was lying on his side, watching the afternoon shadows begin their long crawl through his open door when a pair of legs came into view at the lodge entrance and Dances With Wolves' voice floated inside.

"Grandfather? Are you in there?"

Pushing himself up to a sitting position, Ten Bears answered, "Yes, yes. Come in, Dances With Wolves."

The tall warrior ducked through the flap, followed by his two children, and for a moment they all stood awkwardly.

"Sit down in my home," Ten Bears urged. Dances With Wolves said nothing to his boy and girl but indicated the ground with the flat of his hand and the three sat, the children just behind their father.

"Do you have any tobacco?" Ten Bears asked. "Mine is almost gone. It seems everyone is coming to see me today."

"Of course, Grandfather, we can smoke my pipe."

Dances With Wolves slipped his pipe out of its beaded case and went about the business of loading it. In those few moments, Ten Bears had an opportunity to study his face and felt profound concern at what it told him.

The whites of his eyes were stained red. The face was creased with lines and the lips gave the impression that they might be permanently pursed. His hair was unkempt, his face unwashed, and his fingers quivered as if seized with palsy as he pushed tobacco into the pipe's bowl.

When it was filled, he passed it respectfully to Ten Bears, who lit it with a brand from the small fire he had built.

"You've got two good children there," Ten Bears remarked, passing the pipe back across the fire.

"Yes," Dances With Wolves agreed, "I'm lucky to have them."

The children stared mutely at their crossed legs. Dances With Wolves did not speak anymore and Ten Bears felt an unexpected shudder of pity for the sad trio.

"Do you sleep?" he asked Dances With Wolves.

The question seemed to stir the warrior's lethargy. He stared across the fire as if he had never heard such a question.

"I don't know," he replied. "Awake, asleep . . . it's hard to know the difference."

He gazed, trancelike, at Ten Bears and for a moment the headman thought Dances With Wolves' face was going to break apart.

"Oh, Grandfather . . ." he gasped, closing his eyes and letting his head fall until his chin touched his chest.

"Snake In Hands . . . Always Walking," Ten Bears called in little more than a whisper. The children looked up. "You know that boy Rabbit, Smiles A Lot's little brother?"

Snake In Hands nodded and his sister followed suit.

"He's lonely for friends these days. He lives just across there. Why don't you go over and see if he's home?"

Both children looked to their father. He hadn't moved.

"Go ahead," Ten Bears prodded gently, "have some fun."

Hesitantly the children began to rise.

"Go ahead," Ten Bears encouraged. "Go."

They turned and went out and Ten Bears looked once again at the downcast warrior with the closed eyes sitting across from him.

Dances With Wolves still had not moved and it occurred to Ten Bears that the way he held himself, so still and defeated, told the full story of his suffering. He reached across the fire and laid a leathery hand on the pair hanging limply in his visitor's lap.

"Dances With Wolves," he whispered.

Dances With Wolves slowly lifted his head and stared dully at Ten Bears.

"I'm glad you came to see me," the old man smiled. "What is in your heart?"

"I am only waiting."

"Waiting for what?"

"I am waiting for Wind In His Hair to make his war on the whites. I will ride with him."

"Hmmm," the old man grunted.

"Then I will keep riding," Dances With Wolves intoned.

"What do you mean?" Ten Bears was suddenly puzzled.

"I mean to get my family back."

"But that is not possible."

The simple act of talking seemed to refresh Dances With Wolves. Color was returning to his face and little explosions of light shone in his eyes as he spoke.

"I alone can move among the whites and not be seen."

"But you are a Comanche."

A small, sly smile spread across Dances With Wolves' lips.

"That is true," he said, "but the color of my skin has not changed."

Ten Bears' face tightened in concentration. He had never heard such a wild idea.

"But how will you talk? How will you eat?" He looked Dances With Wolves up and down. "You cannot look as you do now."

"I won't look like this."

Ten Bears dropped his gaze to the flickering fire. That men could turn into animals or animals to men was not unheard of, but such a thing as Dances With Wolves spoke of now—this he could not imagine. To think that a Comanche could turn into a white person was beyond him.

The children suddenly burst through the door. Rabbit was with them.

"Father," Snake In Hands started breathlessly, "Rabbit knows where to find snakes near the stream—lots of snakes. He wants to show me."

"Go then," Dances With Wolves said. "Take your sister."

Snake In Hands pushed Rabbit and Always Walking through the door and they hurried off to the stream, shouts of excitement fading in their wake.

"Have you spoken to your children of this?" Ten Bears asked.

"No."

"What will you do with them?"

"They will stay in camp."

Ten Bears shook his head.

"I always thought that one parent is better than none," he said.

"There will be two when I return. That is the best."

"I cannot see how that can happen," Ten Bears said stubbornly. "All I can see is two Comanche children with neither mother nor father."

"But, Grandfather . . ." Dances With Wolves leaned forward a little, with more life in his voice and eyes than Ten Bears had seen since the ranger attack. "They are alive. If they were dead we would continue. They are not dead, but speaking their names only brings sorrow. No one can live like that. I know the whites. I can do this thing. I can get her back. I can get Stays Quiet back. Maybe I will die, but we cannot live as we are living now."

Again the sly smile flitted across Dances With Wolves' face. "Maybe I will succeed, Grandfather . . . maybe we will all be together again."

For a moment Dances With Wolves looked like a mischievous boy and Ten Bears chuckled at his audacity.

"Maybe you will," the old man said, "maybe you will. Who am I to say you won't? I am not the Mystery."

CHAPTER XXII

*W*HEN KICKING BIRD DEPARTED, TAKING THE STAUNCHEST advocates for peace with him, Wind In His Hair's war agenda, having nothing to blunt it, became the single topic of discussion in Ten Bears' village. As always there was debate, but the open, free-flowing talk of war with the whites seemed to invigorate everyone's spirits.

Talk alone, however, was not enough to pull people out of the stagnancy they had become accustomed to. A spark of ignition—some sign or event that would set off the frenzy necessary to take the war trail—was missing. There was nothing inside a village laden with grief to provide combustion, and the likeliest possibility for such impetus lay to the north. That was where White Bear would be coming from. But a week after Kicking Bird had gone, there was still no sign of them and war talk began to flag.

Wind In His Hair grew more and more frustrated. Though most warriors agreed that a war must be made, the majority had assiduously avoided the kind of blazing commitment that would galvanize the village, and seeing that his zeal alone would not be sufficient to move men out of their lodges, Wind In His Hair curtailed his advocacy of war. If he kept on and the talk did not boil into action, the idea of war would never amount to anything more and his standing would plummet.

The great warrior seemed to become more sullen with each day the Kiowa did not turn up. His conversations were curt and acerbic, and instead of spending his evenings calling on fellow warriors, he withdrew to his lodge. There he chewed bitterly on his fading prospects, wondering if the Mystery was abandoning the Comanche. It had been almost a moon since he had sent his runners north, and Wind In His Hair began to think that if he had stayed in the becalmed camp much longer his smoldering frustration might catch fire and consume him.

On a day when his restlessness was near the breaking point a runner appeared with the exciting news that the Kiowa were coming. A powerful line of horsemen from the north were sighted that afternoon, and an hour later the Comanche band that had suffered so terribly was in a delirium as nearly eighty solemn Kiowa fighters, led by the formidable White Bear, entered the village.

The heavily armed warriors were painted, many of them from head to toe, in the brilliant reds and blacks of war. Their ponies were decorated with symbols of hail and lightning and, as Ten Bears' people swarmed around the procession that snaked its way through the village, the Kiowa maintained the bellicose expressions of men determined to meet and vanquish any enemy.

For the remainder of that day and long into the night, fear and doubt were suspended as the village recalled the unchallenged supremacy they had enjoyed for generations.

A huge group of women and children, carrying all that was needed for a temporary camp, had traveled in the van of the great procession, and a large Kiowa camp was erected adjacent to that of Ten Bears.

Feasting and visiting were conducted almost as an afterthought as the combined camps exulted in a feverish daydream of a war against the whites that would bring honor to individuals and retribution for a whole people—a blow delivered straight to the heart that would send the enemy reeling, wounding him so vitally that all thought of further incursion would be forgotten.

Women worked with revitalized spirit as they made sure their men would lack nothing when they went into battle. Gangs of children staged mock battles all over the outlying prairie, and cells of warriors met constantly to trumpet their worthiness and compare strategic experience in fighting whites.

Toward twilight, women and children put finishing touches on the huge fire that would blaze in the center of the village while the war party's leaders, Wind In His Hair, White Bear, and a dozen others including Dances With Wolves, paid a visit to Owl Prophet.

The prophet handed out pinches of mole dirt to each man, instructing them to sprinkle the grains of freshly excavated earth over the withers of their ponies before engaging the enemy. Then he had them wait outside his lodge while he consulted with the Mystery.

Silhouettes of owl and man glowed behind the skin of the medicine man's tent and a long, indecipherable conversation commenced. Though they understood nothing, the warriors hung on every word until at last, in a cacophony of unearthly screeching, the outlines of man and bird fell out of view.

A few moments later, Owl Prophet emerged to give a short, exhausted account that told the warriors what had transpired.

"You will meet two forces of white men. The first you must let pass. Attack only the second. Attack the first and disaster will befall you. Attack the second and you will kill many whites. Attack the second and you shall have victory."

A chorus of unruly cheers erupted and, as Owl Prophet stumbled back into his lodge, the excited leaders hurried back to their homes to prepare for the great dance of bravado that was to begin shortly.

As darkness fell, the populace watched Ten Bears pause in silent prayer before applying a glowing faggot to the tinder at the edge of the great fire. At the same moment, as flames licked upward and sparks spewed into the blackness of the night sky, four Kiowa musicians sitting cross-legged around a drum began to beat out an ominous cadence that reverberated through the village like approaching thunder. The deliberate cadence grew stronger and stronger, its insistent pulse gradually insinuating itself into the bloodstreams of the waiting warriors.

Hears The Sunrise and a young Kiowa named Trotting Wolf, unable to resist the power of the drum, entered the empty circle first. The men alternated from one leg to another, lifting and dropping their feet in perfect unison with each ringing vibration of the echoing drum.

Many other warriors stepped methodically into the circle and it was soon crowded with dancers moving as one body to the irresistible, repetitive beat.

Imperceptibly, the rhythm picked up speed, gradually animating the dancers and driving some of them to utter spontaneous cries which seemed to spill not from their mouths but from hidden recesses of their viscera.

At a signal not so much seen as felt, the Kiowa drummers suddenly ceased and a waiting Comanche cadre took over, the new arms and hands and hearts seamlessly lifting the concussive rhapsody to new heights. Several drum groups had assembled and as one flowed into another, the furious climax of the last was carried to new heights by the next.

The dancers followed as the drummers led them unerringly toward a sublime oblivion where no pretense is brooked in the abandonment of self. Warriors transformed themselves into namesake animals. They unsheathed their knives and raised their lances and strung their bows and stalked the enemy. Always in time to the drum, they lifted war clubs and smote the enemy. They slashed and scalped and pierced him over and over and over with the points of their spears. All the while their battle cries grew louder and sharper as each warrior played out his destiny in what was more a dress rehearsal for war than a dance.

At unscripted intervals the drums would suddenly fall back to the single grave beat that had marked the beginning. Then the cycle was repeated, again and again.

After several hours, a few warriors began to withdraw. Others collapsed and were dragged, senseless, from the circle by their relatives. The majority danced on, stretching the limits of their stamina to unknown realms, surrendering every measure of energy they possessed in hope of achieving an unconquerable purity of purpose.

The stars were beginning to fade when the outpouring reached its climax. Comanche and Kiowa drummers, ignorant of fatigue, had mingled, feeding off the competitive power in limbs whose muscles were driven by indomitable will. Guided by like forces, the dancers had become a turbulent sea of gyrating bodies whose voices ruled the night with a tumult of howls and moans and cries and shrieks flying heavenward in a single, thunderous, rolling roar.

High-pitched trills of encouragement from the swaying women massed in a huge circle around the warriors joined the gigantic eruption of sound and motion that fused each heart and mind, creating a force free of earthbound constraints, a force straining with all its spiritual might to coalesce with the supreme power of creation.

CHAPTER XXIII

*S*MILES A LOT WAS A MEMBER OF THE GREAT CONGREGATION dancing around the fire that night.

No one had questioned his joining the warrior ranks, an action that, considering his lack of standing, would have been unthinkable in the past. But times were different now. Very young boys like Snake In Hands had gone among the warriors. Every soul was more precious than ever and every soul was welcome.

It had taken courage for Smiles A Lot to move his feet forward to the call of the drums, but once he was in the circle his steps grew stronger with each one taken, and by the time the first round of dancing reached its climax, his body, fixed in the grip of music and fire and the blackness of night, was moving without thought.

Smiles A Lot had been one of the exhilarated warriors left inside the circle when the drums finally ceased. He had danced for hours, but his body had crossed the narrow threshold that normally separates exhaustion from renewal. Far from being tired, Smiles A Lot felt positively airy. His feet were light, his blood flowed unimpeded, and his head was clear as a cloudless day. It was natural that such rapture would guide his gaze to the face in the surrounding circle which brought him incalculable joy, and a few moments after the drums ceased he looked in that direction.

She had been watching all night and when she saw him look her way she flashed the shy, closemouthed smile that had marked the start of his lovesickness. Yet in a subtle way the smile was different. Its shyness was newly tinged with a familiarity that made it knowing, and the effect on him was more entrancing than ever.

Smiles A Lot and Hunting For Something had touched but only in the accidental way people living under the same roof often do. They had not slept together or embraced or nuzzled or even held each other's hands. They had talked of many things, but only obliquely about their feelings for one another. To surmise, however, that theirs was a union of convenience would have been wrong. No young couple was ever happier than Smiles A Lot and Hunting For Something. That they had not touched was of no importance, for reality had supplanted their mutual, despairing dreams of being together with a magnificent new dream, a dream that floated them through each day and laid them down each night in an inconceivably effortless way. Night was the most difficult part of existence because thoughts of each other circled so furiously in their heads that both shuddered at the thought of making a physical overture.

But while she watched him dance, a curious feeling crept over Hunting For Something. She wasn't sure what it might mean, but the sensation was intoxicating. All she knew for sure was that she had never imagined that such a feeling of pride could exist within her for a man. He had danced until the end, but long before that he had begun to attract attention for the compelling way in which he moved. He was so committed and animated in his actions that he had danced all night on the narrow edge of disaster. But he had never gone over, and to Hunting For Something he distinguished himself as one of the few who abandoned themselves to the dance with the relentless, unstoppable bravery a true warrior exhibits in battle.

Her observation that experienced warriors noted his commitment reinforced the honors he had received for killing two of the enemy, erasing all traces of doubt she might have had in his ability to provide the security every Comanche woman expected from a man.

And to see him boldly take his place in a pair of moccasins, a set of leggings, and a battle shirt fringed with the scalps of slain foes she had fashioned with her own hands swelled her heart to bursting. She even had an intimate connection with the bow and arrows he carried on his back all night. The first time Smiles A Lot hunted for her he had killed a large panther and carried it all the way back to camp. She had skinned it and cleverly constructed a bow case and quiver from its hide. There was nothing like it in camp and it had drawn many comments for its beauty and uniqueness.

Hunting For Something's happiness was so complete that she could not bear to look his way for long, and, leaving him to converse with the other warriors, she hurried back to their lodge to recheck the items she had gathered for the dangerous journey he was to embark on the next day.

Her heart jumped when she heard him coming in but she continued tidying his bed and poured fresh water into a bowl before she felt composed enough to look at him.

His face was painted black with red half-circles around his eyes. In the separate world of the dance it was fitting, but here it made her uneasy.

"You scare me now."

Smiles A Lot touched his face with a finger. "The paint?"

"It makes me afraid."

Smiles A Lot grinned and nodded his head. "Good," he said, "maybe it will make the enemy afraid, too."

He reached down for the water bowl and she handed it up. Then he sat in front of her and splashed water on his face.

"Are you tired?" she asked, handing him a cloth.

"Yes, I feel good."

While his eyes were covered with a cleaning rag, Smiles A Lot heard her say, "You were the best."

"I was just dancing," he said and shrugged.

For reasons that mystified the new warrior, Hunting For Something seemed suddenly frustrated.

"I thought you were the best," she said, rising defiantly off the floor. "Good night."

Helplessly, he watched her step past the bed where Rabbit was sleeping and slip huffily into her own.

Smiles A Lot wanted to ask what was wrong but she had turned her face away. All he could see was the back of her head. He finished rubbing the paint off his face, slipped out of his clothes, slid under the covers of his own bed, and tried to think of tomorrow.

But he could not maintain a single line of thought. The girl lying a few steps away kept intruding and he had just begun to think of how he might find the courage to go to her when he heard a rustling of covers.

A moment later she was standing over him in the half-light of the dying fire, staring down with an odd look on her face.

"I want to sleep with you," she said emphatically, and before Smiles A Lot could respond, she was pulling her dress over her head. In what seemed one motion she dropped the dress and lay down beside him, stretching her long, skinny frame straight out as she nestled against his chest.

"There," she sighed, snaking an arm under his and pulling herself closer. "This is how it should be."

He could feel her moist breath as she whispered against his shoulder. He could smell the fragrance of her skin. The pressure of her lithe body was the most wonderful thing he had ever felt.

"You make me happy," he whispered. "I don't want anybody but Hunting For Something."

As he said this he pulled her closer and he could feel her lips brush the skin on his shoulder. Her free hand stole softly onto his chest and didn't move, and Smiles A Lot thought briefly that he might levitate off the bed.

"I want a baby," she murmured.

One of her legs slipped between his, and Smiles A Lot's mind ceased to function under the barrage of tactile sensations that overwhelmed it. His body lost its tension as it melted into hers and they writhed under the covers as two snakes entwined, groping, twisting, undulating in celebration of instinct. The awkwardness of novices was flung aside as they feverishly searched out one another, and even as she cried out, Hunting For Something urged him on. By then Smiles A Lot was past all need of encouragement, and the perfection of the collision that came soon after left them stupefied.

After a few minutes he rolled to one side but she did not move. Her glistening eyes stared into space while her shoulders and chest heaved for breath.

He watched her dreamily, his fingers playing with a thick strand of her shiny, black hair.

"I think I have it," she whispered blankly.

"What?"

"A baby."

A look of puzzlement appeared on Smiles A Lot's face.

"How do you know that?"

"I feel different."

"Maybe we should do it again."

She shifted her eyes to his and smiled. "I would like that," she said.

"I've heard that some people have to do it a lot to get a baby," he said, laughing.

Hunting For Something turned her face to the shadowy rafters overhead.

"You have to come back," she commanded.

Smiles A Lot lay back then, and together the lovers contemplated the nothingness above them.

"Warriors die sometimes," he said softly.

"I'll pray to the Mystery every day," she countered. "I'll pray to the Mystery all the time you're gone."

She talked on a few minutes more before she realized her husband had fallen asleep. Hunting For Something lay as she was, swathed in the fertile, pungent odor of their lovemaking, her sleepy, unfocused eyes staring into the Mystery as she marveled at the incontestable change that had taken place deep in her body.

Then she, too, fell into a leaden sleep, which passed uninterrupted until first light, when she woke to find Rabbit's bright, inquisitive eyes gazing at her. Sometime during the night the boy had wedged himself between them.

"What are you doing here, little brother?" she asked drowsily.

"I got lonely. Is this how we will sleep from now on?"

"Where's your brother?"

"He's here."

Rabbit turned impulsively and began to shake his sleeping brother.

"Smiles A Lot, wake up. . . . Smiles A Lot!"

While Hunting For Something packed his food and accoutrements, Smiles A Lot chose three excellent ponies from his herd and set to work in front of the lodge painting crow symbols on the tough little dapple-gray that had carried him to the Medicine Bluff and back.

At mid-morning, Dances With Wolves appeared with his dejected children to ask Hunting For Something if she would look after them in his absence. Her heart opened to the gloomy children being left behind and she promised to take good care of them.

Smiles A Lot had been selected, along with Dances With Wolves and a few other seasoned warriors, to scout the advance for the main column, and they disappeared to make final arrangements with their compatriots.

In the time they were gone, Snake In Hands and Always Walking sat as listlessly as the condemned, a demeanor they maintained through the riotous, village-wide send-off for the more than one hundred cherished warriors who rode onto the plains a few hours later.

This time a score of warriors, among them several Hard Shields, had been left behind. The village was secure, and Hunting For Something was happy when Rabbit, Snake In Hands, and Always Walking went on an egg-hunting expedition, leaving her free to daydream about Smiles A Lot through the afternoon.

But she began to worry when there was no sign of the children at sunset and her heart jumped with fear when Rabbit came in alone just after dark.

"Where are Snake In Hands and Always Walking?"

"They're gone," the boy answered impassively.

"Gone? Where?"

"They went after Dances With Wolves."

"What?" cried Hunting For Something, her voice rising. "When did they go?"

"Oh, a long time ago."

"Why didn't you tell me?"

"They made me promise not to tell anyone till after dark."

Hunting For Something's hand had gone over her mouth and she was staring wide-eyed at nothing as her mind ran with all manner of tragic possibilities.

"Were they on foot?" she asked, suddenly hopeful.

"No, no, they took ponies . . . and food, too."

Rabbit's attention was momentarily diverted to a kettle hanging over the fire.

"Can I have something to eat?"

But there was no answer and when he turned to see why, all he caught was a glimpse of Hunting For Something's backside as she ducked out of the lodge.

CHAPTER XXIV

*B*ECAUSE HIS MOTHER WAS A KIOWA HE HAD VISITED THE
Medicine Bluff country often as a boy and knew it almost as well as his
own homeland.

Kicking Bird was thinking of his mother as he passed by the great
bluff. He could not remember much of her now, but her cheerful nature
came to mind, and suddenly he could see her doubled over in laughter at
the telling of a funny story.

She had been killed, along with many others, in his eighth summer,
when the Pawnee overran the village they were visiting, a site easily visible from the top of the bluff he was passing just then. Much of the village
had gone out to cull buffalo from the first big herd of the season, but his
mother had stayed behind to care for a dying aunt. The Pawnee killed
them all, chopping off their heads, which they stuck in cooking pots.
These they lined up in front of the village, a macabre greeting for the
hunters when they returned home. The attack was avenged, just as bru-
tally, two years later, but Kicking Bird remembered that it had done little to assuage his loss.

Strangely, the bitter recollection of his good-natured mother's death
spawned a host of other, more pleasant memories. At the top of the bluff

above him he had first drawn a girl into his blanket, a girl whom he sub-
sequently lost to a worthless man she later divorced. A stand of oak at the
spot where the creek turned just ahead had yielded his first deer. A mile
or two to the south he had won a hotly contested horse race, riding
against the finest ponies on the plains. And a few miles ahead, eerily near
his destination, Kicking Bird had first slain an enemy.

That so much of his own life had been played out in the area he was
now passing through had meaning for him personally, but to the Kiowa
nation the importance of the great Medicine Bluff and its environs was
far greater. It was the beating heart in the body of a country they had
dominated through all living memory. For the whites to have taken root
in this of all places was practically inconceivable. That he, Kicking Bird,
a Comanche warrior, was actually going to call on a white representative
living within sight of the shrinelike bluff was so outlandish as to be hard
to believe, even when the odd-looking box made of wood that the whites
called a "house" came into view.

It was situated at the top of a rise, and to Kicking Bird's eyes it looked
like a very square, very white rock. Surrounding it was a white fence
made of stitched-together wood with tips shaped like arrowheads. He
could see vegetation growing in a large plot behind the house. Nestled in
several neat rows among the green mass he recognized a commodity
called corn, which the Comanches sometimes traded for with tribes who
lived far to the west.

The house was fronted by a long, shady porch. A group of white
men, some of them wearing soldier coats, their faces sunk in the over-
hang's shadow, stood expectantly, and as he started up the hill, Kicking
Bird saw the diminutive figure of Lawrie Tatum raise an arm in greeting.

The gesture, however, did little to reassure Kicking Bird. A group of
armed soldiers were hanging around some wagons a few paces from
Lawrie Tatum's house, and the presence of so many white men, including those clustered on the porch, had the effect of shrinking the Quaker
down to nothing.

At the same time, Kicking Bird's sense of being Comanche expanded, and as they pulled up in front of the bright white box, the dis-
tinctiveness of the two races, and the gulf dividing them, seemed too
enormous to ever be bridged.

Had he been alone, Kicking Bird would likely have been unable to come this far, and though he could not know their minds at this unprecedented moment, he took courage from the company of strong, wise warriors who surrounded him: Touch The Clouds and Little Mountain and Eagle Head and Pacer of the Kiowa, Sitting In The Saddle and Shield and Big Bow and Gap In The Woods of the Comanche.

In the face of the most perplexing situation they had ever encountered, the confederation of warriors approached the porch as a solemn, single body, and when the little Quaker with the ecstatic smile stuck out his hand, Kicking Bird took it.

Introductions were made all around, and despite not knowing who the hodgepodge of military and civilian hair-mouths were, or what their standing might be, Kicking Bird and his fellow peace-seekers took each white hand that was offered before being ushered off the porch and guided down the hill to an expansive tent that had been pitched in a shady spot to receive them.

Ever astute, Kicking Bird's mind worked furiously as they walked to the meeting place, rapidly sorting the bits of information that were flying into his head, but by the time they had begun to seat themselves in the big soldier tent, he realized it was useless to strain for enlightenment as to what role the strange men he was meeting with would play.

As he lit his pipe and passed it to Touch The Clouds, his deceptively impassive eyes trolled for any flicker of behavior in the whites that might throw light on what sort of men they were. The first thing he noticed, a thing so obvious that it was evident to all, was the configuration of the whites. The man who knew the Indian words was sitting off to one side while the rest placed themselves in two rows: a large grouping in the second row but only two men, a soldier and a civilian, in the first.

Lawrie Tatum was insinuated in the back row of hair-mouths and, seeing him there, Kicking Bird realized at once that the genial Quaker did not possess the power of the two men sitting at the forefront.

A heavy, gray-flecked beard covered the whole of the civilian's face. It circled his lips, accenting the dark, moist cave of his mouth. His skin—what little could be seen of it—had an unhealthy-looking, reddish hue, his eyes were small, and it was impossible to ignore the pitted, corpulent nose that seemed less a part of his countenance than it did an attachment.

His belly filled his shirt to bursting, his fingers had the appearance of fatty stubs, and he wheezed audibly with each breath, as if something were stuck in his throat.

The other white man, the soldier, had a smooth, unblemished face. His soldier clothes were as trim as his body and the buttons and bars clinging to his coat gleamed golden even in the murky summer light filling the tent. He had dark, shiny hair that covered his head like a cap, and his light-blue eyes were partially crossed and seemed not to move. Exceedingly thin lips were drawn neatly over hidden teeth, and his nose, in sharp contrast to that of his counterpart, was long and sharp as a fox's.

Taken together, these visual details conveyed a sense of quiet command, but for Kicking Bird and his friends one salient feature of the soldier's appearance outstripped all others combined. Three fingers of his left hand were no longer fingers but uneven stumps which peeked out angrily from the sleeve of his coat.

Even more intriguing was the fact that the ruined fingers made sounds. At irregular times during the talk that afternoon, at the prompting of some hidden cue in the soldier's heart, they were rubbed together to produce an odd, clicking noise. Where this sound came from, whether from skin or mangled joints, one couldn't say. The quirk impressed the Indian delegation for it deepened the mystery of the delicate, cross-eyed soldier, and though he remained Mackenzie to the whites, from that day forward the aboriginal people of the plains knew him as Bad Hand.

When the smoking, which every white man respectfully took part in, was finished, the white civilian whose name was Hatton rose to make a talk, which, owing to the labor of translation, took most of an hour. Hatton explained that he had been sent by the Great Father in Washington to seek peace with Indian people and outlined in general terms what the Kiowa and Comanche could expect from concord with the whites.

He then laid out the key elements of the offer. The initial inducement was a promise of presents by the wagonload. Among the incredible array of items offered was tobacco, clothing, cooking utensils, weapons, mirrors, trade cloth, farming implements, sugar, coffee, building materials, candy for children, hats for men, combs for women. Hatton told them there was more but that the list of goods that would flow unceasingly from the cornucopia of white civilization was too long to recite.

Washington was also offering to set aside a vast tract of land called a reservation that would constitute a permanent sanctuary for the Kiowa and Comanche. In this place they and their families could peacefully prepare to take the white man's road, a road which was open to all the red children of God.

Education would be open to everyone, especially children. The standing of headmen would be preserved. Food would be provided in the form of rations, including the fresh meat of cattle. People could camp together in traditional bands. Soldiers would be garrisoned nearby with the twin tasks of keeping order among Indian residents and protecting them against white incursion. Interpreters, agents, merchants, and many others working for the welfare of Indian people as they assimilated were already being mobilized to support the effort.

By a single action, all these things could be made available to peace-loving people. Those who touched the pen to a thing called "enrollment" would find themselves free to pursue a new life in which no one would go hungry and no one would be attacked by enemies.

The Kiowa and Comanche had listened to all this with mute attention and the abject silence continued for a few moments after Hatton had finished. Then Touch The Clouds rose, his nearly seven-foot frame requiring the white emissaries to gaze upward at an uncomfortable, neck-bending angle.

"I have heard this talk," he began. "It is good to hear and makes me glad I have taken your hands."

When this was translated, the white emissaries, sensing acceptance, smiled at one another in congratulation. But as Touch The Clouds continued, their smiles gradually faded with the realization that their feelings of satisfaction were premature.

"Touch The Clouds is only one man," he said. "I have but one voice, but I think we do not need what you want to give us. I love my country. The bones of my ancestors are everywhere in it. It has everything we need. Kiowa people are happy to walk on it. Why should we give up something we love so much? I can see no good reason for me or my people to throw away happiness."

The faces of the whites turned blank. Some of them had become restless and there was a persistent shifting in the two rows of listeners.

When Touch The Clouds sat down, Kicking Bird rose, and in his imagination he felt his upward motion carrying him into the sky and beyond. The well-being he had felt when he got off his pony in front of Lawrie Tatum's house had been growing all afternoon. Now, as he paused to look over the crowd of whites he was about to address, Kicking Bird's psyche expanded and rose until it was floating over the heads of the hair-mouths, and his natural curiosity was displaced by a stone-hard resolve to speak exactly what lay in his Comanche heart.

"Touch The Clouds has spoken as I would speak. His words are good and it makes my heart glad to hear them. I love my country as a child loves its mother. I love my people in the same way a father loves his son. I was born out on the plains and that is where I want to die."

Kicking Bird detected a small smile in the beard that covered most of Lawrie Tatum's face but the slight expression of support barely registered. The words poured from his mouth with a fluency that made it seem as though someone else might be speaking them, and as he stood before the white men, he imagined that what he was saying was rolling over his listeners like some magical vapor.

"It is good that the Great Father in Washington looks for peace. It makes me happy to take the hand of white men in friendship, because I seek peace as well. But we do not need what you are offering. All we need from white people is to be left alone. We need white people to stop killing the buffalo. I have been told many times that the white man loves money above all things. Maybe you can understand when I tell you that the buffalo is our money. What would white men feel if all their money was taken away? The buffalo was given us by the Great Mystery to feed and clothe ourselves. The buffalo is more than money . . . he is our brother . . . blood-related to all of us. When he is carried away, our hearts go with him. This must stop before there can be peace between us."

Commissioner Hatton wriggled his sizeable bottom from side to side and cleared his throat.

"The Great Father and all his people decreed several summers ago that no one can hunt buffalo south of the Red River."

"Then it must be that the Great Father's promises are no stronger than any other white man's, because there are more of these hunters in our country than ever before. They are hard to kill because they have far-shooting guns, but we do what we can. What does the Great Father do to stop people he has forbidden to come into our country? I have never seen them punished."

What Kicking Bird said begged a response and, in the silence that followed, all eyes turned toward Bad Hand. Moments before his soft, thin voice sounded, the mangled digits of his left hand made the odd clicking sound.

"My soldiers cannot be everywhere at once," he said flatly.

Kicking Bird met Bad Hand's stare with equal force, never averting his eyes through the response and translation.

"What the soldier chief says is true," he began, his gaze still unwavering. "The country of the Kiowa and Comanche is vast. It makes all men puny. The country of the Texans is as big, but when one of our warriors kills a single, bony cow to feed his starving children, soldiers saddle their horses and come after him to avenge the white man whose worthless cow was lost. Your white hunters come without permission. They kill our buffalo . . . more than can be counted . . . as fast as they can, taking the robes and tongues and leaving the rest to fester on the plains. No soldier saddles his horse or blows his trumpet when this is done."

Bad Hand remained still during Kicking Bird's talk, so still that the Indian delegation, who were impressed with his warrior-like bearing, could not be certain if he had blinked during all that time. But beneath this tranquil surface were currents of emotion that were expressed once again in the clicking of his ravaged fingers.

"Tell me when you find them and I will send soldiers to punish them."

"If we make a ride of one or two sleeps to tell you this what good can it be? The hunters will have quit their camps when your soldiers arrive. These men must be stopped before they come into the country."

Bad Hand shook his head.

"That is not my job," he said. "I am a soldier, not a politician."

Kicking Bird turned his head and looked down on Hatton. But the commissioner also gave a little shake of his head.

"I do not have the power to keep people from going where they want to go."

Kicking Bird looked from Hatton to Bad Hand and back again but nothing more was forthcoming.

"Our young men will kill as many hunters as they can," he declared. "So long as these men take our money without asking, there will be trouble. That is all I have to say."

In the hours that followed, warriors rose again and again to address unfulfilled promises, while the whites, with equal obstinacy, returned unfailingly to their plan for peace that would deny the aboriginals all freedom of movement. It was nearly dark before the meeting broke up.

Nothing of substance had been achieved, yet by virtue of having met, a certain progress had been made, and there were handshakes all around as the deadlocked delegations took leave of each other in front of the lodge tent.

The warriors said little as they followed Lawrie Tatum back up the hill to their horses, having decided only that since the moon was up they would travel awhile rather than camp close to the whites. Though none of them said so, each man was hungry for open space after the grueling talk in the stuffy tent.

If Lawrie Tatum was disappointed with the meeting he didn't show it, for he was his usual ebullient self as he took each man firmly by the hand, making it clear to all that he was glad they had come and would continue to pursue the friendship he so eagerly desired.

After he and Kicking Bird clasped hands, the Quaker pulled the Comanche aside and showed him into the place he called a "house." Passing over the threshold, Kicking Bird was astounded to find that a single footstep could transport him into a foreign, confounding world.

As he stood fixed to a floor of wood, his head turned slowly, allowing his uncomprehending eyes to absorb fully the numbing wonder of what he saw. This was the box that Lawrie Tatum lived in, and the sight of four walls, a roof, and a floor sent a tremor of horror up Kicking Bird's spine.

How a person could exist in such a place was difficult to believe. The Quaker was completely sealed inside the box. The air inside did not move, and although the things called windows admitted the moon's light, they seemed completely unnecessary. The whole world was only a few feet away! Who could possibly want to look outside when the opportunity of being outside was as easy as walking?

Tables and chairs were placed in the room, as if in wait for a large child. A heavy piece of soft material obscured much of the floor's planking. The fire was hidden in a metal box, where it could not be enjoyed. But most startling of all, macabre images of hair-mouths hung in several spots on the walls. For a beat or two of his leaping heart Kicking Bird thought they might be living beings whose faces had somehow been manipulated onto the sides of Lawrie Tatum's box. Then he thought they might be representations of slain enemies, but he quickly realized that Lawrie Tatum could not be capable of killing anything more than a rabbit . . . maybe a deer.

The blur of visions was further complicated by the little white man's frenetic behavior. The moment he entered his box, Lawrie Tatum began gesturing and talking in a vain effort to explain every item to a man who had never seen them before, nor even knew of their existence, and what little Kicking Bird learned of the objects the Quaker was describing was canceled out by the haste with which he drew his visitor across the floor to a far wall, where a tall, dark box, fronted by a similarly colored chair, stood.

His host sat in the chair, reached up, and opened the box. The inside was littered with pieces of paper stuffed into holes that had been carved into the box's top. The Quaker reached down, took hold of something with two fingers, and pulled out another, smaller box. As he began to dig through it, Kicking Bird interrupted his search to ask what the tall box might be.

"Oh," chirped Lawrie Tatum, looking up earnestly. "Forgive me . . . desk . . . this is a desk. Make words here."

Still unsure what it might be, Kicking Bird could manage only an affirmative grunt as the Quaker laid out several small cases on the desktop and began to inspect them. Inside were the glass discs suspended by wire and, as Kicking Bird stared down on them in awe, Lawrie Tatum suddenly turned to him again.

"The man . . . old . . . Ten Bears . . . Ten Bears."

"Uhhh," Kicking Bird snorted. "Tin Bares."

"For his eyes," Lawrie Tatum said eagerly, pointing to his own. "Eyes . . . Ten Bears."

"Uhhhh," Kicking Bird answered, lifting a finger to one of his eyes, "aye."

"See far," Lawrie Tatum asked, holding a cupped hand at arm's length before drawing it quickly to his face, "or close?"

He repeated the motion and a moment later Kicking Bird took the Quaker's hand and brusquely stretched his arm straight.

"Thisss," he said, shaking his head.

"Ah, nearsighted!" Lawrie Tatum grinned. He turned once again to the desk and went on with his examination.

The Comanche and Kiowa warriors rode far onto their beloved prairie that night before finding a shelf of sandy soil where they could stretch out and sleep a few hours in the shadow of a looming cut bank.

Wrapped in a blanket, his head resting on the occasional bag he used for a pillow, Kicking Bird lay awake, his mind crowded with all he had heard and seen. It was thrilling to think of the surprise for Ten Bears wrapped in deerskin just behind his skull but, as he watched the orange trails of stars streak across the heavens, he gave the surprise the same passing attention that other, vivid impressions of the previous day received.

They were pushed aside by a single, overwhelming question. It was a question about the whites he had long contemplated and had always believed a firsthand encounter like the one in the Quaker's home would provide a simple answer to. Instead, a hundred different potential answers whirled in his mind, while the question itself continued to float in his consciousness, heavy and persistent as a pendulum.

How could Lawrie Tatum, or any other man, in exercise of free will, eschew the sun and stars and wind, spurn the earth itself, to sleep and eat and laugh and cry and bathe and smoke and procreate in a box?

Kicking Bird thought to himself, *I am glad I have never dreamed of such a thing.*

But then he thought, *Now that I have seen it, perhaps I will dream about it. That would be bad.*

He shut his eyes and tried to push the possibility of dreaming out of his head.

CHAPTER XXV

*T*HE NIGHTMARE CAME IN STORMY WEATHER AND CLEAR. IT CAME in good health and bad, and it came with every sleep.

There was a box within a box and people were trapped inside. People slept in the box. Often they defecated and urinated in the box. The stale air they breathed was hard to filter and made them cough.

A small square had been cut in one of the box's walls and glass had been sized to fit the square. Thin, metal spikes driven into the outside held it fast so that the glass would not open.

On the opposite wall another, larger square had been cut then filled with a large, similarly shaped plank that reached to the floor. Attached to this plank was a round, metal knob below which a small hole was visible. Every night, as the sun started behind the earth, measured footsteps sounded outside the box within a box, and moments later the sound of metal on metal was heard. Something turned and clicked and, no matter how much the knob was turned, the plank would not open.

Footsteps came again when the sun's light began to reveal the world. The metal in the plank turned and clicked as it had before; then the plank opened and the dream reached its chilling climax as an expressionless white man or woman appeared.

What made the nightmare especially horrible was not that it came each night. What gave the nightmare its terror was that it was not a nightmare at all. Everything in it, as far as she could tell, was real, and as the bad dream nights began to pile up behind her, Stands With A Fist feared that her mind was no longer able to tell her what was real and what was not. Sometimes she smiled inwardly at the irony, and when she did, those whose custody she was in would purse their lips in sympathy at the poor woman who had been so diminished by her lifelong ordeal that she smiled when there was no reason.

They were allowed out in daylight, and Stands With A Fist tried to work as often as possible in the garden beside the big box where she lived. Though she was always watched, her captors were often out of earshot when she was in the garden, and she could talk to Stays Quiet in hushed Comanche. She could fill her nose with earthly things as her hands worked the rich loam in an effort to coax flowers and vegetables to life. Despite her inexperience she was extraordinarily successful, and the luxuriant Gunther garden growing at the hands of Christine, the for-mer captive, quickly became a regular topic of conversation among the survival-minded citizenry dwelling in the rough-hewn settlement called Jacksboro.

But the talk about Christine ranged far beyond her skill at garden-ing. The presence of one so unusual—and famous—held the town in continuous thrall, and no day passed without reference to the other-worldly woman who had landed in their midst. The hem of her dress, the tone of her skin, the way she threw her hands around in the rare mo-ments when she uttered words, the wild-born child constantly at her side. All these things and many more were discussed through every wak-ing hour. A lion caged in the center of town could not have evoked more interest.

But as her residency passed thirty days, a change took place. Passing comments and trivial anecdotes gave way to an issue of far greater weight that inflamed and divided the populace. It was becoming apparent that she was having problems adapting, and the question of whether she would ever fit in split the people of Jacksboro.

A large number of citizens believed that she would eventually em-brace her white heritage, arguing persuasively that no one could predict how long it might take for someone who had lived with savages for twenty-five years to reenter the fold. Through God's guidance and the generosity of His flock, assimilation might yet be effected. The Lord had taken her away and the Lord had given her back. That was proof enough to believers that she belonged among them.

But nearly an equal number of colonists had come to the conclusion, after careful observation, that she was an unredeemable heathen and a racial embarrassment of no apparent social worth and should be cast out.

Some held the opinion that she should be institutionalized, this despite a visit from a representative of the governor, who eloquently argued that the reclamation of Christine Gunther was of the highest priority in that it would provide hope for other captives' families, who were constantly appealing to the governor's office for help. He also reminded the inhabitants of Jacksboro that should they lose the battle to win back Christine Gunther it would have national repercussions. It might leave the impression that the people of Texas did not take care of their own.

Though the governor's position did not change many minds, it blunted the drive to remove her to an asylum, while at the same time giving rise to a variety of other wild schemes. A tiny knot of Comanche-haters pointed out that she had already attempted to escape twice, and that it would be best to incarcerate her. A plan to make her a kind of townwide domestic, rotating from home to home, was advanced by a group of women who advanced the notion that hard work would speed her rehabilitation. A cabal of enterprising businessmen proposed a plan designed to capitalize on both her celebrity and her obstinacy by turning her into an attraction for visitors. A dwelling of three walls, one wall being left open for viewing, could be erected for her and her issue to live in, with regular hours for viewing established and ample daily breaks provided in the name of privacy and humane treatment.

None of these ideas found much in the way of popular support, and so, faced with no other option, the townspeople simply continued to watch as the Gunther family attempted to restore their long-lost relative to Christian respectability.

Most of the family she had known as a little girl were dead and the authorities had consigned her to the care of a cousin and his large, relatively prosperous family. The Gunthers' original euphoria at her arrival was, to their great consternation, shockingly short-lived. The lovely bedroom they had created for her, complete with a metal-frame bed, a ceramic wash basin that had survived the crossing from Germany, a lady's vanity painted light pink, two bottles of recently purchased scents, a refurbished wardrobe with three oversized dresses inside, and an array of cheerful bunting that encircled the room, had, by her second day in Jacksboro, been utterly destroyed.

The bed's mattress she had pulled to the floor; the scented water she had poured out; she was using the dresses for blankets; and the basin, now filled with a mixture of bunting and wooden shards from the legs of the vanity—a precious Old Country heirloom—now stood in the center of the room, perched on its metal stand. In it she made her fire, and when, upon smelling smoke, the elder Gunther raced to her door, he found he could not get through. Knocking, then pounding, to no avail, the taciturn cousin to Stands With A Fist put his shoulder to the door and burst into the room, only to find her seated cross-legged in the middle of the floor, Stays Quiet in her lap, rocking lunatic-like in front of the blazing basin.

At the first family dinner, conducted at a long table in the formal dining room, her cousin was somberly carving a roast when she lunged across the table, snatched a fresh-cut slab of meat, and stuffed it into her mouth.

She would defecate or urinate in public, refused to bathe except in a nearby stream, cried without warning, hardly spoke, and, after only a few days, had driven the entire Gunther family to distraction. Not a moment seemed to pass without crisis. Children complained about the interminable labor of "watching Cousin Christine," a steadfast wife's nerves began to fray, and the cousin who had so righteously stepped forward to claim his kin now found himself lying awake at night, vainly wondering how life could be returned to normal.

Faced with a dilemma beyond his ability, the elder Gunther, with the eager support of his family, turned to a higher authority, who appeared a few days later in the pallid, squeamish form of a man named Tooey, reputed to be the most mesmerizing preacher in the district.

Firm and soft-spoken, Reverend Tooey assured the rattled Gunthers that there was nothing to worry about because while he taught Christine the rudiments of English he would be instructing her in the basics of scripture—a potent formula in which he had every confidence.

But by the end of the second full day of "instruction" he had stretched the narrow limits of his imagination to their fullest. The woman in his charge seemed unable to grasp any of what he was trying to teach. When he was certain that she was poised for a breakthrough, the dull-witted creature would lapse into a litany of mumbles and grunts that comprised the only language she seemed capable of speaking. At last he turned to God, expecting that if she were anointed with the power of prayer, the light of understanding was sure to fill her eyes. For twenty minutes he tried to explain what he wanted, talking, cajoling, and pantomiming until uncharacteristic beads of sweat appeared at his hairline and ran downward in tiny, determined rivulets until they reached the reverend's brow, causing the single-minded preacher to swipe constantly at his face as he tried to prepare Stands With A Fist for a profound encounter with the Almighty.

At last the beleaguered Reverend Tooey, fearing the onset of his own derangement, sank to his knees, and was pleasantly surprised to see his refractory subject settle next to him. The emaciated man of God smiled wanly at his wide-eyed pupil, lifted his head, closed his eyes, and launched into a dirgelike recitation of the Lord's Prayer. Almost at once a mantle of warmth descended onto the reverend. All worldly anxiety vanished as he steeped himself in the word of God, and, as often happened when ministering to distraught members of his flock, one of his bony hands lifted into space to search out and give comfort to his needy partner in worship.

But the pastoral hand that settled on Stands With A Fist's landed with the devastating impact of a bomb. She leaped to her feet, emitting a long, violent, ear-splitting shriek that rattled the panes of the closed window. Dropping into a crouch, she began to back up, one slow step at a time, all the while spitting a stream of Comanche expletives at her molester.

His mouth agape, the Reverend Tooey got to his feet and made the near-fatal mistake of advancing, his upraised hands signaling peace.

When he had closed to within a few feet of his would-be convert, the cooing preacher saw her crouch even lower and an instant later her lips peeled back in a sneer. An unearthly howl flew from her mouth, and she charged, striking the Reverend Tooey's meatless chest with all the force her two clenched fists could muster.

Lifted clean off his feet by the blow, the Reverend Tooey shot backward onto the far wall, which he hit so hard that great flashes of light erupted in his head. He sank to the floor like a sack of grain, and as breath flowed once more into his emptied lungs, he raised his head and was horrified at what he saw.

With unmitigated violence she was assaulting the metal bed, alternately kicking and grappling at it with such demonic force that the entire frame was being pulled this way and that. Every hair on the Reverend Tooey's body sprang to terrified attention as he realized she was trying to secure a weapon.

Frantic to escape, he crawled along the floor, scooped up his Bible, and scuttled, crablike, toward the salvation of the door, which, to his frenzied despair, he could not open. The door was locked.

"Help!" bleated the Reverend Tooey. "Open the door! In the name of God, open the door!"

Fortunately for the panicked Tooey, Cousin Gunther and his family had gathered at the door on first hearing the commotion, and he flew out when it finally opened, landing face first at the feet of the aghast family. With the help of many fumbling hands, the reverend's sticklike frame ascended from the hallway floor amid a clamor of succoring voices.

The reverend didn't respond to their solicitous remarks but glanced back at the open door, where he saw that the object of his fright still concentrating her fury on the unyielding bed frame.

"Close the door," he intoned. "Lock it!"

Again he was peppered with inquiries as to his condition.

"I am all right," he announced, hoisting a hand to silence the Gunthers. Then he gazed over the heads of the anxious clan, and in a tone both distant and final, declared:

"The woman is a hopeless idiot."

Reverend Tooey's failure drove the Gunthers away from miracle cures and into a more utilitarian realm. A modified version of the plan to make Christine the town domestic was put into motion, but because Stands With A Fist knew nothing about maintaining a box and seemed incapable of grasping even elementary tasks, like where to empty a chamber pot, that, too, was a failure, so much so that ultimately no one in Jacksboro would allow the repatriated Gunther in their front yard, much less their home.

People altered their path of travel to avoid contact with the family. The local pastor asked them, in the interest of preserving decorum, to sit in the last pew of God's house, a request to which the family glumly acceded. Visits to the Gunther habitat quickly trickled down to errands of necessity, and the family felt the sting of its pariah status for the first time in their long and unstoried tenure.

All of them wanted desperately to rid themselves of the cancer they had unwittingly embraced, and when Cousin Gunther's wife struck on the idea of somehow marrying her off they realized a perfect candidate existed in the person of Axel Strunk, a dimwit far past marrying age who lived with his mother only a few miles away.

Certain overtures were made to the simpleton's mother and expectations soared when Cousin Gunther's discreet inquiry was greeted with unalloyed zeal. Nearing the end of her life, the old woman had long dreamed of seeing her son married before she passed on, and the contrived courtship was commenced when the Strunks came calling a few days later.

Unfortunately, the first close-up view of the prospective groom reminded the Gunther clan of how pitiful his condition was, and their spirits dipped.

A futile attempt had been made to drag a comb through his thick, yellowish hair. His clothes were reasonably tidy but a clue to his implausibility lay in the fact that he was wearing two left boots. Though his hands had been recently washed, the stunted sleeves of his jacket showed that it had been some time since his arms had encountered a cleaning agent.

Hygiene aside, it was the essence of Axel himself that caused a momentary deflation in the family's hopes. His small, close-set eyes peered out of a bony promontory that was more ledge than brow and was complemented by a wide, impenetrable jaw. In rustic parlance he was what was called a "mouth breather," and he shuffled wherever he went in the short, careful gait usually associated with advanced age. His great paws hung lifelessly at his sides and, aside from an occasional expression of glee at some childish stimulus, he rarely spoke unless by way of a response to some simple instruction.

It was patently clear to all who saw him that for a dullard of Axel's magnitude to conduct a courtship was impossible. Nor was it conceivable that he could form any kind of proposal, even if his unknown desires were to hit upon the idea.

But nothing could deter the Gunthers in their desperation and, despite the suitor's total lack of qualification, they pressed forward. After a short-lived repast, they managed, through a flurry of hasty, bald-faced maneuverings, to isolate the trio of Axel, Christine, and her undemonstrative offspring on a porch bench. Once the players were in place, the Gunthers retreated into the house to monitor developments from behind a curtained window.

Stands With A Fist's back felt their eyes, but the surveillance did not bother her. To sit alone on the porch freed her from the constant and annoying presence of the whites, whom she had come to regard as incessantly antic. Here she could think and dream and feel without interruption. Nor was she concerned with Axel's presence. Far from being ostracized, the feebleminded of Ten Bears' village were fully accepted, and there was nothing unusual about sitting next to one of the "slows," whose behavior was harmless and easily predicted.

To be alone in thought also gave her the opportunity to muse about her secret. When she thought about it, she indulged herself with an inward smile. It was hard not to smile openly, or even laugh out loud, when she considered the monumental foolishness of the whites.

It had surprised her when it all came back during the long ride as a prisoner of the rangers, and she remembered thinking at the time that such a thing, coming so easily and so completely, must have emanated not from her own mind but from the Great Mystery.

There were words she still could not understand, but the gist of everything had been plain almost from the beginning. She knew who the Gunthers were supposed to be and was aware of political and social divisions in the town. She had not expected Reverend Tooey to touch her, but she had known who he was and why he was coming long before she faced him. She also knew why the slow one sitting next to her had come.

The secret had made it possible for her to navigate the trials of captivity one step ahead of her keepers while allowing her to use her own language, in fact her entire being, as a part of the subterfuge, and even now, sitting in the still, heavy air of summer, it infused her with hope.

To the consternation of the ever-vigilant Gunthers, more than an hour passed in which the thrown-together couple shared neither word nor look. Once or twice Stays Quiet made brief inquiries of her mother but that was all and it is likely that the couple, both of whom were quite content to sit, would have continued in silence had not Axel happened to lay one of his huge hands on the trouser pocket in which he kept his sizable collection of marbles.

He loved his marbles completely, and the simple act of rubbing them back and forth inside the pocket was enough to produce a ferocious-looking, gap-toothed grin on his face. The light clacking sound drew Stays Quiet's interest. When she gazed first at the pocket, and then at Axel, the moron nodded smugly. Gurgling happily, he lifted his bulk off the bench and shuffled down a short flight of steps to the yard. There he selected a patch of bare earth just below the porch and tamped it gently with one of his left boots.

Stays Quiet was now hanging over the railing, peering down inquisitively at the moron's ritual. Axel knelt in front of the spot he had chosen, and, using the side of his hand, spent a minute or two smoothing the surface with extraordinary care. Satisfied at last, he made a fist, then flipped out an index finger as if it had been sprung from a jackknife, and, marshaling all his concentration, began to draw a circle in the ground he had so assiduously prepared. When the circle was complete, Axel leaned back to better regard his effort, and, pleased with it, started a hand into the marble pocket with a delicacy that gave the impression he was after something fragile as a flower.

The girl on the railing watched, spellbound, as Axel closed his eyes to all distraction and let his fingers search out the treasured cache. Stays Quiet didn't see the marbles when Axel first drew them out in a cupped hand. But when he opened his fingers and let the perfectly round, multi-colored stones dribble onto the dirt inside the circle, Stands With A Fist's daughter fell into a trance that pulled her along the porch and down the steps to Axel's side. There she stood, her light, hazel eyes drifting from one magical sphere to another, as Axel tucked his shooter into the crook of his thumb and scanned the playing field for the most promising opportunity.

Settling on a nearby cat's-eye, Axel crouched low, bounced his eyes from target to shooter several times, and fired. The shooter sped across the pancaked ground, made a loud pop as it impacted, and sent the larger marble rolling out of the circle and into the nearby rough.

Axel cried out. Stays Quiet clapped her hands and, in a few bounds, located the marble. She lifted it gingerly out of the grass, stared at it in a brief spasm of awe, bounded back to Axel, and placed it in his yawning palm.

Stands With A Fist was now standing at the rail, and as she watched Axel ready himself for the next shot, the moron's concentration was suddenly broken. He lifted his eyes to the girl standing next to him. Then he glanced at the shooter wedged against his thumb, plucked it daintily away, and offered it to Stays Quiet.

For the first time since her capture, Stands With A Fist's soul was invaded by a good feeling as Axel positioned the girl next to him, tenderly fixed the marble against her thumb, and generously provided his expertise in the selection of the most likely target. Though Stays Quiet's first attempt skipped across the circle without hitting anything, Axel yelped happily and stroked the girl's shoulder as if she were a puppy.

The rest of the afternoon transpired without incident. Stands With A Fist sat stoically on the porch while the two competitors below her, who proved to be quite evenly matched, played game after game, each contest conducted with a joy that made winning and losing irrelevant.

From then on, Axel didn't miss a day, often waking in the dark to walk the miles that separated him from Stands With A Fist and Stays Quiet. He was always at their side and one look at the contented threesome, whether at work or play, suggested a familiarity that might have spanned years rather than days.

The Gunthers watched all this with pleasure, for even the most careless observer could have detected a bond between the disabled man, the former captive, and her child. In a sense it was better than a marriage, the arrangement of which would have taxed the family's skimpy reserve of emotional energy.

Without the rigors of public sanction, a family unit had been created and the effect on Christine's kin was evident. The coming of Axel Strunk seemed to sedate the Gunthers' wild charge and the family dropped most of its efforts at rehabilitation to let her life follow its languid, routine course of eating and sleeping and work and play.

Everyone was happy except Stands With A Fist, but true to the form that made her captivity bearable, she kept her feelings hidden from all but Stays Quiet. When the key turned in the lock at twilight, they invariably sat together at the west-facing window, watching the sun make its fiery exit.

In the terrible days following their arrival in Jacksboro she had explained to her daughter the purpose of the ritual. The same sun was shining somewhere on her sister, brother, and father, and it was important to wish them good dreaming each twilight. In that way their family could stay together.

Stays Quiet often asked her mother when Dances With Wolves would come and get them, and her response was always the same.

"He'll come, little girl," she would whisper.

"Tomorrow?"

"Maybe tomorrow."

Then she would stare out the window, wondering if her hopes were foolish. Sometimes she thought he might be dead or too badly wounded to ever come. But she never indulged despair for long, and as darkness descended at the wane of day, she would close her eyes and imagine her family whole once more.

CHAPTER XXVI

*T*HE VALLEY WAS LONG AND FLAT, BROKEN OCCASIONALLY BY oak trees in various stages of growth and a few stunted mesquites. It was covered with tawny grass a few inches high. Etched along its center were the twin depressions set close together that indicated a white man road. Scouts had crept down the night the main war party reached the area and, after close inspection, pronounced the road frequently and heavily used.

Hills rose like shoulders on each side of the valley and it was on the westernmost of these, on the upper slopes overgrown with ash and scrub oak and sumac, that the great party of Comanche and Kiowa warriors awaited their prey.

Just after sunrise, scouts had come in from the east to report that white men had taken the road and were coming their way. A council was immediately convened. The admonitions of Owl Prophet were remembered and it was decided that the very small party of soldiers and one wagon would be allowed to pass unmolested, while a fresh group of scouts was sent east once again with orders to look for the next white people that might be coming along.

The whites who had been spotted, though they were to be granted life, would be passing very close, and this prospect of proximity to the enemy stirred the warriors. All of them, trained from birth to risk their lives in battle, were aware of the end of existence, and for some the moments they were living now would be their last.

Who might fall could not be known, but it was likely that some of the younger men would not come home. Young men were often foolish. They wanted honors and they wanted to impress young women. They weren't afraid of death, but few, if any, thought they would be killed. They were teenagers who had ridden on few raids and the finality of life was an abstract idea to them. Youth had ordained them bulletproof.

Yet in each there was a mysterious trembling that often led them into peril. The trembling made for an odd sort of giddiness that none was able to confront. They had to ignore the fear rattling up and down their bodies, because those who paid fear too much attention were sure to die. Every boy marshaled his fighting spirit in hope that he might survive.

For men like Wind In His Hair and Iron Jacket and White Bear, men who had fought the enemy a hundred times and survived, the emotions were much the same, though years of combat in every imaginable circumstance had reduced the mysterious trembling they felt before battle to a barely perceptible palpitation. Experience had taught them that the death they courted with every engagement was a thing so sudden and random that to fear it was an unaffordable indulgence.

The responsibilities of people like Left Hand and Whirlwind and Hears The Sunrise and Little Raven, distinguished warriors who had lived to see middle age, left no room for contemplating mortality. They would be charged with seeing to the execution of strategies, to rallying young men at decisive moments, and to fighting a delaying action in the event of a retreat.

At mid-morning the little covered wagon with a red cross first came into view. Half a dozen mounted soldiers were escorting the wagon and it was only through the repeated admonitions of leading warriors that the young men were held in check.

Still, it was something of a miracle that the temptation of the single wagon and its insignificant escort was avoided. All the white men would have died within minutes and in less time than it takes to skin a rabbit their scalps would have been waving from the coupsticks and lances of warriors. But the whites passed in full view, the creak of wheels, the snorting of horses and casual human utterances all clearly heard in the self-imposed silence along the wooded slopes of the hill.

When the slow-moving prize finally disappeared from sight a scout from the east pounded in with the exciting news that a second group of white men, the group Owl Prophet said they would be successful in attacking, had taken the road.

Perhaps twenty white soldiers were in the lead, followed by a dozen big wagons driven by hair-mouths. Each wagon was filled with yellow cargoes of corn and in the rear a herd of fifteen good horses was being tended by only three blue-coated soldiers.

Wind In His Hair, White Bear, and a dozen others quickly devised a simple plan for attacking the enemy. The small horse herd in the rear would be hit first as a ruse to lure the main body of soldiers. Most likely they would give chase to the handful of warriors trying to drive off their animals. Once the soldiers had cleared the line of wagons, Wind In His Hair and a large contingent of warriors would swoop down, cutting them off from the corn train, leaving it vulnerable to an overwhelming assault from White Bear and the remaining fighters.

There was no talk of anything going wrong. Neither Wind In His Hair nor White Bear had ever gone into battle wondering what might go wrong. Both men had known bad feelings before riding against an enemy in an ill-advised fight, but there was nothing of that kind in the backs of their minds on this day. They were supreme warriors of unexcelled bravery, and once the plan of attack had been struck, both gave full rein to the innate instincts, polished fine with time, that had carried them so far in life.

Immediately after the council broke up, the hillside that hid the warriors became active as a hive as final preparations were made. Those not in mourning touched up or reapplied the paint they had chosen for themselves and their ponies. Everyone stripped to breechclouts and moccasins to afford maximum freedom of movement. Hair was oiled and heads were adorned with the proper number of feathers set at the proper angle. Scalplocks and the amulets braided into them, a grizzly claw taken in an individual encounter, the talons of a hawk snatched bare-handed from the sky, the canine tooth of a wolf who had entered a lodge—all these charms were fingered repeatedly to make sure they were secure. Warhorses were charged back and forth, made to back up, spun in circles, and guided in all directions to assure the riders who would shortly risk their lives that their animals were sound.

In some cases, horses were switched. Late additions or deletions were made to accoutrements. Lances were changed from one hand to the other. Primary weapons were shuffled, and last-minute changes were made in the fighting units as men jumped from group to group according to the power of intuition.

Dances With Wolves was thankful his intuition had been silent, because he did not want to make any changes. The men under White Bear were all Kiowa but his wish to ride with them had been granted. The wagon drivers presented an easy chance for scalps, but everyone understood that the light-skinned Comanche was after something other than scalps, something only the drivers could provide.

Unfortunately, the arrangement did little to help him apply the single-mindedness so vital to fighting, and even as he smeared blue paint on Smiles A Lot's chest and back, doing his best to create the semblance of an owl, Dances With Wolves struggled to keep his mind from racing off elsewhere.

It was hard to think of killing the enemy while a higher mission consumed him. Added to that was the ever-present distraction of the children who had so disobediently followed him. The anger he first felt at the enormous complication of their presence had subsided but he still felt pangs of irritation at having to constantly consider their welfare, making certain at the same time that nothing he did for his children would compromise the war party. Even in the chaos of going to war, he could not help glancing up the slope for a glimpse of them through the trees where they were helping a handful of older boys watch the reserve horses.

Dances With Wolves agreed with his brothers in arms. It was no good to have a woman—much less a little girl and her nine-year-old brother—with a war party. But everyone also agreed that nothing could be done under the circumstances and they had been permitted to stay with the tacit understanding that Dances With Wolves would be responsible for keeping them out of the way. So instead of singing a silent mantra of courage he was looking up the hill for them every few minutes, or shuddering at the prospect of failing to get his wife and daughter back, or wondering if he was going to die in battle and make it all moot.

Miraculously, these trepidations vanished as three returning scouts were suddenly sighted. The riders flew up the valley at a full run, quirting their lathered horses up the slope, and announced excitedly that the enemy, still unaware of their presence, was just behind them. The war party erupted in a near-soundless frenzy of action as a hundred men swung onto their ponies and galloped in different directions to join their respective groups.

As he leapt onto his pony, Dances With Wolves caught a last glimpse of Smiles A Lot, the azure outline of an owl standing out against the red that coated his legs, torso, and face as he hurriedly guided his pony through the trees.

Thinking of his friend Smiles A Lot and the amazing transformation he had undergone, Dances With Wolves took up his position in the line of Kiowa warriors hidden among the trees. A few yards ahead, poised under a large elm near the tree line, Dances With Wolves could see the broad back of White Bear. He and the two warriors flanking him had gone ahead for a better view of the action.

Suddenly, the big warrior turned his massive head and scanned the warriors behind him. Then his wide, thick-lipped mouth opened as he barked out a name in Comanche and Dances With Wolves rode forward. One of the warriors next to White Bear sidled his horse and Dances With Wolves drew even with White Bear.

"Ride with me," the Kiowa signed.

Dances With Wolves nodded.

A grin broke on White Bear's face as he signed again.

"Some of these young Kiowa," he said and gave a backward tip of his head, "they get crazy when they fight. We are older. We should stay together."

Dances With Wolves grunted mirthfully but a more elaborate reply was interrupted by the sudden whispering of one of White Bear's lieutenants. The man lifted a finger and every eye followed.

White soldiers had appeared at the far end of the valley. No flankers seemed to be out, and when Dances With Wolves counted heads, he saw twenty-one, just as the scouts had reported.

Behind the soldiers appeared the ears of mules, and in a few moments a line of open-topped wagons moved into view. Nine of the big wagons entered the valley and Dances With Wolves was heartened to see a wide gap between the loads of corn and the dawdling horse herd bringing up the rear. Now there were four soldiers minding the trailing horses, but one more man, unless he was very good, didn't matter much. It seemed the whites were doing all in their power to accommodate the plan of attack.

The soldiers had yet to come abreast of the Kiowa position when White Bear slipped from his pony, an action mimicked by his entire force, and pinched the animal's velvet nostrils closed to stifle whinnying. Like slowly turning screws every muscle in every warrior tightened as the soldiers passed below them and under the trees blanketing the slope stillness was absolute.

Moments after the first wagon began to go by a shrill whistle split the silence and Dances With Wolves leaned forward, looking toward the horse herd farther up the valley. He could hear the whooping of warriors, and seconds later they burst into view, charging the loose horses. A few animals broke free but the soldiers were disciplined enough to try to hold most of them as the handful of warriors raced toward them. When the Comanche fighters hit the flats, the horse herders opened fire, causing them to zigzag to avoid being hit.

But one warrior took no evasive action. Never flinching, he rode straight on, quirting his pony furiously. A hundred yards from the enemy, the solo warrior astonished all who saw him by rising to a standing position on the back of his running horse. As if his extraordinary horsemanship were not enough, the warrior, still standing, began waving a blanket over his head. Dances With Wolves could make out a splash of blue against the red of his back and realized the rider was Smiles A Lot.

The main body of soldiers was already heading down the wagon line, racing to give aid to the horse herders. When they were clear of the teamsters another whistle blew, and with catastrophic screams Wind In His Hair and the Comanches flooded down the slope to attack the soldiers from behind.

But the Kiowas and Dances With Wolves barely noticed, for as soon as the soldiers had cleared the wagons, all eyes settled with calm, predatory intent on the objective below.

White Bear turned and bellowed, "Brave men to the front, cowards to the rear!" and the trees exploded with a full-throated roar of humanity as the Kiowas surged from their cover and streamed riotously down the slope.

Dances With Wolves was side by side with White Bear as they reached the bottom of the hill. From the corner of his eye he saw a pony go down, cartwheeling headfirst over the prairie as his rider catapulted into space. Whether the pony had tripped or taken a bullet from the sporadic fire commencing in front of them he did not know. Nor did he know what was happening farther up the valley. The pop of heavy fire in the distance was swamped by the rush of wind in his face, the straining of his pony as it dug across the level valley floor, and the panic he could see, between his horse's ears, unfolding before him.

Most of the hair-mouths had jumped down to take cover behind their vehicles and were firing their guns with all the effect of spittle against a gale. A few of the drivers, horrified at the wave of death about to engulf them, had broken out and, like leviathans struggling in a bog, were trying to raise enough speed from their lumbering wagons and panic-tangled teams to escape.

Dances With Wolves saw these things without any real awareness, for he was barely cognizant of the fight. He no longer felt the pony under him or heard the cries of his fellow fighters. He heard, yet did not hear, the high, metallic whine of a slug passing near his head, for every sense he possessed was concentrated on the search for a man his size.

Reaching the wagons seconds ahead of the unbroken line of warriors charging in behind him, Dances With Wolves fired at an enemy crawling under one of the beds. Before he could fire again, however, he spied what he wanted farther out on the prairie, and as men swarmed in around him, he wheeled his pony out of the tumult of wailing and shooting to pursue a tall, rangy white man trying to drive his heavy wagon to safety.

As he closed the hundred yards that separated him from his quarry, Dances With Wolves began to yip as a coyote does when running down a rabbit, and the tall man turned in his seat. The whites of his eyes shone clearly as Dances With Wolves raised his rifle, but before he could squeeze the trigger his prey took flight.

Plunging over the side of the wagon, the white man landed awkwardly, buckling his ankle, and Dances With Wolves could have killed him then with a single shot. Instead, he tossed his rifle to the off hand, drew a long-shafted club from his belt, and pressed his pony forward.

Cantering slowly alongside his victim he swung the stone-headed club in a lazy arc and brought it down on the crown of the driver's head. It was a glancing blow, for the skull did not open, but it was enough to knock the man senseless. As he crumbled in the grass, Dances With Wolves vaulted off his pony, rolled the driver over, and began to peel off his clothes, taking the jacket and shirt first.

He gripped the heel of the man's boot and noticed that a shard of ankle bone had pierced the leather. When he ripped the boot free with a powerful jerk, the man screamed himself awake. In any other circumstance Dances With Wolves would have killed him immediately but the white man was helpless and, wanting nothing more than the remaining boot and trousers, he focused on removing them. The last boot seemed to take forever to pull off, and when he tugged the pants leg over exposed bone the driver screamed once more and tried to crawl away.

Still in no hurry to kill him, Dances With Wolves picked the light cotton jacket off the ground, slipped his arms into the sleeves, and found that it fit perfectly. In turn, he held the shirt and trousers up to his body and was certain they, too, would serve him. He was starting to give the boots a try when he heard White Bear's deep, distinctive voice barking commands.

A few yards away, the driver he had clubbed had apparently gotten back on his feet only to be roped, and he was presently being dragged back to the other wagons by a pair of mounted Kiowa warriors. White Bear was riding alongside the man, striking him over and over with his coupstick.

Beyond them, Dances With Wolves could see the fight was over. Warriors were scampering over the wagons and cutting away the teams. Some were swirling around, still mounted, raucously displaying the scalps they had taken.

The reserve ponies had been brought up and were grouped near the bottom of the hill. He could see Snake In Hands and Always Walking sitting quietly on their ponies, watching the aftermath of victory. Farther up the valley and out of sight he could still hear firing, but now it was intermittent and he wondered if Wind In His Hair had managed to finish off the soldiers.

Whether he had or not, all seemed well and, cradling the driver's outfit, he remounted and trotted back the way he had come. Passing by the scene at the wagons, he saw several mules lying dead in their traces. The bodies of drivers, already stripped and hacked open, were strewn about in the grass. Several of the wagons had been set afire and the flames sent roiling clouds of black smoke skyward.

The bulk of Kiowas had massed at a single wagon. There, two white men, still half-alive, had been tied to separate wheels and were about to be roasted, to the immense satisfaction of the jeering warriors. As the tinder around them was ignited the unlucky white men made plaintive, sobbing cries for mercy and Dances With Wolves, who had not heard a white man speak in many years, was shocked at how well he understood the words. He trotted on to where Snake In Hands and Always Walking were waiting and the three rode back up the slope, intending to push east as fast as possible.

There was no time for good-byes. Everyone knew that Dances With Wolves had but one ambition and that was to rescue his wife and child.

CHAPTER XXVII

*A*S IT TURNED OUT, WIND IN HIS HAIR CAME TANTALIZINGLY close to wiping out the blue-coated soldiers. Pressed on all sides, their commander had ordered a running retreat, which, by some miracle of fate, carried them straight to a formation of huge boulders at the entrance to the valley. The collection of ancient stones provided a redoubt from which the desperate soldiers were able to keep Wind In His Hair at bay and thus save the lives that for a time looked certain to be lost.

Once the soldiers had dug in, the Comanches, wary of their rifles, had withdrawn beyond range, content to spend the rest of the afternoon drawing the fire of trapped white men in hope that they would deplete their ammunition.

When White Bear and his Kiowas arrived, the leading men went into council to discuss what they might do next. There was talk of charging the soldiers and overrunning them but Wind In His Hair was opposed. Given the cover the soldiers enjoyed, and the steady aim it provided, too many more Comanche warriors might be lost. He had six wounded, two of them badly. A young man on his first raid had been killed, and the body of Left Hand was slung over his pony's back.

The idea of laying siege to the whites was dismissed when it was pointed out that more soldier traffic was sure to be coming down the heavily used road, and at last it was decided to break off the fight. They would pull out quietly an hour after sundown, leaving the soldiers to suffer in suspense through the night.

The war party traveled for many hours before finally making a long halt on the open plains at noon of the next day. Triumphant spirits were still running high and though a few of the exhausted warriors dozed, most sat smoking around a score of fires, recounting all that had happened.

The Kiowas had not lost a single man and had taken thirteen scalps. The Comanches had taken only three, but all belonged to fighting men, and both forces were well satisfied with the proof of their victory.

Conversations returned again and again to the exploits of Smiles A Lot. He had dazzled all who had seen him and was rewarded with first choice of the stolen animals. Among the horses was a slim, all-black gelding. The horse proved exceptionally fast and quick on his feet and Smiles A Lot seemed glued to his back all the way home.

Only one man eclipsed the unlikely hero as a topic of conversation, and he, ironically, had been far out on the plains in the midst of a long afternoon nap when the attack on the corn wagons took place. Nonetheless, it was Owl Prophet's name that was most often on the lips of the warriors as they rode home. It was his prophecy that had led directly to the death of so many whites, to the whipping of the soldiers, and to their own comparatively light losses. Owl Prophet, the warriors agreed over and over, must be an agent of the Great Mystery, for his simple instructions had delivered victory and averted disaster.

But no one, not even Owl Prophet himself, could have foretold or guessed or dreamt the depth of the disaster that had, for the time being, been avoided in the place whites called the Great Salt Prairie.

The tiny group of soldiers who passed unmolested before the eyes of Wind In His Hair and White Bear had possessed a prize of incalculable value in the common ambulance they were escorting. Under the canopy of that spartan vehicle, next to the ordinary soldier who was driving, was the chief of every hair-mouthed blue-coat in the United States, the general known as Sherman.

Had Owl Prophet not spoken, General Sherman would surely have been killed—stripped, scalped, and dismembered—and his demise would have provoked total war, bringing the powerful wrath of a united white nation down on the heads of the Kiowas and Comanches with sledge-hammer effect.

The man they had spared was taciturn as a stump and bilious in the extreme. It was he who had championed the strategy of "scorched earth" and brought the Confederate States of America to its knees. His face was scarred by battle and his small eyes, by any standard, looked inordinately cruel. It was his unalterable goal that in his presence, politicians should quake, subordinates should tread softly, and commoners, whether sol-dier or civilian, should be struck dumb with awe. He was the steadiest, most brilliant General of the Army the United States had ever produced.

On the fateful morning he had skirted death, General Sherman had said nothing to his lowly companion in the ambulance, because nothing could be said. The country was as desolate as any other on the Texas frontier.

Worthless, he had thought to himself as he stared ahead at the bleak landscape, the stub of a cigar clenched in his teeth. *Just like all the rest. How long have I been here? Almost three weeks. Inspecting what? The stingi-ness of my budget? Listening to whom? Broken-down farmers and backwoods-men wringing their hands, begging for protection. From what? Half-naked men with bows and arrows that they see behind every tree. I served with the president. He wants peace. A drunk who wants peace. Who doesn't want peace? That's why we fight. He was better as a soldier. Goddamn Indians. I haven't seen a one. Just the same, I'd clear the country that fast if I had the authority. Then these people's carping would cease and the army could get on to other busi-ness. Goddamn, godforsaken country. Who would want to live here!*

General Sherman had taken the road from Fort Richardson to the new post at Fort Sill against the advice of everyone with the courage to speak. The country was too dangerous to traverse virtually alone. Dou-bling his token escort would not have made the general any more secure, and more than one officer had prudently suggested that he travel with the corn train, which was bound also for Fort Sill.

But Sherman did not take the danger seriously and his bile rose at the questioning of his wish to travel early and light. He was eager to inspect the construction of what was to be an enormous installation, and was looking forward, after sharing the mess tables of so many dubious officers commanding far-flung posts, to the company of Colonel Mackenzie.

Mackenzie was a queer one, to be sure—unmarried, moody, and given to oddly timed fits of temper. But his talent for leadership, his reliability, his energy, and his terrier-like pursuit of the enemy raised him above other officers when it came to field command. General Sherman was looking forward to the breath of fresh air Colonel Mackenzie's competence would bring him.

He was hurrying through breakfast with Mackenzie the next morning, anxious for a firsthand look at the new construction, when a first sergeant knocked at the door so violently that both soldiers started out of their seats. A squad of tired, terrified cavalrymen had come in, he informed them, with news of the wagon-train massacre. Within an hour's time, the two officers were riding toward the site at the head of nearly fifty mounted troops.

The timing of their arrival at the Great Salt Prairie coincided with the appearance of a large group of aggrieved civilians from a settlement named Floyd, which had been home base for most of the unfortunate drivers whose bloated corpses were now turning black in the noonday sun. Since no one had as yet been interred, General Sherman had the opportunity to view the charred, eyeless bodies, which were still lashed to the wagon wheels, and, after squatting a few moments in front of the grinning carcasses, expressed the wish to speak with civilian and soldier alike.

The general told his somber audience that he took this travesty as a personal affront and, so long as he was General of the Army, punishment of the perpetrators would be his highest priority. Nor would he stop at atonement for the innocent lives so wantonly destroyed. The material wealth of the Indians would be confiscated until every ear of government corn had been compensated.

A few days later General Sherman, standing ready to travel a hundred miles to the railhead, where he would board a train east to Washington, lit his cigar and whispered to Colonel Mackenzie:

"I'm going to work on the president as soon as I get back."

"Yes sir."

"Keep your troops in readiness."

"Yes sir."

"You'll be going after these people as soon as I can clear channels."

"I'll serve you in any way I can, sir. We'll be ready."

"We need to end all this."

"Yes sir."

CHAPTER XXVIII

*T*HE GREAT WAR PARTY MADE ITS VICTORIOUS RETURN A FEW days after Kicking Bird's, but as revelers ruled the village with dancing and feasting, the man who had spoken so effectively for his people stayed in his special lodge, gazing morosely through the hours of the day and night at the flames of his fire.

His wives brought food and drink, and his children popped their heads in from time to time for a look at their father, but otherwise they let him alone. It was obvious that he was troubled as never before, and to the regular queries from his wives as to what troubled him, he offered the same reply again and again:

"I am thinking."

The state of mind he had fallen into was a devastating reversal of the euphoria he had felt when he spoke to the white men from Washington. The good feeling began to fade on the morning he awoke from the nightmare of the box, and by the end of the first full day's march home, it had evaporated completely. In its place was a sickness that had seeped into his blood and taken root there.

Again and again the words he had spoken invaded his solitude, and a few times they almost drove off the cloud of despair that enveloped him.

The words were true enough, as true now as when first spoken. But time and distance had given Kicking Bird the opportunity to reflect, and when he regarded the meeting objectively, only one, inescapable conclusion could be reached. It was obvious, in Hatton's squirming and Bad Hand's deadened eyes. It was manifest in their outrageous offer of slavery for a free people.

The whites were unconcerned; they were perfectly comfortable with their position. When Kicking Bird thought hard about it, he understood that every physical movement they made, every word they uttered— even the excited ramblings of Lawrie Tatum—boasted of their superiority. The whites behaved as if they knew something he did not, and Kicking Bird, searching the depths of his malaise, guessed correctly what it was. That the Comanche and everyone like them were doomed.

Men who were also looking to the future, men like Gray Leggings and Island, would stop by occasionally to smoke and talk, but for almost three days Kicking Bird remained in the special lodge. Finally he ventured out after White Bear had taken his Kiowas north, and the first place he went was Ten Bears' lodge.

The old man was in good spirits and was obviously feeling good physically for he climbed to his feet almost in one motion when he heard Kicking Bird announce himself.

"I have been wondering when you would come," Ten Bears cried happily as Kicking Bird came through the door. He spread his arms and embraced the traveler and walked him to the fire.

"What have you been doing?" the old man asked.

"I have been thinking."

"Ah." Ten Bears nodded, his eyes widening. "You have been back for several sleeps. This thinking must be important and strenuous ... hmm?"

"It's hard thinking. I had to stay in my lodge to do it."

Ten Bears lit his pipe.

"The village has been happy. People like to celebrate a victory ... especially against the whites. The young men need to feel good about themselves, and the women and children are happy that almost everyone came back."

Kicking Bird puffed somberly on the pipe and handed it back.

"I took a different path," Kicking Bird said.

"Yes . . . tell me about it. I am eager to hear."

He started at the beginning, leaving nothing out about the journey and his meeting with the whites. Ten Bears interrupted him rarely but had to ask for details of the white offer to be repeated because it was so hard to believe. For the most part, however, he listened intently to Kicking Bird's story. The former medicine man revealed his conviction that they were all doomed, and when he was finished, Ten Bears sucked at his pipe for a long time before speaking.

"How could anyone do as the whites ask?" the old man said. He had said this to his lap, and when he raised his eyes, Kicking Bird saw the same plaintive disbelief that inhabited his own heart.

The visitor lowered his eyes, pursed his lips, and shook his head.

"How could we give up our country?" Ten Bears asked, incredulous. "How can the whites expect this?"

"I don't think your question matters to the whites," Kicking Bird said. "They want our country, and if we don't give it up they mean to take it from us."

"But they will have to kill every Comanche to do that."

Kicking Bird heaved a sigh. His eyes roamed Ten Bears' lodge as if he were taking it in for the last time. Then he settled his stare once more on the old man sitting across from him, and when he spoke, his words carried the weight and gravity of absolute truth.

"The whites have enough bullets and enough soldiers to kill every Comanche a hundred times."

Ten Bears thought hard for a moment but such a thing was difficult to grasp.

"Have you seen that many bullets and soldiers?"

"No."

"How can you know for certain they have the power to do this?"

"Their eyes told me so."

Ten Bears knew that Kicking Bird was an astute reader of the evidence behind men's eyes, and there was no doubt in his mind that he had heard truth. The old man closed his eyes and let his head tip back. In a prayer he had known since childhood he petitioned the Great Mystery.

Do not leave us, Mystery, he thought. *Your Comanche children need protection. Take pity on us, Creator of All Things. Do not leave us.*

When he opened his eyes, Kicking Bird was looking straight at him.

"We must council," Ten Bears declared.

"Ummph," grunted the visitor.

Ten Bears had noticed something strange between Kicking Bird's fingers. He had never seen anything like it.

"What's that?" he asked.

Kicking Bird gazed down at the little case Lawrie Tatum had given him.

"For Ten Bears," he said, handing the case across the fire.

As Ten Bears turned the unknown object in his hands, Kicking Bird circled the fire and settled on his knees next to the puzzled headman.

"What skin is this?" Ten Bears wondered. "It's rough."

"I think cow . . . look." Kicking Bird pointed to the case's seam. "It opens, Grandfather."

With a slight trembling of his fingers, Ten Bears pried open the case and peered down at the delicate blend of wire and glass inside.

"The agent, Lawrie Tatum, said you should put this thing on your face."

Suddenly startled, Ten Bears snapped his head up and cocked it at Kicking Bird.

"What for?"

"It makes old eyes new."

"What?"

"Whites with poor eyes put this on their faces."

"What whites?"

"All kinds. Even young ones."

Ten Bears tentatively pinched two fingers on a section of the wire and lifted the strange object in front of his eyes.

"Are they beneficial to women, too?"

Kicking Bird thought for a moment.

"I haven't seen a white woman yet."

Ten Bears had begun a close inspection of the spectacles but could find nothing familiar enough in their makeup to provide a clue as to how they might work.

"How do they function?" he asked.

"They have arms that fly out." Kicking Bird's hand instinctively reached for the glasses. "May I help you, Grandfather?"

"Yes, yes."

Kicking Bird took Lawrie Tatum's present in both hands, and, with the exactness of a surgeon, slowly unfolded the device. Turning the spectacles around, he lifted them toward Ten Bears' face.

"The arms rest on the ears and the glass on—"

Ten Bears threw up a hand and Kicking Bird stopped.

"Do they cause pain?" the old man asked.

A worried expression fixed itself on Kicking Bird's face. "Not in the whites."

For a moment the two men gazed helplessly at one another. Then Ten Bears gave a little, resigned wave of his hand.

"Oh, put it on. I'm not afraid of it."

Kicking Bird bent forward once again and the spectacles landed softly on Ten Bears' face. The lodge had grown murky in the twilight, and the old man, unsure of what he might be seeing, brought one of his hands in front of his face.

"Ah!" he cried and, brushing at his face with both hands, flipped the spectacles onto Kicking Bird's legs.

"It's awful! My hand is blurry! I can always see my hand."

"They are for far-seeing," Kicking Bird explained hastily. "We should go outside. Let me help you up, Grandfather."

Ten Bears let Kicking Bird help him to his feet and tottered to the door rather sheepishly, silently scolding himself for making a fuss over some trivial white trinket. The whites possessed some useful objects, some of them quite decorative, but nothing along the lines of the miracle Kicking Bird had described.

Determined to observe the decorum that befitted his age and place, Ten Bears let Kicking Bird place the white man's invention on his face, thinking he would make a polite comment or two if he saw interesting colors or odd patterns. He did not expect to see a teenager on a horse at the far end of the village and was astounded to find that he recognized the young man.

"How did Sun Boy get in here?" he exclaimed.

"Look to the right," Kicking Bird suggested.

"It's Otter Belt. He's leading some horses."

"Look left."

"Bird Woman shaking out a robe . . ."

Ten Bears pulled the glasses off his face and looked down at them with a mixture of respect and awe.

"This is a good trick . . . but how do they get people inside these discs? And how do they know what the people I see look like?"

"You don't understand, Grandfather . . ."

"No."

"Put them on."

Ten Bears did as his friend asked.

"Everything you see is here in camp. Sun Boy was riding his horse just now. Otter Belt was bringing in his animals. Bird Woman was shaking out a robe. Looking through the discs makes your eyes new."

Ten Bears fixed the glasses over his nose and ears, this time without help, and commenced searching out a succession of objects both living and inert. All the while he kept his fingers on the frames, tilting the glasses up to check the indistinct images in his eyes against the ones he was seeing through the little discs of glass.

A profound calm settled over Ten Bears as he moved his gray head from one place to another. He stopped tilting the glasses and for a long time stared through his new eyes exclusively. At last he turned to Kicking Bird. The spectacles hung on his face as if they had been there for years.

"You are right . . . my eyes are new. I'm going to keep this thing."

"Good, Grandfather."

The old man resumed his gazing. Looking over the village so keenly seemed to take the stoop out of him. The addition of the glasses had made him appear straighter and stronger. So intent was he on looking that when he spoke again it sounded like he was talking to himself.

"We must council on all you have told me."

"Yes, Grandfather."

"We must talk tonight."

CHAPTER XXIX

SMILES A LOT WOULD HAVE SPENT MUCH MORE TIME IN HIS lodge had it not been for the demands of others. Almost as soon as he got home, men started coming by to smoke or invite him out, and after a full day and night of constant interruption, he and Hunting For Something decided to leave Rabbit with one of his uncles, strike the lodge, and move a distance from camp, where they would be left alone.

They had returned at twilight on the day Ten Bears received the miracle of new sight and had just started to unpack when they heard the crier announce an important council that night.

Not long after they had started a fire the voice of Wind In His Hair sounded outside the door and Smiles A Lot was stunned to see him come inside. The great warrior walked to within a pace or two of the boy.

"Sit among the Hard Shields tonight," Wind In His Hair said. "The bravest should always sit together."

Smiles A Lot was too shocked to respond.

Wind In His Hair smiled thinly, reached out, and gave Smiles A Lot's shoulder a few light taps.

"Someone will come by and bring you."

Then he turned and, a moment later, ducked out the lodge flap.

Smiles A Lot and Hunting For Something had known Wind In His Hair all their lives. They saw him almost every day he was in camp. The history of his life was well known to them and yet they stood mutely, as if they had been poleaxed and would at any second crumble, senseless, to the floor.

As usual, it was Hunting For Something who found her tongue first.

"Sitting with the Hard Shields . . ." she said, turning her face to his. "What does it mean?"

"I don't know."

"Does Wind In His Hair want you for the Hard Shields?"

"Maybe."

"He wants you to sit with them."

"Yes," he answered. "Anyway, I have to make ready."

"I'll help you," she said excitedly and skipped across the floor for the occasional bag that held Smiles A Lot's things. "What is this council about?"

"Kicking Bird is going to make some talk," he answered, settling himself in front of the fire.

As she brushed his hair and oiled it, and found the new moccasins she had just finished for him, she questioned him, but Smiles A Lot, who was usually happy to converse, answered in one-word replies. It was evident that some problem was occupying his thoughts.

"Do I look good?" he asked after he was standing again.

"You look like a warrior."

Somehow Smiles A Lot was not pleased. With a wince he cast his eyes down and thought a moment more before gazing unhappily into her face.

"I have nothing for my scalplock."

Hunting For Something was more concerned with his sadness than she was with his scalplock. She wanted to pull him close but did not. Smiles A Lot began to pace.

"That white man I killed . . . I should have taken his rings. I think he had some."

"A white man's ring," she muttered cynically. "Why would you want something so awful in your hair when you have that black racer standing outside?"

"I can't put a horse in my scalplock," Smiles A Lot laughed.

"A piece of him," she countered. "A piece of him."

Smiles A Lot cut a hank of hair from the black racer's tail, and when Hunting For Something was done braiding it into his scalplock, the horsehair flowed along one temple, over his shoulder, spread down his back, and spilled over his buttocks like a living talisman. As he walked back and forth, in the way a haberdasher's client might take a few steps to check the fit of a new suit, the voice of Shaking Hand called from outside.

Hunting For Something moved with him as he started for the lodge flap.

"You can speak if you want," she reminded him.

"Why should I speak?"

"People want you to."

Smiles A Lot couldn't fully grasp that he had become a man of distinction. Everything had happened so quickly. He stared at her vacantly but Hunting For Something only smiled.

"I won't go to sleep," she said matter-of-factly, and he stepped outside, the long swath of black horsehair moving behind him.

Ten Bears' tent was already packed with warriors when he came inside. Smiles A Lot still felt he was dreaming as a place, only a few men removed from Wind In His Hair's side, was made for him among the Hard Shields.

He had never sat in the front rank of a council, and as he let his arms relax on crossed legs, a flash of clarity lit inside him. Taking in the scene around him, Smiles A Lot realized suddenly that he knew what was about to happen.

Though the council had not started, the lodge was abnormally quiet. Flanked on either side by Kicking Bird and Wind In His Hair, the figure of Ten Bears provided a clear line of demarcation. The lodge was physically split by the followers of each warrior, yet each of them shared a uniformly apprehensive look on his face. There were always disagreements in council, and at times heated words were exchanged, but Smiles A Lot understood, even before anyone had spoken, that the division that would rend this council was something completely unprecedented.

Extraordinary as the tension was, it was surmounted in spectacular style by the appearance of Ten Bears. Every man made some whispered comment about the bizarre apparatus on his face, and the fact that it was a thing from the white world passed from warrior to warrior until it was known to all.

Smiles A Lot's eyes fell toward his lap, then onto his hands, fingers, and wrists. He noticed the elegant curve of his fingers for the first time, and the supple, miraculous movement of his wrist. A prominent artery ran over his thumb, and where it stood at its highest he could see the steady pulse of his blood.

All at once he felt whole, the connection of everything that made him one person suddenly evident. The wavering flames in Ten Bears' fire were interchangeable with himself. They burned in concert for life—just as his own mind, body, and heart burned. And like himself, they were subject to the vagaries of wind and water, sun and air, wholly dependent on the Mystery for existence.

In the moments before the council convened, Smiles A Lot's surprising transformation reached its climax, and by the time the pipe had traveled twice around the first circle, the boy who knew horses had shed an old, hindering skin. His perception had shifted from himself to the world around him. He was no longer self-conscious, and as Ten Bears made ready to speak, Smiles A Lot tuned his senses to receive the headman's every word.

Ten Bears understood that the tension in his lodge was coming from an invisible fissure beneath his feet, a rift that separated Kicking Bird and Wind In His Hair and their followers from one another. To feel it troubled him, but as he looked out over the warriors gathered around him, he felt his heart and mouth come together, and felt secure that his words, even if they fell short of unifying the opposing factions, would soar high above earthly cares, for he was sure they had been touched by the Mystery.

In silence the old man turned in a circle, passing his eyes over the crowd. When he had completed the first rotation he briefly lifted his face to heaven before beginning his address.

"We are all together," he began. "It is good for Comanches to be together. Our power is always greater when that happens."

As he spoke Ten Bears began to move, constantly shifting his attention from place to place, making contact with everyone sitting around him.

"You can see my face," he continued, "and you can see this object I have lain over my nose. You may find it strange but do not fear it. It is a magical apparatus, for with it I can see you just as you see me."

To demonstrate the proof of what he was saying Ten Bears picked out warriors all over the lodge, identifying them by name and alluding to unique items that adorned them.

"But I do not need this to see that the men in my lodge have two minds. One mind is for peace and one is for war. These two minds trouble me because peace and war cannot sit together comfortably, and my heart goes to the ground when I see Comanches divided.

"We know about the wagon raid and the great deeds that were done there," he said, directing the words toward Wind In His Hair. "But Kicking Bird has been walking a different path and he has yet to tell us about it. We should hear what he has to say."

Kicking Bird rose as Ten Bears descended. He, too, scanned the entire gathering, but as he began to speak he kept his face turned toward the Hard Shields and their sympathizers. Without embellishment or prejudice he described the meeting with the whites, taking care to personify the participants by giving their names and detailing their appearances.

But as he began to outline the substance of Hatton's offer the Hard Shield contingent grew visibly restless and a sneer began to grow on one of Wind In His Hair's lips. When Kicking Bird related the proposal for the Comanche and Kiowa to live in a single, restricted area, Wind In His Hair was finally compelled to interrupt.

"Put a Comanche in a pen and the Comanche will die."

As if ignoring a heckler, Kicking Bird held up his hands for quiet and pushed on.

"I think Bad Hand and his soldiers would not mind if we defy him. I think he would be happy to make war on us. But he will not come to steal our horses or robes or weapons. They want only to drench the prairie with Comanche blood. White people give their soldiers money to do this."

Again Wind In His Hair interrupted.

"If Bad Hand comes out here it might be his blood that goes into the earth. That might happen to any white man who dares to come into our country. I am ready to kill as many as I have to."

A flutter of approving grunts and murmurs flew up around Wind

In His Hair, and Kicking Bird waited for them to die down before he continued.

"I do not think all the whites are bad . . . not all of them should be killed."

Several shouts of derision sailed across the fire, but for the moment they succeeded only in hardening Kicking Bird's reserve. He pointed sharply at Ten Bears and his voice rose.

"The white who knows how to make eyes new . . . the one called Lawrie Tatum . . . his heart is good. He wants only to serve us . . . and the Kiowa, too. He wants to help us and take care of us."

"Take care of us!" Wind In His Hair shouted, jumping to his feet. "Put a Comanche in a pen and the Comanche will die! What do you say to that, brother?"

A hush followed Wind In His Hair's outburst and, as all eyes fell on him, Kicking Bird seemed suddenly placid and majestic in the lonely silence that surrounded him.

"I agree," he said quietly.

Wind In His Hair grunted haughtily.

"How would you die, my brother?" Kicking Bird asked.

"Like any man—as a warrior."

"What of your wife, your children? How should they die? Fatherless? Starving? Helpless?"

"In a pen?" Wind In His Hair retorted.

Kicking Bird appealed now to everyone.

"I do not want my children to die. I want them to grow."

"And what do you want them to eat? White man biscuits that soften the teeth and make them fall out?" Wind In His Hair threw his arms out declaratively. "I want my children to grow on buffalo!"

A smattering of cheers erupted around the lodge and Wind In His Hair turned his fearful gaze on Kicking Bird once again.

"Comanche warriors defend their country and everything in it. They defend their brother the buffalo. What does Kicking Bird do? He sits at the feet of the whites like a child. He takes the puny hands of the enemy in his own while his relations fight and die. You are dirty with white men. You talk like a woman . . . like a coward!"

The two warriors rushed each other but their charges were blunted by the lightning appearance of Smiles A Lot. His recent integration of self allowed him the freedom to move without thought, and he had started up as Wind In His Hair's verbal assault reached its apex.

Now he stood spread-legged between the warriors, his hands grasping each of their shirts.

"You cannot fight!" he shouted. "Not in our grandfather's lodge! Do not bring disgrace on him."

The warriors understood the rightness of Smiles A Lot's words and, as their tempers cooled, they looked down on Ten Bears. The old man was the picture of serenity. The would-be combatants glanced at each other sheepishly and offered apologies to Ten Bears.

"Forgive me, Grandfather," they both said, almost in unison. Ten Bears acted as if he had not heard and did not look up as Wind In His Hair bent close to his face.

"Do not take offense, Grandfather, but the air in your lodge tonight has grown too stale for me to breathe. I wish you good night."

With that the one-eyed warrior swept out, followed by the Hard Shields. The rest of the council was breaking up as he departed, but, unlike the many warriors who shared Wind In His Hair's views, there was no unity among those who thought of peace. They walked out in mute little groups of two and three without speaking to Kicking Bird, who in the end found himself alone with Ten Bears.

The old man continued to smoke serenely, the glasses still fixed on his face, and after rejecting a multitude of parting comments, Kicking Bird settled on a simple good night and walked alone into the night.

No one could give him comfort, and Kicking Bird dragged his wounded heart into the special lodge, where he sat long into the night, struggling to recompose his shattered spirits. His dream of a workable rapport with the whites lay in pieces. He had lost the support of his staunchest adherents, men who had trusted his initiatives. Worse, he had lost face and could no longer expect that anyone would listen when he spoke.

In his misery, Kicking Bird let his mind drift into the past. There his memory drew out the glory of difficult hunts, hairbreadth escapes, successful defenses, and a succession of enemies fleeing before the tidal might of Comanche warriors. Sifting through strong-hearted memories salved his despair and reminded him of the central role he played in the history of his generation.

It was true that he had always been curious about what lay beyond camp and had sought to find ways of living that would make his people more secure. But the memories he had sought as a balm told him emphatically that he had always been a warrior, and as he smoked into the night, he heard Wind In His Hair's harsh words so often that he began to believe there was truth in what his old friend said. Perhaps he had capitulated too soon. Perhaps he had deceived himself into throwing his warrior's heart away. Perhaps he had forgotten to defend his country and everything in it, especially the buffalo. Perhaps he had taken the coward's trail.

Restless, he stood up, and as he rose, found himself acutely aware of the vitality that still coursed through his body.

My legs, he thought, *my arms, my hands and feet—they are all here but I use them hardly at all. And my heart . . . where has my heart been? Isn't it here in this lodge? Isn't my heart with my people, just as it was when I met Hatton and Bad Hand? It is here . . . it will always be here.*

A few minutes later Kicking Bird summoned runners to carry a message to the Kiowa and Arapaho and Cheyenne. He woke the crier and instructed him to spread the news at first light. Kicking Bird was getting up a party of all who wanted to follow. This party was to strike a blow for the buffalo. It would sweep the prairies clean of the scourge that was destroying the animal without whom free people could not live.

CHAPTER XXX

*T*HOUGH HE HAD WORN THEM FOR MANY DAYS HE COULD NOT get comfortable in the white man clothes. They bound him in places where his joints met, scratching, chafing, and itching his flesh.

But the irritation of strange clothes was nothing in comparison to the processes of thought. He had not expected the pressure to be so great. It suffocated and squeezed him in every waking moment. It danced in his sleep, and no matter how much rest he got, there was no sensation of renewal in waking. His mind was so exhausted by the rigors of navigating an alien world that it was sometimes impossible to close it down and go to sleep.

Locating her, he thought, would be the easiest part of his mission. But it was not, and the white man pretending to be a white man quickly realized that he could not inquire about her whereabouts without knowing her white name. Without that his search was entirely dependent on luck.

The dying men of the corn train had swung open long-closed doors to remembrance with their cries for mercy. Like Stands With A Fist, he was startled at how easy it was to find his mother tongue and use it. But he had also recalled how huge the white man's country was. She might have been sent to one of countless villages and towns far to the east. The rangers might have killed her and Stays Quiet. Maybe they had contracted a white man disease and died and been put into the ground. Thoughts like these intruded without warning and had to be beaten down with the same vigor a fire is beaten with a blanket. The one scenario he did not torture himself with was the possibility that Stands With A Fist might want to remain among the whites. That was inconceivable, and he never thought of it.

It had been difficult to cut his own hair, more so his son's. The boy had begun to cry, something he was not known to do, as the knife sawed through handfuls of his hair. He had continued to sob off and on through the whole of one day, then became sullen, speaking only when spoken to. If his father called him by name, he would answer, "Snake In Hands is not here. He's lost."

Always Walking continually pestered him with the complaint, "Father, I don't feel good."

Trying to keep his children content was, however, the least of his problems. From the moment he began the charade, Dances With Wolves felt the penetrating stare of white eyes. Wherever he went he felt watched, as if he were moving about the white world unclothed.

In the early days of their search the trio had kept to themselves, traveling at night to avoid contact with the whites. They had stolen saddles for their horses from a farmer's barn, and the theft went unnoticed until they were well away.

But as they journeyed deeper into the country of the enemy, clothing the children became essential, and on the fourth day of their quest, after secreting them on a high hill, Dances With Wolves swung into the saddle and rode down to the settlement that lay below. He rode with as much confidence as could be expected. He had practiced the old language to the point of tedium and had discovered a wad of white man paper money in a pocket of the dead driver's trousers.

As he passed the crude buildings that comprised the settlement he saw dry goods through a window and turned his pony in that direction. Stepping off, he straightened himself, brushed his jacket, and went inside.

The storekeeper, a short man with red hair on his face, eyed him but said nothing, and Dances With Wolves browsed the shelves for a minute or two, rehearsing what he would say. The corpulent merchant's attention had sharpened at the sight of a stranger. Strangers were an uncommon commodity. Sometimes they meant trouble. The stranger's hair was odd, more chopped than cut, and his skin looked scorched, as if he had been sleeping in the sun. A drunk often did that, and drunks never had money. This man didn't look like a drinker, and he didn't stink of liquor, but he seemed tentative in his every movement, whether he was fingering some item or just gazing at the shelves. By the time his strange customer paused in front of the modest supply of clothing on hand, the shopkeeper had seen enough. He slipped around the counter, walked up to Dances With Wolves, and stopped.

"Help you?"

Dances With Wolves slowly turned his head and stared down into the storekeeper's eyes. He could see the words in his head but was fearful that his tongue would not know what to do. When he spoke, his voice seemed to come not from his throat but from someplace deeper, and the flat, ominous sound of it sent a shudder up the merchant's spine.

"Need clothes."

For a moment the red-bearded man could not find his own voice, and when he did the words came out tangled.

"Clothes . . . uh . . . yes . . . clothes for whom?"

Dances With Wolves had not taken his eyes off the white man.

"Boy," he said slowly. The word was so weighted that it seemed suspended in the air between the two men. "And girl."

Having never encountered a man like this, the merchant stood transfixed, as if hypnotized, his urge to turn away overridden by the stranger's spell.

"A boy and a girl," he repeated mechanically. "How old?"

Dances With Wolves shifted his view from the corpulent man to the empty space in front of his face. He had not thought of numbers. He searched frantically now for the memory of them and how they might work, but his mind remained blank.

After a few seconds he looked down at the storekeeper again and raised a flat hand level with his ribs.

"Boy," he intoned, "like this." He lowered the hand to a spot just above his waist. "Girl, like this."

With trembling hands, the shopkeeper pawed through the stock and succeeded in picking out a woolen shirt and trousers and a light plaid dress that Dances With Wolves found acceptable.

Hugging the garments to his chest, the confounded shopkeeper hurried around his counter, quickly ripped a length of wrapping paper, and folded it over the clothes. As he was binding the packet with twine he glanced up to see Dances With Wolves advancing toward him. The customer's eyes were devoid of all expression yet relentless and, in an instant of horror, the shopkeeper imagined himself a deer paralyzed at the closing of a panther.

Somehow managing a knot, he slid the package toward this otherworldly figure and smacked his lips, trying to get some moisture into his mouth. Though the day was clear and unseasonably cool, beads of sweat had broken out on the fat man's face.

"Ah, let's say . . . three dollars."

Dances With Wolves let his eyes slide down to the pocket that held the paper money. Using one hand to hold it open, he slid the other in and drew out the rolled bills. He could not remember what three looked like but hoped it would come to him as he deliberately peeled a bill away and placed it on the counter.

Once again he lifted his menacing gaze, hoping to find a clue in the red-bearded man's face, but all he saw was a widening of his eyes.

"More . . . ," the merchant whispered, "please."

Dances With Wolves unrolled another bill and slowly placed it next to the one already lying on the counter.

The shopkeeper was gripped with the notion that the stranger's eyes were looking through him. The man across the counter was staring with the unmistakably quiet, potentially lethal, expression of a wolf.

The merchant's heart began to pound audibly in his chest. His breathing became rapid.

"Mister," he gasped, "where are you from?"

Dances With Wolves blinked calmly and the shopkeeper recoiled at the heavy, mystifying words that marched out of his mouth.

"Far . . . away."

His mouth agape, the perspiring storekeeper, certain that he was in the presence of something he could not understand, lurched backward, only to find his progress halted by the solid wall behind him.

He bobbed his head at the packet on the counter and tried to cry out but the words came in an urgent hush.

"Take it . . . I give it to you for nothing . . . take it . . . take it!"

Dances With Wolves' serene and deadly gaze fell on the packet, then rose once more to the terrified man behind the counter. The storekeeper's hands now held the shelving at his side in a death grip.

"Take it," he gasped again. "Nothing . . . you owe me nothing."

Dances With Wolves ran a couple of fingers through the twine, hoisted the parcel, and turned for the door. A few steps later he passed outside and his image disappeared in an explosion of blinding, morning light.

Pressed against the wall, in the throes of apoplexy, the shaken storekeeper struggled a few moments to recover. Then he hurried to the door, locked it and pulled the shade, then staggered for the sanctuary of his back room and the earthen jug of spirits he kept there. He was fully inebriated before noon, by which time Dances With Wolves and his newly outfitted children were on their way to the next settlement.

For more than a week they searched with no success. Unable to make inquiries without giving himself away, Dances With Wolves clung to the thin hope that he might catch sight of her. He talked to a few white people as they wandered from town to town, and his fluency in English improved. But as one futile day ran into the next, he despaired more and more.

At the same time the oddness of the dark-skinned man with the two shoeless, speechless children elicited notice wherever they went. It seemed only a matter of time before they would be found out, for no day could be completed without a near-disaster of one sort or another.

They tried to take their breakfast in a crowded eating place, but when a piece of beefsteak hit his palate for the first time, Snake In Hands spat it onto the floor and cried out in clear, concise Comanche, "It tastes awful, Father!"

Because Always Walking could not be deterred from defecating in public any time she felt the urge, Dances With Wolves was often accosted by irate citizens who demanded that he control his child.

On one hot morning, they had just entered a sizable village of several hundred souls when, drawn to the commotion of women screeching on a boardwalk, they saw a large rattlesnake, obviously in flight, slithering along a crease where the ground met the walkway. Townsmen were racing from several directions to aid the screaming women, but before Dances With Wolves could react, Snake In Hands had scissored off his pony, and, arriving first in the vicinity of the big snake, startled everyone in view by reaching down and deftly picking the serpent up by its tail. Then, with no more care than a boy might take to shuck an ear of corn, he pinched the snake's head between the fingers of his other hand, coiled it twice around his neck, and, cradling the reptile, pulled himself back into the saddle.

Snake In Hands was so intent on calming the snake with soft strokes along its back that he didn't realize the impact of his simple act until his father nudged him to attention and motioned for him to start moving. It was only then that Snake In Hands discovered that the handful of white people around him had ceased all activity.

Rattlesnakes were universally thought of as deadly pests, to be eradicated wherever they might be found, and the sight of a mere boy picking one up and fondling it in a way usually reserved for a favorite pet had produced looks of confused wonder on those who were watching. It also produced a quick exit from the vicinity for the odd trio.

The white man money was quickly used up and they had been surviving on a dreary diet of rabbits, squirrels, and other small game for several days when they reached the outskirts of a large settlement called Vernon.

Like his children, Dances With Wolves had grown weary of a search that seemed more implausible with each day's passing. He was tired of reminding his son and daughter not to behave in the way they were raised. He was sick of white man clothes, white man talk, squalid white man towns, ugly white man roads, and gameless white man country. Most of all he was sick of pretending. It made him feel dirty, and after repeating the distasteful chore of cautioning the children once again, he led them into Vernon with the thought that if they did not find Stands With A Fist in this place, they would turn for home and be done with it.

The outskirts of the town were strangely devoid of life, as were its main street and the mismatched collection of structures that fronted it.

They were halfway down the muddy thoroughfare and had not seen a single resident when Dances With Wolves spied a large congregation massed at the far end of town. He halted his pony and listened to the faint hum of voices in the distance. Something special enough to interrupt routine life was happening up ahead.

What might be taking place was no clearer when they pulled up at the fringes of the crowd, whose animation was strangely muted. Men sat their horses in little groups, gangs of children roosted on wagons, while others milled aimlessly through a considerable crowd of pedestrians who had gathered in front of a strange edifice which provided the center of attention.

Traders moved through the throng, promoting the sale of drinks, fans, and colorful flags, but their excitement was strangely muted, too, and it occurred to Dances With Wolves that the people were like children at play, fearful of raising their voices lest they wake some powerful entity sleeping nearby.

The hushed buzzing of the crowd rose as a small group of men ascended a flight of steps attached to the platform and faced the onlookers. One of them, a huge man with black skin, stood still as the others, who were white, scurried about performing small chores of readiness.

A white man wearing a metal star on his breast stepped forward, and, looking at a sheet of paper in his hand, began a short talk which silenced the audience.

The man with the star was quickly followed by another man, dressed in black, who clutched a book of the same color. As he spoke, a loop at the end of a stout rope hanging from a beam was slipped over the black-skinned man's head and tightened against his neck. The white man who did this stepped back a few paces, gripped a lever, and, at a signal from the man with the star, depressed the long stick.

Suddenly the black-skinned man fell straight down, and when his feet were just inches from the ground, the rope went taut. As he had dropped the crowd moaned, but as his neck broke with an audible crack, all breath seemed to go out of the audience. Spontaneous cheers erupted from some of the watchers as the black-skinned man hung lifeless. Others broke into applause, and shortly after, the casual chatter of friends and neighbors filled the air as a handful of somber men, working in the shade beneath the wooden platform, fussed around the body of the black-skinned man.

It had happened too fast for Dances With Wolves to analyze, but as he watched the incongruous scene before him he remembered the thing called hanging. It repulsed him to see men, women, and children kill a man without fighting him, and he instinctively turned to his children. They were sitting, ashen-faced, on their horses, their expressions helpless, and at that instant Dances With Wolves decided they should go home.

But before he could move, something extraordinary happened. The breeze, which had been lifting and falling all day as if it could not decide what to do, suddenly made up its mind in the spectacular form of a titanic surge that knocked both children off their horses and nearly sent Dances With Wolves to the ground.

For a split second he saw his children up and chasing their horses, but he was already in the air and, as he pitched to and fro on the bouncing, stiff-legged pony, the refuse that the audience had scattered over the ground filled the space about his head.

At the same moment he got his pony under control the wind inexplicably died, and when Dances With Wolves looked up, trash was still flying, the crowd was gathering itself in stunned disbelief, and the children had recovered their ponies. He was as dazed as anyone and was wondering where such a wind could come from when a stiff aftergust shuddered past.

Again refuse swirled up and a broadsheet of newsprint wrapped itself around his pony's face. Before the pony could explode, however, Dances With Wolves reflexively snatched the paper off his animal's eyes and was about to toss it into the breeze when his glance fixed momentarily on the paper.

A drawing of a woman stared up at him. It was Stands With A Fist. Stays Quiet was sitting on her lap.

CHAPTER XXXI

*F*OR THE NEXT THREE DAYS, DANCES WITH WOLVES RUMINATED over what to do. He studied the article under the drawing of his wife and daughter, reading it constantly in hope that he could fully understand it. But eleven years had elapsed since he had read words. The jumble of names and places and events tumbled like confetti in his mind, and he could make little sense of what was written. Though he could not be certain, he felt reasonably sure that the writing did not tell where she was and, with no other option than to risk discovery, he decided to step forward.

After bathing and grooming themselves to present the most convincing front possible, the three rode into Vernon at mid-afternoon and tied their ponies in front of the town constable's office.

Dances With Wolves whispered a final reminder to Snake In Hands and Always Walking. They should stay near at all times and under no circumstances utter a word. Then he climbed a few steps to the uneven boardwalk and knocked at the door.

It opened and a scruffy-looking white man with a puzzled expression asked, "What?"

"I want to see the con*sta*ble," Dances With Wolves stated.

As soon as the word came out he knew it was somehow wrong. But he could not remember how to make it right.

"Wait here," the man said, receding into the darkness of the office.

Inside, the constable, his feet propped up on his desk as he reclined to enjoy a good chew, peered up at his deputy.

"There's a fella standing outside with two kids who says he wants to see the con*sta*ble. He knocked at the door. . . ."

The constable stopped chewing when he heard the odd pronunciation of his title and was interested enough to rock his chair forward when he was informed that the visitor had knocked on a public door instead of coming inside. Something strange was afoot.

Unlike his peers on the frontier, the constable of Vernon was constantly on the alert for the tiniest ripple of intrigue that might cross his path. He had held his position for several seasons and performed the duties of his office well, but his true ambition was to master what he called the "science of criminality." He considered himself to be rather more intellectual than the average frontier lawman, and prided himself on being the only man within a hundred miles to possess a subscription to *The Police Gazette*. Normally, he read each issue from cover to cover, embracing the most lurid aspects of crime in his quest for expertise. The magazines were so precious to him that they were secured with lock and key and read by others only within view of the owner.

The constable shifted the tobacco in his mouth and resumed chewing. Folding his hands together on the desktop, he briefly drifted off in thought.

"Have them come in," he said at last, too consumed in the mechanism of weighing clues to make eye contact with his deputy.

A moment later, Dances With Wolves came inside with the children in tow and was ushered to the constable's desk, where he met the lawman's look with his implacable, unsettling Comanche gaze.

The constable, faced with an unknown presence, narrowed his eyes slyly.

"What can I do for you today?"

Dances With Wolves reached into his white man pocket and pulled out the sheet of crumpled newsprint.

"I am looking for her."

He spread the paper on the constable's desk, flattened it, and jabbed a weathered finger at the image of Stands With A Fist.

"The white captive."

The constable leaned forward and stared down at the drawing for a long time. Of course he knew about the woman in the paper, but he wanted a few extra seconds to think. The man before him was quite out of the ordinary, and the constable, ever eager to throw light on darkness, was already turning suppositions around in his active mind. The most obvious explanation was that the man standing on the other side of the desk was a family member of some kind. But there was something so odd about his visitor that the constable decided to conduct a careful, yet casual, interrogation.

"Christine Gunther," he said with the lightest touch he could manage. "What do you want with her?"

"I want to find . . . Christine Gunther."

"Uh-huh. . . . And who are you?"

Dances With Wolves had noticed half a dozen loose cartridges lying on a corner of the constable's desk when he first came in, and one word sprang into his mind like a huge sign.

"Bullet . . . Gunther."

The constable's eyes narrowed even more.

"Bullet? That's your name."

"Yes," Dances With Wolves answered placidly.

"Well, who are you, her brother?"

"Yes."

Suddenly one of the children, whom the constable had already noted were extraordinarily quiet, startled him by stepping up to the desk and grabbing one of his spare revolvers. The girl, who couldn't have been more than seven or eight, walked nonchalantly to the center of the floor, the revolver swinging in her hand with practiced ease, squatted in front of a large scorpion, and smashed it with the butt of the gun. Apparently, the insect was not dispatched with the first blow and the little girl hit it again, this time with more force than might have been expected of a child. Then she rose off her haunches, retraced her steps to the desk, returned the revolver to the spot where she had found it, and resumed her place next to the boy.

Evidence was mounting, and though it was still too soon to draw a conclusion, the constable suspected he was dealing with people who had suffered some unknown trauma of the severest type. The actions of the little girl were disturbing, and the dull-witted behavior of her father was even more alarming. To the practiced eye of the constable, the look of the man who called himself Bullet Gunther was one of the most predatory he had ever seen, and were it not for the presence of children, he could easily have imagined his visitor as a habitual killer.

"Where are you from?"

"The east."

"And where in the east would that be?" the constable questioned.

Dances With Wolves' memory whirled in his head and suddenly stopped at a place called St. David's Field, the place where he had tried to end his life during the Great War.

"Tennessee."

The constable whistled.

"You're a long way from home."

"Very far from home."

The words were so remote, so cold and chilling, that they seemed to pass straight through his body. The constable recoiled as he tried to remember if trauma could induce dementia. The constable rose out of his chair and faced Dances With Wolves at eye level.

"Have you lost someone?" he asked bluntly.

"Yes."

The constable glanced cagily at the unmoving children.

"Did you lose your wife?"

"Yes."

The constable was certain that the clever line of questioning he had adopted would bring him to the truth. He leaned forward.

"Did you lose her to the Comanches?"

Dances With Wolves blinked for the first time. He was trying to think of what to say when he was seized with an urge to follow where the white man led.

"Yes."

"Your name isn't Bullet Gunther, is it?"

"No."

"And you want to find Christine Gunther?"

"Yes . . . I want to find her."

As if he had solved a difficult combination lock, the constable was thrilled to feel the tumblers in his mind click into place and marveled at the simple answer he had formed to what had seemed a complex riddle.

He had never encountered a "revenger" before, but they were not uncommon and he had studied several cases that had come to his attention during conversations with other lawmen scattered along the frontier. Revengers were difficult to deal with because of the universal empathy for families who had been victimized by marauding Comanches. So many were so deeply disturbed that the revenger's true intent was nearly impossible to ascertain. That's what made them dangerous.

To the constable's agile mind, the visitors in his office fit the profile to perfection: homicidal gaze, halting, twisted speech, children rendered numb through barbaric brutality. He remembered reading about some cases in which repatriated captives were murdered. An eleven-year-old boy had his skull crushed by a revenger bent on destroying not only Indians but anyone who had had contact with them. On more than one occasion, former captives had been kidnapped and tortured for information as to the whereabouts of an abducted family member. He even remembered reading a celebrated case in which a revenger, whose entire family had been slaughtered in his absence, persistently courted a former captive, a fourteen-year-old girl, in a misguided quest for matrimony.

He felt profound sympathy for the shattered family standing in his office, but at the same time he was thrilled—in a professional sense—to have a firsthand encounter with a revenger to add to his lexicon of criminal experience. But a higher calling superseded these emotions. The constable's oath was sacred. Law and order must be upheld, and the presence of a revenger was a clear threat to the peace. The unwritten rule in managing such individuals was to employ a firm hand. Revengers were best controlled by keeping them moving, and that tried technique would be employed with this one.

While the constable thought, Dances With Wolves' mind had been working on a different line. He had decided that if he had to kill the white men, he would take the man with the star first. He was hoping to cut his throat with such speed that he could reach the man who had answered the door before he knew what was happening. He was already tensed for action, and as the constable came around the desk, his hand drifted almost imperceptibly to the skinning knife tucked in his belt.

His fingers closed around the handle as the constable lifted a hand and brought it to rest on his shoulder. Had the pressure of his touch been stronger or the look in his eyes slightly less benign, the blade would have passed under the constable's chin in a single, perfect stroke. But the touch on his shoulder was light, and there was no malice in the eyes.

"I don't know your name," the constable began, "and you don't have to tell me. I can't know how you feel, but I want you to understand that I'm real, real sorry for all your trouble."

Dances With Wolves' eyes had turned to slits as he listened to what he could not understand. Perhaps it was his own clumsy English, but he could not imagine what the man with the metal star was talking about.

The constable couldn't read his listener, either. The stranger seemed disoriented instead of comprehensive and the look in his narrow eyes was mindful of sudden death. The skin along the constable's shoulders rippled with terror and for a split second he thought he might have miscalculated. But the homicide in the stranger's eyes suddenly evaporated and the shuddering along his shoulders ceased. The constable sighed.

"You get your children and get on your horses, 'cause I'm gonna need you to leave town. I'll ride along with you myself."

The constable's hand left Dances With Wolves' shoulder. He turned his back, snatched a fedora off its peg, and started out of the office. He paused when he saw that his revenger had not moved.

"Come on, friend . . . let's go."

Before he reached the door Vernon's constable glanced quickly over his shoulder and saw with satisfaction that the stranger had begun to shepherd his children along in compliance with the order.

They rode in silence until they reached a fork in the road almost a mile out of town.

The constable indicated a track that curved northeast. "You folks take your business that way."

Dances With Wolves looked perplexed and the constable sidled his horse closer.

"Lemme tell you something, mister . . . just a little piece of advice. Whatever happened to you I wouldn't wish on a dog, but the way you're goin' isn't gonna get you anywhere. You need to take care of these children. You need to find yourself a wife . . . get yourself a new life started. Huh?"

Dances With Wolves nodded.

"As far as Christine Gunther is concerned . . . you need to give that up. Nothin' good can come from it. Now, you can take my advice or not, that's up to you. But if you don't take it, I've got a warning for you. Soon as I leave you, I'm sending word to the law in Jacksboro to look out for a man traveling with two kids. You go down there, you'll find nothing but trouble."

Gathering up his reins, the constable made a little shooing motion at Dances With Wolves and his children.

"You get movin' now. Good luck to ya!"

Dances With Wolves moved forward obediently and the constable turned back down the road to Vernon.

When they were out of earshot, Snake In Hands and Always Walking brought their ponies even with their father's.

"What is happening?" the boy asked. "What did that white man say?"

Dances With Wolves glanced back down the road to Vernon. The constable was nearly out of sight.

"I don't know. I think he was confused. He seems to think we want to find your mother and hurt her."

The children looked at him in shock for a few seconds, and then, for the first time in recent memory, smiles broke over their faces.

"Why does he think that?" asked Always Walking.

"I don't know," Dances With Wolves replied.

"He was mixed up." Snake In Hands laughed. "Are all white people mixed up like that, Father?"

"Maybe."

Always Walking's round blue eyes looked up hopefully at Dances With Wolves.

"Do you know where mother is now?"

"She is in a place called Jacksboro."

"Are we going there?"

"As soon as we meet someone who can tell us the way."

"How can white people get along being so mixed up?" Snake In Hands wondered aloud.

"I don't know," Dances With Wolves said.

"Is that what makes them so dangerous?"

"I don't know white people anymore," Dances With Wolves explained, "but I think the answer to your question is yes."

CHAPTER XXXII

A CHORD WAS STRUCK THAT REVERBERATED UP AND DOWN the southern plains like the tolling of a great invisible bell, for not one free village on the prairie failed to heed Kicking Bird's call.

The Cheyenne under Wolf Robe, the Arapaho under Young Dog, the Kiowa under Touch The Clouds and White Bear, and hundreds of other proven warriors fired with the prospect of taking up arms against the clearest threat to their existence eagerly answered the summons.

The war party swept north, constantly gaining strength through the addition of roving warriors and, as almost a thousand fighting men approached the hunting grounds white hunters had entered with complete indifference to all but their own ambition, they moved like a deadly wind that sent everything in its path rushing for cover. In sheer size the body of defenders far surpassed what anyone had experienced and presented a front of unity that few could have conceived.

Owing to the necessity of obtaining food for themselves and forage for their ponies, the party did not travel en masse but in several sections. They stayed in touch through the use of runners, who reported the smallest development with an urgency that fully reflected the significance of having more warriors in the field than could be counted.

Even Owl Prophet was caught up in the thrill of a gathering of such historic proportion. With Kicking Bird's call to arms he had sensed an instantaneous change in the atmosphere and, as warriors streamed into Ten Bears' village by the hundreds, he found himself unable to think of anything but driving the whites out of the buffalo country.

Knowing his advice would be solicited, the prophet withdrew to his mysterious lodge while the warriors made frenzied preparations to march north. When all was ready, they converged on Owl Prophet's lodge and were amazed once again at the spirited, unknowable babble that comprised the conversation of the prophet and his owl.

When the now familiar silhouettes fell away, the spent prophet, running with sweat, staggered from his lodge with upraised arms.

"The Mystery has told of the skunks!" he screamed. "They are not to be harmed. If this is done, the whites will be driven out!"

The warriors, euphoric with the promise of success, surged in around the prophet, while he, collapsing into their arms, cried out as if it were his last breath.

"Owl Prophet will ride with you . . . die with you!"

The Comanche seer proved as good as his word, riding with Kicking Bird at the head of a large contingent of warriors from Ten Bears' village that also included Wind In His Hair and his Hard Shields.

The one-eyed warrior had been one of the first to volunteer his services, ducking into the special lodge shortly after the crier had begun to trot through the village with Kicking Bird's proposal.

"Wind In His Hair and all the Hard Shields will ride with you," he had declared.

"You make my heart good," Kicking Bird had replied.

Since then the two rivals had barely spoken. But there was no lingering trace of the divisions that separated them. All animosity lay buried deep beneath the common cause that had brought them together at the behest of a man who seemed to have changed his skin.

From the moment they set out, Kicking Bird, resplendent in battle dress, led with the cool, unhesitating hand of a veteran general. It was he who had designed the novel line of march that would bring the various discrete elements of his force together again at the edge of the hunting grounds. It was he who had counseled secrecy, night rides, small fires, and evasion instead of engagement if white soldiers were encountered. It was he who had devised ever-revolving cadres of scouts carrying messages every few hours between himself and the Cheyenne, Arapaho, and Kiowa. And it was Kicking Bird himself who had declared that the war party would stay out until the country was cleared, no matter how long it took.

Shortly after the great force rendezvoused, on a day when the plains that spread before them were spotted with the shifting shadows of the cloud world, Kicking Bird lifted a hand and a thousand fighting men halted their ponies.

A group of four scouts were flying toward them from the north. The great party watched as the scouts grew larger, each warrior aware that the speed at which the scouts were traveling meant that they bore urgent news. Something had happened.

A Comanche named Blue Turtle leapt from his pony and dashed up to Kicking Bird, gasping for breath.

"On the earth ahead . . . the ground is covered with dark bumps. Some are streaked with pink."

"What are these bumps?"

"We didn't go close enough to see them. Maybe they are dead buffalo."

"Many?" grunted Kicking Bird.

Blue Turtle nodded, then turned his head away as he spoke.

"Yes," he said, "many."

Blue Turtle had averted his eyes because he was not certain he could trust what he had seen. He could not believe what his mind said his eyes had found on the prairie. The scale of it was too enormous, and even as he made his report to Kicking Bird, Blue Turtle still wondered if he might be hallucinating.

An hour and a half later, when the army of confederated warriors reached the place Blue Turtle had described, there was no man among them who did not feel as if he were in the throes of dementia. Most of them had seen the work of white hunters before, but this was beyond conception.

Ahead, in a country of unbroken plain, the dead lay in uncountable numbers. As far as the human eye could see, corpses of the revered, indominatable buffalo blanketed the prairie. At first glance it seemed inconceivable that anything but the Mystery could have produced such

a startling panorama of death. Yet as soon as Kicking Bird and his feathered warriors began to cross the ocean of slaughter, they knew it was
the work of the people they had come to fight. Only white men killed
like this.

Birds in numbers that occasionally darkened the sun rose from the
carcasses in massive clouds as the warriors passed through, their deafen-
ing shrieks obliterating the hoofbeats of a thousand ponies.

Rising from the floor of the prairie were the yips and growls and
snaps of four-leggeds as the smaller predators were evicted from one car-
cass by teeming clans of coyotes and wolves only to arrive at another for
a few frantic seconds before being driven off again. The entire animal
world, it seemed, had been driven mad by the tragedy of the buffalo.

The stench of decaying flesh quickly became so great that many
hardened warriors, men who had endured injury and deprivation, found
their hands involuntarily flying toward their faces to shut out an odor
that seemed to have become the air itself.

It was only when the corpses began to thin that the body of warriors,
weighed down by an invisible, incomprehensible anchor of woe, gradually slowed and stopped. The men fell out to wander the nearby prairie,
trying to clear the concussive haze of what they had seen through their
eyes. Some sat in numb groups of two or three, and in many of these cells
no words were exchanged until the light began to fade. In others, a few
low sentences were uttered but it amounted to nothing that could be
called conversation.

The majority of warriors sought out little patches of individual space
to reflect on the damage inflicted upon their hearts and, in opening
themselves to grief, they inadvertently created a spectacle of their own.
Fires were kindled and pipes were lit and a wide array of prayers were
spoken, beseeching the Mystery to relieve their misery. Everywhere men
sat cross-legged, their arms outstretched toward heaven, their innermost
thoughts sealed behind pursed lips. Some, for the first and last time in
their lives, wobbled, then collapsed in uncontrollable sobs.

At twilight, hundreds of tiny fires twinkled in the vast prairie night,
and an hour after the lonely plain was cloaked in darkness, one sorrow-
ful man lifted his voice and began to sing his death song. Spontaneously,
others followed, and in a short time hundreds of sad voices were singing
about how they had lived and how they hoped to die. The short, simple

laments were repeated many times before the singers, satisfied that the Mystery had noted their pleas, lay their heads down and rested.

Kicking Bird was no less affected than any other man, but all night his mind hummed with the responsibilities of leadership, and shortly before first light he was presiding over an extraordinary council of half a hundred warriors. Once the men were seated, Kicking Bird rose to address them. The pipe had not been passed, but no one thought of smoking.

"We have seen what cannot be seen," Kicking Bird signed. "A monster walks our land."

The warriors watched his words in unblinking silence.

"I have never fought a monster. I have wondered all night if such a thing can be done. It must take the strongest men with the bravest hearts, men who are not afraid to die, to fight a monster . . . men like ourselves."

A ripple of affirmative grunts coursed through Kicking Bird's audience.

"Is any man here afraid to die?"

A chorus of *no*'s rose in the dawn.

"Is any warrior among us afraid to die?"

Louder and more confident, the chorus was repeated as light spread over the prairie.

"Then we must fight this monster!"

Kicking Bird's words were what every warrior needed. They shifted restlessly on the ground, muttering and grunting their approval. A few jumped to their feet and shouted out their disdain for all enemies, regardless of size. More warriors were streaming in from the surrounding prairie, and in what seemed no time, a gigantic circle had formed around the men in council.

"We must fight this monster with care if we are to defeat him," Kicking Bird continued. "We must fight him as he sleeps in the night."

"Yes . . . yes . . . at night," the voices of his listeners rejoined.

"The monster is of many parts. We must kill it a little at a time. We must kill it whenever, wherever we can find it. Death to the killers of our brother!"

It would have been useless for Kicking Bird to sign more because pandemonium had overtaken the council. Every warrior was on his feet.

Some had begun to dance and sing. Others were racing onto the prairie to gather their horses.

Kicking Bird stood calmly at the center of the upheaval. He did not know what would happen now, nor did he want to think about it. But for the moment he felt good. The hearts of the men who followed him were beating again.

CHAPTER XXXIII

*T*HAT SAME AFTERNOON, OUTRIDERS OF THE GREAT PARTY DIS-
covered the first camp of hunters. The scouts had not actually seen their
bivouac, but the distant boom of the long-barreled, far-shooting buffalo
guns of the whites told of its existence. Following instructions, the scouts
hurried back to the main body of warriors and, shortly after their arrival,
the leading men went into council.

No one had ever seen a party of white hunters that consisted of more
than ten or twelve men, and their camps never had fortifications. Their
heavy, fast-firing rifles presented the most difficult problem. A warrior
might not even see the man who was firing before losing his life an instant after he heard the hollow report of the big gun. A handful of such
rifles were enough to deter large forces. A night attack, however, reduced
this threat to practically nothing.

As the men in the circle talked these things through, it quickly became apparent to all that Kicking Bird's strategy was wise. A few men
wondered aloud at the lack of honor in killing enemies as they slept, but
they were quickly reminded that the whites were not so much an enemy
as a scourge, and a scourge, as everyone knew, must be eradicated by any
possible means.

Ever mindful of the niceties of diplomacy, Kicking Bird suggested that each tribe select fifteen warriors by lot to ride in the first wave, an approach embraced by every man in the circle. The timing of the attack was set for an hour before dawn, and as the sun dropped below the horizon, the warriors concluded their talk and returned to their followers, certain that by the time the sun returned, the prairie would be soaking up the hated blood of the buffalo-killers.

Around midnight a force of sixty-five warriors, augmented by Kicking Bird, Wind In His Hair, Young Dog, Touch The Clouds, Wolf Robe, and White Bear, who, by virtue of standing, had been exempted from the random draw, moved to within striking distance of the hunters' camp.

After an hour's wait, two scouts returned to report that there were eight white men in the squalid camp and that all of them, even the guard they had posted, were asleep. Two wagons were parked near the fire, but otherwise there was no visible impediment to the attack.

A few young men whooped with anticipation but their cries were quickly stifled by the reproaches of elders mounted next to them. Only a signal from the man who had created the war party could send it into action, and Kicking Bird was sitting calmly on his pony.

Like any good field commander who strives to leave nothing to chance when the lives of his fighters are in the balance, Kicking Bird decided to wait a few more minutes. It was possible that the scouts' maneuverings had caused a light sleeper to open his eyes, and the Comanche leader wanted to give the camp time to slip back into the deepest slumber possible.

But even the shrewdest commander cannot anticipate all of the infinite chance deviations of life, and it was no different with Kicking Bird. That one of the hunters might have a toothache never occurred to him, much less that the man who sat up in his blanket shortly after the scouts departed had done so at the instance of a throbbing jaw and not because some sixth sense had alerted him to danger. Nor could Kicking Bird have foreseen that the pain in one man's mouth would have such devastating consequences for himself, his warriors, and those whose prayers for success they carried. Had he been able to divine any of these things, Kicking Bird might have concluded that the fate of the Comanches and all other free people on the plains had turned cruel.

The man whose aching jaw was a key element in the destiny of an entire people had been suffering for several days. His fellow hunters had done all they could for him, trying that same afternoon to yank it out with a bullet mold, but their latest effort had only succeeded in breaking off a chunk of the afflicted molar.

The sufferer had tried to hasten sleep with a few long gulps of whiskey, but now, as he sat in the night, staring at the slovenly camp, which stank continually with the odor of rotting blood and skin, he decided impulsively to ride for Adobe Walls.

It pained him to do so because he was going to lose a lot of money, but the hurt in his head was too great. He grabbed up his Sharps rifle, scooped his bedding into his arms, and in minutes was riding north across the prairie.

Half a mile out he heard gunfire at his back and turned to look. The fire at camp was only a pinpoint of light far off in the darkness, and though he couldn't make out the action at that distance, he knew instantly from the volume of rounds being fired that the camp was under attack.

Then, as he sat listening, the gunfire suddenly diminished and a different sound rolled across the prairie. It came to his ears and traveled into his brain with a creeping recognition that stood his hair on end. He was hearing the primal, horrifying screams of Indians. With the finality of a trip-hammer, the hunter whirled his horse around and, even after reaching a full gallop, didn't stop kicking.

CHAPTER XXXIV

*T*HE BUFFALO-KILLER WHO LIVED THE LONGEST MANAGED TO get off one round before his head was split in half with an ax. The others barely had time to stir before they died.

But as warriors buzzed over the camp, firing everything but the body parts of the dead, Kicking Bird sat his pony with little sense of satisfaction. The scouts were certain they had counted eight white men, but only seven lay dead. The surrounding prairie was hastily searched for the missing enemy but no one was found, and Kicking Bird sensed they must move quickly in case the missing hunter had somehow escaped to spread an alarm.

Twenty minutes after they attacked, the thousand warriors were ploughing the darkness of the plains, hoping to catch more camps unaware of their presence. As they sped north they saw many more dead buffalo but little of the men who had killed them. By noon of the following day, they had encountered but one recently abandoned camp, and, certain that their presence had been announced, the great force hurried on, clinging to the prospect of overtaking isolated parties of fleeing hunters.

Judiciously alternating between all-out flight and periodic brief rest, the man with the toothache maintained an hour's lead over the huge war party. He had roused one camp of men, who spurned his advice and dashed east instead of following him to Adobe Walls. But he encountered no one else, and as he urged his weary horse on, the sore-jawed man assumed that by a miraculous stroke of luck all the other outfits must be out of the country or laying over at "the Walls."

His assumption was confirmed when, only a few miles from his goal, he happened upon three white men—two riding side by side on a buckboard, one mounted on a horse. Though he had never been introduced he knew the bearded, well-appointed men on the buckboard to be the brothers Rath, the wealthy, energetic financiers behind the frontier buffalo trade. The man on horseback was well known to him as the manager of the brothers' holdings at Adobe Walls.

The three men listened to the hunter's story of narrow escape and flight in shocked silence. All of them were unnerved to hear that what seemed to be a very large party of heathens was abroad and obviously bent on murdering whatever lay in their path.

For the Rath brothers, however, the Indian threat represented something other than mere bodily harm. Being inveterate creatures of commerce, the siblings' minds naturally leapt to the problem of how best to protect their investment.

They exchanged a few whispered words, then climbed down from the wagon. The manager dismounted and the three men held a brief conference out of earshot of the surviving hunter. In the tall grass of the prairie a number of quick decisions were reached. A lull in the buffalo slaughter had concentrated many hunters at the Adobe Walls installation. There were at least twenty-five guns there, maybe as many as thirty, but if they knew a large party of marauding savages were headed their way, many were likely to bolt. That would leave the saloon and hotel and processing sheds the Rath brothers owned vulnerable.

In the interest of preserving the empire they had labored so mightily to construct, an empire that produced a juggernaut of wealth to which there seemed no end, a conspiracy between the Rath brothers and their reliable manger was hatched.

Minutes later, assured that he would obtain proper care for his inflamed molar away from Adobe Walls, the hunter traded horses with the manager and struck east in the heady company of the Rath brothers.

The manager started back for the holdings at Adobe Walls, entrusted with executing a plan sure to guarantee that his masters' vastly lucrative industry would be maintained. None of the hunters at "the Walls" was to be informed of the impending threat to their lives. But that night, through a subterfuge of the manager's devising, the temporary settlement would be caused to prepare for an attack that was sure to come.

The manager was confident in the plan's simple brilliance. He was also certain that the presence of so many crack shots working behind the solid fortifications of the recently erected company town could blunt any hoard of screaming, arrow-shooting wild men.

CHAPTER XXXV

KICKING BIRD AND HIS ARMY OF WARRIORS WERE ABOUT ten miles from the place called Adobe Walls when its presence was reported and, in the lengthy council that followed, the discouraging news brought by the scouts was discussed in detail. It seemed that the head of the monster had been located but almost every piece of information spoke against attacking it.

The buffalo-killers had congregated in alarming numbers. The scouts had counted twenty-eight white men with far-shooting guns, guns which could be fired from the cover of several large earthen houses which had risen on the plains. The settlement lay in a denuded bowl of land upon which there was nothing to shield an attack. Four white men seemed to be camped around a wagon perhaps a hundred yards from the shelter of the buildings. They would be an easy target, and that was the only attractive aspect of making an attack.

But a door had closed behind each of the thousand warriors and there was no going back. No one talked against going ahead, despite the fact that everyone knew men were bound to die in the face of guns that could tear holes in flesh as big as a gourd, and that the chances for victory could not be great. Since they had taken the war trail, the party's reason for being and its avowed mission had swelled to something larger than its parts. They could not now shrink from what had become a holy duty. The only question that needed to be decided was how they would assail the monster's head, and Kicking Bird's strategy was so simple and straightforward that it was adopted after a few minutes of perfunctory discussion.

They would attack as one body, slamming their full might against the objective in the hope it would collapse through the sheer weight of their assault. They would not attack in the dark but come out of the sun, using its first, blinding light as a screen. Kicking Bird and half a dozen handpicked warriors would overwhelm the men camped around the wagon in the open while the vast bulk of warriors threw themselves against the hunters' fortifications. They would wait until an hour before dawn to position themselves, thus giving each warrior ample time to smoke and recite prayers, prepare his accoutrements of battle, and sing his death song.

Whether these decisions might have altered the outcome could never be known, but one thing was certain: no warrior heard the shot, fired in the early hours of morning, that woke the entire population residing at Adobe Walls.

The manager had retired earlier than usual to ensure he would be wide awake at the precise time everyone else would be steeped in slumber. The round had come from his own pistol, which he reholstered immediately after firing. To the sleeping, disoriented hunters inquiring what was the matter, the manager explained that the sound had come from the prime supporting beam that spanned the "hotel" in which they were now standing.

Fearful of the roof's possible failure, the hunters compliantly set to work shoring up the beam under the manager's careful direction. Toward dawn, as the useless task neared completion, a number of workers, including the men who had been camped outside, returned to their beds, but, to the manager's satisfaction, the majority either continued to tinker with the refurbishments or loiter over coffee, watching and commenting on the labors of their fellows. He had hoped the men from the wagon would stay but felt no culpability when he saw them pass out into the dark. He had encouraged them to stay, and so, he decided, they were making their own funerals by disregarding his advice.

Shortly after the morning sun cleared the horizon, a strange sound, like that of a distant roaring crowd, momentarily froze all human activity at Adobe Walls. Seconds later all eyes had flown to any crack or crevice that afforded a view of the outside. What greeted them was a spectacle so incredible that it squeezed the breath from their lungs.

A sea of mounted warriors was streaming in their direction, surging down a long gentle slope several hundred yards away in a movement so massive as to resemble the graceful, inexorable sweep of an ocean wave. So stunning was the image that at first sight the men inside Adobe Walls could not understand what their own connection to the rushing tide of warriors might be. Time stopped as their brains tumbled incredulously, trying to make sense of the unbelievable message from their eyes.

But when time moved again, barely a split second later, the watchers reacted with a mechanical swiftness. They could not dread or even fear what was bearing down upon them. They only had time to reach for the most obvious instruments of deliverance from certain death. In a mad, strangely silent scramble, each man jumped for the salvation that dwelt in the long barrel of his buffalo gun.

Kicking Bird was charging down the slope at the crest of the human wave, the long, feathered lance he had chosen for the close-in fighting around the wagon leveled against his hip. He pressed a knee against his pony's shoulder and, without breaking stride, the little horse swerved in the direction of the wagon. The metal ribbing bent over its top was only half-covered and, as he closed on the vehicle, Kicking Bird could see the forms of the enemy stirring beneath and above the wagon bed.

Over the last yards of his rush, time began to slow and, picking out a single foe, Kicking Bird raised his lance. A second later the air in front of him was obscured with white smoke and his ears rang painfully as a volley of concentrated fire coming from the wagon seemed to blow it apart.

Most animals might have jumped or twisted away but the pony Kicking Bird rode in war had never been headed. The pony shivered momentarily as the concussive shock buffeted his face and neck and chest. But he never strayed from his course, and an instant later, almost at full speed, he crashed against the wagon. Then Kicking Bird felt his lance point penetrate the soft flesh of a man's body as his own lifted into space. The moment he collided with the earth he was shot in the face from a range of inches.

The pistol slug tore off one of his earlobes, but, like his war pony, Kicking Bird was so used to the primal intensity of battle that he was unfazed and, before the white man could fire another round, his gun hand was in the grip of his attacker's. A split second later Kicking Bird's sharply honed knife drove into the hunter's midsection and ripped upward, opening his belly. As the enemy jerked spasmodically, Kicking Bird mounted his chest, grabbed a hank of long hair, pulled his head off the ground, sliced into the skin at his hairline, and tore off his scalp.

He tucked the bloody hair in his belt as he scrambled from under the wagon and dashed for his pony, which, though pirouetting with excitement at the steady boom of the big buffalo guns being fired from inside Adobe Walls, was waiting obediently. Kicking Bird caught him, swung onto his back, and galloped on into the furious fight ahead.

Mounted warriors were circling the settlement like living rope, trying to draw fire away from the masses of warriors who were clamoring about the doors of the two main buildings. Kicking Bird galloped from one building front to the other and found the same situation at each. Though they were lunging in against the big doors with all their might, the warriors could not break through and the big guns were bringing people down.

Two enterprising warriors, having found a way to separate the tongue from the wagon Kicking Bird had attacked, rode into the mêlée dragging it behind them. Grabbing it up as a battering ram, the frantic warriors began to hurl it against the door but by now the whites inside had found good holes to shoot through and men in front of the entrance began to fall.

Kicking Bird glanced over his shoulder and saw that some of those among the ranks of the circling riders were falling, too. Men were lying dead or wounded on the ground and riders were breaking off in pairs to perform the sacred duty of carrying their brothers off the battlefield.

When Kicking Bird saw one of these saviors shot from his horse, only to tumble onto the man he was endeavoring to rescue, he knew he must call for a retreat. With an eagle bone whistle between his lips, he desperately signaled his men, and after a few minutes of charging within earshot of every fighter, he managed to effect a pullback.

Once the withdrawal was under way, Kicking Bird kicked his heaving pony back up the long slope to the attackers' original staging area, where many of the dead and wounded were being gathered. Pausing beyond the shade of the only tree in the area, Kicking Bird tried to tally his dead as other warriors rode in and stood beside him. But when he had counted to twenty he stopped. There were too many more to count, maybe three times as many.

"We can burn those houses," White Bear signed.

"No fire," pronounced Owl Prophet.

He was sitting on his pony with arms folded across his chest, and the sight of him piqued Kicking Bird's ire. He pushed his pony roughly through the men immediately around and sidled next to Owl Prophet.

"Your power is false," he snapped.

"My power comes from the Mystery!" Owl Prophet snapped back.

"Look at our dead," Kicking Bird shouted. "Who will take their places? You said we would kill all the white men. We have four scalps."

"Some Cheyenne killed a skunk," the prophet retorted. "I heard it."

"Your power is useless," Kicking Bird roared. "You are useless. You should be thrown away!"

He was about to strike Owl Prophet with his quirt when one of the big guns far below boomed, and at the same instant Kicking Bird saw the smoke he heard a slug's distinctive whistle rend the air.

The bullet struck a nearby tree and the lead ricocheted into Owl Prophet's chest, the force of it sending him tumbling straight over his pony's hindquarters. What would have been a killing shot at a shorter distance merely stunned the prophet. He lay on his back for a moment, then pulled himself to a sitting position and groggily gained his feet.

Everyone was thunderstruck. Agitated warriors milled around their leader and Touch The Clouds said the words everyone was thinking.

"The hunters have a rifle that can shoot around objects!"

Touch The Clouds had barely made the words when another gun boomed and the prophet's pony sank onto its knees with a hole in its forehead.

"No rifle shoots that far," White Bear cried. "Maybe they have a gun that can shoot from yesterday."

But the words were seen by only a few because Kicking Bird and the others were already moving away.

The great war party did not survive much longer, only long enough to put its dead to rest. Then it splintered into large, tribe-oriented groups and broke apart, its stupefied members spreading across the open prairie in all directions.

Some still possessed enough fight to drive east for the outlying settlements, where they wreaked havoc for several weeks. Others headed west and north, searching out pockets of remaining buffalo. Kicking Bird, leading a large contingent of dispirited fighters, charted a southerly course that would carry him home.

CHAPTER XXXVI

*T*HE ROAD TO JACKSBORO WAS BROAD AND EASY TO FOLLOW. IT was also well traveled, such that Dances With Wolves had to keep himself and his children clear of human traffic whenever possible. That they kept out of sight slowed their progress, but taking their time fit well with Dances With Wolves' plan. Nothing could be gained by haste and much could be lost. He wanted to leave the impression with anyone they encountered that the threesome was on a routine errand. Any suspicions that might be transmitted to the local counterpart of the Vernon constable would be disastrous.

Though it was only sixty miles from the spot in the crossroads where they had parted company with the lawman, three camps were made and slept in before they reached the outskirts of Jacksboro on the morning of their fourth day out of Vernon.

Mindful of their past lapses in obedience, which reflected so well the stubborn wills they had inherited, Dances With Wolves reminded his children of the necessity for absolute adherence to his instructions so often that he provoked protests from both of them.

Even as they passed the town's outlying buildings, Dances With Wolves was mumbling in Comanche.

"Remember—no talking."

Neither child looked at him. They stared ahead glumly, as if his constant pestering had made them weary to the point of exhaustion.

"And do as I say."

"Father," began Snake In Hands, "I cannot think when you talk. You talk all the time."

"Let's just find Mother and the baby and go home," added Always Walking. "All we do now is talk."

Two horsemen, coming at a canter, emerged from a bend in the road.

"No more," hissed Dances With Wolves.

He could see that they were both men and, as the riders drew closer, Dances With Wolves instinctively checked to make sure his rifle was resting in its scabbard.

When he glanced up again he could see the glint of a metal star on one man's breast and his heart jumped. In a few seconds he would know if the constable had carried out his threat. He hoped desperately that he would not have to kill the approaching riders, because it would give him so little time to locate his wife and daughter. But readying himself as the riders came up, he leaned down along the side of his horse, pretending to check his girth while he gripped the stock of his rifle.

The man with the metal star brought his fingers to the brim of his hat as he and his companion loped past without breaking stride, and to Dances With Wolves' profound relief the ordinary drum of hoofbeats began to fade behind him.

"Do not look at them," he whispered in Comanche to his children.

When the hoofbeats of the lawmen's horses had fallen away to nothing, carrying off the clearest, most dangerous impediment to the success of his mission, Dances With Wolves' heart quickened with the feeling that the Mystery had come forward to aid him. But as he tried to decide whether or not to turn up a side road, new doubts crowded his mind. Perhaps his wife and child were being kept indoors. They might, for some unknown reason, be in another settlement miles away. Maybe they were ill. Maybe they were dead.

Still, he took the sidetrack, and as soon as he made the turn, the trepidations he had labored under for so long lifted off his shoulders in the same way a morning mist vanishes under a powerful sun.

A hundred yards ahead three people were walking up the middle of a hard-packed earthen track. A small child was sandwiched between a large shuffling man and a woman. The child was holding the woman's hand and no amount of white man clothes could obscure their Comanche identity.

Dances With Wolves shouted, "Follow me! Don't stop!" and as his horse leaped into a gallop, he was a warrior again, uttering the series of high, sharp barks of a man charging to battle.

When Stands With A Fist turned to face the oncoming sound, she was momentarily confused by the sight of a white man racing toward her and reflexively stumbled backward for the safety of the roadside. But the white man was screaming out her name in Comanche and all at once she knew it was him. Sweeping Stays Quiet into her arms she jumped back into the center of the road.

He was coming at a full run and when he leaned along the charging horse's shoulder and extended an arm, Stands With A Fist planted her feet and reached out. His hand slammed into her arm, locked itself on her bicep, and suddenly she was swinging up in a high, smooth arc that brought her down behind the saddle.

But as she landed on the horse's rump the animal bucked and she listed to one side, almost going over. Struggling to right herself, she lost her grip on Stays Quiet and the little girl tumbled off, landing prone on the road.

Stunned by a rush of action he could not comprehend, Axel Strunk had stood still as a post, but when he saw Stays Quiet on hands and knees, shrieking in the road, he bellowed in anguish and lumbered toward her. He had taken only a few tottering steps however, when he was hit from behind by a force that sent him sprawling to the edge of the road. When he looked up he saw two children, a boy and girl on horseback, galloping after the man who had grabbed Stands With A Fist. And between them, suspended in space, a foot or two above the ground, was his little friend.

Unable to absorb what had happened, Axel sat crying on the side of the road. Several citizens had witnessed bits and pieces of the rescue, but despite their entreaties, Axel Strunk was unable to enlighten them with further information concerning the bizarre incident.

As more curious inhabitants were drawn to the scene, it soon emerged that it would be impossible to inform the town constable, for he had already departed on official business to an outlying community. It was quickly concluded that it would be logical to repair immediately to the Gunther home, and it happened that Cousin Gunther himself was in residence when the small mob of worried townspeople, pushing the bewildered, grief-stricken simpleton in front of them, ascended the porch.

Cousin Gunther had no better luck in extracting an intelligible account from Axel Strunk, who refused to do anything but sit on the bench and sob into his hands.

It was obvious that Cousin Christine and her child had been abducted, though for what purpose and by whom remained unclear. The kidnapping had only been witnessed in its final stages and those who had seen it were certain that white people, a man and two children, had been the perpetrators. Yet all within earshot were just as certain that they had heard the unmistakable howls of an Indian.

Before a search party could be formed, the searchers would have to know what they were looking for, and thirty minutes passed before the notion was put forward that a "revenger" had snatched them. That led to an animated discussion concerning the dangers of fooling with someone so crazed, and as Cousin Gunther listened, he became more detached, withdrawing into a dreamy, altogether balmic glow. The regular earnest application of prayer had worked a miracle, releasing himself and his family from their unbearable burden.

"Yes," he agreed, "a revenger is nothing to fool with."

The litany of excuses for inaction continued until, at last, a woman who had said little before now shook her head and, in a rare patch of silence, offered the inescapable conclusion no one had yet dared to express.

"If they're not dead already, they will be by the time anyone catches up. I'm not letting my husband get killed over that."

No rescue party was formed that day, and when the constable returned to be apprised of what had taken place he soberly echoed the sentiments of his constituents.

"Naw, I can't waste a minute's time tryin' to get them people back. Far as I'm concerned, we're a lot better off without 'em."

Weeks passed before news of the once-famous captive's disappearance at the hands of a revenger saturated the frontier. But it evaporated rapidly. Alive, Christine Gunther was something to talk about, but death quickly reduced her to an arcane memory of times past.

CHAPTER XXXVII

*T*HE FIGHT AT ADOBE WALLS, LIKE OTHER REPORTS OF SKIR-
mishing along the frontier, elicited little excitement at Fort Sill. That the
free tribes had managed to raise such a large force prompted considerable talk, but the fact that a small group of civilian hunters had triumphed over hundreds of warriors only served to confirm the belief that the dismantling and subjugation of the wild societies of the plains was inevitable, and Colonel Mackenzie continued to devote his seemingly depthless reserves of energy to raising the great installation that would function as a clearinghouse for the changeover to come.

He had been in regular telegraphic contact with General Sherman, who rarely failed to express his ongoing consternation at the massacre on the Great Salt Prairie while he kept Fort Sill's commander up to date on every appreciable shift in the political winds of Washington.

The president still clung to a policy of pacification, but the General of the Army was certain that adjustments were sure to come. The Quaker plan, for all its scope and sincerity, was not yielding significant results, and fruitless projects supported by public monies were something no politician, no matter how highly placed, could suffer for long.

Colonel Mackenzie, glad as he was for the biweekly wires, did not have to be told from afar that the assimilation initiative was not working. The proof was in front of his face.

On balance, he had a high regard for Lawrie Tatum. The little Quaker possessed boundless determination and had consistently attacked his impossible task with the zeal of a terrier unearthing a bone. His honesty was as sincere as his faith, and Colonel Mackenzie could find no fault with all that he had created from virtually nothing. He had erected a school and recruited a Quaker teacher for Indian children, built stockpens to hold the government-issue beeves, had systemized a line of trade for the goods offered by the post sutler, and was even conducting daily classes in the art of agriculture.

But Lawrie Tatum's naïveté could be annoying, and it regularly occurred to Colonel Mackenzie that the shiny-domed, arm-waving little man cut a ludicrous figure. It was as if the agent had mounted a grand party to which no one came. School attendance fluctuated between zero and four or five. Agriculture classes were often canceled because no one showed up, and most of the aborigines who frequented the sutler's store rarely had anything to trade, but merely loitered in the shade of the porch, trolling for handouts.

Like a wilderness doctor on rounds, Lawrie Tatum rode his mule in a daily circuit of camps scattered through the vicinity, doing his best to indoctrinate and minister to the tiny fraction of wild people who had taken the white man's holy road.

But despair nagged at him, and it required the Quaker's entire reservoir of faith to continue. There were no leaders among the enrollees, who were comprised of the aged or infirm, the opportunistic, and, in some cases, the feebleminded. Those who had answered his call were merely stragglers. Even Lawrie Tatum knew that his efforts would be fruitless so long as the core of the Comanche and Kiowa nations ran free.

The first tremor of change arrived at the end of summer, when Colonel Mackenzie was promoted to the rank of brigadier general. At the same time he had been summoned east for the broad purpose of "consultation." Though he could not know the exact nature of his summons, during the long trip to Washington he became convinced that the military was about to assume a more active role in the affairs of the wild tribes.

General Mackenzie spent a week in the capitol. His evenings were exhaustive gauntlets of social gatherings which did not provide much leisure. The parties and charity functions he attended were packed with military brass, and General Mackenzie, who had never grasped political life or its intrigues, felt uncomfortable in the top-heavy presence of his masterful fellow generals.

He was even more out of place in the company of women. Perhaps because he had been brought up in a houseful of aunts who had raised him as if he were a little girl, as an adult he ran from anything having to do with the female sex.

For years he had worried that his lifelong bachelorhood would be an impediment to promotion, but now that he had the stars on his shoulders, he was confident that no amount of whispered asides or late-night pillow talk between man and wife—or mistress—could take them away.

The peace of mind his generalship afforded him brought with it a clarity, and despite the memories of so many old wounds, he found his powers of concentration at full capacity during the many important policy meetings he attended during the day.

The round of conferences reached a crescendo on the last full day of his stay, when, in a party that included General Sherman, his number two, General Sheridan, and four other men of field rank, he met with the president.

At first General Mackenzie was lulled into believing the meeting was of no particular importance. The president and his generals behaved more like old acquaintances than they did men of stature. They bantered among themselves for a time, and even when they got down to business, the agenda seemed to provoke no urgency. Gradually, however, it dawned on the new general that any interview with the commander in chief must, despite the collegial atmosphere, be paramount.

He listened keenly as General Sherman laid out the state of affairs on the frontier and was taken aback when the General of the Army suddenly turned in his direction and announced, "General Mackenzie, provide the president with a firsthand account, if you please."

A bolt of panic surged through the new general, and in the second or two it took to subside, Mackenzie's athletic mind formed a plan. He would be clear, succinct, and objective. And he would not try to hide his deformity. If the stumps started their odd clicking, as they most likely would, he reasoned that it would be best if the president not only heard them but saw them as well.

Thus General Mackenzie placed his forearms on the tabletop, taking care to fully expose both hands, and began a concise report of his experiences in the field. He prefaced his remarks about the activities of the Quaker agents with a brief declaration of the high respect he held them in before outlining the miserable results of their struggle. He related his observations on the massacre of the corn train and a few other examples of outrage that had recently come to his attention. He concluded with a short but dramatic account of the fight at Adobe Walls.

When the stumps on his hand first began their disconcerting syncopation, the president dropped his eyes to the source of the sound. Mackenzie had paused long enough to provide the commander in chief's gaze a graceful exit, and from that point on, the odd disfigurement ceased to be disruptive.

The president, who had listened attentively, sat back in his chair and glanced into space before fixing the new general with his smallish eyes.

"What do you think of those buffalo-hunters?" he asked flatly.

Again Mackenzie was taken aback.

"As a race, sir?"

Everyone laughed, and the president was still chortling as he said, "I can only imagine what they're like as a race—a bad dream!"

The generals laughed until their eyes ran, and when the guffawing had finally dwindled into snorts and chuckles the glassy-eyed president looked at Mackenzie again.

"I mean, what do you think of them being there?"

"Well, I believe it's unlawful, sir."

"Are you doing anything to uphold the law?"

"In my opinion, sir, it's impossible to enforce the legislation."

"How can that be?"

"Sir, the buffalo trade is popular and lucrative. It's something like a gold rush. Every prominent restaurant in this city has buffalo tongue on its menu."

"That's right," the president agreed, "and it costs an arm and a leg."

The room was silent as the president rubbed his eyes with both hands.

"Well," he said, dropping his hands, "the army is convinced that the peace policy is a failure."

"On most accounts, sir," Sherman answered.

The president rose out of his chair, signaling closure. "Come up with an alternative and we'll schedule another meeting."

"We have an alternative, sir."

The president stood for a moment longer before descending again to his high-backed chair.

"Let's hear it, then."

"Actually, sir," Sherman explained, "it's more a variation than it is an alternative."

"All right, all right."

By way of introduction, Sherman indicated the small, bullet-eyed man next to him and said, "General Sheridan has been the primary formulator, so I'll let him speak to it."

"Good," grunted the president.

Sheridan was known to the president as a master at applying lethal pressure on a weakening foe, and his ideas for dealing with the "Indian problem" were cut from the same cloth. As he listened, the president quickly realized the plan was smart, simple, and, best of all, politically adroit. The Quaker agents would deliver a clear message to all camps on the plains: all would be required to enroll on reservations within thirty days of receiving the message. Those not enrolling would then be considered hostile and subject to pursuit and punishment by the forces of the United States. The public would believe that the government was offering the olive branch to all peace-loving natives, while serving notice to the hopeless incorrigibles. In less than five minutes General Sheridan had layed out a reasonable, workable solution to the whole unrelenting mess, and as the president rolled it over in his mind, he could find no good reason to reject it.

"How soon would you be able to mobilize?" he asked Mackenzie.

"In a week, sir."

Encouraged, Sheridan leaned forward.

"If I might just add, Mr. President . . ."

"Yes?"

"As the ultimatum is delivered . . . might it not be wise to invite the most amenable leaders to visit Washington. We know from past experience that a trip to the capitol has a sobering effect, even on the most intractable chieftains. And the timing might prove quite advantageous."

"Excellent idea," the president remarked, rising out of his chair again. "Let's get some of those people out here."

Ranald Mackenzie returned from Washington wearing stars and girding himself for battle. He immediately called together the Quaker agents and instructed them to disseminate the War Department's ultimatum to the tribes of the southern plains in any manner they felt prudent. Then he hunkered down on the veranda of his quarters to plan his campaign. One of the hallmarks of the general's field operations was meticulous and canny planning. His attention to detail had enabled him to carry the day on numerous occasions, and he would spare no efforts as he laid his nets for the subjugation of the primitives.

Sheridan seemed to take a campaign for granted, and though Mackenzie had not known him well before his trip east, he departed Washington with the impression that General Sheridan knew quite well what he was talking about. They had shared a brief but memorable conversation as they left the White House and crossed Pennsylvania Avenue.

"You handled yourself well, General," Sheridan had said. "I particularly liked what you did with that silly question about the buffalo-hunters."

"Thank you."

"The president has been sensitive to this business of the buffalo-hunting. Half of Congress—half of the congressional wives, anyway—they're bitching constantly about the 'slaughter of the buffalo.' I don't think a day goes by that he isn't assaulted by some plea to save the buffalo. To hell with the buffalo! Those hunters are saving the army time, trouble, and money. They're killing the Indian commissary. No buffalo, no Indians, no problem. Simple as that."

"You think there'll be no need of a campaign?"

"Of course there'll be a campaign," Sheridan replied jovially. "There'll be some diehards . . . and you'll have to go after them."

CHAPTER XXXVIII

ONLY ONE AMONG THEM UNDERSTOOD PRECISELY WHAT THE defeat at Adobe Walls signaled, and that was Kicking Bird. Though he was as brokenhearted as any man, the leader of those who strove to look beyond the horizon had settled on a final, unalterable course of action that would begin to unfold as soon as they reached the village.

In the meantime, however, an insistent voice began to speak in his head. "Go west . . . find food."

They were still several days from home when the detour to the west was made, and they had traveled but a few hours when they met the party led by Wind In His Hair. After debating the possibility of continuing the war trail, the remaining Hard Shields had at last discarded it and turned their horses for home.

As the leaders of the two groups councilled in the open, under a cloudless sky, a brief reestablishment of brotherhood was effected. Wind In His Hair had also sensed that the village would be hungry and, while they could never make up for the terrible losses they suffered, bringing in food would fill empty stomachs and provide some relief for the hearts of everyone.

The parley was more like a meeting of old, trusted acquaintances rather than actual band members who had known each other all their lives. It was better that way, for the animosity between the two groups was momentarily suspended in the space between them. The smoking was leisurely, the talk was casual, and there was even a little of the joking that had always been a feature of such meetings.

Kicking Bird and Wind In His Hair and even Owl Prophet shared laughter over the visionary being knocked off his pony, and when Kicking Bird offered, "I guess your power is pretty good . . . you're still alive," a reconciliation of sorts was effected. The council broke up with more comraderie than anyone had felt in a long time and the two groups rode west together with common purpose.

The country that was once home to buffalo in huge numbers was nearly devoid of game, but after a full day of traveling, the party located a herd of several hundred animals. They were spaced for several miles along the breaks of a wide stream, hiding like refugees from the agents of holocaust, and when the warriors started them they ran not as a herd but like a flock of frightened birds, scattering helter-skelter.

Enough of the big creatures were taken to load every spare pony with hides and meat, and women who might ordinarily have shaken their heads at the sloppiness of the butchering did not complain when the humbled war party returned. The village had been living on scraps for many days, and the arrival of meat had the hoped-for effect.

But the prospect of full bellies did little to offset the present grief. Twenty-two warriors had been left on the slope above Adobe Walls, and ten more had serious wounds that, if not fatal, would incapacitate them for the rest of their lives. Shrieks and moans for the dead and wounded overtook the village even as the meat was being parceled out and, as daylight faded, the communal gloom deepened.

Not a single lodge was spared the anguish. Those who had lost family members were inconsolable, and even as some sheared off their hair and others hacked at their own limbs, relief was no closer.

At twilight the mourning had yet to peak, and it was at this time that a lone rider was spotted coming off the prairie. Unfortunately for the little Quaker on his mule, the first riders to reach him were a group of angry young men who ignored his upraised hands and the words of peace and friendship with which he spoke to them in their own language, and contemptuously ripped the small bald man off his mount.

Providentially, the young men began to argue, shoving each other roughly around in a contest to see who would have the right to strike the fatal blow. As the squabble continued, Lawrie Tatum tried to wriggle away through the grass. When a few observant boys pounced on him, the Quaker suddenly found his legs held fast against the ground and several knees pressing into his chest. His head was jerked so hard that his neck cracked, and the merciless face of a young warrior peered, upside down, into his. He saw metal flashing in the sun and he felt a blade cut into his temple and slice backward along the side of his head. Just as he made the realization that he was being scalped alive, the knife halted and his body was suddenly released.

He shut his eyes, trying to comprehend what was happening, and when he opened them again he was looking in the gruesome, one-eyed countenance of Wind In His Hair. The warrior stared at him silently for a few moments. Then the face of Kicking Bird appeared and Laurie Tatum was certain he had received deliverance.

"You want this pitiful creature?" Wind In His Hair asked.

"Hmm," Kicking Bird grunted.

"Better keep him in your lodge . . . better watch him. If he comes out these young men will kill him. If I see him, I'll kill him."

There was still a gauntlet of knife-wielding widows and taunting, stone-throwing children to navigate as they passed through the village, and Lawrie Tatum was struck on the head with several projectiles before he was whisked into the safe haven of Kicking Bird's family lodge. While Kicking Bird's wives applied compresses and bandaged his torn and bleeding scalp, the shaken Quaker watched and listened as his host tried to explain that he should stay put until he could be spirited out of the village.

But Lawrie Tatum had not risked his life only to abort his mission, and Kicking Bird was taken aback when his white acquaintance began to converse in passable Comanche.

"Bring Ten Bears," he petitioned. "You . . . Ten Bears . . . me . . . we talk now."

"Now?"

"Yes . . . now."

A few minutes later, the old man, whose spectacles now rested on his nose through every waking hour of the day, took the hand of a white man for the first time.

Fearful of the danger in having the little agent in his special lodge, Kicking Bird shooed his family out and the three men settled on the floor. They smoked Kicking Bird's pipe, and as it began its fourth revolution, the Quaker shook his head negatively. He let his gaze wander fitfully over the floor for a few seconds before glancing first at Kicking Bird, then Ten Bears, then back to Kicking Bird.

"I talk," he said, jabbing a stubby finger against his chest. "I talk now."

Kicking Bird and Ten Bears exchanged puzzled looks. This little man, his face coated with sweat and grime, blood caked in jagged lines along his jaw and throat, his bandaged head giving the impression of an impoverished potentate, and the bent frame of his eyeglasses causing the apparatus to list wildly on his face—what made him think he could simply ride into their village and demand to speak with Ten Bears?

Yet Lawrie Tatum's eyes burned with a bright purpose that would have registered on anyone. The urgency of his mission was so great, in fact, that it transcended his ridiculous appearance, and Kicking Bird and Ten Bears, curious to hear him, nodded for him to go ahead.

Clearly and concisely, the Quaker relayed the new ultimatum. All Comanches must enroll on the reservation within thirty days or suffer the consequences of war with the whites. He also made it clear that while he personally abhorred war, there was nothing he could do to stop it, and he stressed that to take up arms against the whites would be fruitless. He concluded by telling both men that he had spoken truly.

Kicking Bird stared at him, shocked.

"Everyone must come in?" he asked, disbelieving.

"Yes."

"In one moon?"

"Yes."

Ten Bears had pulled out his pipe, packed it, and, in the silence before Kicking Bird and Lawrie Tatum spoke, had began to smoke.

"One moon not enough," Kicking Bird stated flatly.

"One moon," Lawrie Tatum repeated helplessly. "One moon."

Kicking Bird leaned in toward his visitor.

"Some Comanche fight."

"You . . . stop them."

"No, Kicking Bird cannot."

"If you go . . . people follow."

"Some . . . maybe. Each man decide. Not Kicking Bird."

Frustrated, the Quaker tacked in another direction.

"The buffalo . . ." he began solemnly, "buffalo gone."

Kicking Bird's eyes widened. So did Ten Bears'.

"Gone!" Kicking Bird exclaimed. "Where?"

"Trains."

Lawrie Tatum sighed as Kicking Bird tried to grasp what he was saying.

"East," the Quaker offered.

Direction didn't matter much to Kicking Bird, who was still preoccupied with the concept of buffalo on trains. "How many trains?" he asked.

"Oh," Lawrie Tatum gasped, "I do not know. Many, many, many. All day. All night."

"The buffalo are dead on the prairie," Kicking Bird stated firmly. "Not on trains."

The Quaker's rudimentary Comanche was adequate but, reverting to simple signs, he easily made Kicking Bird and Ten Bears understand that he was not talking about whole buffalo. Only the tongues and skins of the buffalo were being carried east on trains.

Ten Bears took the pipe from his mouth and said something that Kicking Bird quickly translated.

"Buffalo not die. Buffalo holy."

Lawrie Tatum pursed his lips and softened his voice.

"Comanche no eat . . . no food. Comanche must come."

Again Ten Bears spoke and Kicking Bird translated.

"We talk in . . . in council . . . tonight. Ten Bears will not go. Born on prairie. Die on prairie."

Kicking Bird glanced at Ten Bears as the old man continued.

"Ten Bears old," Kicking Bird said "Too old for white man's holy road."

"Kicking Bird?" Lawrie Tatum asked. "Kicking Bird come in? Touch pen?"

Though his mind was already set, Kicking Bird could not find it in himself to admit his decision.

"Maybe," he answered.

The Quaker agent was crestfallen. He had ridden far into unfamiliar country, risking his life to deliver a distasteful ultimatum. The response to his personal plea had fallen far short of the hopes he harbored, and as he tried to articulate the last part of the offer, he did so with none of his normal verve, certain that this, too, would be rejected.

"Come to Washington."

Kicking Bird's face jumped.

"Washington?"

"Great White Father wants . . . meet Comanches."

"Who?" Kicking Bird asked.

"You," Lawrie Tatum answered. Then he tilted his head in Ten Bears' direction. "And Ten Bears."

"Kicking Bird . . . Ten Bears . . . go Washington? Meet Great White Father?"

"Yes."

Kicking Bird translated the startling invitation for the old man, but Ten Bears, after a moment's reflection, shook his head as he spoke.

"Ten Bears say no. Can't ride horse. Can't walk so far."

"Ride train," Lawrie Tatum countered.

Kicking Bird spoke to Ten Bears again and, for the first time, the headman sent his reply directly to Lawrie Tatum.

"White people kill Comanches," he said.

"No, no, no. Great White Father say no. No . . . no."

"Catch Comanches . . . put in cage."

"No," the Quaker said emphatically. "Kicking Bird, Ten Bears go Washington. Make five, six, seven sleeps. Come home."

Kicking Bird translated and the old man picked up his pipe. He lit it with a brand from the fire and puffed intently. Then he laid it across his lap and, when his reply to Kicking Bird was finished, looked good-naturedly in Lawrie Tatum's direction.

"Ten Bears say he like new eyes Lawrie Tatum give him. Wants new eyes to see what white men do. He go."

"Kicking Bird?" the Quaker asked breathlessly.

"Kicking Bird go."

"Wonderful!" Lawrie Tatum exclaimed in English. The two Comanches gazed at him quizzically and he quickly added in Comanche, "Good . . . good!"

The excitement in the lodge was palpable for a few seconds. Then Ten Bears spoke his second thoughts.

"Train safe?" Kicking Bird asked.

"Yes, quite safe."

"No kill Comanche?"

"No," replied the Quaker, who, for emphasis, reached into his saddlebags and pulled out the black book he worshiped. He placed one hand flat on the book, raised the other, and swung his head from side to side.

"No kill Comanche."

CHAPTER XXXIX

a COUNCIL WAS HELD THE NIGHT OF THE FATEFUL INTER-
view with Lawrie Tatum, and it was perhaps the most unlikely ever
convened.

As the warriors filed in, the wailing of women and children outside
continued unabated, but the men stuffing themselves into Kicking Bird's
special lodge would have been no less morose had there been no mourning to dampen the atmosphere. Each took his place, and the pipe re-
volved around the first circle in a silence so complete that each could
hear his neighbor breathing.

Finally, Ten Bears laid the pipe in front of him and started up from
the floor. Pushing the spectacles higher on his nose, he gazed wistfully
over the assembly.

"Hear me, brave-hearted Comanche men. My heart is glad to see
you here. It fills with pride at the sight of fine warriors sitting together."

Choking with emotion, Ten Bears paused. In the absolute quiet, he
stared at his feet until he regained his composure.

"The little white man agent has asked Ten Bears and Kicking Bird to
make a long journey east. The Great Father in Washington wants to
meet us and take our hands. I have told him I will go. Kicking Bird has

said the same. I have often wondered how white people can live in this world and I want to see it. We will visit the white people for maybe ten sleeps and then we will come back.

"This journey will be my last. When I return I will leave this beautiful earth I have been walking so long and cross the stars to be with all those who came before me. I am looking forward to crossing the stars. I have traveled the circle of life. My life has been good. My heart is good. That is all I have to say for myself."

There was not a sound as Ten Bears sat back down, with help, and the few seconds of stillness that followed seemed to last forever.

Then Kicking Bird stood up.

"I have seen what you have seen," he began. "Our brothers lying dead on the earth. I have fought what you have fought. I was not afraid to fight. I was not afraid to die. I took a white man's scalp. It hangs in my lodge . . . but Kicking Bird is finished trying to fight the white man's guns. It is useless. More fighting will only make more dying . . . more weeping."

He paused long enough to let an upwelling of sobs from outside wash eerily through the lodge.

"The little white man says the buffalo are being killed so the white people can have their tongues. Maybe they are making medicine with the tongues of our brothers. Maybe they are using them for ceremonies. I do not know. Soon there will be nothing for my wives and children to put in their bellies. I want my wives and my children to live more than I want to fight.

"Before I go to Washington I will go where the white man asks and take his pen in my hand and touch it to the paper that promises to make no more war. I will follow the 'holy road.' This I will do in the morning.

"I ask no one to go with me. Each man here is a warrior. Each man will know his heart. I have no rancor toward any man who disagrees with what I do. My heart is good."

Wind In His Hair was starting up as Kicking Bird settled back down but, after reaching his feet, he seemed in no hurry to speak. He stood, imperious, for a few moments, his good eye unblinking. Then he laid a fist gently against his chest.

"There is no bitterness in Wind In His Hair's heart," he began. "Our minds may choose different paths, but some part of every heart will always be as one. All my life I have been a warrior, and I will not change. I will not die as anything else.

"The whites have taken much from me. They have taken my brothers, my wives, my children. Now they want to take me off the earth upon which I walk. Maybe they will kill me now, and if they do, so be it. I will not take their hands. I will keep my ponies' tails tied up for war."

Wind In His Hair had made his quiet, measured statement in silence, and it prevailed as he resumed his seat.

The council did not stir for a minute or two and then, as spontaneously and mysteriously as a school of fish shifts direction, men began to rise and file out. No one talked because there was nothing left to say. Each warrior walked back to his lodge alone.

CHAPTER XL

*T*HE YOUNG MEN WERE ESPECIALLY TROUBLED. THEY HAD PLANNED and dreamed and striven all their lives for opportunities to prove themselves, but the perplexing rush of events that culminated in the most recent council denied them the chance to live fully. If there were no buffalo, how could anyone hunt? Or feed a family? Or have a family? If there were no horses to steal, how could a man grow rich? How could a man win honors if there was no enemy to fight? How could any young warrior just starting out aspire to membership in the Hard Shields? How could Hard Shields exist? What could a man do on a "reservation" except watch the sun go up and down? The questions haunted every young man, and that agony was felt by Smiles A Lot.

When he stepped into his lodge and Hunting For Something asked him what had happened, he said nothing. His mind was being pressured from all sides with pros and cons. To be a Comanche was suddenly a strangely confusing thing.

He stood with his back to her, working loose the braid that attached the black cascade of horsehair to his head. When he had returned the decoration to its place of safety, in an occasional bag, he walked to the fire and sat down, but still he did not speak.

248 · MICHAEL BLAKE

Sensing that he should not be pressed, Hunting For Something waited patiently for him to come to the fire. Normally, he sat across from her but tonight he sat beside her, as if offering himself, and she knew he was ready to talk.

"Tell me," she said softly.

Smiles A Lot told of the ultimatum Lawrie Tatum had brought to the village and related what Kicking Bird and Wind In His Hair had said in council.

"What will you do?" she asked.

"I am a Hard Shield. I will fight."

He had hoped she would embrace his decision but she said nothing. He gazed at the bulge in her dress where the baby they had conceived was showing and stroked it lightly.

"Maybe you should go in," he whispered.

Hunting For Something shook her head.

"Are you sure?"

"Yes."

Taking her time, she stretched out on her side and laid her head in his lap while Smiles A Lot looked across the fire at the sleeping head of his little brother.

"I am going to send Rabbit with Kicking Bird," he said.

"He won't go," she retorted.

Smiles A Lot didn't argue because he knew she was right. Rabbit could never be induced to leave.

"What did Grandfather say?" she asked.

"He is going to meet the Great White Father."

Hunting For Something raised her head.

"The Great White Father?"

"Yes."

"Where will he meet him?"

"In the place called Washington."

"When?"

"I think they are going tomorrow. He says he will die when he returns home."

Hunting For Something didn't move, but her husband felt a tensing in the parts of her body that touched him.

"I must see him," she said, her voice suddenly a whisper.

Then she got up, and, because the nights were turning colder with the advent of fall, she pulled a robe over her shoulders and wrapped it around her reedy frame.

She started out of the lodge, then hesitated, and looked back at Smiles A Lot.

"I might stay with him tonight."

CHAPTER XLI

*F*ATIGUE HAD SO OVERWHELMED HIM THAT HIS BODY SEEMED TO weigh nothing. He could imagine it as a cloud, suspended just above the ground, and each time he drifted into the warm haze of unconsciousness he saw himself in effortless ascent, a phenomenon of the psyche so compelling that it kept him half-awake.

But the old man knew that his tired body was not wholly to blame for keeping him from sleep; rather, it was his mind that made rest impossible. It was crackling with an energy that he would have been hard-pressed to describe. Disconnected ideas and images and statements and even entire scenarios appeared out of nowhere to glide through the portals of his mind, and all Ten Bears could do was watch helplessly as the spectacle went on and on.

From time to time he would—for how long he did not know—slip into the twilight edges of sleep, but he was constantly waking with closed eyes to some new entertainment, the latest of which was a dizzying series of moments from his boyhood, when he perceived the soft tones of a girl's voice whispering, "Grandfather." In his mind he could see her soft, unwrinkled lips moving as the word was formed.

The whispering would stop for a few seconds before the word came again, tunneling into his head like a call from afar.

When in addition to hearing the whisper he imagined he might be smelling the speaker's breath, Ten Bears suspected he might actually be awake. His eyes fluttered and opened. A form was in front of him. It was opaque and, because he was lying on his side, he could not tell if it was that of a man or a woman, but it seemed as if someone must be in the lodge with him.

"Grandfather?"

It was the same voice, and now Ten Bears was sure it belonged to a girl. With a grunt of acknowledgment, he pushed himself up on an elbow, at the same time opening the bony hand that clutched his spectacles.

Fumbling with the arms of the frame, he slipped the miraculous things onto his nose and the luminous eyes of his granddaughter stared down at him.

"Grandfather?"

"Hunting For Something."

"Are you all right?"

"I'm having difficulty sleeping tonight."

"I won't disturb you, then. . . ."

"No, no," the old man said, waving off the notion with his free hand. "I'm fine. Stay awhile. Spread your robe and lie down and we will talk. I'm tired of trying to sleep."

Hunting For Something did as he suggested. She laid the robe down like a blanket, stretched out, and, in imitation of her grandfather across the fire, propped herself on an elbow. They looked like bookends.

"You like the cool air?" he asked.

"Yes. . . . Are you going to that Washington?"

"Yes."

"Aren't you afraid they will kill you?"

"Noooo," Ten Bears laughed, "I'm to be a guest. I don't think even the whites kill their guests. I've never heard that they do that. Are you afraid for me, Granddaughter?"

"Maybe I should go with you," she said. "I could take care of you."

"I think I'll have plenty of help. Kicking Bird is coming. I think Touch The Clouds is, too. And some Cheyenne and Arapaho men."

"Will they make your pemmican?" she asked slyly.

"No," Ten Bears replied, laughing again, "but you can make up some for me to take."

Hunting For Something's affection for her grandfather was apart from what she felt for anything else. It was purer, and, with the simplicity of a lover, she nodded at him dreamily. She would do anything for her grandfather.

"When that's gone," Ten Bears continued jovially, "I guess I'll be at the mercy of white man food." Ten Bears raised his eyes in a comic, knowing way. "Whatever that is."

As they laughed together, Hunting For Something blurted out, "I would be afraid to eat white man food."

"I'm curious about it," Ten Bears said, smoothly shifting tone. "It's strange . . . a man with as many winters as I—all those seasons behind me—I'm still wondering. I'm very curious to see what I can see in Washington with these new eyes."

Unable to resist the constant temptation, Ten Bears let his eyes roam the lodge, and he marveled at the clarity of objects and the shadows that shrouded them. While he was gazing, Hunting For Something's hushed voice came to him once more.

"I don't want you to cross the stars yet."

The old man swung his head back. He reached over and patted her hand.

"The Mystery has been calling me for a long time. I have to answer."

"I want you to stay with us."

Ten Bears smiled.

"We will all be together someday."

Hunting For Something did not look reassured.

"You love the Mystery?" he asked.

"Yes."

"I have always loved the Mystery. In between birth and death there is life, and I have tried to stay close to the Mystery for all of mine. There are only two times when a person is truly with the Mystery: birth and death. . . ."

He stretched out his elbow and laid the side of his head against the ground.

"My mother said I came out easily. I think I will go out of this life in the same way." He lowered his voice in a conspiratorial hush. "I'm looking forward to it!"

She couldn't help but smile at her grandfather's intrepid enthusiasm. Her worries always seemed to melt in the warmth he radiated.

"Is that grandchild of mine kicking yet?"

"A little," she said. "It kicks hard. It must be a boy."

"If it kicks hard, it's probably a girl."

She laughed, but Ten Bears was only half-joking.

"I mean it," he said, "you were the only girl your mother had, and she always said, 'Hunting For Something kicked the hardest.'"

"I did?"

"Yes."

Hunting For Something pulled her robe aside and ran a hand over her belly. She pushed at the bulge with her fingers, but there was no response.

"Asleep," she announced, looking at him again.

Ten Bears stared at her belly, then lifted his eyes up toward her face. She was yawning.

"Has Smiles A Lot decided which path to walk? Is he going to take the white man's holy road?"

"He's going to stay out."

Ten Bears nodded.

"I thought that's what he would do. Keep together . . . you never know when you might need each other."

"We will, Grandfather," she said, yielding to another urge to yawn.

"Are you comfortable?" Ten Bears wondered.

"Yes, Grandfather," she answered, closing her eyes.

"Then sleep here tonight."

"Yes, Grandfather," she murmured.

Still, he could not sleep. He kept his glasses in place as he alternated between shadow and light. That way he could gaze whenever he wanted at the slumbering, fresh-faced flower of a granddaughter he loved so well.

CHAPTER XLII

*B*Y MID-MORNING OF THE NEXT DAY ALL WHO HAD DECIDED
to go in with Kicking Bird pulled out. More than half the village trudged
north for the country of the Kiowas and the unpredictable future awaiting them. There were many young. There were widows and a few wid-
owers and a dozen prime warriors and their families. Ten Bears was the
last to fade from sight, his travois at the rear of the column tracking over
the earth's every wrinkle.

It had been a bitter, wrenching departure, oddly devoid of all but the
most poignant sound: a stifled shriek of agony or a sudden fit of muffled
sobbing. People who were staying behind milled mutely through the
slow-moving column as it left the village, reaching up to touch relatives
and friends with trembling hands. When they were gone, people seemed
stuporous as they tried to pick up the tasks of everyday life. Their hearts
were dragging and tears were constantly being wiped away as they
moved about.

Even Wind In His Hair was weeping—to his surprise—and, hoping
to clear his head, he jumped on a pony and galloped alone onto the
prairie for a distance of several miles before halting at the top of a little
berm.

There he slipped off the pony, started a fire, and smoked in silence under graying skies that threatened rain. Seeing so many people go was difficult. He knew in his heart that he was not likely to see them again. He also knew that with their leaving, Comanche sway over the domain they had controlled was broken.

But as he stared over a prairie whose surface was pierced here and there with the last, errant rays of the sun, the shock of separation began to recede, clearing space in his mind for contemplation of how he would defend his country.

Seventy strong warriors followed him but they would never be enough to fight the many soldiers coming out. As the first drop of rain struck his forehead, Wind In His Hair realized that it would be well to be moving all the time. In that way soldiers might be kept off balance and contact with itinerant bands of people who might be absorbed into his force was more likely.

In the meantime, scouting parties would have to be sent out to keep an eye on the hair-mouth soldiers while the village went about the work of trying to make enough meat to see it through winter. Food was paramount, especially with the buffalo so scarce. Men could not fight long on empty bellies, and if children began to cry for food, all ears would be cocked in their direction.

The clouds were hanging close to the ground and rain was falling steadily when Wind In His Hair reentered the village. The wet and cold had driven the dispirited Comanches inside their lodges. He guided his pony to the center of the lifeless village and sat on his horse for a minute or two. He could hear no talk or laughter, not even the whine of a youngster, and, hearing only the dismal cascade from above, it occurred to Wind In His Hair that the sooner the village shook off its lethargy, the better would be its chances for survival.

Within half an hour every warrior in the village was filing into his lodge, and when Wind In His Hair rose to speak, every face looked to him, yearning for guidance.

"Hear me now, Brothers," he exhorted quietly. "We must turn ourselves inside out from this moment. Every warrior's heart must be brought out. We must cover our skins with bravery, because from this moment we live only to defend our country.

"Myself and three others are all that is left of the Hard Shields. But

I will not pick from among you to replace warriors who have been destroyed. From now on, all of you, and all who join us, will fight as Hard Shields."

Wind In His Hair had just told his listeners of the plan to move the village north and west, in search of meat, when the lodge flaps flew open and the rain-soaked heads of several women appeared. Each had a look of horror on her face and each was shrieking the same thing at once.

"White people! White people outside camp!"

Half-trampling each other, warriors spilled out of the lodge and scrambled over the muddy ground for their horses. As was his habit, Wind In His Hair had his pony tied immediately outside and he was one of the first to get mounted. The one-eyed warrior did not wait for a force to form behind him but galloped out of the village with a handful of others in the direction indicated by the frightened women.

The rain was driving across the grasslands in thick, waving sheets and it was hard to see anything. But a half mile out of camp, Wind In His Hair glimpsed the first ghostly outlines of four people on horseback.

He kicked his pony harder and the silhouettes ahead were just beginning to take shape when Wind In His Hair jerked at his pony's mouth and sat back. The horse's hind hooves planted in the watery earth and skidded to a stop. The warriors behind him halted too, peering intently through the rain at the figures a hundred yards ahead, reconfirming what had caused Wind In His Hair to pull up.

The people weren't running away and they weren't coming forward. They were standing perfectly still and, for a moment, Wind In His Hair considered the alarming idea that they might be ghosts. The outlines ahead were shimmering through the rain in vaporous waves.

Overcoming the fear sparking at the base of his neck, he nudged his pony forward, and as he drew closer, Wind In His Hair discarded the idea of ghosts. The people were wearing white man clothes, and in the shrinking distance Wind In His Hair was momentarily caught up, trying to discern a few details of their appearance.

But when he swung his gaze again to the foremost of the riders, the one who seemed to be a man, the features of his face suddenly came together. Peering out from under the dripping brim of the white man hat were a pair of unmistakable eyes.

It was Dances With Wolves.

CHAPTER XLIII

*T*HE RETURN OF THOSE WHO HAD BEEN GIVEN UP FOR DEAD was universally accepted as a good—and long-overdue—omen.

But the giddy first reaction was quickly replaced by doubts and speculations. What would Dances With Wolves' decision be? Could he possibly go in? How could he stay? When the white soldiers chased them, as they were sure to do, what would he do? His dilemma seemed intractable, and a few people came to the conclusion that he should leave.

Stands With A Fist was more withdrawn than people remembered, and even after the trauma of her captivity was taken into account, there were some who wondered at the integrity of her Comanche spirit.

The most jittery people in the village, people who worried constantly over their lives and bellies, looked at the Dances With Wolves children and saw the burden of three more mouths.

Stays Quiet had come home with a deep cough and a high fever, but Owl Prophet, who had great skills in the application of medicine, quickly cured her. Yet there were still those who thought that it was a bad idea to have let anyone with a white man disease into the village.

Dances With Wolves and Stands With A Fist—and, to a lesser degree, the children—could not help but sense the subtle shifts in attitude. He had felt it from the moment the village saw him in white man clothes. People had regarded him with a tangle of astonishment and confusion, and for a few minutes it was hard for them to believe he was speaking Comanche.

There were still traces of doubt and hostility when he counciled with Wind In His Hair and a dozen others the night he came back. He gave a brief review of his journey, and even though the men laughed heartily over humorous highlights of his adventure, a few left the distinct impression that they were uncomfortable to have him sitting among them.

Wind In His Hair told of the white ultimatum and Kicking Bird's departure with half the village, and even after he responded unflinchingly with the simple declaration that he was a Hard Shield, Dances With Wolves was certain that some who had seen him in the white man clothes were having a hard time seeing him any other way. Ironically, the only man he was certain regarded him as a brother was Wind In His Hair.

To the dismay of many friends, Stands With A Fist was close-mouthed about her abduction and captivity at the hands of the whites, responding to the gentlest inquiries intractably.

"I don't want to talk about it," she would say. "I'm home."

She, too, had worn the white clothes and it was clear that some were having trouble letting that image pass. At first she was unsettled but, like her husband, Stands With A Fist had never felt complete acceptance and quickly realized that things were the same as they had always been. One realization led to another, and a few days after their arrival a peace she had never experienced before overtook her. She was too Comanche to be white and too white to be Comanche, and there was nothing to be done about it. It was useless to fight or fear what she could not control.

They were going to stay out because they had no choice and, once they had discussed it, she and Dances With Wolves felt a renewal of their reliance on each other and their children. Whatever awaited them they would leave to fate. They shared their feelings on the shifting attitudes of fellow tribesmen and found they shared a mutual conclusion. They didn't care much what anybody thought. Living the Comanche way suited them.

Naturally, they were concerned about their children. The ranks of friends and playmates had thinned but neither Snake In Hands nor Always Walking seemed to mind. The mobilization of the village affected them little and, though their parents dreaded the possibility of leading them into pain or misery, Dances With Wolves and Stands With A Fist agreed that the family was better off together than apart. They would do all they could to keep the young ones from harm, but they had no illusions. Death always had a place on the prairie, at all times.

The more they talked of these things, the closer they got. Snake In Hands and Always Walking had heard of the ultimatum and the threat it posed, but they asked few questions and the family was united as never before.

In the days the village marched north and west in search of buffalo the doubts other people harbored began to evaporate. The family who had always lived in a lodge set apart went about the business of their lives as if the monumental dilemma they faced did not exist and, instead of engendering doubt, their presence began to achieve the opposite effect of fortifying confidence.

By the time a herd of several thousand buffalo was located and the village made enough meat to sustain it through the winter, there were no longer reservations about the Dances With Wolves family. All talk had shifted to the white soldiers everyone knew would be coming into the country and impromptu councils seemed to dominate the social life of the village.

Not knowing white culture, however, left many gaps which were filled with unquenchable conjecture. What weapons might the soldiers bring with them? How many blue-coated men might be sent out? Would they be good riders? Would they have good scouts? Would they be willing to fight? Invariably, the speculations focused on a single name that was spoken so often that men, women, and even children invoked it as if it belonged to someone they knew. The white people always followed one man in war and it was widely agreed that the one called Bad Hand was likely to lead them. But no one knew what kind of man he was and talk of what he might do led nowhere. Even Dances With Wolves knew nothing about him.

CHAPTER XLIV

*T*HE DEFENDERS OF THE PLAINS GAVE NO THOUGHT TO THE personal life of General Mackenzie. His marital status, his fondness for certain foods, the highs and lows of his young life—none of these was the sort of issue Indians pondered. They were concerned only with the practical question of how brave he might be, how shrewd and how determined he would prove to be in the field.

The answer, had they known it, would have been unsettling.

In the field, General Mackenzie was a living fusion of strength and perseverance. He faced the most heinous weather, the roughest terrain, the severest privation with equanimity, regarding them as mere annoying impediments to bringing the enemy to heel. Though his marches routinely strained human endurance, and despite his frequent, inexplicable explosions of rage, many men were eager to serve under him because Mackenzie's name was synonymous with success.

Yet for all that was known about the handsome officer who performed so brilliantly, his true identity was a mystery. Beneath the surface of his existence ran a dark, angry river of pain, unseen by all but the man whose life it ruled with unrelenting cruelty. Pain was Ranald Mackenzie's sole and constant companion. He ate and slept with it, laughed with it, defecated with it, and dreamt with it. It accompanied him through every waking moment and released him only for brief naps at night.

His face was untouched but beneath the uniform his body was covered with a latticework of wounds and attendant scarring, a secret world throbbing with torment. An angry tear that made the stumps on his hand trivial in comparison ran in a jagged line down the middle of his left pectoral and along the rib cage. The jumble of scar tissue twinged with every breath as did the tenuously grafted breaks in his ribs.

Several pieces of lead, embedded in his knee and hip, grated against bone at the slightest movement and provided him with advance, if painful, knowledge of changes in the weather. A twice-broken shoulder often ached as if a knife blade were embedded in bone and gristle, cutting him repeatedly as he rocked back and forth in the saddle.

For years he had gotten no relief. Often the pain would radiate across his torso with such vengeance that he was forced to lie down on some pallet and match his own steely reserve to the demons bedeviling his flesh.

At first he had experimented with painkillers but only the most powerful had any effect, and these he could not take for they made his mind too fuzzy to perform his duty. His only weapon against the grievous attacks that tormented his body was his clear, incisive mind, a mind which he trained to combat his suffering while he functioned. He fooled the doctors who administered his yearly physical, and while the men who worked closest to him knew of his infirmities, no living being guessed at the depth of the daily torture that was his life.

Defeating pain had become his reason to be. Every phase of his existence was based on the never-ending competition between mind and body for dominance, coloring every action he took. All that he did, whether it was conducting a field operation or merely getting out of bed, was a mortal challenge to the tenacity of his will, which he used in every instance with unflagging dexterity, elevating mind over matter.

He personally supervised the care of the elm trees that were planted on the perimeter of the parade ground, insisting, to the consternation of the soldiers who plodded back and forth to the creek, that they be watered regularly. Otherwise, it could not be said that the general had anything approaching a hobby. He drank lightly, slept alone, eschewed games of chance, did not smoke, and had no friends. Pursuit of pleasure was unknown to him.

His characteristic lack of passion was nowhere more evident than in his reaction to the various Indian leaders who were preparing to embark for Washington. Twice he met with them, smoking the pipe and sharing a meal of venison on one occasion. Mackenzie said little at either meeting. His most pronounced expression was a thin, noncommittal smile that followed several good jokes. He noticed a high degree of intellect in an old Comanche man and was impressed by the adequate command of English in another, younger Comanche but that was the extent of his feeling.

The general saw no value in discourse with a group of primitive men on their way to meet the president. Such things were simply not part of his job, and Bad Hand was delighted when the delegation of twelve tribesmen departed for the eastern railroad. With all distractions cleared away, he could immerse himself in applying the finishing touches to the coming campaign.

His excitement in taking the field was high. General Sherman had cleared the way for the mountains of provisions and munitions that flowed into the fort. His staffing was only a few souls shy of one hundred percent, and the rank and file could count quite a few veterans among them.

Best of all, General Mackenzie knew that once he was at the head of a column seeking to engage the enemy, his pain would become more manageable. He had never pondered the connection, but when he was in the field the torture never failed to wane.

There was a sharp drop in his pain the same day the Indian delegation ventured east in a convoy of open wagons, and later that afternoon Bad Hand composed a thorough set of orders to be transmitted by wire to Fort Richardson, a post far in the south.

The orders were directed to a young captain by the name of Bradley, the same man who, as a lieutenant some months before, had been humiliated by Wind In His Hair. His narrow aversion of disaster on that occasion had seasoned him, and Captain Bradley was proud to receive instructions directly from General Mackenzie.

Though the orders appeared to call for a routine reconnaissance scout into Indian country, they were, in reality, much more than that. The force under Captain Bradley would be large, more than a hundred men, and it would scour the country for a month, far longer than the usual week or ten days. Instead of traveling in a loop, the command was directed to weave to and fro, constantly angling north in a sweeping fashion.

The directive clearly stated that engagement of the Indians was to be strictly avoided, unless, of course, Bradley and his men were fired upon. Nor were Indians to be chased. In fact, the orders stated repeatedly that a primary feature of the captain's mission was to conduct the action as peacefully as possible.

But Captain Bradley understood that the true object of his mission was to gently herd the savages north, bringing them closer to General Fordike's column traveling down from the northwest and General Mackenzie's advancing from the east. Pressed from three directions at once, it was hoped the hostiles would be constricted into a shrinking, inescapable circle of resistance which could be efficiently annihilated.

No one wanted a long war.

CHAPTER XLV

*A*T THE FIRST FORWARD LURCH OF THE TRAIN, ITS SPECIAL passengers, in a coach reserved exclusively for their use, made a mighty effort to hold off the temptation to panic. Their eyes shot everywhere at once and their car echoed with spasmodic grunts of fear at the unknown.

All were mesmerized at the speed of the land flashing past their windows and the unearthly power of the great engine pulling them along the tracks. Had they been alone they might have spontaneously jettisoned themselves through the first available exit, but the constant reassurances and relaxed manner of the whites traveling with them kept the tribesmen at rigid attention in their seats.

In a remarkably short time the novices acclimated themselves to the velocity and motion of the alien conveyance and were able to turn their attention to the many other mysteries surrounding them. They were inducted into the use of an onboard toilet, tutored unsuccessfully on the mechanics of time, and given a demonstration of the wonders of writing implements. Before long they tested their palates on white man food and filled the car with smoke from the white man's hand-rolled cigarettes.

They remained on the train throughout the first long leg across the plains, for their safety would have been at risk in the rough settlements of the frontier. In eastern Missouri, when they were allowed off to stretch their bodies on the unmoving platform of a sizable community, a surprising phenomenon presented itself for the first time—one that would become more common the farther east they journeyed.

Despite the early hour, the platform was crowded with white people who had gathered in anticipation of their arrival. As Kicking Bird and Ten Bears and their friends alighted, the throng drew back in momentary awe, then crept slowly forward, entranced by the living embodiment of their imaginations.

The escort had prepared the twelve exotic men for the experience of crossing the Mississippi River, but as they started over the bridge, one of the Cheyenne, a man named Hollow Horn, was suddenly seized with the certainty that they were going to fall into the water. With a curdling cry he leaped to his feet and chopped at the inner flanks of the car with his ax, hoping somehow to slay the monster before it carried the party to a watery death. He was restrained before he could do much damage, and after the crossing Hollow Horn remained seated in a cocoon of mortification.

For some reason no one traveling with the befeathered men from the prairies had anticipated what effect passing through a mountain in total darkness might have on their charges, and when the idea did occur it was too late.

The train had been climbing through a range of low mountains for about half an hour and several of the tribesmen were dozing when it rounded a sharp curve and disappeared into the black maw of a long tunnel. For a full minute, shrieking Indians flew about in the pitch, the racket they raised drowning out the thunder of the engine ahead.

After a sixty-second eternity, a dim but growing light began to suffuse the car, then all at once they were outside again. Most of the men recovered immediately, but one Arapaho, a man named Striking Eagle, was still on the floor in serious difficulty. His long frame was drawn up in a trembling, fetal ball, and after all attempts to rouse him failed, it was concluded that Striking Eagle had suffered a breakdown. Still encased in his imaginary womb, the stricken Arapaho was carried from the train at the next stop. Adamant in his refusal to go any farther, Hollow Horn also disembarked, leaving ten shaken but stalwart comrades to face the wonders that lay ahead.

Oddly, the one among them who took the new world most in stride was also the oldest. Ten Bears had been asleep when the train entered the tunnel, and though he was jarred awake by the ensuing tumult, the old man simply assumed he had slept through sundown. He had been remarkably composed from the trip's outset, and as light again washed into the car, he followed form. He barely glanced at the aftermath of chaos strewn about him and for several minutes was oblivious of Striking Eagle's collapse.

Instead, the old man gazed serenely through his spectacles at the receding tunnel.

We went through a mountain, he thought to himself. *It was made to open its body to this snake of metal and wood we are riding. The whites possess incredible magic.*

A few moments later, Kicking Bird slid into the seat next to him and related the trouble with Striking Eagle. Ten Bears peered over his spectacles.

"Maybe a ghost got into him."

"I think he is afraid," Kicking Bird replied. "Someone heard him yell about the sun being killed."

"It's shining now," Ten Bears observed.

"Striking Eagle's mind can't see it. He can't move."

"He needs to get off this thing," Ten Bears said, a hint of condescension discernible in his tone.

Kicking Bird's chin vibrated with a quick succession of reassuring nods.

"They're going to put him off at the next stop."

"How will he get home?" Ten Bears inquired.

"They will wait for a train going west. Then they will put him on that."

Ten Bears stared briefly at the seat in front of him.

"Poor man," he sighed, his voice falling away to silence. A moment later, when he tilted his face toward Kicking Bird's, a smile was hovering about his mouth. "He'll have to go back through that mountain."

Kicking Bird managed to avoid laughing out loud but his shoulders heaved convulsively.

"Are we going to pass through more mountains?" Ten Bears wondered.

Kicking Bird's levity vanished. He hadn't thought of more tunnels.

"I don't know," he said.

"I wonder if this thing goes through water, too. Someone better tell us so we can close these openings. Otherwise the water will come in and we'll all drown."

Starting to the edge of his seat, Kicking Bird eagerly scanned the car's interior, searching for the little Quaker.

"Lawrie Tatum will know," he said absently.

"Oh, leave him alone for a while," scolded Ten Bears. "All you want to do is make that white man talk."

"What if water does come in?" Kicking Bird retorted.

"This thing has gone over lots of water," Ten Bears grunted dismissively. "If it does go into water, the whites will close these things in time. I'm sure none of them wants to drown. How much farther is it to Washington?"

"Lawrie Tatum says it is one more sleep."

"Is it the biggest white man village?"

"Lawrie Tatum says it will be bigger than anything we have ever seen. He says our eyes will see many things that do not seem real."

"I believe him," Ten Bears said, nodding solemnly as he placed his moccasins on the footrest just above the floor.

The old man slid his pipe from its case.

"We should smoke for poor Striking Eagle."

"Hmm," Kicking Bird agreed.

"I hope the food is better in Washington," Ten Bears said, tamping a pinch of tobacco into his bowl. "They have so much magic, yet they can't make good meat. It's stringy and filled with grease."

Kicking Bird nodded mutely.

"It goes right through my bowels," Ten Bears groused.

"Mine, too," Kicking Bird sighed.

CHAPTER XLVI

*A*SIDE FROM THE INCESSANT, UNSEASONABLE RAIN WHICH swamped the southern plains, the signs had been good for Wind In His Hair and the hostiles. They had been fortunate in striking several more small herds of buffalo and, despite having to dry the meat indoors, they had made enough to last beyond winter.

Everywhere their odyssey led them they met contingents of wanderers with like minds and, as the days until the deadline melted away, Wind In His Hair's camp swelled steadily. People from Comanche bands like the Antelope and the Liver-Eaters and Those Who Move Often had come together, as had significant groups of Kiowa, Cheyenne, and Arapaho.

With warriors in the hundreds to guide, Wind In His Hair was in constant council. Ten sleeps before the deadline, half a dozen parties of warriors had been selected, formed, and dispatched to specific corners of Comanche territory, there to keep an eye on the hair-mouth soldier forts.

Wind In His Hair and his advisers had anticipated the army's plan, thinking the soldiers would try to push them from the south, and it seemed likely that the first enemies would come from the place called

THE HOLY ROAD · 269

Fort Richardson. Owl Prophet, whose standing had been shaken but far from destroyed, declared adamantly that soldiers would be coming from the south.

Three Hard Shields—Dances With Wolves, Smiles A Lot, and Blue Turtle—had been chosen to make the far ride to Fort Richardson. The distance was great, as was the difficulty of sitting undetected under the soldiers' noses until their movements could be learned, but the hardest part was the unrelenting rain.

Descending the caprock required a man to be alert in the best of times but after a week of intermittent deluge the steep ground was greasy and the horses fought for footing all the way down. The riders had to jump on and off constantly to give the animals a chance to stop sliding or gain their balance. Halfway down, Blue Turtle jumped off his pony, lost his feet, and might have gone over a precipice had he not been able to hang on to his horse's tail.

Bucolic streams had become racing, churning rivers, and at one crossing Dances With Wolves and Smiles A Lot were unhorsed when a large, thick log they were trying to avoid suddenly veered and struck both horses at once. For a quarter mile the warriors and their animals struggled in the current. Miraculously, both eventually made it to solid ground and were reunited with Blue Turtle. But Dances With Wolves lost his food, and from then on rations for two had to be shared by three.

Once they reached the vicinity of the white man fort, the three warriors were dismayed at how little spying they could actually accomplish. The best vantage point to be had was a thick growth of oak a quarter mile from the soldier fort, but with the incessant rain it afforded only fractured glimpses of enemy movement.

The sound of the rain, which dripped from every leaf of every tree, squashed all but the loudest noises coming from the fort, and for three days and nights the soaked, cold scouts huddled under the trees with their horses, nibbling at their dwindling supply of jerked meat.

They were too despondent to converse much, but when they did say something it usually pertained to the task at hand, and midway through the third day of their surveillance Smiles A Lot wondered if they should try to get some white man clothes, put them on Dances With Wolves, and let him go among whites.

Blue Turtle correctly pointed out how risky it would be to obtain the clothes and when they looked at Dances With Wolves for a response, he spat, "No more white man clothes," then rose from a squat and walked off through the drizzle.

On the morning of the fourth day, when the fog lifted a few hundred feet off the ground and sunlight was endeavoring to penetrate the gloom, the scouts were astonished to see the first riders in a long column starting out of the fort.

Seconds later the distinct cracking of twigs caused the three Comanches to turn. Only a few yards behind them was a large buck. Flanks heaving, he stood nervously and, as he craned his neck for a furtive look behind, the report of a gun exploded in the stillness.

A slug whistled through his antlers and, as the buck bounded away, another round was fired. The Comanche scouts could see white men, two of them, in civilian clothes, coming through the woods with rifles. And the white hunters could see them.

Fortunately for the spies, they had gathered up their weapons and made ready to move as soon as they saw the column starting out from the fort, intending to shadow it for a day or two before hurrying home with news of its existence.

But there was no time to shadow anything now. The hunters were already firing at them as Dances With Wolves, Smiles A Lot, and Blue Turtle leapt onto their ponies. They charged along the tree line until it ran out. No one was hit by the hunters, and if the soldiers saw them now, it couldn't be helped.

On hearing gunfire in the nearby woods, the column halted. But Captain Bradley was not overly disturbed. Since his initial, disastrous encounter at the dry streambed he had clashed with Indians several times and the results had been far different. He had vanquished several small groups of Comanche and Kiowa raiders, overrunning and killing half a dozen warriors. His naïve, bungling commandant had been replaced by an astute field officer, and since winning his captain's bars he felt supremely confident. Late experience told him that if he took the necessary precautions, kept a clear head, and thought on his feet, the hundred men he led now could keep a whole nation of Indians at bay.

He had met General MacKenzie and held him in high regard. Mackenzie's obvious grit was something the captain wished to emulate, and he felt honored to be given the opportunity to play a vital role in the grand campaign to sweep the plains. As he sat squinting at the tree line for a sign of what might be causing the disturbance in the woods, Captain Bradley did so without a hint of trepidation.

A tiny knot of riders burst into the open at the end of the trees. They galloped up a long incline toward the naked brow of a low hill several hundred yards distant, and the captain noted with satisfaction that his chief of scouts, a levelheaded former ranger named Cox, had already raised his field glass to follow the runaways.

"Comanches?" Bradley asked casually.

"Sure are, Captain," Cox replied, the glass still pressed against his eye. "Three of 'em. They seen us . . . they're ridin' like hell."

"Good," the captain said cooly, "that's the whole idea."

The chief of scouts suddenly lowered his field glass, squinted at the three riders for an instant, then raised the glass again.

"I'll be goddamned!"

He abruptly passed the glass to Captain Bradley.

"One of 'em looks like a white man. Take a look, Captain."

Bradley raised the glass in time to see the three Comanches crest the little knob of a hill. One of them—his hair was cropped and he was appreciably taller than the others—happened to glance back a moment before he disappeared behind the rise. At first sight he might have passed for Indian, but, seeing the structure of his face and the roundness of his eyes, the captain was inclined to agree.

"Probably a deserter," Bradley theorized, handing the glass back.

"I've heard there's a few white men with 'em, but I never seen one before."

"Me neither," the captain replied.

"I wouldn't want to be in his hide when we catch him." Cox chuckled.

"No," the captain remarked, picking up his reins, "he won't have any skin to be in after the army gets him."

CHAPTER XLVII

*A*S THE DELEGATION DISEMBARKED IN THE POLITICAL HEART of the white nation they found themselves at the center of a wild, unthinkable scene.

Aboriginal visitors had been coming to Washington for many years, but such appearances were hardly routine, and the platform was overflowing with a gaggle of government functionaries and citizens eager for a look at the alien personifications of the "Indian problem."

Having grown used to being objects of curiosity, the men who called themselves Cheyenne, Arapaho, Kiowa, and Comanche snaked through the mass of whites pressing around them with pronounced aplomb, their faces utterly impassive, speaking rarely and then only in low murmurs to one another. The whites fell silent when the free men passed, the drama of their appearance heightened by the light clink of jewelry and the gentle scrape of moccasins that filled the vacuum of sound.

Exiting the station, they were greeted with a pageant-like spectacle that stretched the limits of their comprehension. A great hatted crowd waited below them, flanking both sides of a long, open patch of stones leading to a road filled with wagon traffic. Between the path and the crowd, standing shoulder to shoulder, were two solid lines of blue-coated policemen. Like the throng they were charged with controlling, the police were gazing up, their expressionless eyes barely visible in the brim shadows of their strange uniform hats.

Everywhere the visitors looked there were white man houses, some reaching so high into the sky that they grazed the clouds. The sun still hovered in the heavy, smelly air but the earth was nowhere to be seen. All that was left of the natural world were columns of green scattered over the vista, trees growing in straight lines on either side of the white man's many roads.

After receiving a brief explanation regarding the function of steps, the warriors started down. Waiting at the bottom of the steps were several open wagons, all drawn by fine, sleek horses. They climbed into the carriages and set off through the streets, stopping traffic and turning heads, until they arrived at their place of residence, something the white men called a hotel.

Here they were shown the room where white men filled their bellies and were casually informed that the white man had a machine that told him when to eat. It turned out that the device, which the white men mounted on walls, erected in streets, and even carried in their pockets, told them far more than when to eat. The machine told them when to wake and when to sleep. It dictated the moment at which one man could visit another, when he could perform duties, when he could relax.

No one could understand the necessity of such a thing. Ten Bears put it most succinctly when he remarked to Kicking Bird, "How can a man be a man when he enslaves himself to a circle of glass and metal?"

The visitors, who were housed in separate suites according to tribe, were indoctrinated in the uses of furniture, the function of water closets, the intricacies of beds, the opening and closing of windows, and the procedures for summoning hotel staff members.

When the thing called a bathtub was demonstrated, the men from the plains were amazed to see a pond magically take form before their eyes. They were equally horrified, however, when the plug was pulled and the water drained away through a black, evil-looking hole in the bottom of the pond. Something down in the hole made disturbing sounds as it fed on the water. No one wanted to bathe on top of the creature, nor did anyone want it getting out, and for the duration of their stay, the tubs' drains were jammed with knife blades or stuffed with linen and regularly monitored for any sign of whatever dwelt inside.

Because they were only two, Kicking Bird and Ten Bears were provided with a sumptuous but smaller suite at the rear of the hotel consisting of a sitting room, a bedroom, a water closet, and a bathroom.

Leaving Ten Bears stretched out on one of the beds, Kicking Bird made a thorough and energetic inspection of all that the rooms contained. He was vibrating with excitement, not only for the many wonders at his fingertips but for the prospects for knowledge as well. His ability to communicate was increasing every time he spoke white words, and though he understood relatively little, he was pleased with his progress. He knew innately that having the words would increase his power in negotiations when he returned to the reservation. Without knowing the words, the Comanche would be as dependent on the white man as the white man was on his clocks. Learning the language was the first and most essential tool to navigating the bizarre terrain of the white world and Kicking Bird embraced the study of it with zeal.

As he drifted through the rooms, he was constantly intrigued by all that the white man had wrought—from the fixtures on the bathroom sink to the glass transoms that opened over the doors. Like the others, he feared the bathtub and was baffled by the concept of time, but, taken as a whole, he was deeply impressed by the accomplishments of white culture.

He was tired of traveling but could not think of resting. A walk through the streets of Washington was to take place shortly and he was anxious for a closer look at the huge, strange town, so alive with human endeavor.

Returning to the bedroom, he found Ten Bears lying faceup on the bed, in the same position he had left him. The old man had draped a forearm across his eyes. The other arm lay at his side, his hand delicately clutching the precious spectacles.

The room was very still, and as Kicking Bird stared down at the still form of his mentor, he imagined for a moment that Ten Bears had passed out of the world.

Without moving, the old man's lips suddenly parted and his voice sounded.

"When are those people supposed to come?"

"Soon," answered Kicking Bird. "Will you go with us?"

"No." Ten Bears took the arm away from his face and sat up. "I'm going to rest. My body is still swaying like that crazy thing we rode out here."

"Train," Kicking Bird said in English.

"Tren," Ten Bears repeated. Then he lay back down. "I'm going to sleep."

"All right, Grandfather."

Kicking Bird moved closer to the bed.

"Do you want to be covered?" Kicking Bird asked attentively.

"Yes, that would be good."

Kicking Bird unfolded the blanket near the foot of the bed and spread it gently over the old man.

"Sleep well, Grandfather."

Ten Bears didn't answer. He was already floating in twilight and didn't know if the voice of Kicking Bird was real or part of a dream. He was turning into something . . . a great bird . . . maybe a hawk or an eagle, and he soared and dipped and climbed in the heavens as it scanned the world below. It was the white world, for he could clearly see houses and trains and dark networks of roads running in every direction.

He dove closer to the ground and flew at tremendous speed toward the artificial landscape of a large city. For a time he flew over streets choked with white people. Suddenly, he arched into a graceful ascent and when he glanced again at the streets he saw immediately that the white people had turned into insects, bustling up and down their avenues in a disciplined frenzy.

Rising higher, the city below transformed itself into a red anthill. The barren landscape around the hill was steadily expanding away from the nest as its residents harvested everything in sight. No matter how high he flew, the insect metropolis stayed in view, enlarging perceptibly, as if it were pursuing him.

A shaft of light struck him, and Ten Bears woke to find that a slanting ray of afternoon sun had crept across the bed. He yawned and stretched and sat up feeling fresh. The dream, which he remembered clearly, was disturbing, but all that flying must have been invigorating because he suddenly felt restless.

I wish I could do some more of that flying, he thought, swinging his feet onto the floor and rising off the bed. Thirsty, he went to a dresser across the way and drank from a tall vessel standing next to a bowl. The white man water looked like water but didn't taste like anything.

As he replaced the pitcher on the dresser top Ten Bears felt a shudder of panic. Inside the white man world, in this place called a hotel, it was as if life had ceased. Except for the irritating noise of the machine that told the whites what to do, there was no sound.

Ten Bears made straight for the window, hoping he could remember how to make it open. He worked the latch free, pushed up with both hands, and took great draughts of odorous air into his lungs.

He had closed his eyes as he sucked in air, and when he opened them again, he found himself staring down at a large rectangle of green bordered by a high fence. In the center of the green strip was a body of water.

Ten Bears walked back across the room and pulled on a soft rope hanging next to a wall. How it could summon white men he did not know, but in minutes there was a knock at the door, and when Ten Bears opened it he found a white boy in tight-fitting clothes decorated with golden buttons standing in the hall.

"Yes, sir?" he asked cheerfully.

Ten Bears motioned him into the room, took the puzzled boy by the elbow, and guided him to the open window.

"Ten Bears," he said in Comanche, pointing an index finger at his chest, before thrusting it at the green below the window.

"What?" the boy inquired, not understanding.

"Ten Bears . . ." he began again, repeating the gesture. "Go," the old man blurted, remembering the English word for moving. Once more he pointed out the window.

Light washed over the boy's face. "Oh!" he exclaimed. "You want to go down to the garden."

Ten Bears sat at the side of the pool for a long time. The water was green and tasted rotten and had plump, golden fish living in it. Noises from the city crept steadily over the fence and sometimes curious white people stared or tried to ask him questions but, all in all, the setting was superior to the suffocating boxes the white men seemed so excited about inhabiting.

He still had some of the incredible little sticks whose red tips made fire when they were scratched in the proper way so he filled his pipe and smoked through the twilight as he revisited the dream of that afternoon.

Ten Bears believed in the purpose of dreams and concluded that this one was instructing him to behave as an eagle in the days to come. He would fly above the many forthcoming talks and social activities they were scheduled to have with the white men. If he could watch these things from the heights a truer picture of white people might emerge. Being an eagle, Ten Bears decided, would be the best way to proceed.

When the garden was saturated with shadow he heard familiar voices and turned to see his fellow warriors coming down the stairs at the rear of the hotel. They, too, preferred the garden and related various anecdotes of their walk around Washington as they lounged beside the pool with Ten Bears. At last light, Lawrie Tatum and some other white men came out and told them the clock said it was time to take food.

But no one was hungry and Kicking Bird asked instead if they could have fuel for a fire. Lawrie Tatum looked perplexed but told him to wait and returned a few minutes later to say that a fire would be all right, but only on the condition—and he emphasized this several times—that it be small.

Several of the warriors retrieved the last of the food they carried with them, and the delegation sat around their tiny conflagration, staring fixedly into the flames as they passed the pipe and devoured the last of their jerked meat.

Naturally, all thought drifted toward home, and the men wondered aloud about friends and relatives who had come into the reservation and how they might be faring on the white man's holy road.

Since each man was a warrior, the talk eventually gravitated toward those who had stayed out to fight. These were their friends and relatives, and they speculated at length on the chances so many good fighters might have in battle with white soldiers. The more they talked about it the more convinced they became that the distinguished body of hostile warriors could not help but have success, and by the time some members of the delegation began to yawn, the idea that the buffalo might return was being discussed enthusiastically.

CHAPTER XLVIII

S IX DAYS AFTER THE DEADLINE FOR THE ULTIMATUM PASSED, Captain Bradley's command was hit by a large, combined force of well-armed warriors.

The attack came a few minutes before dawn, and though it had been repulsed, four troopers were dead and six were wounded. Seven of the enemy had been killed. The captain was certain that more Indians had died but he listed only the bodies that had been recovered.

Enemy wounded weren't counted. A lesser officer would have been tempted to embellish his report, but Captain Bradley was a rare bird. He laid out only the plain facts of the engagement in the official report he scribbled to General Mackenzie barely an hour after the fighting had ceased.

The night before, his command had bivouacked in a small valley nestled in rolling, mesquite-covered country. The site, which was spotted with growths of cottonwoods at its deepest point, had been chosen because a large spring of pure, clear water had been discovered there.

He didn't mention it in his report, but Bradley had began to feel restless as soon as they made camp. In the days before, they had encountered more and more Indian sign, much of it fresh. None of the hostiles had been sighted, but having led his column so deep into enemy territory, the captain was on high alert.

The wide ravine was, from a military point of view, neither the worst nor the best place he might have chosen to spend the night. His ambivalence about the spot left him vaguely queasy, and after dark he ordered the herders to move the horses and mules closer to camp. Once this was accomplished he ordered that a half dozen more men be detailed to guard the livestock. Auxiliary fires were lit and tended through the night. Sentries were doubled, and instead of reporting once an hour, they were required to signify their presence to the sergeant of the guard every fifteen minutes.

Despite these measures, Captain Bradley found himself unable to rest and spent the balance of the night in sporadic checks of the camp. He had just returned from an inspection of the guard when, according to best estimates, nearly half a hundred screaming savages charged out of the blackness and attacked the horse herd.

Captain Bradley remained coolheaded through the ensuing ripple of chaos, giving strict and specific orders for the mounting of no more than twenty-five soldiers, who sped to aid the defenders of the precious herd. As firing echoed up the ravine, Bradley ordered the deployment of skirmish lines on either side of the bivouac and instructed the Gatling gun crew to set up their weapon in a position facing east.

The young commander had not guessed that an attack would come that morning, nor did he have any inkling of the Indian plan of battle. But his few engagements with the aboriginals had been enough to give him a feel for the enemy. Bradley understood, as did few of his peers, that to fight Indians effectively required leadership of an instinctive sort. In a land bare of all but the most natural elements it behooved any commander to make himself as much a part of the landscape as possible. He had realized after his initial debacle that the only individual he should rely upon was himself and to do that he had better "listen" to the enemy and to the country as much as possible. The captain had listened attentively in succeeding months, and though it could not be said he understood the language of nature, he was open to it and responding instinctively.

Captain Bradley had organized his defenses with little analytical thought and it was well that he did for in deviating from normal practice he successfully parried the surprisingly clever strategy of his native adversaries. The attack on the horse herd was no more than a ploy to divert attention from the real attack, which came a few moments after the sky had lightened, when a legion of warriors, estimated at more than two hundred, thundered out of the east, seeking to overrun the bivouac and kill everyone in it.

In a state of calm he could not have explained, Captain Bradley had his waiting troops hold fire until the charging wave of Indians was within a hundred yards. When he did give the command, the line of rifles exploded as one, lashing the first ranks of horsemen with a fiery, galelike blast that shattered their momentum. As riflemen reloaded and the enemy tried to gather itself, the Gatling gun sprayed a lethal curtain of bullets over the field. In less than a minute it malfunctioned, but by that time critical damage had been done to the enemy, who were withdrawing in disarray.

For more than an hour afterward, Indian snipers shot into the camp but the firing dwindled steadily until, at mid-morning, it was ascertained that the enemy had forsaken the field.

Aside from the three enlisted men and one officer who had been killed, the only material loss was a significant portion of stores and this was due entirely to bad luck. A stray enemy round had struck a keg of gunpowder packed on a mule and the crazed animal, exploding in flame, had careened into the tents, setting several on fire.

Included among the completely and partially destroyed tents were two belonging to the quartermaster which contained a large supply of rations, and Captain Bradley concluded his report to General Mackenzie by expressing doubt that his command could remain much longer in the field without being resupplied.

He was tempted to include the interesting anecdote of a white man riding with the savages who attacked the horse herd, but, deciding that it was not germane, omitted the strange sighting attested to by several of the horse-herd defenders. He did add that, while he was impelled to detach some manpower to escort the wounded back to Fort Richardson, he would stay in the field and continue his mission for as long as was feasible, or until he received contrary directives.

As his dispatch was carried east by two good horsemen, accompanied by a pair of Tonkawa scouts, Bradley turned his energies to sorting through the fight's aftermath and the Indian bodies collected for examination. There were four Comanche, two Kiowa, and one Cheyenne, which led to the quite logical conclusion that the hostiles had formed a working alliance.

The Tonkawas requested the bodies, and despite Captain Bradley's refusal, they eventually managed to purloin one. The remaining six were left where they lay and after burying his own dead and salvaging all useable goods, Captain Bradley marched his column back onto the prairie. Though he knew he would not go very far that day, he wanted to impress the enemy with his resiliency.

As they angled west, the latest in the never-ending series of storms lifted, a break in the weather that mirrored a rising of the young commander's spirits. Morale was high and he perceived a renewed snap in the attention to orders and their execution. The attack on the horse herd had resulted in the loss of only six animals, and despite the necessity of reducing rations by half, it was likely that the command could last another two weeks in the field without being seriously compromised.

Three days later, as the command was meandering about in broken country adjacent to the great caprock barrier to the Staked Plains, the captain's spirits received another boost with the return of his messengers.

With them was a reply from Fort Sill, signed by Mackenzie's adjutant but obviously dictated by the general. The new instructions acknowledged receipt of Captain Bradley's report and directed him to march north and east to a point where he would rendezvous with a supply train being sent out from Fort Belknap. Once refurbished, he was to continue his long sweep up from the south for an eventual rendezvous with a column from Fort Sill under the command of General Mackenzie, whose departure was imminent.

Best of all, there was a postscript floating below the adjutant's signature which read as follows:

"The general wishes to convey his complete satisfaction at results of the late engagement described in your report. Additionally, he wishes to express his affirmation of the initiatives you have taken subsequent to the skirmish with hostile forces."

Captain Bradley had his own adjutant read the postscript aloud at roll call the following morning. The rank and file greeted the reading with cheers and, as they marched off to the northeast after breakfast, all recent privation was forgotten. The campaign's foundation had been unerringly laid. Now it was going into full motion, and for Captain Bradley it was easy to believe that the final outcome would be total victory.

CHAPTER XLIX

*T*HOUGH HE REMAINED THE MOST RESPECTED MAN OF THE DELE-gation, Ten Bears' purposeful maintenance of a certain attitude set him apart from the others. From the old man's vantage point, even Kicking Bird operated far below him as the visitors from the plains proceeded through their exhausting Washington itinerary.

Each day was packed with meetings, receptions, and sightseeing, all carefully orchestrated by an army of white officialdom. Its purpose was to overwhelm the peace leadership with an endless array of devastating impressions which would keep them reeling. Washington had practiced the same bloodless warfare for decades with striking success. Few Indians left the city without recognizing they had already been defeated by a culture whose size, energy, technology, and appetite altogether eclipsed their own.

Supposedly predicated on substance, the meetings with various government agencies followed the theme of producing an unforgettable show of power. Invariably, the men of the prairie were conducted through an inconceivably grand public building before meeting their human hosts in a room furnished with excessive and lavish distractions.

There were spirited exchanges at the Interior Department where many pointed questions about the mechanics of reservation life were asked, and at the War Department, where Kicking Bird lectured General Sherman on the limited control any elder can expect to exercise over the young. And the meetings were, of course, bracketed with eating sessions and demonstrations of magical apparatuses which effectively overshadowed the substance of the official discussions.

Apart from showing him deference owing to his age, the whites paid little attention to Ten Bears. It was a neglect the old man welcomed, for he had little to say on the issues of war and peace, and he was often seen dozing during the weightiest conferences.

That was not to say that the Comanche headman was bored. His interest in white civilization was profound, and his apparent lack of engagement was merely a way to stay focused on his more elementary agenda.

On the third morning of the stay in Washington, following a tour of the city's waterworks, he stayed behind to question the director while the rest of the delegation hurried off to see a horse race. Standing next to a set of huge turbines which pumped water to those who could afford it, Ten Bears' interpreter filtered the Comanche words into English for the director of public works, a fat, florid, and genial man who rejoiced in his work. He stood with one hand cupped to an ear, intent on all that the old man had to say.

"When refuse grows in our camp, we move," Ten Bears stated.

"Uh-huh . . ."

"White men stay in one place."

"Uh-huh."

"Where does this refuse go?"

"Ah!" the director exclaimed. "Good question! Would Mr. Ten Bears like to see?"

Ten Bears nodded without hesitation and a few minutes later they were riding toward the outskirts of the city in an open carriage.

Long before they reached the dump, Ten Bears noticed a change in the sky's complexion that could not be linked to any natural element of weather. In the distance columns of dark smoke curled in the atmosphere, merging, then flattening out in a single, great blanket that dulled the sun.

All manner of conveyances piled high with garbage clogged the approach to the dumping ground, and when at last the carriage came to a stop within its confines, Ten Bears found himself surrounded by hillocks of smoldering waste, each the size of several lodges.

"Does the smoke stay here?" Ten Bears asked.

"No, no," the director replied eagerly, "it goes away . . . it disappears. But I suppose you could say it's here all the time. The dump is always open."

"Too much smoke," Ten Bears observed absently.

His every word was translated, and upon hearing his casual aside, the director was prompted to look skyward for a moment of inconclusive meditation.

"Well," he began earnestly, "eventually there will be too much smoke. The population is expected to double in the next twenty-five or thirty years."

When this was translated, Ten Bears asked that it be repeated, and when he heard it again he was still unsure if he had heard right.

"Two times as many white people? . . . In twenty-five snows?"

"Yes," the director assured him, "but we are working on alternatives. We don't possess the means yet, but it seems likely that in the future trash will be buried."

"In the earth?" Ten Bears questioned, his face frozen in shock.

"Why . . . yes."

"The earth is alive."

The director didn't fully grasp the concept.

"Well . . . uh . . . yes," he stammered, "but it has to go somewhere."

The men were silent for a time as their team jogged smoothly back in the direction of the city. Ten Bears had closed his eyes, but just when his white hosts thought he might have drifted off, the old man's head jumped forward and his eyes flew open.

"I didn't see any feces or urine. Where do you put that?"

The director's stare was so incredulous and intense as to cause Ten Bears to wonder briefly if his question had not provoked a spell of insanity in his companion. But a moment later a grateful smile spread across the director's small mouth.

"Thank you, Mr. Ten Bears, thank you for asking," he said.

The director's thankfulness was heartfelt. Not a day went by that he didn't long to hear the question Ten Bears had asked. His longing usually went unrequited, for the disposal of human waste was not a topic that excited public interest. But here was a man who wanted to know. It didn't matter to the director if he spoke a language of grunts or dressed in the skins of animals or attached eagle talons and eagle feathers to his head. The director was happy to share his excitement.

The sewer system, which had finally become operational only six months before, was the crown jewel of his career. He launched into an animated technical explanation of the system but had barely spoken a few sentences before the translator threw up his hands and explained to the director that most of what he was saying could not be turned into Comanche.

"Ask Mr. Ten Bears if he would allow me to show him the system."

The translator passed this on, listened to the response, and turned again to the director.

"He says he would like that very much."

Shortly after arriving back at the administrator's office they were off again, traveling for only a few minutes before turning up a broad residential avenue flanked by enormous houses that Ten Bears was astonished to learn held but one family each.

Halfway up the street they pulled behind an empty wagon apparently belonging to a pair of burly, taciturn workmen who had taken up a position in the center of the street. Ten Bears noticed that one of the men was shouldering a length of stout metal and, when they reached the middle of the street, he discovered that the men were standing over a large metal disc fitted perfectly into the roadway.

"Have you defecated in a water closet, Mr. Ten Bears?" asked the director.

"Yes."

"And have you pulled the chain and seen your feces disappear?"

"Yes, I did that. It went down a hole and didn't come back."

"Good. Now . . ." Here the director paused to pick out the first mansion he chanced to see. "If you were in that house and defecated in its water closet and pulled the chain, your feces would disappear into a tube. The tube would carry your feces out here."

Ten Bears understood the various parts of the director's explanation but could not put them together, and, thinking he might have missed something, glanced regularly at the interpreter.

"If you please, gentlemen, lift off the manhole," the director commanded, as if he were about to reveal a fabulous jewel.

The man with the steel bar inserted it into the disc's edge and, in a show of prodigious strength, levered the heavy plate high enough to be grasped by his companion. Together they rolled the huge wheel of metal to one side, leaving a hole in the street.

Ten Bears peered into the hole and caught the unmistakable odor of excrement. At the same time, he picked up the sound of moving water.

Ten Bears glanced at the director. The white man smiled knowingly, as if in concert with Ten Bears, and began to gesture expansively at the houses of the rich.

"Every house has such a tube and all the tubes flow into this big one."

"A river," Ten Bears offered.

"Exactly," the delighted director replied. "We have made a river to carry away the waste from our bodies."

Ten Bears gazed deeper into the hole.

"But where does it flow?" he asked.

"Ah-ha!" the director exclaimed, raising an emphatic finger in front of his face. "I will show you."

They clambered back into the carriage and in a few blocks turned east on a road parallel to the brooding river that hugged the city, following it to the desolate outskirts of town.

The carriage pulled up to a fenced portion of the adjacent waterway's banks and Ten Bears was escorted to a spot where a door had been made in the fence. The director pushed a key into the door and a few steps later Ten Bears was gazing down at four enormous tubes, all of them spewing effluent into the river.

Though the air was heavy with stink, Ten Bears stood mesmerized. At last he looked at the director and lifted an arm over the Potomac River.

"Is this a river of feces, too?"

"No, this river only carries the sewage away."

"Where does it go?"

"To the ocean."

"The great water that goes forever?"

"Yes."

Ten Bears looked downriver. He regarded the gushing tubes once more and sank into thought.

"What will happen when the great waters fill with feces?"

"Oh, no," the director chuckled. "The ocean cannot be filled."

CHAPTER L

*T*EN BEARS WAS STILL AWAKE WHEN KICKING BIRD CAME BACK and they talked about the events of the day over a pipe.

Kicking Bird had been impressed with the races. Just like Comanches, the white people got very excited when the horses ran, though some were demonstrably sad or angry when wagers were lost. Both men agreed that it was one more sign among many that the whites lacked pride.

"What did you do, Grandfather?"

"I was shown a river," Ten Bears answered.

"That big river we saw?"

"No, this one runs under the earth. It was made by the hair-mouths. I think one of its streams runs below this place where we are sitting."

Kicking Bird was too stunned to speak.

"Do you know what it carries?" Ten Bears asked.

Kicking Bird moved his head numbly back and forth.

"It carries the white man's excrement."

Kicking Bird's mouth fell open and the blood drained from his face.

CHAPTER LI

*T*WO DAYS BEFORE THEIR SCHEDULED DEPARTURE, THE MEETing with the generals at the War Department took place. As the delegation filed out, Ten Bears paused at a balcony while the others started down a long line of steps to a convoy of carriages which were to carry them to an afternoon portrait session at one of the city's leading photographic studios.

His position behind the balcony's stone railing afforded a comprehensive view of the sprawling city, and as Ten Bears filled his eyes with the evidence of white proliferation, he was struck with a question that had been haunting his thoughts.

A high-ranking, crisply groomed colonel had escorted the delegation to the exit, and, seeing Ten Bears standing alone, he sidled over and commented on the grandeur of the view.

Ten Bears responded with an uncomprehending nod, then thought to himself, *Maybe this soldier knows.*

The old man caught the attention of one of the interpreters, calling him over with a few flicks of a hand. Out of courtesy Ten Bears asked for a translation of the colonel's remark.

"Yes," the old man replied, "I have never seen a village of this size."

He glanced at the colonel, then at the interpreter.

"There is something I do not understand," he announced.

"Perhaps I can help you," the colonel offered.

"I have seen the white people feasting in the rooms where they pay money. I see them eat lots of meat. I see this in the pay money rooms. Do the families eat meat in their lodges as well?"

"Yes," the colonel affirmed. He waved a hand over the city. "Almost every house you see has a room for cooking meat and other foods."

Ten Bears squinted skeptically at the vast settlement.

"But I see no one hunting. I see no game being brought in. How does the white man make meat?"

"We slaughter it," the colonel answered matter-of-factly.

"Slaughter it?"

"We kill animals in a big house."

"Where is this big house?" Ten Bears asked and the colonel pointed north across the city.

"The biggest one is over there," he said.

"I will go there," Ten Bears stated.

The colonel and the interpreter looked at one another helplessly.

"But you are to have your portrait made this afternoon," reasoned the colonel.

"I don't care about that," Ten Bears grunted, looking in the direction the colonel had indicated. "I want to see how the white man makes meat."

Leaving Ten Bears to wait outside with the interpreter, the colonel disappeared into the offices of the War Department, where he relayed the visitor's request. After twenty minutes of bureaucratic maneuvering it was decided to grant Ten Bears' wish.

To the colonel's consternation, no one else could be persuaded to go and, within an hour, he, the interpreter, and the old Comanche man were breezing through the city streets on a course for the great slaughterhouse that supplied much of Washington's meat.

End-of-day shadows were beginning their march across the landscape when Ten Bears' carriage came to a stop in front of a sprawling maze of stock pens, many of them crowded with the condemned.

Two unhappy-looking men, their clothes lightly spattered with blood, waited for the visitors at the head of a track that cut between the pens and terminated in front of a cluster of massive, dark, almost windowless buildings.

"You Colonel Bascom?" one of the men asked dully.

"Yes, and this is our guest, Ten Bears, and his interpreter, Mr. McIntosh," the colonel replied.

The man who had spoken made a little nod of acknowledgment and, with his companion, turned up the track leading to the gloomy set of structures.

"He want to see anything in particular?" the dull man asked over his shoulder.

"I don't think so," Colonel Bascom replied.

"We're doin' hogs right now," the man offered, a remark to which Colonel Bascom did not reply.

Ten Bears had not been able to imagine the white man's place of making meat and was totally unprepared for what he saw as they passed pen after pen. He had never seen so many animals enclosed in one place, nor had he ever encountered such wholesale misery.

Many of the pens held what he recognized as the four-leggeds the whites held in high regard and called "cows." A large number of the enclosures held a much smaller, hairless four-legged the whites called "pigs." He came upon a pen of horses and paused to stare in shock at the forlorn animals. Ten bears had eaten the flesh of horses a few times in his life, but only to keep from starving. To think that any race would willingly kill and devour horses was incomprehensible, even if they were as poor as these.

That they would soon be killed was evident from the attitude of the animals themselves. Like the cows and pigs, the horses seemed fully cognizant of their fate and stood about in pronounced gloom, their heads hanging sadly a few inches from the ground, moving only when jostled by other animals. Some of them were suffering from broken limbs and a few carried ghastly wounds on their flanks or hips or chests where slabs of flesh hung open as if a butchering had been interrupted.

The strongest animals churned incessantly about the pens, whinnying, snorting, lowing, and squealing in abject terror, their eyes bulging to the whites as they danced in the ankle-deep quagmire of communal waste.

Ten Bears had killed animals all his life yet he knew them as brothers, and he pitied these, for the expressions on their faces were the same he had seen in his village when a child died in sickness or a warrior failed to return from a raid or a mother succumbed in childbirth. It was the same expression of abandonment he had seen on the faces of the men who returned from the battle at Adobe Walls, the men who had witnessed a nation of buffalo dead on the plains.

Through helpless eyes the animals in the pens asked the same questions over and over: Where is the Mystery? How can life end in this way?

As they neared the entrance to the gigantic box that was the largest in the group of sullen buildings, the dull man stopped and pointed to the end of the structure. Ten Bears was barely aware of Mr. McIntosh's translation, for he had already seen what the man had pointed out and was watching it carefully.

A long path, enclosed on both sides, angled up from the holding pens and went through a hole high up on the box. On the path were the beasts called pigs. They were moving forward in a single line, being driven by men on either side who were hitting them repeatedly with heavy sticks. The white men yelled angrily as they beat the animals, but this rough encouragement was muted by the shrill, cacophonous screams of the pigs themselves as their round, thick bodies vaulted and twisted and bucked in hopeless denial of what was about to happen.

Colonel Bascom did not want to go inside. Neither did Mr. McIntosh, and a brief squabble ensued before it was decided that Ten Bears would not need an interpretation of what he was about to see.

The old man followed the two men with bloodstained clothes through the doors of the slaughterhouse. Inside, they climbed a long stairway which led to a catwalk that gave a comprehensive view of everything going on below.

But all that Ten Bears saw could not be taken in at a glance. And it could not be absorbed, even over time. The sight was too bizarre, and in the course of his watching, the images that settled in the old man's eyes had the sharp, surreal quality of something dreamt.

The natural light entering through a series of small, square windows mounted high on the walls of the cavern-like place steadily lost power as it drifted downward and was swallowed by the nightmarish, yellow glow of work lamps spaced at regular intervals along the walls.

Hatted men were moving about in the tawny, submerged light.

Splotches of white shone through on clothes streaked with red as they went about their gruesome work with an air of impunity.

At the far end of the trileveled floor, men wielding axes chopped mechanically at the bodies of pigs, severing heads and limbs which were then cast with practiced ease into huge wooden tubs.

At the next level, Ten Bears saw a team of three men in the act of disemboweling one of the short-legged, flop-eared animals. One worker slit open the pig's belly and, with a few quick swipes of his long-bladed knife, emptied the abdomen of what little viscera had not already spilled onto the floor.

Another member of the team grasped the animal's hind legs and spun it across the slippery, metal floor to the lip of a slide. With a push from a glistening black boot the heavy body cascaded down the slide, coming to rest in close proximity to the choppers. A third man pushed the animal's viscera with an implement Ten Bears had never seen. The tangle of intestines and other vital organs disappeared over the edge of the floor and plopped into a large barrel already half full with the bowels of countless predecessors.

Directly below him, on the third and highest work level, two big white men waited on an expansive metal floor at the foot of another slide. No white at all could be seen on these men's clothes. Though they wore extra covering, every inch of their attire was covered with blood, as was the floor they stood on.

The man holding a thin-bladed, slightly curved knife stared up at two workers looming near the top of the slide. He nodded and, following a clank of metal and a thump, a living pig, its piercing screams echoing off the walls, slid across the floor to where the two big white men were waiting. Grabbing the crazed animal by its ears, one of the white men jerked the animal's head back while the other's knife sliced through its throat. Jets of blood struck the men's chests, and a moment later, they were guiding the still-bucking body to the slide that would carry it to the disembowelers.

Ten Bears saw the process repeated again and was astonished at how quickly and smoothly the white men worked. They seemed oblivious to their surroundings and its nature, to the stench of so much blood and flesh, the earsplitting cries of their victims, the eerie light and barely breathable air.

A third pig tumbled down the chute, but as the man who held its ears tried to stretch its throat for the knife the animal unexpectedly threw its head back with such power that its human captor was knocked to the floor, losing his grip.

Ten Bears heard sudden laughter and turned to see that the man who had brought him up the stairs was laughing. He shouted something out and the man who had fallen looked up from the floor and made what Ten Bears took to be a sign of anger with one of his fingers.

The man's partner had caught the pig and was still trying to restrain it when the one who had put up his finger wrathfully pulled another knife from its place on the wall.

The laughter next to Ten Bears grew louder as the angry white man rushed across the floor. Bellowing words of rage at the struggling pig, he drove his knife into the animal's face. Then he stabbed and slashed until blood seemed to be squirting everywhere.

For some reason the man was treating the animal like an enemy and it was then that Ten Bears' head began to reel. Sound and smell and sight seemed to merge as he pushed away from the catwalk rail and followed the tops of his moccasins down the stairs.

He hardly glanced at Colonel Bascom or Interpreter McIntosh when he got outside. He tried to keep his eyes on his feet as they walked past the pens, for every time he looked up the same thing would happen. The faces of the animals, the tint of their coats, the heaving of their nostrils—all that he saw would swirl together like multicolored ripples of grease on the surface of a boiling cook pot.

As they drove away, Ten Bears asked if they could make the horse go faster and when the breeze began to pass over his face he could see clearly again.

He spoke only once more on the trip back to town, and that was in answer to a question from Colonel Bascom. The colonel recognized that the old man was shaken, and, certain that any Indian was inured to the sight of blood and death, assumed that he was overwhelmed by yet another achievement of modern civilization.

"You have seen how the white man makes meat," the colonel stated rather smugly. "What do you think?"

Ten Bears never looked at Colonel Bascom, directing his reply instead to the space in front of his face.

"I do not believe it," he said.

As he sat talking with Kicking Bird that evening, Ten Bears tried to describe the way the white men made meat, but what he had seen so violated the basic tenets of his life that no portrayal seemed adequate.

Kicking Bird listened to Ten Bears' description in horror. To see blood, to smell death, to kill an enemy without mercy were aspects of life with which he was intimate, but hearing what had gone on in the white man slaughterhouse frightened him, and when Ten Bears told him about the choppers he had to stop the old man.

"They don't use all of the animal?" he asked, his voice hushed.

"Maybe half. They throw the rest away."

"You saw this?"

"Yes, I saw it. They didn't say any prayers, either."

"No prayers?"

"No. And one of the animals was attacked by one of the white men . . . like it was an enemy."

Kicking Bird could not make sense of such a thing and the thought crossed his mind that Ten Bears might be afflicted with some sort of dementia. People of great age were often invaded by transforming spirits.

"The white man must have been insane," Kicking Bird theorized.

"I'm certain of that," the old man retorted. "There's no understanding this white man's holy road. I wouldn't be surprised to see Comanches in those pens next."

"The white people do not eat the flesh of other people, Grandfather."

"How can that be known? The river of excrement was not known. The place they make meat was not known. I don't care to find out any more about the whites. I want to go home."

"We are meeting the Great White Father tomorrow."

"Of course we are meeting him. I will sit with him and hear his words. But I will have nothing to say. I want to go home."

CHAPTER LII

*T*HE DELEGATION ARRIVED AT THE GREAT WHITE FATHER'S RESI-
dence in the early afternoon of the next day. The temperature had
plunged overnight and the bundled warriors peered out from the hoods
of blankets as they drove up, uniformly impressed with the size of the
place called the White House. Various dignitaries fell into step with the
party as it made its way through the vast rooms and corridors, all of them
appointed with splendorous articles of white culture.

The men from the plains were at last shown into the enormous room
where they were to council with the Great White Father. Its center was
dominated by a table the length of several horses and surrounded by the
things called chairs. Above the table were the sparkling glass trees the
whites liked to attach to their ceilings, and at either end of the room
huge fires were blazing.

The warriors were seated at the far end of the table. Ten Bears was
given the honor of the biggest chair, which faced the one standing empty
at the opposite end, the one reserved for the Great White Father.

Many civilians and a few high-ranking soldiers took the remaining
places. A dozen of the white man's black-skinned slaves were posted at
various points on the perimeter of the room, and shortly after all was in

readiness, the Great White Father himself, a covey of assistants traveling in his wake, entered the room. The whites rose from their seats, but the Comanche, Kiowa, Cheyenne, and Arapaho, thinking that the rising was some kind of occult facet of encounters between the whites and their chief, stayed seated.

The Great White Father was not quite what they expected, for despite the hair on his face being extraordinarily thick and his eyes being unusually small, he looked about the same as most other white men. But it was clear that he possessed incredible power. With a simple lifting of his hand he induced the other white men to resume their seats, and when he began to speak, his followers leaned forward as if their lives depended on his words.

At the direction of the Great White Father the members of the delegation were made to stand up and arrange themselves in a line against a bank of windows. The Great White Father then started down the line, taking each man's hand and saying a few words of welcome. Over the men's necks he draped one of the heavy peace medals, each bearing a likeness of himself. When he reached Kicking Bird and saw that the Comanche was already wearing a medal stamped with the face of one of his predecessors, the Great White Father seemed especially pleased.

"Here is a man who knows peace," he said.

"I have always loved peace," Kicking Bird confirmed.

"And what is your name, sir?" the Great White Father asked.

"Kicking Bird."

"Kicking Bird, uh-huh . . ."

The Great White Father shook Kicking Bird's hand and hung a second medal around his neck. When he was finished with the line, he returned to his place at the head of the table as the delegation drifted back to their seats.

At some unseen signal the black-skinned slaves came forward to pour coffee into large white cups and lay thick, dark cigarettes called cigars in front of each man. The slaves fell back to their positions and the Great White Father commenced a talk, expressing gratitude to his "Indian children" for coming so far to meet him and hoping that their visit had been pleasant and informative. He spoke a long time of the need for peace and assured his guests that the key to peace and prosperity depended on their willingness to embrace the new world of the reservation and avail themselves of its many advantages. He closed his remarks by inviting each man to speak, pronouncing himself ready to hear their hearts.

For more than an hour the tribesmen took turns sounding the familiar themes of contention between the races, concerns that the Great White Father deflected with paternal benevolence, constantly returning to the declaration that his greatest desire was to ensure the welfare of his children.

The sharpest questioning came from Kicking Bird, who iterated a long list of conditions for a successful transition to the reservation, including freedom from assault by whites, limited sovereignty, hunting rights, and proper instruction in the ways of the holy road.

The Great White Father proclaimed repeatedly that he would never abandon those of his children who promised to behave themselves, and Kicking Bird's questions, like those of his brethren, at last collapsed under the weight of platitude.

Only Ten Bears was left to speak. He had sat placidly in his chair through the afternoon, listening attentively but expressionlessly to every exchange, and the Great White Father, though he was anxious to get on with his schedule, was curious about the old man.

"The oldest of you has not spoken," he said, pointing out Ten Bears. "I would like to hear what is on his mind."

Laying a hand on each arm of his chair, Ten Bears pushed himself up.

"You made us an invitation to come to Washington, and we accepted. You have taken our hands and made us presents and cared for our needs with generosity, and no harm has come to us. We never invited the white man into our country but he came anyway, not looking for game to hunt but for people to kill. Comanches did not fire the first shot . . . the white man did.

"Why the white man wants our country I do not know. He has more than enough for himself. I do not understand why the white man wants to kill everything in our country and make it poor. When the Comanche resists, the white man says he is misbehaving and must be punished.

"We have never tried to take over your country. All that we have ever asked is to be left alone. You will not grant that wish. Instead you want us to give up everything we love and come to live in a small space and wear your clothes and eat your food and pray to your god. You want us to walk with you on what you call the holy road. I will not do that."

As Ten Bears paused to wet his lips with a sip of coffee he could see and hear the whites shifting in their seats. Only the Great White Father did not move but kept his eyes steadfast on the speaker.

"I was born upon the prairie," Ten Bears continued, "where the wind blows free and there is nothing to break the light of the sun. I was born where there are no enclosures and everything draws a free breath. I want to die there. I would rather wander the prairie eating dung than live on a white man's reservation."

Silence continued a few seconds after Ten Bears was seated again. At last the Great White Father rose.

"There is a poet among you," he announced, directing his gaze upon Ten Bears. "His speech is beautiful. Thank you for sharing it with us. And thank you for coming to my home today. I wish you all a swift, safe journey home."

CHAPTER LIII

*E*VER MINDFUL OF LASTING IMPRESSIONS, THE WHITES SUR-
prised the delegation by moving them to an even grander hotel on the
eve of their departure, where they, their agents, their interpreters, and a
host of Washington dignitaries were fêted in a private banquet room.
Before the meal was served the primitives were treated to the spectacle
of gaslight as two black-skinned men entered and went from lamp to
lamp, creating light out of a metal valve and the application of a spark.

The depth of conviviality that had been reached between Indian and
white was amazing. After only a few days of intimacy, white and Indian
were familiar enough to sit side by side at a dinner table. They talked,
and in several instances Ten Bears noticed they were easy enough in each
other's company to poke fun.

Ten Bears did not find fault with any of it. Nothing was better than
peace and goodwill. At the same time, however, he found himself detached, as if he were viewing everything from a distance. He was no
longer interested in human affairs. His motivation for living had been
reduced to a single, powerful drive, and that was to go home.

The appearance, toward meal's end, of a white man priest, only
increased his desire for the prairie. The priest made a long talk, during

which he often referred to the black book which the white man said contained instructions from the Mystery. Ten Bears listened attentively, concluding, as did everyone else, that there was much in the book that made sense. But to the old man the appearance of the priest and the talk he made were final confirmation that the holy road should not be walked.

Though it no longer seemed important to do so, he shared his misgivings with Kicking Bird after they retired for the evening to their suite of rooms. Kicking Bird had been taken with many of the priest's ideas about brotherhood and not wanting other men's wives and loving neighbors and not stealing.

"Yes," Ten Bears agreed, "the words were good. But he didn't smoke the pipe. He didn't acknowledge the Mystery. These things have to be done."

"The whites have a different way of doing it," Kicking Bird answered resignedly.

"They think the Mystery lives in a book. Even a fool knows the Mystery is everywhere. The whites tell us they love the Mystery's instructions, but so far as I can see they don't do anything the Mystery tells them to do. I think the whites believe they are the Mystery."

In his heart Kicking Bird agreed with Ten Bears, but understanding that the whites were wrong about the world would not aid his cause of helping people adjust to the reservation.

"You're probably right, Grandfather," he sighed, "but the whites will not change."

"No," Ten Bears replied wistfully, "they won't change. And neither will I. I want to go to sleep now. Sleep will bring tomorrow, and tomorrow we start for home."

Ten Bears found the bed to his liking. Kicking Bird, who preferred the floor because it was closer to the earth, performed his nightly ritual of clearing away the rugs to make a place on the wood to spread blankets.

As he was executing this chore, one of the departing rugs revealed a rough spot on the floor about the size of two men laid side by side. The flooring was so cracked and rotted that in some places light shone through. The white people had used the rug to hide the eyesore but for Kicking Bird it was just right. He was tired of perfect surfaces and happily spread his blankets over the rough spot. Though the night was cold and there was much on his mind, Kicking Bird willed himself straight to sleep.

Ten Bears had a more difficult time of it. As on the night of the council when his village was split forever, he could not shut down his mind. It flitted, uncontrolled, from one disconnected thought to another, teasing the old man toward the border of sleep only to pull him back again.

Exasperated, Ten Bears turned his mind exclusively to landscapes of his homeland but something was still distracting him and, when he opened his eyes, the old man realized that the little fires on the walls were keeping him awake. He swung his feet to the floor, pushed himself off the bed, and went from one fire to another, opening the little glass doors and extinguishing each irritating flame with a puff of his breath.

Back in bed he felt much better. In the darkness his mind began to slow and as he tumbled toward unconsciousness, he saw the prairie in its limitless glory. The grass was waving, the sun was high, the sky was blue, and in the far distance he could see the distinctive dark forms of buffalo grazing. He also saw something coming toward him.

Nothing more than a speck at first, the object came at great speed and suddenly the face of an eagle filled the whole of Ten Bears' vision. Its keen, unblinking eyes were focused solely on Ten Bears but the old man felt no fear.

An instant later Ten Bears realized he was astride the eagle's back. Powered by the great levers of the eagle's wings, they were rising through the mist of earthbound clouds.

Sudden as the turn of a dream, eternal blackness stretched above them. Glittering stars, more stars than could ever be imagined, stood out like particles of dust spinning in a ray of afternoon sun. They covered Ten Bears like falling snow.

Then they went out.

CHAPTER LIV

*T*WO DAYS LATER, KICKING BIRD AND LAWRIE TATUM BOARDED
a westbound train, and, though he had made a full recovery and had not
been damaged physically, the Comanche was still shaken when he took
his seat.

Having no idea how he had been spared made the entire episode impossible to reconcile. How was it that his nose had found and pressed itself into a crack in the wood that provided enough oxygen to keep his
body from succumbing to the gas? How was it that he had been found
and pulled from the room with what the whites said were minutes to
live?

How could it be that Ten Bears' body lay on the floor of a coach a
few behind his own, his remains enclosed in one of the white man's death
boxes? How could it be that an old man's humble wish to die on the
prairie had not been granted? How could the Mystery let it come to this?

Kicking Bird had never felt more helpless. He could not exist in his
present state, yet he was powerless to change it. The past was gone, the
future was overwhelming, and his life, as he sat inert and shattered, was
being measured out minute by minute.

The train jerked ahead and, with each revolution of its wheels, a healing miracle began as well. Knowing that he was moving west drove Kicking Bird's soul forward, and by the time they crossed the span over the Mississippi River, the far-seeing Comanche realized that he was nearly whole again.

Perhaps he was intact once more because he was also feeling a new, exhilarating sense of purpose. The Comanches, whether they knew it or not, had their greatest protector in the man Kicking Bird. It was Kicking Bird who was best qualified to see them through the struggle of change, and this he was resolved to do even if it meant the sacrifice of all he possessed, even his life.

Now he was ready to lay himself down and let his people cross over to the future with all the security his body and spirit could provide.

CHAPTER LV

*T*HE ABORTIVE RAID ON CAPTAIN BRADLEY'S COLUMN HAD plunged the hostile camps into chaos, and the news of Ten Bears' death, transmitted by spies filtering in and out of the reservation lands, was marked by a shorter period of mourning than would have been observed in better times. In the frenzy of trying to mount a defense on the run, every day was a desperate struggle, and grief was a luxury that no one could much indulge.

Hunting For Something hacked off her hair, as did Stands With A Fist, and both women gashed their arms and legs. But the cuts were fewer and not as deep as they might have been.

Owl Prophet was vehement in his conviction that the whites had murdered Ten Bears through the use of some magical agent but his ire was quickly shoved aside by demands from the many wounded men who had managed to make it back from the attack. It seemed that every other lodge held someone who needed attention and, in the coming weeks, the prophet was perpetually applying spells, potions, and even surgeries as his family picked the surrounding prairie clean of healing medicines.

Like many others, the Dances With Wolves and Smiles A Lot families had doubled up. It was the only way to meet the increasing demands of cooking and cleaning, hauling food and water, tending to the needs of exhausted husbands, and organizing the lives of Snake In Hands, Always Walking, Stays Quiet, and Rabbit.

In addition to their clearly defined and dangerous roles as providers and protectors, warriors were burdened with a staggering onslaught of decisions, all of which had to be made in the ever-shifting circumstances of evasion and escape. Owing to new movements on the part of the white soldiers, camps were erected only to be struck a day or two later. Keeping every camp supplied with the basic elements of food and fuel was a herculean task that never seemed fully accomplished. In addition, huge expenditures of energy were surrendered in restraining factions of young men, eager for combat, from running amok.

Some people went into the reservation, only to return disillusioned, while a few hardened warriors packed up their families and possessions and took the white man's holy road, never to return.

The one thing the Comanches and their allies did not need was the rain, which made every obstacle that much harder to overcome. It never seemed to stop, and after weeks of inundation, the people native to the land wondered if they hadn't miscalculated in supposing the Mystery had abandoned only them. It seemed the whole world was gradually submerging under the deluge.

Ponies sank past their ankles in the sucking mud that coated the prairie everywhere they traveled. People were never dry and their skin became so sodden that this time of their greatest trial was referred to through succeeding generations as "the wrinkled-hand chase."

Ceaseless traveling in difficult conditions took its toll on possessions as well as people, and long before the running and fighting ended, people were often forced to sleep in the open. For a time, the comment that it was "cruel to wake a man before his puddle was warm" enjoyed wide popularity. But the joke quickly played out. There was too much struggle for levity. Every day of life was a grand achievement for the grim souls who had committed themselves to defiance.

Yet, if asked, it is certain that the people branded hostile would have agreed that the fierceness of their determination elevated them to a previously unknown spiritual plane. Mourning for the warriors who had fallen in the unsuccessful first attack of the campaign was conducted inwardly, privately. The desperate search for food and forage went on without complaint. Even the coughing sickness many had contracted from the wet and cold was ignored in the set-jawed atmosphere of defense.

Stands With A Fist and Hunting For Something and Wind In His Hair's wife, One Braid Trailing, rose unheralded to positions of leadership in the phalanx of women who kept the village intact and moving. Somehow they managed to nurture children, prepare food, provide shelter, create warmth, and strike or set up camp at a moment's notice in the muck and rain. The women organized and maintained a semblance of life in vague hope that the warriors, already overtaxed by the neverending search for food, would find a way to defeat the white soldiers.

The fact that Captain Bradley's troops had repelled them so effectively forced Wind In His Hair and his inner circle to suspend plans for further attacks on the invaders. The fast-shooting guns of the whites were too powerful. Sixteen warriors had been lost in a fight that yielded no scalps and caused but a momentary halt in the enemy's advance.

Bad Hand had taken the field with hundreds of blue-coated men. They were driving down from the northeast while Captain Bradley's smaller force moved steadily up from the south. A third army of soldiers was coming from the northwest, but, fortunately, they were being held up by large groups of Cheyenne and Arapaho.

The situation was growing more dire by the day for Wind In His Hair's community. They knew they could not evade the white soldiers forever, nor could they fight them effectively. Groups of decoys, sent to draw the hair-mouths off the scent, had succeeded only in causing slight delays in the enemy advance. The warriors agreed that the best they could hope for was to stay out of range until the soldiers ran out of ambition, or food, or both. Sooner or later they would have to leave the country.

But even that strategy disintegrated on a rare, rainless night when Dances With Wolves, Smiles A Lot, and Blue Turtle returned from a long scout to report that a train of perhaps twenty soldier wagons, undoubtedly intended to resupply those already in the field, was driving toward them from the east. Dances With Wolves said he had not seen any of the fast-shooting guns and only a small force of soldiers was escorting the train.

That same night, after a council remarkable for its brevity, Wind In His Hair gave the order for camp to be struck. The whites had opened the only avenue of action available to the warriors. They had to move east and engage the wagon train. It was their best and, as each warrior knew in his heart, only chance.

CHAPTER LVI

*E*ARLY IN HIS LIFE AS A WARRIOR, WIND IN HIS HAIR HAD nearly been killed several times on a single raid into Mexico and on his return home had sought the counsel of an old woman reputed to have the power to turn bad luck to good.

When the old woman learned that Wind In His Hair had recently begun to eat with metal implements, she advised him to cease the practice. Wind In His Hair had followed the advice unerringly, and not once in the intervening years had his lips touched food tainted by the metal of a white man's spoon or ladle.

Even in the chaos of the wrinkled-hand chase, he had scrupulously monitored the preparation of his food, but in a temporary camp sequestered in a stand of cottonwoods several miles from the wagon train, the taboo was violated.

That morning had been particularly confusing. Camp was erected as men prepared for battle, and while trying to organize the warriors, he had too hastily accepted and devoured a bowl of broth and meat. A few minutes later One Braid Trailing had brought him a second breakfast. Tracking the first breakfast back to its source, Wind In His Hair discovered a large metal ladle submerged in the pot that had produced his meal. If he led his warriors that morning he was certain to die, so he watched sourly as two hundred warriors disappeared into the east to confront the wagon train.

Careful to avoid casualties, they swooped down from all sides and put the mule-driven wagons to flight, killing several soldiers and knocking down a few mules in the process.

The ungainly wagon train fled in the direction of a nearby stream, hoping to make its stand in reach of water, but the warriors quickly surrounded it, forcing the wagons to halt short of their objective.

The whites drew their vehicles into a tight circle and began to throw up breastworks of wet earth as the Comanches and Kiowa, following Wind In His Hair's strategy of weakening them through hunger, thirst, and attrition, settled in to snipe at long range.

But it was not long before the simple plan began to unravel.

In days past the discipline of a siege would have been carried out, but now the buffalo were dead, the army was coming after them, families had little to eat, and every warrior felt constant pressure to do something. No one was content to sit still, especially the young men, and when Smiles A Lot impulsively and suddenly rode his black horse toward the encircled wagons, roars of approval followed him.

He moved at a walk until close enough to draw the enemy's fire. Then his horse rose into the air, came back to ground, and, with a great leap that made a projectile of both horse and rider, charged into the fire coming from the wagons.

At fifty yards, Smiles A Lot veered to a parallel course and inaugurated a demonstration of horsemanship for which the Comanche were famous. At full speed he grabbed a hunk of mane, swung down along the racing animal's side, struck the earth with both feet, and vaulted high into the air before coming to rest again on the animal's back. He repeated this astounding maneuver several times before pulling up, wheeling, and sprinting back the way he had come. To the amazement of all who could see, he rose and stood on the horse's back, dropped down, swung over the speeding horse's side, passed under the animal's neck, swung up the other side, and stood once again.

Though unrivaled in its mastery, Smiles A Lot's daring exhibition was part of a long tradition practiced by bold warriors of preceding generations. It was always good to do such things: it swelled the courage of brothers-in-arms while disconcerting the enemy and making him waste ammunition. But as Smiles A Lot halted to give his heaving mount a chance to catch its breath, his heart and mind fused in an indescribable entity. The blood pumping through his veins resounded like the beat of a great drum. It filled the open prairie around him with an irresistibly primal call, and the circle of wagons ahead suddenly grew as transparent as the enemies he had seen in the vision at the great Medicine Bluff.

Smiles A Lot charged the wagons again but this time he did not veer, and as he swung down along the side of the running black horse, his fellow Comanches could not believe what was happening. Smiles A Lot was going through the enemy.

The black horse took flight over one of the wagons with Smiles A Lot still hanging at his side. Scattering white men as they landed, horse and rider dug across the open ground, cleared a wagon on the other side, and streaked back onto the prairie.

When Smiles A Lot pulled up again the screams of his fellow fighters overwhelmed all sound. The voices did not abate. They rushed into his ears and spread through his body like fire. The black horse pivoted on his hind legs and charged again. This time Smiles A Lot did not conceal himself but rode into the oncoming fire from the wagons straight up. Again they leapt a wagon, tore over the ground occupied by the whites, flew over a second wagon, and sped back across the prairie until they reached the ranks from which they had come. The feathers on Smiles A Lot's head had been shot to pieces. The toe of one of his moccasins was missing. Both reins had been sliced in half. But the bodies of horse and rider were untouched by white man bullets.

The power and magic of Smiles A Lot electrified the Comanches and Kiowas surrounding the wagon train. The young men could no longer be held in check, and even veteran warriors knew that something must be done. Smiles A Lot's charge had brought their pride to a boil, such that when the warriors talked excitedly about what course to take, it quickly became apparent they could not act without the one who was the soul of resistance.

Riders were dispatched to the village, and, less than an hour later, overcoming his best instincts, Wind In His Hair answered their call.

"We will ride over them," he bellowed, riding up and down the lines of warriors. "We will ride over them again and again until they are dead."

Seeing that the Indians were attacking in full force, the wagon train's commander ordered everyone to take cover. Soldiers and civilians were instructed to go to small arms once the Indians penetrated the defenses, but one among them, a former buffalo-hunter named Arbuckle, had no intention of using a peashooter when he possessed the best rifle a man could own. He slid under a wagon and started firing at the oncoming horde, taking aim at the figure out in front, the one with the big, trailing bonnet of eagle feathers.

Arbuckle emptied a couple of saddles but was unable to get a clear shot at the one he wanted. As the Indian charge broke overhead, Arbuckle about-faced under the wagon to fire at those who had gotten inside the circle.

Suddenly, the mass of horses and men parted and Arbuckle sighted down his rifle at the back of his prize. He squeezed the trigger and the warrior with the bonnet jerked. A hand went to the small of his back and the Indian slumped forward. The man with the eagle feathers disappeared, and Arbuckle's disappointment at not being able to shoot him a second time was fleeting. He knew he had gotten him good with the first round.

CHAPTER LVII

*D*ANCES WITH WOLVES AND A MAN NAMED HE WHO DOES NOT Listen To Them were the first to get to Wind In His Hair. Together they lifted him off his pony, and when they were clear of the wagons, Dances With Wolves pulled the mortally wounded warrior up behind him.

"I am fighting no more!" Dances With Wolves screamed, and as he broke off the battle to carry Wind In His Hair back to the camp, most of the holdovers from Ten Bears' village followed.

White Bear and his Kiowas wanted no more, either, and though a few pockets of young Comanche and Kiowa pestered the wagon train with sniper fire until dusk, the main force of fighters left the field without fulfilling their last, desperate hope. If the whites could kill Wind In His Hair, there was no point in fighting.

The one-eyed warrior was still alive when they reached the temporary camp, but the bullet that had lodged in the bone of his back made it impossible for him to move his legs or even feel them.

As he was carried to bed, Wind In His Hair heard Dances With Wolves calling for Owl Prophet.

"No," he commanded, "I do not want to be doctored. I will not live like this. I am dying now . . . let me die."

Propped against a backrest, he lingered until moonrise. Then he closed his eyes and let his chin slump against his chest as the last trace of breath passed out of him.

In his last hours of life the leader had made but one demand. He wanted his body secreted from the enemy, and as soon as he was dead, his remains were carried away from camp, buried in a deep hole, covered with earth, and carefully camouflaged with brush and stones.

No ponies were killed over him and only a few personal items, hastily grabbed up by his friends, were placed in the grave with him. One Braid Trailing cut her hair and slashed herself, but she was the only one who mourned. There was no time for the others.

Word came that yet another column of soldiers was coming, this one from the east. Some families had already started for the reservation and many others were making ready. Those who felt compelled to stay had no idea what to do next. White man soldiers whom they could not hope to fight were converging on them from all directions. If they stayed where they were, they would be annihilated. But where could they go?

In the council convened shortly after the return of Wind In His Hair's burial party, it was decided that a single option was left. They must flee west before the soldiers could catch them, surmount the great caprock barrier, cross the trackless wilderness of the Staked Plains, dive into the Great Hole In The Earth, and hide.

But they would have to escape the net closing around them before they could hope to hide, and, on the night Wind In His Hair passed over the stars, his heirs started west—three hundred men, women, and children pushing almost a thousand ponies, frantic to make themselves invisible.

CHAPTER LVIII

WHEN LAWRIE TATUM AND KICKING BIRD DISEMBARKED AT the terminus of the train line, they were given a large spring wagon to carry Ten Bears overland to Fort Sill.

At mid-morning of their journey's second day, Lawrie Tatum mentioned that he had been thinking of a suitable site for Ten Bears' interment and had concluded that a place of prominence at the post cemetery would be the best solution.

"Not at Fort Sill," Kicking Bird replied flatly.

"Then where?"

"On prairie . . . old way. You go Sill. Me . . . Ten Bears go on prairie."

For a time Lawrie Tatum tried to talk his friend out of it, reminding him that they had much to accomplish on the reservation. But Kicking Bird was unmoved and the two parted, Lawrie Tatum angling north on his mule as Kicking Bird swung south, then west, to Comanche country.

He had been told of the heavy, unremitting rains, but though the earth was still soggy, he encountered nothing but fair weather. The sun was bright, the breeze stiff, and the wagon's two mules had little difficulty navigating the trackless plain.

The deeper Kicking Bird penetrated his homeland the more he wondered how it could be that the free ways were gone. The country looked the same as it always had—vast, ever-changing, and empty. It was hard to believe that white people were taking over the country and that their soldiers were chasing his friends.

He hit a stream swollen by the recent rains, and instead of trying to cross, he followed it, trusting that the Mystery would lead him to the right place.

He had camped but twice when he happened on the perfect spot, an exquisite glade of high grass and soft soil surrounded by sentinels of cottonwoods whose leaves were tumbling.

As he stood watching the place, Kicking Bird heard a thumping in the air, and with only the strange sound as warning, he felt waves of motion suddenly crash over his head. He ducked reflexively, and a split second later saw the forms of two golden eagles sailing across the glade at low altitude. Simultaneously, they arched into an effortless, elegant climb and landed their big bodies with ease on the uppermost reaches of one of the cottonwoods.

He could not believe they had passed so close to him, and as he watched the eagles get their bearings with quick twists of their heads, Kicking Bird understood that since his parting with Lawrie Tatum, the Mystery had been guiding his progress.

For the rest of the afternoon he constructed a burial scaffold under the vigilant eyes of the eagles. When all was in readiness, Kicking Bird pulled apart the wooden box, lifted out the old man's corpse, and laid it on a blanket.

Ten Bears was quite stiff, so there was little Kicking Bird could do to make him more presentable, but he gave the body a cursory inspection anyway. As his eyes traveled to one of the old man's hands he was surprised to see the white man spectacles. They were held in the fingers and Kicking Bird's first reaction was to give the alien apparatus a tug. A second thought quickly seized him, however, and he relented. The hand and the spectacles seemed perfectly at ease. They were welded together in the same delicate way Kicking Bird had observed on so many occasions when Ten Bears was alive.

He rolled the old man up in the blanket, hoisted him onto the scaffold, tied the body fast to its moorings, and stepped back to see if all was right. Then he tossed a few offerings of tobacco into the air and thought of leaving.

But his body would not move. Kicking Bird stood transfixed, trying to understand what might be happening to him.

Perhaps I am meant to stand here awhile longer, he thought.

The breeze rose. Soon it was whistling through the burial scaffold, and as he listened to the eerie music, Kicking Bird realized the full depth of what he was saying good-bye to. He looked over his shoulder and the white man wagon was suddenly more than just a wagon. It was the life awaiting him, and, to his horror, Kicking Bird understood with crushing finality that he could never live successfully in a world of wagons. He looked again at the scaffold swaying in the wind and the pair of eagles high in the cottonwood and realized that he was saying good-bye to the country that had been his whole life.

Feeling a rising in his stomach, he said to himself, *It is a beautiful country . . . the most beautiful . . .* and a torrent of sadness flooded in on him. It permeated his skin and swamped his heart, and with his next conscious thought Kicking Bird found himself sobbing on the ground.

Wiping his face with his hands, he stumbled back to the wagon and climbed onto the seat. He kept his eyes down as he picked up the team's reins and didn't look up until they were turned around and headed out of the glade.

He drove many miles that night before finally making camp.

CHAPTER LIX

*T*HE REMAINDER OF THE COMANCHE AND KIOWA HOSTILES MOVED
as one great body, employing every known tactic to evade the soldiers
who were chasing them. Despite being encumbered with a huge horse
herd, dismantled homes, and the women, children, and elderly, they had
managed to stay out of the enemy's reach for weeks. Every day the warriors risked their lives trying to distract and annoy the soldiers. They
backtracked miles up swollen rivers. On dry days they built and set fires
far from their true line of march. Parties large and small constantly tried
to decoy the soldiers by showing themselves or harassing the enemy with
sniper fire. They harnessed artificially weighted travois to their ponies
and created miles of false trails.

Audaciously, they struck Bad Hand's horse herd in daylight, and
though they captured only a few animals, many broke free in the attack
and scattered over the drenched prairie in every direction. They suffered
few casualties, but Bad Hand pursued them so relentlessly that only by
splitting themselves over and over, until they were fleeing in groups of
twos and threes, did the warriors save themselves.

On another occasion, a party led by Dances With Wolves and White
Bear boldly doubled back on a group of Bad Hand's scouts and attacked

them within earshot of the main column. They killed two Tonkawas and an Osage and would easily have overwhelmed the others had not Bad Hand dispatched a squad of rescuers at the first sound of firing. Dances With Wolves and Blue Turtle were the last to break off the action and escaped only because they were able to jump from one back to another of the five ponies between them.

Actual battle against the soldiers was practically nonexistent because every warrior was consumed with trying to keep people out of harm's way. But the success they had in keeping their friends and families from being killed or captured was so miraculous that each man knew it could not be sustained without intervention from the Mystery.

Owl Prophet had said that if they could reach the Great Hole In The Earth they might yet achieve deliverance from their tormentors. But reaching the Great Hole seemed more implausible with the close of every day. They had tried every strategy and trick but still could not shake Bad Hand and his soldiers. Even if they reached the great caprock barrier, the soldiers were too close now for them to climb over undetected. The soldiers would pursue them onto the Staked Plains and there would be nothing to keep them from following the Comanches straight into the ancient winter sanctuary.

The tenuous stalemate which threatened the hostiles with destruction was finally broken when they were within sight of the caprock. At any other time the weather's lifting would have been greeted with relief but the sudden clearing of the skies finally forced the hostiles' hand. They were hemmed in by Bad Hand's column from the east and Bradley's from the south, and the sunshine washing over the prairie left them with but one alternative. They would have to make a run for the caprock in broad daylight, a maneuver sure to be seen by the soldiers swarming over the country in their rear.

A desperate plan, concocted by the warriors in the predawn, started with a squad of children, including Rabbit, Snake In Hands, and Always Walking, driving the thousand ponies toward the brooding outline of caprock that vaulted skyward from the prairie floor. Close on their heels came the women and elderly, dragging the essentials of the village behind them.

Several detachments of warriors tried to create a diversion by opening fire on the waking soldier camp. The main body of warriors daringly positioned themselves between the fleeing village and the soldiers sure to pursue it.

The distraction provided by the snipers bought them little time. White man scouts quickly spied the horse herd and the village behind it, and with only hours to make up, the hair-mouth force started in furious pursuit.

Dances With Wolves, White Bear, Smiles A Lot, Blue Turtle, and their compatriots fought as they retreated, sometimes engaging the soldiers from cover, sometimes throwing themselves in feints against the enemy flanks.

But as the morning wore on it became clear that the soldiers would not be stopped, and, to the dismay of the warriors, they found the ground they were backing over increasingly littered with lodge poles and cooking pots and other miscellaneous articles of camp. The women ahead were losing pace.

Just as the curtain of total defeat lowered, the long-hoped-for intervention of the Mystery made its appearance, with the spectacular timing of a last-minute reprieve.

The village was barely a mile ahead of the warriors when the air temperature started to plummet. Moments later, an unbroken wall of gray crested the looming caprock and swirled down the face of the great natural divide.

Knowing they now had a chance, the warriors stiffened against the onrushing blue-coats, who were nearly upon them when the first particles of sleet began to sting their faces. Minutes later the storm slammed into them and Bad Hand had no choice but to sound recall as he watched his quarry vaporize into a maw of ice and snow so thick that he was soon unable to see beyond his horse's head.

CHAPTER LX

*W*HILE HIS FRIENDS AND RELATIVES FOUGHT FOR THEIR lives on the plains, desperation of a different kind gnawed at the hearts of Kicking Bird and his fellow leaders on the reservation.

The passing of the ultimatum had swollen the reserve's population with anxious people utterly ignorant of how to navigate the holy road. The former free roamers knew nothing of the structure upon which the white man's culture was based and, though the wild people of the plains responded to peer pressure, to follow instructions from any type of central authority was as alien to them as celebrating a birthday.

People weren't used to camping in one place, often adjacent to other clans or tribes, and men of standing like Kicking Bird and Touch The Clouds found themselves struggling against a constant stream of problems.

While they tried to instill basic principles of sanitation, they also were called upon to settle disputes over pasturage of horses between feuding neighbors. When they tried to convince mothers to let their young be treated by white man doctors, they incurred the enmity of traditional medicine men. Getting people to bring their children to Lawrie

Tatum's school was difficult enough, but keeping the pupils in class was even harder. Young men were constantly counseled against leaving the reservation to raid, but no inducements were offered to convince them to stay. Those in defiance of the ultimatum regularly slipped in and out of the reservation to visit family, creating even greater unrest. And though the sale of liquor to reservation residents was strictly forbidden, some people had already begun to blot out their misery with inebriation.

Confusion, uncertainty, and fear were a palpable presence inside every reservation lodge. In making a journey of little more than a hundred miles, the Comanche, like the other tribes, had stepped literally from one age of humankind to another, and while Kicking Bird had expected many problems, he could not have fully anticipated his own impossibly demanding role in the transition.

His far-seeing nature isolated the former medicine man. He alone could speak the white man tongue, and he was the only one with the knowledge and influence to assure that the walk down the holy road was safe and sound.

But Kicking Bird had not been long on the reservation before he realized that the holy road was not a point of confusion for Indian people only. The whites seemed confused too. After only a few days of official dealings he was forced to conclude that for nearly every white there was a different perception of the holy road, and it came to him, in a queasy, haunting recognition, that the whites did not know how to operate the system they had invented. Few of them obeyed its tenets, and it was Kicking Bird's fate to engage in a long, lonely struggle against these puzzling powers.

Only half of the promised cows arrived on the first ration day, and instead of fat beeves, the hungry Indians saw a collection of half-dead animals of skin and bone. Kicking Bird complained immediately, but no one could tell him what had gone wrong. The cows could neither be rejected nor replaced. The people would have to make do, and in the end Kicking Bird was forced into the unenviable position of making certain that everyone got a fair share of nothing.

The crazy water was finding its way into lodges at an alarming rate, and Kicking Bird objected vociferously to the military and civilian authorities. The colonel in command of Fort Sill told him he had no authority to ban the sale of liquor and that the issue would have to be taken up with General Mackenzie, who, as he knew, was in the field.

The civilian who owned the store that sold the whiskey had transferred ownership to another who lived far away, and when Kicking Bird took the matter up with the head clerk, he, too, replied that he was not authorized to suspend the sale of spirits.

Lawrie Tatum shared Kicking Bird's outrage, but as commodities failed repeatedly to arrive as promised, and as the whiskey continued to flow without interruption, Kicking Bird was soon forced to alter his regard for the little Quaker. The man who had offered himself as protector, facilitator, and guardian did not have the power to carry out his avowed duties.

There were a few qualified successes, however. The Quaker agent's school began to fill up, not with children eager to learn about the modern world but with children eager for the food their attendance provided. An edict forbidding reservation-wide religious ceremonies, dancing, singing, and mass celebrations of any kind was rescinded after Kicking Bird absolved himself of all responsibility for the bloodshed to come from such a foolish command. The refugees streaming in from Comanche and Kiowa country needed protection from overzealous soldiers, and after pestering, cajoling, and browbeating the colonel, Kicking Bird was able to put in place a system of safe conduct for those who had chosen not to combat the government.

Important as they were to basic survival, these triumphs amounted to little else, and each night when Kicking Bird slipped under the covers in his lodge, he craved only the rest his body and his mind needed desperately. But the day to come would be fraught with a new tangle of events, and, invariably, he lay awake trying to anticipate all that he would have to do.

Though he tried hard to keep his thoughts from drifting in a direction he dreaded, sleep never came before an agonizing contemplation of those who were still out fighting the soldiers. Judging from the bands of disheartened who were appearing in greater and greater numbers on the edge of the reservation, the time when hostilities would be settled was fast approaching but, as much as he wanted the fighting to end, Kicking Bird felt a new river of heartache spreading across his chest each night.

He loved his people, and a part of him especially loved those who were defying the white man's army.

Every grueling day of his reservation life he asked nothing. But every night, on the threshold of sleep, he cried out mutely for the Mystery to deliver from destruction the ones who still fought.

CHAPTER LXI

TWO AFTERNOONS AFTER THE MASSIVE STORM SWEPT OVER THEM, the remnants of Ten Bears' village stumbled, hungry and half-frozen, down a well-worn buffalo trail and into the great canyon. With the last of their energy, the exhausted hostiles threw together shelters and fell asleep, relieved at finally reaching a place they regarded as impregnable.

The most pressing need was for food and next morning a large group of the most able-bodied warriors, including Dances With Wolves, Smiles A Lot, and Blue Turtle, went hunting. Sixty miles long and several miles wide, the canyon had been a favorite winter sanctuary for the buffalo and, two hours after they started out, the hunters found a small herd of several hundred in a side canyon. They killed a dozen of the animals, and the makeshift village spent the rest of the day feasting on the meat. Sated, the people retired early to their lodges for the restorative of another long sleep.

Just before dawn a single, distant shot stirred the Dances With Wolves lodge, but thinking a hunter must be out early, the family turned in their robes and slept on.

Minutes later, however, Dances With Wolves and Stands With A Fist were standing outside in the chill, listening to the sound of more gunfire. Peering through the half-light, they could see a disturbance at the front of the village. Dances With Wolves jumped onto the back of the nearest pony, and as Stands With A Fist rushed out of the lodge to thrust a rifle into his hands, Blue Turtle rode up.

"White soldiers in the canyon!" he screamed.

Dances With Wolves stared down at his wife and children.

"Run!" he commanded. "Where is Snake In Hands?"

"He's with the ponies," Stands With A Fist answered, terrified.

"Run," he repeated. "Run now!"

People were scrambling past them as he and Blue Turtle galloped toward the front of the village. Dances With Wolves could see the silhouettes of warriors already firing from perches on the sides of the canyon, and, as the fleeing people began to thin around him, warriors on foot and on horseback sprang into view, firing desperately at an oncoming enemy that seemed to be everywhere.

Hundreds of blue-coated men were advancing on the village. Half a mile away a large column of hair-mouth cavalry was disappearing into a side canyon, but Dances With Wolves had no time to think. He and Blue Turtle had been joined by many other mounted warriors in their dash, and just as they reached the village's perimeter, the soldiers made a charge.

Firing as fast as they could, the warriors blunted the charge, but they could not stop the forward movement of the soldiers. Fighting only for time, the Comanche horsemen kept shooting as they fell back through the village, constantly checking the progress of the women and children, who were now clambering up the sides of the canyon. In a running council of screams and shouts, the warriors on the canyon floor concluded that they would have to seek cover if they were to continue fighting and began to peel back.

But as Dances With Wolves wheeled his pony toward escape, he heard his own name float through the din of gunfire. Turning back, he saw Blue Turtle standing alone, one arm upraised. On the ground next to him a pony was kicking.

Enemy bullets were splashing the ground around Blue Turtle, and as he began to run, Dances With Wolves kicked his pony forward.

He was just reaching for the stranded warrior when a bullet slammed into his chest and passed out his back.

As Dances With Wolves slumped forward Blue Turtle managed to climb up behind him. Slipping his arms around his wounded friend's waist, the young man grasped the reins, turned the pony, and gave him his head.

They had just cleared the village and Blue Turtle was frantically searching out a good spot for hiding when Smiles A Lot appeared along-side and, motioning for him to follow, galloped ahead.

Dances With Wolves was still conscious when Blue Turtle and Smiles A Lot pulled him down from the pony and began to carry him up a steep, clear trail leading to the canyon's rim. A hundred yards later they reached a wide spot on the trail and laid their burden down to catch their breath. The hair-mouths had overrun the village and dark columns of smoke boiled up from the lodges as they were set ablaze.

A gurgling sound swung their attention back to their fallen comrade and the young warriors were crestfallen to discover that the sound was coming from the hole in Dances With Wolves' chest. The bullet had gone through one of his lungs. Blood was bubbling at the corners of his mouth and his eyes were going gray with the dull film of death.

"See to my wife . . ." he wheezed, his voice garbled with blood, ". . . my children."

"We'll carry you to the top," Smiles A Lot insisted. He and Blue Turtle lifted their comrade up but had only managed to progress a few feet before they realized that the man they were carrying had died.

Not wanting his body to fall into the hands of the enemy, the two young warriors searched the side of the canyon until they found a crevice suitable for burial. They wedged his body into the slit and stuffed the opening with rocks and earth. When the tomb had been sealed and thoroughly camouflaged with brush, Blue Turtle and Smiles A Lot continued up the trail.

Once over the rim, they saw that most of the village had escaped. Women and children and warriors were scattered over the plains adjacent to the canyon's edge. Some were huddled in little groups and some were wandering, half-dazed, trying to locate family members. The wounded had been grouped together and Owl Prophet was doing what he could for them.

After a few minutes of looking, Smiles A Lot found Hunting For Something. She was sitting, stunned but unhurt, with Stands With A Fist and her two daughters. The littler of the girls, the one called Stays

Quiet, was crying in her mother's arms, and the one called Always Walking had her hands against her ears.

"The baby?" Smiles A Lot asked his wife.

"The baby's not hurt," Hunting For Something assured him.

"Have you seen Dances With Wolves?" he heard Stands With A Fist ask.

She sat very still, cradling her child, but her eyes were wild with fear and anxiety, and for a moment Smiles A Lot could do nothing but blink.

"Have you seen him?" she asked again, as if he might not have heard.

"He is dead," Smiles A Lot said.

This revelation seemed to have no effect on Stands With A Fist.

"Have you seen Snake In Hands? He was with the ponies."

"No," said Smiles A Lot, but as he replied, a flurry of excited shouts rose around him. Looking up, he saw a small herd of perhaps thirty horses trotting toward him. When he stood, he could see that a single, bloody-faced boy was driving the ponies.

"Here he comes," Smiles A Lot said.

Although his face was streaked with blood, the boy was unhurt. But he had terrible news.

"The soldiers have captured the horse herd!" he announced breathlessly. "They ran off with them!"

Smiles A Lot and his fellow warriors rushed to the edge of the canyon to see if such a thing could be true and were surprised to see that the blue-coated soldiers were withdrawing. They were filing out of the canyon far to the south, and as Smiles A Lot watched the force serpentine toward the rim, something caught his eye on the prairie beyond.

At a great distance they looked like a legion of worms wriggling over the plains, but Smiles A Lot knew immediately that they were the Comanche horses. He also knew that an effort must be made to recapture them. Without the horses they would all be helpless.

CHAPTER LXII

*G*ENERAL MACKENZIE BROKE OFF THE FIGHT, FALLING SHORT OF but one goal. He had not destroyed the hostiles themselves, an action that would have been in keeping with his orders, but in all other respects he had achieved a significant victory in the great canyon.

Rarely had the general been as enamored of the rank and file as he was following the battle in the canyon. The hundreds of men under him had ridden out the terrible storm and marched all night across the frozen heart of hostile country before scattering the foe and reducing their town to ash.

But as Bad Hand's force marched south the general found himself most pleased in the knowledge that Captain Bradley had succeeded in capturing the entire hostile horse herd, almost a thousand in number, and these animals were being driven in front of him now. Indians without horses were like wagons without wheels, and there was no doubt that the last significant pocket of aboriginal resistance had been shattered. The freezing weather was aggravating the general's many old wounds, but there was no way he would let it reduce his pleasure as the miles between himself and the broken enemy piled up.

What to do with the mammoth horse herd was a piece of unfinished business that he dealt with swiftly and decisively when it was reported at mid-afternoon that the column was being shadowed by fifty or sixty warriors.

The scouts were ordered to locate a dead-end canyon large enough to accommodate the Indian ponies. In less than an hour a suitable place, with high walls on one side and an elevated ridge on the other, was discovered, and Bad Hand ordered the ponies driven inside.

More than a hundred men were ordered to surround the herd. Dozens of cartridge boxes were positioned along the line of soldiers and, as afternoon shadows began to stretch over the cold, brittle landscape, the order to commence firing was given.

At the height of the slaughter, the riflemen had wavered. Some had thrown down their weapons and a few had been overcome with nausea, but the incapacitated were quickly replaced with fresh shooters. The plunging, shrieking mass of ponies diminished rapidly, and by last light, no movement could be discerned in the box canyon now filled with the bodies, two or three deep in some places.

As he was eating dinner, a mixed group of civilians and Tonkawas reported that the hostiles had disappeared, confirming the general's suspicion that they were after the horses, and that night Bad Hand settled into one of the deepest, most peaceful sleeps he had ever enjoyed.

A few scattered and impotent bands might wander the prairie a while longer, but, for all practical purposes, the conquest of the southern plains was complete.

CHAPTER LXIII

*L*ESS THAN TWO WEEKS AFTER THE BATTLE IN THE CANYON, on the plains west of Fort Sill, a safe-escort team of warriors met the bedraggled, starving, destitute remains of what had once been a grand confederation of Comanches and Kiowas.

That same afternoon, one hundred and forty-six men, women, and children, many of them former residents of Ten Bears' village, marched drearily past flanking columns of expressionless soldiers. Among them were White Bear, Smiles A Lot, Rabbit, Hunting For Something, the Owl Prophet family, and Wind In His Hair's widow, One Braid Trailing. Stands With A Fist, Snake In Hands, Always Walking, and Stays Quiet were there, too, buried deep in the group that filed through the post.

At first Stands With A Fist had been adamant in her refusal to come into the reservation, saying that she and her children would die before they repeated the experience of Jacksboro. The other women unanimously vowed that they would give their lives before they would let the whites take her or her children, and Stands With A Fist relented, deciding at last that she would rather live out her life as a captive Indian than a free white.

Without prompting, Kicking Bird and his followers kept Stands

With A Fist's secret, but that proved to be the least of the former medicine man's trouble.

When news of the circumstances under which Ten Bears had died spread through the lodges of the former hostiles, Kicking Bird's reputation plummeted. Owl Prophet told anyone who listened that Kicking Bird's infatuation with the whites and their dubious magic had caused Ten Bears' death. From there it was a short leap to making Kicking Bird personally responsible for the collapse of Comanche life, and with that, lines were quickly drawn between the two men. They refused to speak to each other and avoided all contact.

The reservation's inhabitants were divided into two camps, one that would listen to Kicking Bird and one that would not, and a grating antagonism between the groups became a predictable aspect of daily life.

The intractability of the new residents might have been overcome but their free-roaming ways could not, and shortly after their arrival it was evident that they would not stay put.

The warriors, especially the youngest of them, could not be dissuaded from leaving at their own whim to hunt and raid in secrecy. No matter how carefully they were monitored, gangs of young men regularly slipped on and off their prescribed territory, creating a level of instability that dashed the white-devised system to failure.

Kicking Bird, in addition to his other duties, seemed constantly en route between the lodges of the former hostiles and the headquarters of the soldiers. His tribesmen were rarely pacified, and it was not often that the military could be convinced to relax their rules, but Kicking Bird kept on, certain that his presence was the main impediment to bloodshed between the factions.

As weeks of negotiation turned into months, the optimistic resolve of Lawrie Tatum was gradually smothered. Like Kicking Bird, he was a man in the middle. He disapproved of the former hostiles' attitude and quickly hardened his stance against those who had stayed out, saying that anyone who could not adhere to the rules must be subject to punishment.

At the same time, he found his influence with white authority trickle down to nothing. He did not possess the power to right any wrongs. All he could do was complain, and two months after the last big battle, he resigned in frustration and returned to his family in Iowa.

The little Quaker was replaced by a quiet, complacent man named Parsifel, who was so ineffectual that Kicking Bird quickly realized that all semblance of an advocate had departed with the little bald man who had been his friend.

A month later, during a period of relative calm, Bad Hand commanded all warriors to present themselves on the parade ground in front of his headquarters, and as they gathered, Kicking Bird and Agent Parsifel were called into Bad Hand's house for a council.

"My government has decided to punish those responsible for attacking the army's corn train last summer," Bad Hand announced.

"Many are dead," Kicking Bird countered.

"The government only wishes to punish the living," Bad Hand replied humorlessly.

"What is the punishment?" Kicking Bird inquired.

"Incarceration."

"For how long?"

"That has yet to be determined."

There was a long silence as Kicking Bird searched for a way to diffuse the impending catastrophe, but all he was able to do was ask more questions.

"Who will be punished?"

"Whoever is guilty."

"But how will you know that?"

"I want Kicking Bird to go outside and tell the guilty men to show themselves."

"They will not do that," Kicking Bird said flatly.

"Let's go outside," Bad Hand said, rising out of his chair.

As Kicking Bird predicted not a single man stepped forward. Bad Hand had the government's order repeated, and still no one moved.

"You leave me no choice," he said to Kicking Bird. Then he turned to one of his officers and gave the order for twenty-five men to be selected from the warrior ranks.

"Wait," Kicking Bird interrupted and Bad Hand called back his officer.

"The men who go must take their families," Kicking Bird demanded.

"All right," Bad Hand agreed.

"There will be fighting if the families do not go."

"The families will go," Bad Hand reiterated, extending a hand, which Kicking Bird took. "All right, Captain . . ."

"No," said Kicking Bird.

He stared into Bad Hand's eyes, then scanned the lines of warriors.

"I will pick them."

Kicking Bird did his best, selecting a blend of chronic troublemakers and strong young men whose responsibilities were small to be sent to the faraway white man's prison.

CHAPTER LXIV

*T*HERE WAS STRONG TALK OF RESISTANCE TO THE SENDING OF people to prison but it didn't lead to action. Those selected for punishment were shipped east, leaving only tears behind them.

Owl Prophet had been the most vocal of those who still wanted to oppose the whites but he aimed his wrath at Kicking Bird. The prophet counseled furiously with his owl, and after a climactic, public demonstration, declared, "Kicking Bird is a betrayer. Such a man cannot live. Kicking Bird will die soon."

The prophecy quickly became common knowledge, but if it disturbed Kicking Bird, there was no evidence as he went about his multitude of public duties.

Yet Kicking Bird was changed. His eyes had widened perceptibly, as if some internal shock had frozen them in wonder. The look on his face made people so uneasy that a majority came to expect that the prophecy would be fulfilled.

Four days after the deportees left in chains for the east, Kicking Bird consumed his morning coffee and became violently ill. The pain heightened all day and by early evening had consumed him.

Though he had been nowhere in the vicinity, it was widely believed that Owl Prophet had somehow arranged Kicking Bird's death.

Kicking Bird loyalists might have murdered Owl Prophet in turn, but they didn't have to. Everyone knew that a Comanche who killed a fellow tribesman was certain to die himself, and those who watched for signs of Owl Prophet's demise did not have long to wait.

Three days later the prophet was found dead in his bed, and, like Kicking Bird, the cause of his passing remained a mystery.

CHAPTER LXV

TWO YEARS LATER, UPON THEIR RELEASE FROM AN OLD SPANISH prison in the humid place the whites called Florida, Smiles A Lot, Hunting For Something, their firstborn child, and Rabbit came back to Fort Sill. Some, like White Bear, never returned, dead from the shaking fever.

In their absence the reservation had lost all vestige of rebellion. Some of the people were living in white man houses and all of them were at least partially clad in white man clothes. The old ways were still being practiced but otherwise there was little to remind the returnees of the free life that had once been.

When a lodge had been erected for them Hunting For Something, her infant son, and Rabbit went off for a round of visiting while Smiles A Lot rode to the great Medicine Bluff on a borrowed pony.

He climbed the bluff as he had done before, in what now seemed a long-ago life. This time he would have no visions, for, as he stood on the crest and looked over the country, the view had changed. Spread before him, plain on the knolls of hills and partially visible in the thickets along the creeks, were the impoverished camps of subjugated people.

Smiles A Lot turned and looked to the west. It was blazing with light as the sun flattened on the horizon. The country was still there, limitless and empty save for the bones of warriors and buffalo and his beloved horses.

He gazed down the scarred face of the cliff and thought for an instant how little effort it would take to step into space.

Then he lifted his eyes once more and searched out the lodge that was his new home. The wide world had once been his domain but all that remained to him now was one of the many poor shelters scattered around the soldier fort. The idea that he would be returning to the same place over and over again seemed inconceivable to him, but he would return to it soon.

There was no place else to go.

ACKNOWLEDGMENTS

Marianne Blake

Carter Burwell

Kurt Cobain

James Coverdale

Morton L. Janklow

Doris Leader Charge

Herman Melville

Jimmy "Tumbleweed" Northcutt

Nancy Skandalakis

Barry Spikings

Towana Spivey

Bruce Tracy

THE HOLY ROAD

Michael Blake

A READER'S GUIDE

To print out copies of this or other
Random House Reader's Guides,
visit us at www.atrandom.com/rgg

The novel Dances With Wolves *came out in 1988. It's taken thirteen years for its sequel,* The Holy Road, *to appear. Why such a long gap?*

There are many reasons, but the primary one was emotional and spiritual. I needed that time to summon the courage to write the book. The degree of difficulty in writing a sequel was always going to be high, but it was higher because of the emotional connection I felt with the characters and the story. I didn't want to face the pain.

Why do you think you feel such a bond with the Comanches?

You can't really say *why* you feel an affinity for something. But this is also a contemporary story. It's happening now—indigenous cultures are being overwhelmed all over the world. So everything that happened then was much more than just about that one group of Comanches. It was the beginning of the end of a lot of things. We're still suffering a lot from Manifest Destiny. It has not served mankind very well.

What got you interested in this part of the country's history?

My great grandfather was a soldier in the Apache wars in Arizona and my uncle wrote historical novels about the West, so I was exposed to this stuff from an early age. Also *Bury My Heart at Wounded Knee* was a seminal book for me. When I first read it, when it came out, I had no idea this happened. This book brought all the details home to me and I was stunned. That started everything for me.

And the idea for Dances With Wolves *came from something you read in a work of history, is that right?*

I was reading an obscure history book and mention was made of a wagon driver taking supplies to a far-flung fort and all he found there was a flapping piece of canvas on a sod hut. I thought, What would I have done had I been accompanying that soldier to the fort? Given my romantic inclination, I think I'd stay. The questions began to pile up and I wrote the answers down. That's how *Dances With Wolves* started.

A lot of scenes in The Holy Road *are based on actual events, too, like the battle of Palo Duro Canyon in 1874, for example.*

I knew about the battle. I'd read about it quite a bit. It was the decisive engagement that broke the power of the Southern Plains tribes forever. It seemed a logical place to end the story. When the government sent Colonel Mackenzie out there, he surprised the Indians. No one believed the white people could find them there. The Comanches were unhorsed—and unhorsed they could do nothing—and Mackenzie killed the horses. It worked brilliantly. Less than a year later, everyone was on the reservation.

Three years ago, I kicked around the Comanche-Kiowa country in West Texas and Oklahoma, and I was amazed by the condition of the country. It's all still there. The things I was imagining came to life. Particularly Palo Duro Canyon, which most Americans have never heard of. It's the second biggest canyon in the world and it's amazing both from historical and geological perspectives.

And an Indian chief really was gassed in his hotel room in Washington?

Yes. He was staying with Quanah Parker, the Comanche leader, and they blew out the gas lamps and he was poisoned. Parker fell off his bed and somehow got enough oxygen to survive from a hole in the floor. My son is named after Quanah Parker. My daughter Monahsetah is named for a Southern Cheyenne woman, and my other daughter, Lozen, for a Warm Springs Apache woman who was a healer and a warrior. Lozen could stand on a mountain and hold her hand out and feel the enemy's presence. I used to be skeptical about Indian mysticism but there's nothing in Indian culture I disbelieve—I've seen too much of it.

Are you worried about historical accuracy?

Anyone steeped in the history of the West is going to say, "He's wrong." I mean, I write about a three-pronged assault on the Comanche-Kiowas when really it was five. But I've never taken an anthropological view. I've educated myself, but the main thing has been the human element. *Dances With Wolves* was written to put a human face on these people. That was my only goal: "Look, these are people, too."

Were there a lot of deserters like Lt. Dunbar and captives like Stands With A Fist?

Dunbar didn't really desert the army; the army deserted him! But the scene in the movie when the army's taking Dances With Wolves, who's officially a deserter, in chains to be hung, and the Indians take him and people cheer—it gives me chills still.

But yes, there were a lot of captives. My Kiowa friend tells me they have a special name for the descendants of white captives. If you look at the records, after a year or so, the whites normally didn't try to escape anymore. The Indians captured by the whites never stopped trying to escape. In fact, the white captives who were taken back often tried to return to the tribe who'd captured them. There's a hint of something there. Their lives were primitive and brutal but something worked.

You certainly don't sugarcoat the Indian way of life.

They weren't sweethearts but they conducted themselves in a way that made more sense. War to them was not about conquest. It was a game, it was about depriving their enemy of something. The greatest feat in battle was counting coup. You'd go on a raid and steal horses. Someone would come after you. If you charged this armed enemy and tapped him on the head with your bow and rode away, that was the bravest thing. People would talk about that for years. They had counting coup and we had World War I.

Ranald Mackenzie is a very interesting character in your book. You clearly have more sympathy for Mackenzie than for any other white character, and he was the one destroying the Comanche.

You see this over and over in the accounts. People in the military in that era who had contact with Indians and who fought them had much deeper respect for them and appreciation of their way of life than any other group. They had the most empathy for them. Originally Mackenzie was distant, but he stayed on at Fort Sill and came to regard them much more highly. Certainly more highly than any politician.

In contrast to these military men, there are the politicians.

I see them the same way I see contemporary politicians. They have no idea of what goes on. They know the Beltway and little else. Grant was president at the time *The Holy Road* was set in. He promulgated the Quaker peace policy that I write about but after that he just turned everyone loose. The citizenry had clamored forever to just be rid of the Indians, and Grant finally caved.

There's a sense of inevitability to that process.

People who have read the book have said they couldn't help turning the page but they didn't want to for fear of what they'd read. I feel I've done my job when I hear that.

Tell us a little about your involvement with the Buffalo Commons project.

In conjunction with *The Holy Road* I'm lobbying for the Buffalo Commons, the idea of restoring the Great Plains from Texas to Montana with grasses and buffalo. About thirty Indian tribes have come together to promote the buffalo as well. The Buffalo Commons is the idea of Frank and Deborah Popper, professors at Rutgers. What's really exciting about this is that it's doable. The Great Plains were so coveted in the last century and the people and the buffalo were removed and they were plowed under and now much of it's being left fallow. There's nothing there now so why not restore it to how it was? If we can restore John Wilkes Booth's boyhood home, why not this?

And the buffalo's coming back?

Cattle ranches are going under and the buffalo is coming back. In the 1890s there were less than 500 buffalo and now there are over 300,000. There's buffalo meat and buffalo jerky and robes and shoes. I just bought a pair of buffalo shoes. They're tough, comfortable—marvelous. The manufacturers say they've been "field tested for 1,000 years." I like that.

All this, and your depiction of Washington, D.C., in the novel, would lead one to believe you're not a city guy.

I live on a ranch. City living is so intensely distracting to me. My family still consumes—we use too much water, we make too much trash. But I made a conscious decision after living like a running dog in Los Angeles for thirteen years that if I ever got enough money, I'd go live as far from the madding crowd as I could. I bought myself a little space.

What about a film version of The Holy Road?

I'm writing the screenplay now.

So at what point after the Dances With Wolves *movie did you start to think about a sequel?*

I started writing *The Holy Road* in February 2000 but I'd been research-ing for the book ever since I finished *Dances With Wolves*. When I was driving around L.A. in my car working on the first book I was thinking about the second. In a fanciful way, I'd always envisioned a trilogy.

So there'll be a third book?

There will be a third book, the Great Mystery willing.

Think about Stands With A Fist's former identity as Christine Gunther. From her point of view, what does it mean to be white? To be Comanche? What about in the eyes of the people of Jacksboro?

Contemplate the huge impact of the transcontinental railroad in United States history. Is *The Holy Road* an appropriate name? To what else could the title refer?

Consider the eyeglasses Lawrie Tatum gives to Ten Bears. Are there any parts of the white world that the Comanches admire? Do the whites value any aspect of the Comanche way of life?

How is smoking the pipe an integral part of a Comanche conversation? How does this tradition come into play in their interaction with whites?

Reflect on the Comanches' visit to Washington. Are the whites ever able to see them as human? As equals?

How does the explicit violence throughout the book serve as commentary on the whites' and Comanches' inability to identify with one another? Does either side commit worse atrocities?

Was Ten Bears wrong to allow the tribe to be divided and let each man make his own decision about whether to go to the reservation? If he had survived the trip to Washington, do you think he would have been able to unite his people?

How does the red-haired scalp described in the book's opening pages symbolize the future difference of opinion between Kicking Bird and Wind In His Hair? Which one of them made the right choice?

Consider the relationship between Smiles A Lot and Hunting For Something as well as their improvised family situation with Rabbit. How do extreme circumstances change or negate societal conventions?

Think about Smiles A Lot's transformation of character from the "boy who was good with horses" to a full-blooded warrior. Is his newfound strength and courage diminished by the end of the book?

The final chapter closes with the remaining members of the tribe living on the reservation. Is this the end of the story? How do you picture these characters and their descendants in ten, twenty, fifty, or a hundred years?

In what specific ways has American civilization as a whole been influenced or informed by Native American culture?